RISQUE

He is Sebastian d'Arcy, Marquis of Brecon—and
London's most notorious rakehell.
The author of an erotic book on the art of loving,
he believes the only sensible role
for a woman of spirit and intelligence is that of
a mistress—for a wife is at the mercy
of her husband. To prove his theory, d'Arcy accepts
a wager: he will choose one woman and
transform her into the greatest courtesan the *ton*
has ever seen.

She is Madeleine Foucant. Of dubious parentage,
the impoverished, convent-bred beauty
knows her chances of marriage are slim. Boldly,
she accepts d'Arcy's offer . . . and
succeeds beyond his wildest dreams. Soon all of
England is clamoring for her favor
but it is the hotly sensual d'Arcy whose kisses turn
Madeleine's heart to fire. Passion
will drive her to make a fateful decision—and
bring her a love more dangerous than
anything she could ever imagine . . .

*"Laura Parker is, in my opinion, one of the
finest authors in romantic fiction."*
—Heather Graham Pozzessere

LAURA PARKER
RISQUÉ

ZEBRA BOOKS
KENSINGTON PUBLISHING CORP.

ZEBRA BOOKS are published by

Kensington Publishing Corp.
850 Third Avenue
New York, NY 10022

Copyright © 1996 by Laura Castoro

Zebra and the Z logo Reg. U.S. Pat. & TM Off.

First Printing: February, 1996
10 9 8 7 6 5 4 3 2 1

Printed in the United States of America

The French still confide in long nights to come over
The troublesome ditch betwixt Calais and Dover.
Long nights they may find, and a comfort left still;
They are sure of short days, let them come when they will!

—Excerpt from *Lady's Magazine* for
the year 1812

Prologue

Falmouth Harbor, England, August 21, 1803

The Marchesa de Marconi gazed dreamily down the length of her flushed naked body into the gorgeous male face framed by her luscious thighs. He boldly stared back at her, his clear cherub-blue eyes tucked at the corner by the smile of the very devil.

Sinuously, he disentangled himself and gently repositioned himself by her side. With a delicate finger she traced first the long dimples in his cheeks and then the full tender curve of his lower lip, gleaming now with moisture. His was a very talented mouth, equally adept at conversation in half a dozen languages and the sweet, silent expressions of the libido. Soft tawny curls looped and dipped disarmingly over his forehead, shading the wide cerebral brow of a man whose passion for the flesh was surpassed only by his intellectual endeavors.

"Dolcemento, mio cicisbeo," she murmured as he turned toward her and once more dipped his head to nibble at her. "You are so beautiful you should have been born a woman," she pronounced, stroking his bare shoulder.

Laughing, he lifted himself up and over her. "Ah, but then I would not be so ably endowed to service you." He rotated his hips in the sensitive well between her thighs. "Now would I, Marchesa?"

When the world had once more righted itself after he

again pleasured her to the point of delicious satisfaction, the marchesa smiled lasciviously. "When you wish to prove a point, you do so most admirably, *caro.*"

Her lover lifted his head from her shoulder and smiled. "I knew you would approve."

"Naughty boy!" The marchesa caressed his damp cheek before pinching the fleshiest part of it. No one had ever pleased her as well as this beautiful English boy. Boy? Though young in years, he was truly a *man,* one tirelessly inventive in the intimate ways of pleasing a woman.

Though she was eight years his elder, he made her feel as young and impressionable as a young virgin. When he touched her, she wanted to weep. When he made love to her she wanted to die so that the touch of his body would be the last impression of life she carried with her to the grave. For his constancy she would have gladly paid him any price. In temperament a match for her distant kinsmen, the notorious and amorous Borgias, she found it utterly incomprehensible that he could not be bought.

She did not protest as he slid from her but she watched with a narrowed calculated gaze as he dressed, devouring the faultless symmetry of his insatiable body.

"Why must you leave me?" she cried petulantly, rising up on an elbow. "I wish—no, I command you to stay a while longer with me."

She saw him glance regretfully back at her. After the slightest of hesitations he cast aside the waistcoat he held and came toward the bed. "*Cara,* you've known for weeks that this night would come." He sat down and took her hand in both of his. "We've reached England. I must leave you."

In desperation, she clasped his head tightly between her hands and pulled it down to the perfumed mounds of her full breasts. "You need not go ashore tonight, or ever."

She pressed fervent kisses into his dark-gold curls. "We can sail back down the coast past Gibraltar, to Minorca. I have a villa there where we may spend every day as we like." She pressed her lips to his brow and was annoyed to find it cool and dry now. "You need not wear a single scrap of clothing."

His chuckle was as decadent as the look in his eyes. "I should look like a boiled lobster in three days. Yet I do find a temptation in the picture you present. Another occasion, perhaps?"

"When, *caro*? When? What calls you back to England?" Forgetting herself she let slip the jealous words, "Another woman?"

He passed a hand lightly over the curve of her quivering belly and then allowed his thumb to drift lower into the mossy dampness below. "What woman could call more strongly to me than you, *cara?*"

"What then?" Her berry-red mouth shaped a pout as she flung back her dark head. "What can be more important than— Ah, you fiend!" she gasped as his thumb found a most sensitive place.

"Duty, *cara*. Duty calls me home."

"You . . . do . . . not . . . play fairly."

"No, Marchesa, I do not," he answered as he moved up and over her. "Just one more taste before, alas, I must leave you."

The marchesa fell back among the silk pillows, her arms flung wide in abandon as her thighs opened to his impudent hand. "I shall not soon—*oh!*—forgive your desertion."

"I know," he murmured as he bent to take the nugget of a nipple gently between his teeth. "I know."

Moments later she gasped as he surged powerfully into her. This was not like before when he had inched into her with the disciplined deliberation of a master demanding surrender of his pupil. This time he gave her no chance to catch her breath, to adapt to his rhythm. He catapulted her over the edge of bliss before her mind could even grasp it was happening. A jumble of Italian endearments and more earthy sentiments flowed freely and unwittingly from her mouth.

"I expect to be given the most prominent place in your book of *amore, caro*," she said lightly when once more he had pulled away.

"You shall be in every line, verse and chapter, you ravishing creature," he responded with a note of warmth that any other woman would have believed.

"*Ben trovato*," she responded, and lightly slapped his cheek. "Well said, even if you lie. Promise you will come back to Naples, and me? Someday?"

She saw the truth in those expressive eyes even before he opened his mouth. To keep him from voicing a lie she quickly covered his exquisite mouth with her fingertips. "*Benissimo*. Still, I wish . . ."

She let the thought trail off. She would not humiliate herself by behaving like a cast-off mistress. She was a marchesa, a Neapolitan noblewoman accustomed to all the perquisites of her title and wealth. Wed to an ailing elderly husband so besotted with her that he could deny her nothing, she was accustomed to controlling every detail of her world. But she could not control this man or anything about him, not even when he lay compliant under the expert sensual talents of her fingers and tongue. Always he held something back, some part of him she suspected no one had ever reached. For that reason alone she knew she would always love—and hate—Sebastian d'Arcy.

As she watched him slip on his breeches, a slow smile of contentment curved up her lips. She was luckier than most women. He had shared her bed for a month. There was nothing left for now but to let him go—a sacrifice to the gods and goddesses of *amore*.

French coast, August 21, 1803

That same night, some four hundred kilometers nearly due east, an English frigate commanded by Captain Wright had eluded the British blockade and the French army's shore patrol to reach the steep cliffs near Biville, Normandy.

Just after midnight, eight Frenchmen led by Georges Cadoudal, leader of the outlawed Bourbon royalist Chouans, stood on the ship's unlit deck. A signal was given and returned from the cliffs above. As his men scrambled up ropes lowered by native sympathizers, Cadoudal had but one purpose. Armed with drafts for a million francs with which to organize an insurrection, he had come to France to kidnap Napoléon and, if he resisted, to kill him.

One

Henrice and Justine Foucant, elaborately gowned in lace and silk and thwarted anticipation, waited in their parlor for the suitors who no longer called. Their small brick house in Queen Anne's Gate, which bordered St. James's Park, was surrounded by a large walled garden at the midpoint of a triangle formed by Buckingham Palace, Whitehall, and Parliament. Though still respectable, the aging neighborhood was, like its occupants, slowly if elegantly going to ruin.

French émigrés who twelve years earlier had fled their country's revolution, the sisters were aware that the world outside their modest door was passing them by. They had not been forced from society at the ages of forty and forty-three because of lost beauty or failing health. Far from it. Still attractive in that indefinable way certain fortunate women possess well into old age, the Foucant sisters were victims of the most offensive ailment to affect women of extravagant if faultless taste: they were destitute.

Henrice rose to her feet and began pacing. Her whaleboned bodice, a relic from another decade, still fit her waist as slimly as it had a score of years earlier. "If only we had the use of a carriage, postilion, and groom we might venture forth to the Opéra!" she bemoaned both to herself and to Justine.

She paused dramatically, her gray eyes glowing like the pearls about her throat. Twenty-five years earlier a royal duke had ordered the king's own jeweler to fashion a collar of pearls for her, the newly acclaimed greatest actress to tread the tragic stage since Clairon. Each pearl had been judged by her to be the exact size and lustrous smoke-gray color as her eyes. Now those eyes bespoke a hurt that went deeper than vanity; it struck to the very soul of aging beauty. "How could Lord Jeffreys have forsaken me for a milk-faced trollop? Was it so much to ask for, my own house and carriage?"

"No more than your due," Justine replied. Henrice's loss of her lover to a younger woman six months earlier had been an insult that no amount of sympathy could atone for.

"To replace me over such a trifle?" Henrice shrugged. "Englishmen! *Le bon Dieu* made them only for the Englishwoman *sans âme,* without spirit!"

Justine quietly kept her counsel over the matter. She suspected that it was Henrice's theatrical temperament that had frightened the viscount away. Henrice sought every opportunity to hold center stage in her own melodrama of life. But the French love of the drama had not found a warm reception in England. Englishmen seemed decidedly uncomfortable when faced with a woman's full-flaring passion. With England again at war with France, French mistresses were even less in fashion.

"So then, what are we to do?"

"Give the devil his pound of flesh," Henrice answered.

A sudden chilling thought wrapped its slimy tendrils about Justine. "You are not thinking that one of us should make ourselves amenable to Monsieur de Valmy?"

"I'll enter debtor's prison first!" Henrice's words were firm with conviction.

For all their cash and half their jewels, the mysterious Monsieur de Valmy had helped them leave the blood-crazed city of Paris in 1791. At the time, his help had seemed a boon from heaven. But once in London, the émigré society there spoke of him in horrified murmurs. It was whispered that he had been one of the young radicals who had deserted their aristocratic families to join the *sans culottes* during the early days of revolution. When the revolution became a bloodbath, he led two lives. For the right amount, he smuggled aristocrats to safety. For favors from the republic, he sold other aristocrats to the mob. It was said it mattered equally little to him. When the fortunes of the revolution turned sour and the rebels began devouring their own, he came to England. No one could prove these rumors or, if they could, they dared not. De Valmy was a dangerous and predatory man. He seemed to know everyone's secrets. Now he knew theirs.

Mrs. Seldon, the thin, elderly housekeeper in soiled apron and wilted bonnet, entered and unceremoniously set down the tray with a negligence that made the china rattle.

They paid no more attention to her than they did the wind whistling in the chimney. They were from a world where servants were like furniture, necessary, but when not of use, ignored.

When she was gone, Justine pressed a handkerchief dampened with the scent of lilies to her aching brow. A frequent victim of migraine, she was waiting for the cinchona in pills with ginger she had taken to effect the promised cure. Then she noticed Henrice was pouring a thin amber liquid into a cup. "Tea? The cook knows how I detest the brew! Why are we no longer served wine with supper?"

"Tea is all that is left," Henrice pointed out. "The wine merchant refuses to extend our credit until we pay some small amount on our cheque. I try to explain that the purpose of credit is that we do not need to pay. But, of course, such subtleties are lost on the English."

Justine bent forward to lift the lid from her supper plate,

then wrinkled her nose in distaste. It was the same thin broth of onion soup and crusty bread on which they had subsisted for a fortnight. "How I long for a carp simmered in onions, wine, herbs, and butter!"

"You may as well whistle for it," Henrice answered ruthlessly, then caught her sister's expression. "Unless you have something to tell me, *oui?*"

Justine pinkened under her sister's sharp glance. "I am most embarrassed to confess it, but I—yes *I*—attempted to charm a salmon from the fishmonger's boy this morning!"

"Justine!"

The elder sister tossed her head of carefully maintained blond curls. She confessed to only two weaknesses: love of gaming tables and a coquettish eye for young men. *"Ma foi!* He was a most saucy cherub, so tall with dark curls and pink lips. It was only a small liberty which I intended to permit him. Still, he ran away when I reached out to embrace him. *Enfin,* he took the fish with him."

"Le bon Dieu! Even if we starve, you must not lower your standards," Henrice scolded. "Your arms have embraced princes! For shame that you would waste such charms on a fishmonger's boy!"

"It seemed little enough sacrifice for fresh salmon," Justine remarked in defense. *"Enfin.* It has been too long since a handsome youth clasped me to his manly chest and kissed me breathless."

"It has been two months, exactly the length of time since you lost your nest egg at the faro tables. Always *Maman* would say to us, '*Mes filles,* never drink and gamble together!' Surely you remember her words."

Not in the least ashamed of herself, Justine had long ago embraced her *petite indulgence,* as she called her predilection for young companions, as a natural part of a generous nature, though more and more she had noticed that they sought her money as much as her favors. Not one of them had visited her since word of her calamitous loss had made the rounds of the gaming tables.

Be that as it may, she was adept at turning the finger of condemnation away from her direction. She said without preamble, "This is all the fault of Ondine's English lover. He is the reason we are starving. Even before he showed his lack of consideration by breaking his neck in a fall from his horse, I knew he was the wrong choice for our sweet little sister."

"We should not speak ill of the dead," Henrice responded. "Though, myself, I never cared for him, either."

Completely in accord with her sister's musings, Justine said, "The least Ondine's Englishman might have done was to provide adequately for her. After all, she had us, her family, to consider."

Henrice pulled herself up proudly. "Never have I heard of an aristocratic family disputing the claims of a faithful mistress to a small income and a house. It was such an elegant little house, the square so quiet and shady. And we scarcely took up any space, only the second floor. *Ma pauvre* Ondine, the insult she suffered seeing us all put out on the street! No wonder she ran away to seek out phantoms from her past."

Justine and Henrice lapsed into a short silence, each pondering the wisdom of their youngest sister's decision to depart for France a week earlier to search for a man she had thought dead these last ten years.

"Do you really believe Monsieur de Valmy's claim that Comte d'Artois lives?" Justine whispered finally.

"Jus-*tine!*" Henrice hissed in horror. "England is again at war with France, the fault of that *petit caporal,* Napoléon Bonaparte. Monsieur de Valmy warned us only last week that because we are French the English are suspicious of us. Without an English protector, our loyalty won't prevent us from being dragged out and imprisoned as spies if there should be any rumor against us."

"Very well." Justine shrugged. "I do not care to think so much these days. *Enfin,* there is so little that is pleasant to think about."

"Then we must change that," Henrice said. "We are Foucants, after all. Our great-grandmother was a boudoir companion of the Sun King himself. Great-Aunt Henrietta was the most famous rival of Madame Pompadour for the affections of the magnificent Louis XV. We could boast, if we were not above such things, that we have produced five generations of beautiful women who have won favor in the most noble and royal houses of France."

"You are thinking that one of us must find a protector, yes?"

"Perhaps not 'we,' " Henrice mused, though the thought did not displease her, albeit practical reasoning told her their chances were slim.

Justine sat up sharply, her lethargy completely forgotten. "Henrice, you can't mean Madeleine!"

"But of course I do," Henrice said testily. "It works out quite nicely. I convinced Ondine to send for Madeleine weeks ago, the very day she was forced to leave her house. I thought her daughter's presence would comfort her. But now I believe it was Divine Providence that directed my action. Madeleine's arrival will solve all our problems."

"But Henrice, Ondine has always had other dreams for her daughter." Justine lowered her voice in awe of her own next words. "She wants Madeleine to wed."

Henrice clicked her tongue impatiently. "And waste her beauty on one man? Ridiculous! Did she not ask us to look after her daughter if she did not return in time? Exactly. I am thinking of Madeleine's future." Henrice gave her cooling tea a disdainful glance. "Marriage is not the goal of Foucant women, though at times it has been a convenience. We are born and bred to bear proudly the title of Mistress. Better that than to be cast into the arms of an English husband who smells of horses and the privy."

She shook her head to dispel the picture she had conjured. *"Non!* Madeleine will take her place among us."

"I wonder," Justine murmured as she busied herself smoothing down a flounce of her satin gown. "Perhaps there wasn't money for her fare."

"But of course there was. I clearly recall your comments each time you offered to post Ondine's letters. You always remarked that Ondine was far too generous with her coin."

"Oui, I recall she always enclosed a goodly sum," Justine replied, still not raising her head.

"Don't brood, Sister," Henrice said soothingly. "Madeleine will soon be here to cheer us with her pretty smiles."

"What if Madeleine does not come?" Justine whispered.

"She must come. Her mother's letter would have wrung tears from a stone. You will see, once she is here, we Foucants can regain our well-deserved pride."

Justine began to pick at the lace flounce on her skirt. "What if Madeleine does not wish to be a mistress?"

"Impossible." Henrice snapped open her fan. "She is aware of the family tradition, though I fault Ondine for not encouraging the girl in her intended vocation. Once things are explained to her, she will see she can do no other than her part. The Foucant family honor is at stake. Only Madeleine can save us!"

"Ma pauvre petite," Justine murmured to herself, "who will save *her?"*

Her sister's tone was beginning to whittle Henrice's nerves. "Do not suppose that I would toss her to the wolves. I have given the matter considerable thought." She eased gracefully into a chair. "The choice of a first lover, as we know, is very important. She must have a wealthy patron, a worldly gentleman, a noble of continental polish, of refined appetites and exquisite sensibilities. Someone—"

"Young!" Justine interjected.

"Generous—"

"Gallant!"

"A highly skilled and imaginative lover—"

"Witty and handsome!"

"You ask for a great deal," Henrice said dryly.

"She is so young, Henrice," Justine pleaded in genuine sympathy. "Do you not remember your first lover?"

Henrice's expression softened. *"Oui.* But we must use our heads. An appealing face will not put sausage in the cassoulet. For the sake of her future success, Madeleine's protector must have a respected title and a deep purse."

Her fine gray eyes widened with sudden inspiration. "Why did I not think of it before? *Ma foi!* There is already an Englishman of our acquaintance who answers our needs."

"So I am thinking," Justine answered with a small smile. "His mother was French."

"His father was the very devil!"

The sisters smiled into each other's eyes as they said in unison, "Sebastian d'Arcy!"

"Our plan awaits only Madeleine's arrival. If only that will occur quickly."

"If only," Justine murmured and wondered what would become of them if it did not.

Two

Dressed in the black-and-white robes of a novitiate, Madeleine Foucant climbed stiffly down from atop the highway coach in London's Great George Coaching Yard into the general mill of weary, ill-tempered passengers, lathered horses, and ankle-deep mud. For five long days she had traveled atop the coach in the cheapest seat from the coast at Falmouth. Wet from the late-summer shower that had drenched the outside passengers just five miles from the city limits, she heaved a short-lived sigh of relief as her foot touched the muddy ground.

"Watch below!"

Glancing up, she saw a trunk tumbling toward her and jumped aside.

"Watch 'ow 'ee step, miss!" the coach driver from the next coach warned when she would have backed into his team.

She side-stepped away an instant before the one nearest her kicked out sideways with a hind leg. Frustrated by the flash and mill of the crowds and the rank smell of too many other animals sharing the confining space of the courtyard, all the teams were restless and short-tempered.

"Sorry, ma'am," the first driver called down as he cracked his whip and sawed on the reins of his disobedient team.

Riding atop the coach had afforded her with a spectacular view of the English countryside. Sometimes on new-constructed turnpike roads the driver had raced along at speeds of up to eleven miles an hour. More often, they had plodded along severely pocked lanes, jostled and bumped and jarred until her joints ached even when they were not moving. Difficult as it had been, it had been the easiest part of her journey.

Bewildered by the noise after a life spent behind the peaceful cloistered walls of a convent, she plowed her way quickly through the throng of posting masters, links boys, coach drivers, and passengers who jostled one another as they brayed demands for bags and packages. The chorus of voices was repeatedly punctuated by coachmen's piercing whistles and the vicious snap of whips that made every horse's ears twitch in fearful anticipation.

She had never before been to England. Left behind thirteen years ago in the shelter of a convent when her mother and aunts fled the revolution in France for the safety of England, she had waited patiently for the time when she would be sent for. The waiting had taught her not to expect too much. Her family meant well, she was certain of that, but she had resigned herself to the fact that they often could not be counted on to keep their promises.

Then, a month ago she had received a surprising letter from her mother begging her to come to England. Without two French *sous* to rub together, she had undertaken the dangerous journey with only prayers to help her.

Dressed by St. Etienne's nuns in their own robes for protection, she had walked a good deal of the way across France, sleeping at night in abandoned barns and occasionally by the side of the road. Yet there were things not even a healthy convent-bred girl of nineteen chaste years could accomplish by prayers and determination alone. Crossing the Channel was one of them.

In Brest the only captain who would entertain a bargain

with her was a smuggler. In return for her passage and a few gold coins, she had agreed to row contraband wine ashore once they reached England.

Now, wending her way down a street that offered little relief from the fray of the coaching yard, she tried to shut her ears to the shrill noise of vendors and costermongers who lined the lane with a bewildering variety of products.

Once she reached the corner she paused to gaze longingly at a vendor's pile of turnips. With crisp greens and snow-white upper skins, the southern hemispheres of their bulbous bodies were purpled as if dipped in an inkwell.

A spasm of hunger zipped through her. During her journey, she had often offered up her hunger as atonement for her sins, real and imagined. But, try as she might, she could not do so cheerfully. The ache in her stomach was a reminder that she was selfishly human and lacked the qualifications for sainthood. She had meant to save the rest of her smuggler's wages but gave in to the temptation to satisfy her hunger. She reached for the plumpest turnip.

" 'Ere! Thief!"

Her wrist was manacled by a thick-fingered hand. Startled, Madeleine looked up into the bright-red face of a burly man. His thinning hair stood out from the center of his head like a ruff. A vegetable-spattered apron spanned his protruding belly.

"I do not steal, monsieur. I can pay." She produced a copper coin from her pocket.

The man looked surprised to see the coin, but he did not take it. He sized her up with small blue eyes set in pockets of flesh. "I ken yer kind. There's better ways for ye to square the debt."

With real alarm, Madeleine jerked back. *"Non, non, monsieur.* I change my mind. I do not want your ugly turnip."

"Unhand her at once!"

At the unexpected cry, Madeleine and grocer both

turned toward its source, she in hope and he in consternation.

Inside an open barouche lined in shell pink sat a gorgeous young woman as beautiful as she was angry. Curls the shade of ripe wheat were held in place by a bandeau of gold and foil from which two egret feathers gracefully bobbed. Diamonds sparkled at her ears and throat as she closed the parasol that had been shading her. "Are you deaf, fellow? I order you to unhand that holy woman."

The grocer's chin jutted forward under the push of his anger. "Mind ye own damned business, Jezebel!"

He clamped a meaty hand on Madeleine's waist and drew her toward him. Madeleine averted her face in time to miss having her cheek squashed against the tomato stain dripping seeds on his apron.

The beautiful young woman rose to her feet in the carriage, revealing a shapely form draped in ivory muslin. "Unhand that nun, my fellow, or I shall have you thrashed!" she said breathlessly, drawing every male eye to the low cut of her bodice.

The lady's footman alit from his perch and jammed his tri-corner hat over his powdered wig in anticipation of trouble.

The broad-bellied grocer sized up the lanky footman with contempt. Then his pinched gaze swept insultingly over the beautiful lady. "Ain't frail barks turnin' up proud today? What's it to ye, how I use a whore?"

This description galvanized Madeleine. "Most certainly I am not a whore!"

She twisted violently away from him. When this did not effect the release she desired, she swung her turnip like a ceremonial mace by its wilting leaves. Owing to a bit of luck it struck him right between the eyes.

With a roar of pain he released her and grabbed his nose.

"Come! Here!" Madeleine turned to see the lady beckoning to her. Needing very little encouragement, she did exactly that, reaching the carriage as the footman unfolded the step. With a smile of gratitude, she stepped up into the lovely conveyance. The footman then placed himself directly before it, his fists lifted as the grocer came charging toward them.

"Ere now! 'Ee can't do that!" The irate vendor turned in appeal to the crowd of gawkers that had quickly formed. "Ee all saw it! Stealin' my wares, she was!"

"She's got it still!" exclaimed a boy in the crowd who pointed a finger at the turnip drooping from Madeleine's fist.

Startled, Madeleine cast the troublesome tuber back where it belonged. It landed with a thud atop the pyramid of its mates. Unfortunately, that was enough to dislodge the pile. Turnips rolled and tumbled and fell into the street as onlookers chuckled and a few enterprising souls scooped the multicolored vegetable into their pockets.

"Ye'll pay for that!" the grocer shouted. "Put her down else I'll com' up and get 'er."

"You wouldn't dare." The regally dressed lady brandished her silk-and-ribbon parasol like a cudgel as the crowd roared encouragement to her foe. Suddenly she caught sight of someone in the crowd. "Ha! Now we shall see!" She subsided back onto the satin squabs of her carriage with a tiny smile of triumph.

Curious to know what had subdued the woman, the onlookers swung their heads in the direction of her gaze. A nobleman was coming their way carrying a bag of carrots, the ferny tops of which lay in a bright-green swoon upon the bosom of his fashionable coat of tobacco brown.

He did not have to push through the crowd. Those who had enjoyed watching two unchaperoned women be accosted realized instantly a change in the balance of power with the appearance of a noble. They melted away at once.

The gentleman looked thunderstruck when he recognized the carriage standing in the middle of the throng was his, and that the fashionable young lady adorned in pink and white, known well to him, was accompanied by, of all things, a nun. "I say! What's all this?"

"The blowen there stole me wares!" The grocer pointed in accusation at Madeleine. "Took a turnip."

"I tried to pay him," Madeleine rallied in her own defense.

Though obviously confused, the nobleman's gaze shifted from the shaken nun to the turnips in the gutter. "Fell off the turnip cart, did she? I don't wonder. A nun in Piccadilly. Rare as hens' teeth."

He reached into his pocket and tossed a coin the grocer's way. "Away with you, fellow." To the lady in the carriage he said, "Devil of it, Audelia! Didn't I say I wouldn't tolerate another scene?"

"We were being accosted," the lady replied sulkily. "Not, I see, that it matters to you!" She crossed her arms under her considerable bosom and turned her head away.

The flick of female anger found its mark. Complexion mottling with temper, the young nobleman cast away his bouquet of carrots like rejected tribute where they fell into the gutter. He then directed the footman to open the carriage door.

"Now then, Sister," he said, as he surveyed Madeleine with a glance that managed to be both doubtful and amused, "I believe you are free to go your own way."

Audelia came back to life. "Oh, but I've just taken her up, Richard dear."

With a sigh of resignation, the gentleman climbed in, sat down opposite the pair of women and gave the driver the nod.

The lady smiled charmingly at Madeleine and extended her hand. "We've not even been properly introduced. I'm Audelia."

"My name is Madeleine, mademoiselle," Madeleine replied.

"French!" The young nobleman was not especially handsome but had the benefits of obvious wealth, good health, and pansy-brown eyes in his favor. He removed his top hat. "I am Richard Baltry, baron of Thrawn. Howdy do?"

"Bien, merci. Despite the grocer, it would seem people in London are mostly kind," Madeleine said with a small smile.

"Not true!" Baltry answered crisply. He lazily fingered his gold-and-enamel watch fob. "Best look to yourself while in town, ma'am. There's those abroad as would fleece their own grannies for tuppence and Knock-me-Down."

"Richard," Audelia said in smothered tones, "you will terrorize the sister."

"What?" His sandy brows lifted. "Ha! Right. Don't mean to do that. No, not the thing." He winked at Madeleine. "There's the Watch abroad at all hours. Keeps the peace as much as it will be kept. Still, it don't do for a woman to walk the streets unaccompanied. Don't look right, even for a nun."

"I will remember, monsieur."

"I should like to ride in the park," Audelia said suddenly.

A frown of irritation puckered Baltry's brow. "You know my mind on that matter, Audelia." Yet he looked all done in by the sigh she heaved under the drape of a gown that left her frail sloping shoulders all but bare. "You will persist, won't you?" he said almost savagely.

Madeleine looked from one to the other. The gentleman subsided in a silent snit, while the lady opposite him nervously picked at the bolster beneath her pampered hand. Madeleine suspected they would be quarreling if she were not present.

Feeling quite the intruder, she said, "If it is not too

much trouble, I should like to be set down and given the direction of Whitehall, monsieur."

Her pretense at languor gone, the lady issued a shrill whistle that brought the driver up short in an abrupt stop.

"Devil of it!" Baltry muttered, then darted a rueful glance at Madeleine. "Sorry, Sister. Bad form. But dash it, Audelia! Why did you do that?"

Resuming her demure manner Audelia looked across at her escort through wounded eyes. "Leave us, Richard. I am determined to ride in the park."

"You cannot think of going alone? Or is that to the purpose?" His face swam with indignant color. "I won't have you meeting behind my back!"

"I am not going alone," Audelia answered with a sweet smile of spite. "I will take Sister Madeleine with me." She gave Madeleine an encouraging pat. "I have things I would say in particular to her. Female things."

Quite put out to be so put down, Richard issued a brisk order to the driver who pulled over to the curb.

"Only for you, m'dear," he murmured in resignation before he alighted from the coach. He tipped his top hat to the pair of them, reserving a special smile for his lady. "Until this evening?"

Audelia's eyes, the color of unripe apples, sparkled, and she nodded.

"Your husband is a very kind man," Madeleine observed as the coach rolled along.

"He is the finest man on earth." Audelia's golden lashes swept thickly down. "But he is not my husband."

Madeleine blushed at her mistake. *"Pardon, mademoiselle.* But he is clearly so, *pardonnez-moi,* so enchanted with you. You are very much in love, *non?"*

"Yes, Sister. I believe you are right." Audelia reached out and impulsively squeezed Madeleine's hands. "I knew the moment I saw you that you were a sign. You can't know what you've done for my spirits!"

A smile of satisfaction bloomed on her pink lips. "I was about to throw Richard over for another . . . well, *another.* But you are right. He loves me. He is not as wealthy or handsome as some, but he is kind and generous, and in his way truly devoted."

"You should marry him," Madeleine answered in all sincerity.

"Marry? But he is—" Audelia filled the interruption with self-effacing laughter. "Yes, I should marry him. I most definitely should!"

Madeleine did not quite understand the sudden pain that edged into the laughter in those bold eyes until she remembered the grocer's unkind words. He had called this lady Jezebel and she had not rebuked him. "You are Lord Baltry's amorata, *oui?*"

All animation left Audelia's face. "I am Richard's mistress. Does that offend you?"

Madeleine shook her head. *"Mais non.* In France a mistress often has the place of honor in a gentleman's life. But I am most curious. How did the grocer know you are a kept woman?"

Audelia laughed. "I ride about unaccompanied in the carriage owned by a man who is not my husband or relative. That is how."

"Are matters arranged so simply as that?" Madeleine asked in frank astonishment.

Audelia shook her head. "No, I am being unfair to Richard. I have been indiscreet often enough for word to get about. It is one of the reasons Richard and I quarrel so these days. I press him to take me out in public when we both know I should not be abroad just now. It invites these, ah, situations."

As they turned the corner into Hyde Park all the sundry details spilled out of Audelia, of how she and Richard Baltry had met at the Royal Opera House where she was a chorus singer. She explained how he had courted her until they finally succumbed to the emotion growing between them, of how he had then proposed but she had refused him, knowing his family would never accept her because she was Irish, not of his station, and, worst of all, a Catholic. She was the one who decided that she should become, instead, his mistress. She spoke so proudly of the little house he had bought and furnished for her, of how she filled it with things he loved in order to make him glad to come there, of how she had accepted the fact that he was about to bend to his family's wishes that he marry a distant cousin whom he scarcely knew and did not love. By the time they had made a complete circuit of the park, Madeleine was in full possession of Audelia's story.

"I don't want to lose him." Audelia flushed deeply. "I am terribly jealous of this impending marriage of his. I have created far too many rows of late. That is why I considered leaving him."

She bit her lip until it showed blood. "But I love him!" she ended in a tight little voice. "I fear I shall end up abandoned, but I cannot leave him. So there, I am lost!"

They lapsed into silence, the chastened and the chaste.

Madeleine accepted her hostess's tale in sympathy. Yet, her scant knowledge of the world did not prepare her to play Solomon in a matter so fraught with scandal and moral question. The convent had taught her that the world was a dangerous and wicked place. Even so, she knew—if only indirectly—of another world, a world in which aristocratic mistresses were once the most fashionable and sought-after women in all France.

She remembered well Madame Céline, the former comtesse d'Aixligy, who had for a time sought shelter from the revolution's atrocities at St. Etienne. Bringing with her a full entourage of servants and furnishings, even her private wine cellar, Madame Céline represented a life vastly different from the one the nuns lived. Once part of the most spoiled and pampered and indulged aristocracy

Europe had ever known, she was still beautiful enough to draw envy. She had been whispered about disapprovingly by those who knew about her life outside the cloister walls. They claimed she had had dozens of lovers and had been mistress to Louis XVI himself.

She had brought the scents and sounds of the mortal world into the cloister. Indeed, she had often mimicked the abbess behind her back, observing that the prioress never tired of taking the joy out of the smallest pleasure in life, of using every happy moment as a subject of reproach, and linking even love to sacrifice and suffering.

"Love is the finest feeling a woman can know, Madeleine," she had often said. "It is like an addiction. One taste and one always wants more."

The memory caused a sudden wrenching inside Madeleine, not unlike the onslaught of acute remorse. But it was not that. The longing was a familiar one, so sweet and dangerous that beside it the want of food was nothing. It was her own longing for worldliness. It was the real reason she had left the convent.

"No doubt, you are wishing me to the devil," Audelia declared after a short interval.

"No." Madeleine turned eyes full of new insight on the lady beside her. "I am thinking that you have chosen a most difficult path, mademoiselle. But you love this man, *oui?* What you do about those feelings may cause you pain, but your feelings, so strong and loving, cannot be wrong."

Audelia turned a face free from artifice of any kind to Madeleine. "You are a strange creature for a bride of Christ."

Madeleine leaned forward to whisper, "I will share a secret with you. I am not a nun, only a convent-bred schoolgirl."

With a sensual laugh, Audelia leaned back against the

squabs of the carriage. "I do not wish to lose your friendship, Madeleine. You will be a while in the city?"

"*Oui.* I am just arrived to visit my mother."

Audelia's gaze took in Madeleine's soiled and damp robes. "Your mother would be horrified to see you as you are now." She leaned forward. "You shall come home with me where my maid can remove the travel stains from your garments. It is the least I can do to repay you for your company."

Madeleine looked down at herself self-consciously. She was so weary she could scarcely keep her eyes open. What difference would an hour make? "*Enfin,* it seems I have no choice."

Audelia offered her a dazzling smile. "No, you do not! We shall have a lovely tea with sandwiches and little cakes!"

Madeleine relaxed against the luxurious upholstery thinking that life worked in mysterious ways. In being accused of the theft of a turnip, she had made her first friend in London.

Three

A CANTER 'MONGST THE HILLS

"Ride me, my gallant stallion! Ah! You kill me! I am dying! Dying!"

As my enthusiastic partner and I hurtled ever closer to the precipice by rhythmic motion of our joined bodies, I gently kneaded her heavy breasts, a device which frequently works to heighten the lasciviousness of women accustomed to a man's most intimate caress, and rode her to the conclusion of our mutual needs.

And, indeed, the device sufficed, for at the every acme of our spending she cried out, "My lord! My lord! Oh, you've slain me with your mighty lance!"

Withdrawing after a discreet interval from the heady perfection of her voluptuous body, I lay back among the bedding, my body slicked by the elixirs of our commingled pleasures.

After some moments of quieter heartbeats during which I gauged the rate of her pulse, I then penned a few notes, making use of her exquisite derrière as an impromptu writing desk upon which to prop my parchment.

Despite our exertions, the service of scientific inquiry had required me to bring to bear upon the moment of spending mighty reserves of concentration. I had taken *pains to note her flushed face and her mouth distorted by the low moans of rapture issuing from it. Rising up and away from her a little, I had also detected the high, hectic color that had transformed her pale breasts into ruddy hillocks mounted by tight ruby peaks.*

This, as I had observed before, overcomes every woman of a truly carnal nature, be she chambermaid or duchess. The voice, the words, the writhing, sighs, moans, and feminine extract of love: they may all be counterfeited. The budded nipples and "rash of love" are the unmistakable marks of the aroused woman.

As I labored with my pen in the cause of science, I yet recalled the advice of a former mistress to bestow upon my petite amour *of the moment the occasional tender pat or caress. I have been instructed by my feminine subjects that petting is a custom to which few men beyond the most accomplished rakes or avowed sensualists ascribe. This is a pity, they claim, for it soothes as well as arouses one's partner and may result in the most agreeable sequel. To wit . . .*

When I had tucked my quill away, Lady X rolled again toward me, offering the cushioning of her lush body for my benefit, and said, "My lord, have I pleased you?"

"Indeed, cara mia," answered I, as gallant as truth could make me. Her eagerness to participate as a subject in my experimentation was the most ardent I had yet received. However, such frankness did not seem prudent in the circumstance. "Most superb!"

She smiled prettily, then touched her pouty lips to my chin. Her voice dropped into a more provocative register as her black hair cascaded across my bare chest. "You are as rumor has it, my lord, a well-favored man." Her impudent fingers reached low and encompassed my genitalia. "Is it true also that you are equally superior in stamina?"

As boldly as any courtesan, she stroked and milked without hesitation the object of her desire, bringing it *quickly to a state which best pleased her. But she was not done. To assure its steadiness, she bent her russet-curled head and applied her nibbling mouth with great industry.*

At last, when need and nature were all but bursting from me, she leaned up on one elbow and gazed boldly into my eyes. "There are better uses to which we might put your mighty stallion, my lord. Will you not canter upon my hills yet again?"

Smiling as only a woman can who knows her undeniable attraction for the male, she swept my ever-eager body up into yet another carnal embrace.

These high jinks lasted until dawn touched roseate fingers to enliven the deep purple sky. An hour later, I retired to my own chaste bed, a sated if exhausted man.

The Honorable Mister Peter Eliott, younger brother of the Viscount Priestly, lay aside the manuscript he had been avidly perusing. "B'jove! Capital sport that, d'Arcy!"

Withdrawing a fine linen handkerchief from his lace cuff, he then dabbed his perspiring face. Though he and his companion shared a late supper in a private dining room at White's, yet he felt as if a dozen pairs of prying eyes were watching him.

It was the fault of the scurrilous text, of course. The bawdy tale had made him fidgety and more than a little randy.

"Damme," he murmured under his breath. " 'Tis a raw tale, if true." His furtive gaze darted again to the pages laid out before him. " 'Canter upon my hills,' indeed! Were those the lady's very words, d'Arcy?"

" 'Tis an approximation of sentiment." Turquoise eyes twinkling with amusement, Sebastian d'Arcy, marquis of Brecon, sat perfectly at his ease, swirling an after-dinner glass of claret between his long fingers. "As one of the participants," he continued, "I own that my thoughts were not entirely unclouded by matters at hand."

"Ho! To be sure, to be sure!" Eliott chuckled heartily to disguise his discomfort. He knew d'Arcy but slightly and could not imagine why the fellow had chosen him to dine with from the number milling about the general rooms. D'Arcy was a bit above his social touch.

"Flattered, of course. Flattered as hell!" he murmured under the influence of a surfeit of wine.

Sebastian had also been drinking steadily during the evening, though the effects did not show in his countenance, which was as vividly attractive as his expression was nonchalant. Tender but perfectly lucid blue eyes reflected his continual amusement with the world in which he lived but did not fully comprehend. Soft tawny curls, looped across his high brow like those of a toddler's, belied the broad and often harsh experiences of his twenty-eight years. Judging solely by his sartorial daring in matching a claret-red velvet coat with a gold-embroidered waistcoat of sky blue, a stranger might have thought him a foreigner. A closer association would have yielded the truth that Sebastian d'Arcy was that rarest of all sybarites, a consummate dilettante.

As his body stirred, Eliott's gaze swung back hopefully toward his companion. "I don't suppose you'd be willing to divulge the lady's name?"

"Alas, no." Sebastian smiled, the beauty of it quite disarming. "In any case, unless you are planning a sojourn to Italy, her name would gain you nothing. She is Neapolitan."

Eliott shrugged, resigned to disappointment. He had clamped eyes on risqué diaries before, most notably those of French origin. Yet he had never before been in the presence of the author of licentious material. Conversely, he felt as if it were *he,* not d'Arcy, who had been exposed cavorting in flagrante delicto on paper.

"You must tell me the news," Sebastian remarked in a casual change of subject. "I'm two years behind the times."

"I'd rather peruse a few pages more," Eliott replied.

Sebastian's gaze swung toward the risqué epistle he had penned, a droll smile playing upon his lips. "You must content yourself with these pages. I've taken you far into my confidence by sharing my latest scientific work before it is published."

Eliott started. "Scientific study? You jest?"

Sebastian smiled ruefully. "I admit the epistolary style lends the subject a certain . . . frisson, but this is no rake's Book of Amours. The text is part of a serious work. You did note my attention to the details of the encounter? The female responses to the rapture of spending are duly catalogued."

"Yes, yes they are." Yet Eliott's own responses made him doubt that zeal for scientific inquiry alone fueled d'Arcy's compunction to set down his amatory conquests.

Certainly Sebastian's father had been a devil with women. Everyone knew the late marquis had met an untimely death at the end of a cuckolded husband's rapier. Sebastian seemed to be made of altogether different cloth. And yet . . .

He had heard talk of d'Arcy's duel with Langley, the second to d'Arcy's credit, two years ago. Yet, the details had been so quickly buttoned up that none of his acquaintances could claim possession of the truth. Langley disappeared permanently from London while d'Arcy went immediately abroad. It was supposed that the duel had ended badly, with both men's honor impugned.

Now Eliott wondered if rumor had not greatly exaggerated. One had only to meet d'Arcy's lazy gaze to doubt the supposed intemperate passion that had embroiled him in both affairs.

That was the most curious thing of all. The rumors were

that d'Arcy had fought two duels not *over* women but *for* the women, as a kind of surrogate. The spicy *on dit* had gained him female adoration equal to that of Prinny himself. His own sister spoke of d'Arcy as a *chevalier sans reproche.*

Eliott's gaze edged back toward the pages. He had been initiated into the pleasures of the fairer sex at seventeen. Yet, never in the eleven years since, had he ever caused a woman to scream, "Ride me, my gallant stallion!" to mention nothing of, "Oh! I am dying! Dying! You've slain me with your mighty lance!"

Sebastian observed Eliott with more than passing interest. His real purpose in allowing the reading had been to gauge the reader's response. Eliott's reactions ran true to form. It seemed the nature of men that they could not learn of the sexual exploits of another without it stirring the noxious fumes of envy.

"I take it you disapprove," Sebastian observed mildly.

Eliott pulled on his lower lip " 'Tis not that I disapprove but, damme if I see the purpose. Any man can boast."

" 'Tis not a boast." Sebastian's perfectly arched brows rose in disdain. " 'Tis scientific pursuit with a purpose."

Eliott snorted. "To what purpose?"

"The purpose of advancing human knowledge." For the first time animation fueled Sebastian's expression. "We study the fowl of the air, the orbs in the heavens, and yet remain in abysmal ignorance of the nature of our own species. Unconscionable."

Eliott had never given the subject a thought. That did not prevent him from having an opinion. "Ignorance is expected. Shine the unforgiving light of scientific inquiry upon sexual matters and they might well shrivel!" The analogy provoked a guffaw from him. "Unforgiving light! Shrivel, don't you see?"

Sebastian saw all too well. "Do we not breed faster horses, fatter cattle, richer milk, and better wool by tinkering with the sexual nature of animals? Every good farmer keeps an accounting of the mating of his livestock. The lineage of a racing horse adds value to the unborn foal. How much better might our species be if we were to devote half so much attention to suitability when determining a matrimonial match. London's boudoirs are as much mating barns as Tattersall's paddocks."

Eliott sputtered into his brandy glass, spilling an amber stream down his already soiled ruffles.

"If men and women were more selective," Sebastian went on, "we might soon breed our world into better health and form. For instance, a man who is short and broad might think to wed a tall, thin lady, thus producing tall and hearty progeny."

He paused, fingers playing upon the stem of his wineglass. "I suppose they might also breed a passel of short, scrawny children or tall, excessively broad ones." His handsome face shone with zealous inquiry. "You see the dilemma? Such complexity of possibilities points out the need for so much more study."

"And this is the sole purpose of your scurrilous text, to pair men and women up by their attributes?"

The barest sigh escaped Sebastian, for Eliott had not grasped even the rudiments of his argument. "My work has led me to postulate several hypotheses. Another is that the only sensible role for a spirited intelligent woman is that of mistress."

Eliott paused in midgulp. "Mistress, did you say?"

"After a fashion, yes. You must admit that even the best husband treats his wife as little more than a child. He controls her wealth, her circumstance, where she may go, even whom she may see and receive. If he is a rakehell, a drunkard, or a fool, she can do nothing but endure.

"A mistress, on the other hand, has the potential to be in full control of her life. Is it not her choice with whom she shares her life and her bed? If her protector doesn't suit, does not society expect that she will supplant him with a better prospect? What wife can rid herself of a loutish husband?"

"Mayhap there is truth in what you say," Eliott replied, "but courtesans have no protection from the insults and shocks of the world, no reputation to speak of."

Something dangerous flickered in the depths of Sebastian's eyes. Eliott suspected it was the memory of his murdered mistress. The steely glint was enough to make him hastily revise his theory about d'Arcy's temper.

"Women perish if they believe they have no control. Yet, in every way a mistress has the advantage of her married sister if she will establish her independence and conduct her affairs like a man. A tarnished reputation seems little to exchange for such freedom."

"That is your premise?" Eliott's tone was that of a cleric confronted with a heretic. "That every lady should be taught to be a rake instead of a wife?"

Sebastian's smile was a thin one. "Well, it would bring a quick equality to the sexes. It would eliminate—"

"Half the sport!" Eliott chuckled, more comfortable with this line of conversation. "Damme me! The hunt is the spur to changing partners. The thought that the tender flesh of another's man's bit of muslin might be more tasty, the next pair of lips sweeter, the next pair of breasts, and so forth?"

Sebastian's smile ripened. "Then you will be all sympathy when I have a go at your own sweet Flora?"

Eliott's gaze dipped briefly to d'Arcy's lap. The folded ends of his tailcoat hid what must be, he suspected sourly, loins vastly well equipped. In defense of his own modest means, he said, "Make women equals and you destroy a man's prerogative. Women must keep their place, else what good are we to them?"

"Equality need not negate desire," Sebastian answered promptly. "I would welcome the company of a woman whom I could converse with as I do you, who knew like a man when to speak and when to keep silent, who could judge my every mood and anticipate my desires to our mutual benefit."

"She ain't been born!"

"I wonder," Sebastian replied in all seriousness. "If not, perhaps she could be created."

Envy flickered in Eliott's soul, a tiny hot flame of jealousy at d'Arcy's smug superiority. "I wager five thousand against your success at creating this formidable courtesan."

"You get ahead of me, Eliott. It is but a theory."

Eliott smirked. "Do I hear a lack of conviction in your scientific hypo—hypoth—?"

"Hypothesis. Not at all." The idea seemed to kindle in Sebastian's thoughts. "In theory all things are possible. Let's list the requirements." He ticked the requisites off on his fingers. "She would need be young and as yet untouched by the harsh realities of life. Singularly attractive, it goes without saying. Virginal yet not averse to men. Inquisitive of mind and able to read and write.

"As for her character, she must possess the traits of a lady, the heart and courage of a lioness, the practicality of a man, and the sensibilities of a wanton." He laughed softly. "Where do you suppose I will find such a young woman?"

"No doubt, she has yet to be born," Eliott muttered darkly, hoping against hope in his green-tinged soul that, if such an extraordinary female did exist, Sebastian d'Arcy might never lay eyes—or hands—on her.

Sebastian wandered the notoriously treacherous streets of London with sure footed freedom. The small sword hidden by his velvet coat was seldom used, yet never inaccurately.

A throbbing head had driven him from White's card tables after supper with Eliott. The moment he put a foot on the narrow lane a profound if familiar restlessness had seized him.

As he moved along, the acrid odor of burnt cabbage from one of the houses across the lane twitched in his nostrils. The sound of mice feet in the alley he passed made his nerves tingle. The faint veil of the fog weighed heavily on his ultra-sensitized skin. He could see figures scurrying like phantoms in the moonless night.

These "cerebral storms," as he called the bursts of mental activity, had struck him without warning since childhood. The harbinger was a heightening to an almost unbearable degree of his awareness of every sight, sound, smell, motion, and taste about him. Once they had terrified him and he had run away to hide until they subsided. Fearing his son's behavior was a sign of mental weakness or malignancy, his father had beaten him to discourage the behavior. The tactic failed. When caught by these feverish states, his luminous thoughts held him spellbound until the mood left him. As he grew older he had learned to control them for his own purposes. Sometimes they resulted in brilliant flashes of scientific insight. Other times they plunged him into a deep peace, much like a trance.

Tonight there were any number of burning questions that should have been occupying his roiling mind. For instance, the coded dispatches from the office of the Horse Guards which had been handed over to him upon his arrival in London this morning. The contents were so disturbing that they might set off panic along all the southern coast of England if the details were made public.

The French fleet, once scattered across the Caribbean, Atlantic, and Indian oceans, had gathered to reequip at Brest, Rochefort, Lorient, and Toulon. Spies estimated that upwards of a hundred fifty thousand men and ten thousand horses were massing along the French side of the Channel from Boulogne to Ostend. Invasion of England seemed imminent.

However, matters of national security were curiously absent from the maelstrom of activity that composed his teeming thoughts. The substance—not the amount—of Eliott's wager occupied him as he traversed the foggy streets.

In his eyes, the true abominations against women were the laws of men that made marriage an institution in which men reigned and women served or suffered their tyranny. He had learned that bitter and damning lesson from his father.

A man of insatiable appetites, uncertain temper, and intolerance marked by a streak of brutality, Simon d'Arcy had kept as many as three mistresses while his family went about barely clothed and fed. When his wife's health failed, he had brought a harlot to live under his own roof. The shock and shame had sent his wife to her grave.

The old anger welled up in Sebastian. The years of his father's tyranny had left an indelible mark on him. Despite his best efforts to live a reasonably temperate life, he had to his soul's blackened credit one dead mistress.

"Poor little Meg," he murmured under his breath. At the age of nineteen, he had lost her to an older roué who lured her away with promises of more than he could then provide. Greed had cost her her life. Yet he felt the burden of responsibility. He had not been able to save his mother from his father, nor Meg from her own folly.

The experiences had given him a new understanding of the human capacity for cruelty, not to mention his own deficiencies. He had called out her murderer, whom the courts would not even indict, and had the satisfaction of the man's apology, but that could not bring Meg back to life.

He was a product of the Age of Enlightenment: a scholar, a philosopher, and a student of natural science.

He knew that bloodlines often bred true. He had inherited an ingrained tendency toward vice and dissipation. What if, despite his own best efforts, he ultimately became as thorough a libertine as his detested father? The consequences to any woman he might make his bride would be . . .

"Intolerable."

The word escaped him as a whisper of disillusionment and exactitude. He liked and respected women, even adored them, but he knew that he was not a man upon whom any woman should depend. He could not—would not—burden any lady he cared for with his unreliable nature.

Yet, at the crux of Eliott's wager was the question of whether he could help an extraordinary woman achieve independence from that most unreliable quality in the universe: a man.

As he turned the corner, still steeped in his dark thoughts, he was surprised to find himself in Queen Anne's Gate, a once respectable neighborhood gone to wrack and ruin. His surprise quickened to astonishment when he spotted standing under the faint illumination of streetlight a slight figure dressed in the robes of a Catholic nun.

Her head was slightly bowed and one hand was folded over the dangling end of the gold cross that hung from her neck by a beaded chain. In the other she clutched a paper.

Sebastian felt the shock of her dismay along his spine. He heard her hesitation like the faint hum of an electrical current. The slight sigh of impatience she expressed seemed to be loosed directly into his ear. Thoroughly enchanted by this singular sight, he paused in the dark-blue shadows to watch and listen.

A cursory inventory of her in lamplight told him that she was wealthy—despite the telltale whitish seawater marks on her hem. His well-trained eye recognized the charming spidery design of the transparent veil dipping across her forehead as having been spun by a Flemish lace tatter. Finely woven linen formed the wimple which covered her throat and framed her face from just above her eyebrows to her chin. He was acquainted with the customs of continental nunneries which for centuries had provided a safe retreat for wealthy widows, unloved wives, and discarded mistresses, as well as noblemen's female children and blow-bys. Which, he wondered absently, was she?

After taking what seemed like a deep breath, she climbed the stairs of the first house on the block. Despite the meager light, he saw with unearthly clarity the shape of her arm as, fingers curled into a small tight fist, she lifted it to knock on the front door.

"I wouldn't, if I were you."

He almost felt sorry for her, so badly did she start at the sound of his voice. He stepped from the deepest shadow, removing his top hat as he did so. "The residents of this street have been known to up-end the contents of their chamber pots on the heads of those who wake them," he said in a kindly tone.

With a gasp of alarm she backed quickly away from the threshold. The sound of her sandals against cobblestones scraped lightly along his nerves, sending delicious thrills through his body. He swallowed his surprise. Never before in his life had he ever connected in such instant sympathy with another human being. Ideas had always fueled his brainstorms. Yet, when she glanced up at the tiny window over the lintel, which remained closed, he felt her relief like a light sea breeze on his face.

Though she was enveloped in the shapeless gender-cloaking garments of the clergy, he found the picture she presented to his preternatural vision a completely sensual one. Perhaps, he thought in bemusement, it was the lustrous sheen starlight gave her black cloak. Perhaps it was the delicious rustle of it as she moved. Or, perhaps it was simply the ancient lure of utter innocence. He had been deep in thought over women that—to be quite honest— were best categorized as whores. Now serendipitous chance had presented him with the image of a madonna. What could this mean?

He heard her soft catch of laughter as she again turned toward him, the novice-white robes beneath her black cloak glowing pale as moonlight. "Can you help me, monsieur?"

The small voice that barely escaped the voluminous folds of her robes was French-inflected. It set his thoughts spinning. Nuns were a rare commodity in England. No doubt, she had a fascinating tale to tell. If he could just lure her from . . .

Disconcerted by his own thoughts, he took a backward step. In his present state his emotions were far from governable or his actions predictable.

"Monsieur?" He saw her reach out uncertainly in the darkness. He knew he remained but a shadow to her while she was bathed in the faint but quivering effervescent aura provided by his sensitized vision.

"I'm here, Sister." His voice sounded strained, unnatural to his own ears. He told himself that he simply did not want this experience to end just yet.

He offered her a beguiling smile which was lost in the dark. "How can I help you?"

He heard again the odd catch of her breath, as if expectation came as both a delight and temptation to her. "Oh, monsieur, would you?"

As she approached he felt the breeze pass over him like a quiver of relief. The part of him that was not quite dead to decency deplored the ease with which she had accepted his help. It went to the heart of the matter, revealing as it did the depth of her naïveté that she would accept the word of a stranger in the dark. He almost felt sorry for her.

Telling himself that she was fortunate to have encoun-

tered him rather than any number of other disreputable
fellows who would have cared little for her robes or her
virtue, he gave in to the impulses driving him, dark and
nefarious as they might ultimately prove to be. "What can
I do for you, Sister?"

She whispered as if the night itself had ears. "Perhaps
I have the directions wrong." She held up a small slip of
paper. "I am looking for the residence of the Mesdemoiselles Foucant."

"The devil you are!"

She shrank back at his tone, but Sebastian snatched the
paper from her with one hand and grasped her by the
shoulder with his other. He looked down at her note, seeing a handwriting that was almost as familiar as his own.
Surprised, he lifted his head. "Who are you?"

Madeleine Foucant suspected she had made a serious
error. She had accepted on faith that *le bon Dieu* had provided for her a savior in the form of the stranger who
stood before her. Perhaps it was his voice. Deeply masculine and richly articulate, it had reached out to her in the
darkness with a solid persuasion. He had spoken with
authority, dependability, and humor. But now, as his oath
of displeasure echoed in her thoughts, a sense of dismay
flooded her.

"Don't come the oyster with me now, Sister. How do
you know the Foucants?" He sounded perfectly amiable
again, but the pressure of his hand on her shoulder held
her firmly in place.

"Monsieur?" she asked a little sharply because her
thoughts had dragged her far from the moment. "I am a
relation, monsieur, newly arrived in your city."

"Another Foucant? How delightful." His voice was full
of amusement. "I am charmed."

She jumped nervously, startled by the warmth of his
hand when it encountered hers in the darkness. She tried
to pull away, but he locked her fingers within his.

"Do not fear me, little sister." He drew her hand to his mouth and pressed warm lips into her palm.

The shock of it was so pleasant that for a moment Madeleine did not protest. Unaccustomed till now to such stimulation, her senses blazed in response to the intimate caress. His lips and breath warmed the blood in her cold, cramped fingers, bringing them instantly and painfully to life. Nothing but instinct made her say, "You should not."

"What? Are nuns not permitted even the simplest courtesies? A pity." Despite his words, she believed, in the squeeze he gave her fingertips, that the darkness hid a smile.

"I must go in, monsieur. They are waiting."

The whispered word "waiting" struck Sebastian oddly as her anxiety reached him in gentle eddies across the umber distance between them. Gazing down at her bent head, he caught the rough shadow of her thoughts which, unless his overheated senses betrayed him, were of how best to escape from him unharmed. Had his cerebral storm illuminated a heretofore dark corner of his brain to render him capable of reading minds?

Instinct made him lift his head and scan the darkness. It occurred to Sebastian to wonder if he were being set up for a fleecing. All sorts of scams were used to cozen the unsuspecting gull, as the underworld referred to their victims.

An instant later he heard the faint rasp of another breath. Someone else shared the darkness with them.

The odors of pickled herring, sweat, and sour ale sailed past Sebastian's nostrils on the breeze. What hugger-muggery was this? Perhaps the virginal innocent with him was neither virginal nor innocent.

He swung an arm about her shoulders and pulled her into a narrow alley between two houses. On a moonless night like this, only those of God's creatures blessed with nocturnal vision would have realized the gap was there.

Pressing her firmly to the wall, he wedged his body into the space beside her.

He felt her gather breath to scream and covered her mouth with his hand. As he did so, his senses flamed to the fuel of new sensation. Beneath his palm the shape of her mouth seemed to burn its impression into his skin. It was a delicately sensual mouth. Too tenderly charming for one of Christ's brides, he decided as quite profound and unexpected feelings stirred him.

Quick footfalls passed so close to them now that he could hear the bellows breathing of the man more sharply than his own. She heard it, too, the little nun struggling against his embrace.

She gasped against his muzzling hand. Her fear fluttered about him with the smothering intensity of hummingbird wings, and her vulnerability touched him in a place where he thought he had no real feeling: his heart. Yet, he was cynical enough to suspect that her fear might actually be caused by the fact that her accomplices were abandoning her.

Pressed together, he registered a dozen disturbing details about her. She was a frail bit of womanhood reaching no higher than his nose, and much too thin. Beneath the press of his body her bones were disturbingly prominent, yet their intimate contact yielded up to his ultra-sensitive skin the contours of a being wholly designed as female. The strapping beneath her robes did not successfully hide the natural push of young breasts. Five pounds, no ten; ten pounds would make her Aphrodite.

The man faltered only an arm's length away now. Sebastian heard him sniff, as if the air would offer a scented clue to their whereabouts. "Ye see 'em?" came a whisper.

"Sink me if I do!" came a reply from across the way. "Come on, then. We lost 'em!"

When their bootsteps had died away, Sebastian lifted his hand to hover an inch from her mouth. "I want to know, my little anchoress, why we were being watched."

For the first time since their meeting, Madeleine was afraid of the man beside her. "I cannot say."

"Cannot or will not?" He found her throat and curled his fingers very carefully over the fine linen fabric there, pressing just enough to make his threat appear real. "You are a stranger to these shores, my little French contemplative, if that is what you really are. France and England are at war. Therefore you are my enemy. How do I know you do not mean me harm?"

Madeleine made a small movement with her head. "I had not considered this, monsieur. *Enfin.* You must do as you must."

"Must I?" He leaned in toward her, blocking out even the darkness of the night. "Oh, my little sister," he whispered against her ear, "you don't know how dangerous an offer you make me."

He felt her swallow against the pressure of his thumb, and was astonished to sense that her fear was not an indication of guilt. "I will scream and bite and make you very little sport, monsieur. Spend your lust where it will be more welcome."

Sebastian's shout of laughter startled them both. She knew! This virtuous little penguin understood that he might well be depraved enough to want to possess her, nun's habit or not. And yet she did not fear him as much as he might have supposed.

He released her. "Tell me again who you are. I will know if you lie because the Foucant sisters are well known to me."

He watched in fascination as her hands unfolded like floral petals from about the stem of the cross she had been clutching. "I am Madeleine Foucant, monsieur."

"Madeleine?" The name was unfamiliar to him, but something made him believe her. "Very well, little one."

He stepped out of the alley and handed her the paper he had taken. "You have the right address, though if it be true . . ." He bit off the last of his thought. If this really was the Foucant sisters' new residence, things had changed greatly while he was away. "Go now, I say. I will keep watch until you're safely inside."

"Merci, monsieur." She touched his sleeve with the delicacy of a butterfly's wing, whether by design or accident he could not tell. "Monsieur?"

"Yes, Sister."

"You are a very bad man."

"I know."

"But not so bad as you think!"

Laughing, she lifted her head, a graceful movement that gave Sebastian his first unshielded view of her eyes, and it was as if she touched the core of him with her gaze.

Those eyes! Deep as summer shade and bright as a moonlit sea. Those dark eyes were not merely black or brown but tinged with the deep indigo blue of a star-spattered night.

He closed his eyes. It was a trick of his brainstorm, he told himself, this sudden, certain sense that she had seen into his very soul.

Embarrassed by his cowardice, he opened his eyes. In the blink of an eye the world had changed. He was no longer at Queen Anne's Gate but stood in the shadow of Whitehall. Across the Thames dawn was lightening the sky while behind him Big Ben intoned the hour. Cursing roundly, he realized that his "cerebral storm" had passed, altering as it often did his sense of time's passage. Hours had passed like seconds.

He hailed a hackney and climbed in. Laughter trailed in its wake as it occurred to him that after generations of voluptuaries, the Foucants had at last produced a nun, and a very pretty one at that.

Sebastian, he silently admonished himself in humor mixed with the bleakest of despair, *you are destined to be damned!*

Four

"You have not taken a nun's vows?" Justine reiterated.

"No," Madeleine answered. "The robes were for my protection."

"You see? I told you." Henrice gazed smugly at her sister. "It is a mummery. A mere charade."

Madeleine offered her aunts a dutiful smile. As she looked at these darlings of the *ancien régime,* it seemed as if the Reign of Terror had never been. They wore silk wrappers over their dishabille, Henrice's scarlet and Justine's turquoise, the candlelight revealing a smooth swell of bosom here and a round dimpled thigh there. Henrice's hair of titian red and Justine's of daffodil yellow were tied up in yards of ribbon that trailed from their curls like May Day streamers. Despite the efforts of Audelia's maid, Madeleine felt like a starving crow who had mistakenly flown into the aviary of a pair of tropical birds. She needed the reassurance that only one person could give her.

"Where is *Maman?*"

She saw the glances that passed between her mother's elder sisters before Henrice said succinctly, "Away."

"Away?" Madeleine pressed. "Has something . . . happened to her?"

"Certainly not." Henrice glanced at her in annoyance. "Ondine is as well as ever."

Madeleine swallowed the bile of disappointment at not

finding her mother there. "Is she with her English husband?"

"Alas, Ondine's Englishman has died," Justine answered.

"Died!" A stricken expression crossed Madeleine's face. "Poor *Maman*. She did not tell me this. How sad she must be."

"She is not alone in mourning her loss," Henrice murmured under her breath. "But come, do not look sad. Your mama regrets most terribly to be away at the moment of your arrival, but we will look after you until she returns. Is this not so, Justine?"

"Oui," Justine concurred, but it was clear she was distracted by her own thoughts. "We are, all of us, very much in need of protection. There is so little we can do for ourselves."

Looking at them, Madeleine could believe it. Hothouse orchids could not have seemed more fragile or easily bruised than her aunts, nor less capable of managing for themselves.

As the horrid woman who had answered the door brought in a tea tray, a new thought occurred to Madeleine. "Were you expecting company?"

"Company?" Justine smiled. *"Non,* though we do entertain more lavishly from time to time."

Madeleine glanced surreptitiously about the salon. Tiny and cramped, it was filled to bursting with fine and costly examples of furnishings of an earlier age. The wood of the settees and chairs was gilded. Porcelain bric-a-brac of the finest quality crowded every available surface, along with silver candle holders and marble busts. Turkey carpets covered floors end to end, and paintings hung frame to frame on the walls. Yet the velvet window hangings were badly soiled and streaked with dust. In the dark corners where candlelight barely reached, cobwebs sagged under a thick powdering of dust. Above the mantel the wallpaper had begun to peel away from the masonry. She had lived most of her life in a cell much smaller and austere than this chamber. But that her aunts would tolerate such shabbiness appalled her.

"Is this *Maman*'s house? She described it as much . . . larger."

"Your mama's house is undergoing renovation." Henrice lifted a hand to her brow. "Such hammering and clattering and noise and tramping of feet! It was not to be endured! We retreated here until it is safe to return."

Madeleine wrinkled her nose. "But it is so dirty and damp."

Henrice's eyes narrowed, though she more than agreed with her niece's every word. "Have you then grown so proud, *ma petite,* that you cannot endure a little mildew?"

Madeleine crimsoned. "I mean no criticism, Tante Henrice. I was expecting something . . . else."

"Then you expect too much, *ma chérie.*" Henrice rearranged her Paisley shawl about her shoulders. "Think of the brisk air and spartan conditions as a penance. How much more we will then enjoy the new improvements."

Madeleine doubted that damp quarters were necessary to induce an appreciation of fresh paint but refrained from saying so. Audelia's house had been small but much nicer. She smiled as she remembered the hours recently spent there. She had not meant to fall asleep on Audelia's Recamier but she could not help herself. Audelia had not awakened her for several hours. By then it was dark. Even so, she was still weary. She tried but failed to hide a yawn behind her hand.

Henrice's sharp eyes noticed that hand. She snatched it up for better inspection. *"Ma foi!* You have blisters!"

"And calluses!" Justine added in abhorrence as she inspected Madeleine's other hand. "Such an embarrassment for a Foucant! What tortures have you been subjected to in that horrid convent?"

Madeleine gazed ruefully at her hands which had pained

her for the week since she had rowed wine casks ashore. She suspected that if she told her aunts that she had been bartering with smugglers they would swoon in horror. "At the convent we were taught that we must all do our part of the work," she said evasively.

"Surely one of your position is better suited to embroidery or tatting," Henrice replied.

"I worked in the convent's kitchen," Madeleine answered.

"Kitchen?" A note of complete mystification struck through Justine's inquiry.

Madeleine smiled proudly. *"Oui.* I have become a very good cook, taught by the Comtesse d'Aixligy's personal chef. I will make the best meals you have eaten since you left Paris."

"You will do nothing of the kind!" Henrice snapped.

"But if she . . . ?" Justine began, thinking she might yet charm a salmon from the elusive fishmonger's son.

"Certainly not!" Henrice subjected her sister to a blighting glance. "Madeleine is a Foucant. Foucants never set foot in the kitchen. That is the realm of the *domestique.*"

She rose slowly, dramatically. "Where are your bags, *ma fille?* Did you leave them on the steps? You must have a bath and a change of clothing before you go to bed."

Madeleine looked a little guilty. "I have nothing with me."

Henrice gave a long-suffering sigh. "I see. I will compose a letter at once demanding the abbess send your things."

"I have no things."

"What is this? But that is not possible. We sent clothing every year."

"They were given away."

"The aging things, of course. That's most generous of you. But you will need the gowns we sent last spring. Your mother took great pains to find just the right styles and fabrics to accentuate your youth and coloring."

Madeleine smiled. "They were beautiful but impractical. I sold them."

"Sold . . . ?" Henrice could not bring herself to finish the thought. "You *sold* your clothing?"

"All the silks and velvets and lace?" Justine inquired.

Madeleine nodded. "The money raised was given to the poor."

"Poor?" the two sisters echoed the word together in tones that seemed to convey it was not part of their vocabulary.

"Surely not the gown your mother sent last year for your first communion?" Henrice questioned encouragingly.

Madeleine beamed with pride. "It brought the best price as it was easily altered as a wedding gown. Naturally, I had no further use of it."

"Your own marriage, perhaps?" Justine suggested.

"I do not plan to marry," Madeleine answered.

Henrice smiled. "You see, Justine? Madeleine understands perfectly what is expected of her. But you must be seen in public very soon."

She reached out and took Madeleine's arm, pushing the soiled white sleeve of her robe back to reveal her arm to the elbow. "Just as I suspected. You are much too thin. Gentlemen prefer a little something to hold on to. Never fear, we shall fatten you up with cream soups and egg soufflés. Two weeks at the most and you will outshine all these pale English girls." She snapped her fingers. "Remove this veil so that I may see you."

Reluctantly Madeleine complied, unpinning her veil and then her wimple. A joint gasp of dismay sent her gaze leaping up to the aunts' stricken expressions.

"Mon Dieu! They've shorn her like a sheep!" Justine's soft hands flew up to her eyes to shield them from the sight.

Though she had become a trifle pale, Henrice was made of sterner stuff. "What have they done to your lovely hair? Come here, child. Let me see."

Madeleine put a self-conscious hand to her short curls. "There was an infestation of lice last winter. The nuns sheared all heads to be rid of them."

"The shock value for the lice must have been quite effective," Justine murmured.

Lips thinned, Henrice fearlessly inspected her niece's cropped hair like a farmer assessing the quality of a sheep's wool. She swallowed her disappointment that she would not have at her disposal the yard of mahogany tresses that had once been Madeleine's crowning glory.

"It's filthy," she said crossly as she rubbed her fingers through Madeleine's thick, dark curls. "But it is not a disaster. Come, no more hysterics, Justine. Look at her."

Henrice patted her niece's cheek, then lifted her chin, tilting her face so that the candlelight rendered the high delicate curves of Madeleine's cheekbones in the slender oval of her face. "Look. The bones beneath her skin are perfect! This is where true beauty lies. Comely flesh will wither and drape but good bones endure. Foucant women are known for our bones and our teeth." She bared hers in a faultless display. "But it is the eyes that make the face. Long-lidded and dark as a moonlit ocean. *Magnifique!*"

Justine joined in. "You are right! Those eyes could be her fortune. We shall darken the lashes a little but not enough for even the most sophisticated eye to notice. Cropped hair is all the rage on the Continent, though few English ladies have the features to carry it off. We will make a few crisp curls across that tender brow, and *voilà!* The next toast of London!"

Madeleine listened to them in growing agitation. "I do not want to be a toast!" she said finally. "I do not wish to be a fashionable lady who idles away her days buying hats and trying on dresses and waiting for gentlemen to come calling." She realized she might have been describing her own relatives but she was too tired to master the mulish streak which occasionally caused her trouble.

"Is this the thanks we are to receive in sending for you?" Henrice questioned impatiently. "We thought to brighten your world, to offer you a taste of a life you cannot yet imagine."

"I don't want it," she repeated. "I intend to become a chef."

Henrice paled. "A cook?" she hissed scornfully. "You cannot mean it!"

"Give Madeleine time," Justine suggested. "She's but a child, and road weary."

"Never!" The inflexibility that had made her a diva and the bane of many a theatrical manager's existence, animated Henrice's voice. "I'll have her answer now," she said harshly. "If she cannot be reasonable, she must go back to the convent at once. Today!"

Madeleine closed her eyes against the sight of her aunts. She was not only disappointed and saddened by what she had found here tonight, but frightened as well. There was a cold despair deep inside her. She suspected it was because she did not believe them when they said her mother was away. Away where? Why would she write a desperate letter and then disappear?

These women with familiar names were really strangers, figments of thirteen long years of imagining. She did not really know them, nor they her. She shivered. If only her mother were here to comfort her.

"Well, Madeleine, what is it to be? Are you willing to deliver your future into the safe-keeping of your aunts or will you retreat to the interminable dullness of the convent?"

"Is it your most fervent wish to become a nun, Madeleine?"

Madeleine opened her eyes to the sight of Justine hovering close. "The convent is all I have known and I've not been unhappy there. But no, I did not wish to become a nun. But I feel I must seek *Maman*'s advice before I make any decision."

"And that you shall, just as soon as she returns."

"From where?" Madeleine demanded.

Henrice shrugged. "Why from where she's gone, of course."

Justine enfolded Madeleine gently in her arms. *"Ma petite,* you are not meant for the church or the servants' quarters." She smiled through tears. "I promise you will not regret remaining with us."

"It is settled!" Henrice declared, every frosty line of her strong face thawing. "Now, I hope you have not spent every sou of the money your mother sent you for your journey?"

Madeleine quickly bowed her head to hide her reaction to this statement. There had been no money, only gifts, from her mother in well over a year. Yet she did not wish to reveal this fact while her mother was not here to defend herself. She was certain she had meant to include money.

"I take this silence to mean that you did spend every cent," Henrice said coldly.

Resentful of her aunt's tone, Madeleine produced the last of her ill-gotten coins. "I didn't need it all. I'm certain *Maman* would want me to share her generosity."

As the bright metal fell like a golden manna into her hands, Justine's blue eyes widened to their limit. "It is a miracle! A miracle," she breathed in hushed awe.

"Not so much a miracle, Justine." Henrice scooped the temptation from her sister's hand. "But what is this?"

Her pearl-gray gaze lifted in sharp inquiry from the coins to Madeleine's face. "This is English coinage when we always sent drafts for French francs. How did you come by it?"

A prickly flush once more traveled up Madeleine's neck and into her cheeks. It had not occurred to her that they would question the currency. The incidental meeting outside their door brought forth a new lie. "I exchanged them with an English gentleman."

"Madeleine!" As her aunts stared at her in astonishment, Madeleine experienced the most inappropriate urge to laugh. "I was lost and the gentleman paused to offer me directions."

"I am certain he did," Henrice muttered with a tiny shake of her head. "Foolish, foolish child."

Annoyed to have been cast so completely in the wrong, Madeleine said frostily, "The abbess often admonished us to rely on the goodness and charity of others. Her favorite story is the parable of the woman at the well who offered a drink to a thirsty stranger and thereby secured a place in heaven."

"Ah, but the stranger was an angel," Henrice responded.

"In the disguise of a man," Madeleine added in justification.

"There is another difference," Justine said more kindly. "Men will take advantage."

"Not of a nun, surely?" she scoffed.

Justine rolled her eyes. "I once knew a gentleman who took particular delight in—"

"Justine! Recall yourself. Madeleine is speaking of *les hommes de chevaleresque.*"

"But the gentleman *was* most chivalrous," Justine continued, unabashed. "I have the diamond necklace he gave me to prove it."

Henrice turned from her sister in annoyance. "I will send Mrs. Seldon to the market in the morning to spend a few of Madeleine's English coins on wine, cheese, cream, and eggs."

"Could we have salmon?" Justine put forth. "Then perhaps Madeleine could show Mrs. Seldon how it should be prepared. The English persist on destroying a fish by boiling it." She rolled her eyes heavenward. *"C'est incroyable!"*

Finding at last a family sentiment in which she could share, Madeleine nodded. "I make a broiled salmon with capers and butter sauce—"

"Non!" Henrice snapped. "You must never again sully—"

"I should consider cooking for *Tante* Justine an honor," Madeleine rallied in defiance.

Justine sent a pleading glance between the two. "Perhaps just one small demonstration, Henrice, so that we may judge what she has learned?"

Henrice's lids flickered. "A small knowledge of food may not go unrewarded. I once had the honor of preparing a dish of oysters for Monsieur—Ah, *peu importe.* Prepare your salmon, then. Now up to bed with you, at once."

"What do you think?" Justine asked her sister when Madeleine had left.

"The child has scant manners, no tact, and less sense of her place." Henrice smiled in spite of her censorious tone. "But she has a force of personality much like mine, *oui?"*

When the bell beside the Foucant front door again jangled to life a little before midnight, the Mesdemoiselles Foucant did not even stir. Having spent the last hours in discussion of Madeleine's future, they were now reclining gracefully in a deep state of slumber.

The third ring brought Mrs. Seldon shuffling down the narrow stairs from her attic room. In the best of times, her speech was unpleasant and her manners surly. The required trip from her cozy cot did not endear her to the caller, for she had just about finished her own secreted bottle, that of Blue Ruin.

" 'Old yer fornicatin' 'orses," she muttered.

Grabbing the latch, Mrs. Seldon jerked and pulled and tugged at the old warped door while expending a good portion of her considerable gutter vocabulary in an effort to open it. Just as she was about to give up, the visitor on the other side put a shoulder to the recalcitrant door and it suddenly popped free of its frame with the force of a cork loosed from champagne. Carried backward by the impelling force of its weight, the maid slammed her head against the wall of the tiny hallway.

Cursing roundly, she grabbed her aching head and staggered into the breach, ready to lay Cane upon Abel with the unwelcome guest. Yet the fearsome sight of a tall wraithlike figure on the doorstep with the wind whipping at his black cloak was too much for her gin-fuzzed mind.

With a shriek that loosened a few curls of dried paint from the peeling doorjamb, she staggered back and swung away.

"There's a creature at the door, mam'zelles!" she cried as she passed the salon entry. "The devil's own spawn come to sweep us straight into hell!. Run fer yer lives!" Having delivered her message of doom, she clattered up the stairs.

"Who did she say comes calling?" Justine questioned groggily as she sat up.

"A gentleman," Henrice replied. She reached up to pat her curls in place as she rose to her feet. "I will welcome him."

"Enter, monsieur," Henrice said with great ceremony as she swung the front door open. The note of welcome ended on a choked, "Monsieur De Valmy!"

"You do not looked pleased to see me, Madame Henrice."

Henrice Foucant lowered her thick lashes, eclipsing for

a moment the hated image of the man who stood before her. *"Mais non, monsieur.* I am only surprised. Come in."

But her heart was beating irregularly. Monsieur De Valmy delighted in these little surprise visits. If he had arrived earlier, he might have found Madeleine with them. Thankfully, she was now in bed.

The man with the black mustaches of a French hussar stood so exceptionally tall, he had to dip his head in order to enter. He was, as usual, dressed all in black: coat, waist-coat, breeches, and satin cravat. He said it was mourning for his lost family, aristocrats who had sneezed into Madame Guillotine's basket. A student of the theater, Henrice suspected it was an affectation which dramatized his height and suited his saturnine features.

"You were expecting a suitor, perhaps?" he pressed as he handed her his tri-corner hat.

"A friend, monsieur." She forced herself to smile into those great black eyes that held no pity. "Only a friend."

"I see." He looked about the tiny salon and sniffed. "Nothing like the old days, is it?"

"Nothing is like the old days," Henrice answered carefully. *"Enfin,* we all survive."

His hawklike face, dark and long-nosed, turned toward her. "You may do better any time."

Henrice blinked before that stare. Mesmerizing, chilling. Many women initially found De Valmy handsome. Once, twelve long years ago, she had submitted to his embrace and found him repellent. Better a snake in her bed than he.

"It has been days, monsieur," Justine began without greeting as she rose to greet him. "You have word of Ondine, *oui?"*

De Valmy turned with deliberation toward the younger, prettier sister and subjected her to a long slow scrutiny. *"Je regrette,* madame. I do not have promising word of Ondine." A smile lifted his wide mouth. "In fact, I am most discouraged by the lack of information coming out of France."

"Do have a seat, monsieur," Henrice encouraged with a quelling glance at her overanxious sister.

De Valmy surveyed the seating arrangements in distaste before choosing the chair nearest the hearth. After dusting the seat with his handkerchief, he arranged his long frame on it. He knew the Foucant women were watching him. He liked to be watched, almost as much as he liked watching. He had never yet been able to fully cower this pair of harlots. But, by the looks of things, that moment was rapidly approaching. He would have to devise a special humiliation for them as payment for making him wait so long.

"The world is so much changed, monsieur," Justine said in a sigh of resignation. "Not like before. Never like before."

"It is to be lamented, of course, but we must deal in the present. I have always been a friend to you, have I not?"

"Oui, monsieur," Henrice answered in the hope of steering the conversation her way. "We are most grateful for all you have done."

"Then you will understand if I must press you in spite of the friendship." He sipped a little of the inferior sherry Justine had pressed into his hand, grimacing in distaste as it went down. "Remind me to favor you with a bottle from my cellar," he said, handing it back to her. "Now then, Channel crossings are not easily accomplished. With the renewed war the dangers are greater, the stakes higher. Ondine understood that her diamonds could only take her so far. She was willing to carry a small package from me. But now it appears that she has disappeared, and the package with her."

"Disappeared," Justine echoed, looking quite faint.

"What is to be done, monsieur?" Henrice asked.

"I must appeal to your loyalty to the past and our hopes for the future, mesdames. A royal future."

"We understand, monsieur, we are *loyal en tout*. Alas, we are bereft of the coin of any realm with which to help you."

He looked amazed. "I cannot believe it. Did I not give Monsieur Ferries your direction?"

"He left his card." Justine sniffed. "He is bourgeoisie! A woolen merchant."

"He is a very wealthy merchant." De Valmy's black eyes ranged back and forth between the pair. "He quite understands that under ordinary circumstances, he could never hope to aspire to the favor of ladies of your pedigree. He is prepared to be most generous to the one of you who so favors him."

Justine shook her head. "I cannot. An English merchant? I will not."

"Then perhaps you will reconsider selling your jewels." His gaze turned suddenly chilly, though his tone remained polite. "Or better yet, what of your niece? I understand she is to visit you. As she is a Foucant, she must be quite a beauty by now."

"Little Madeleine? She is but a child, monsieur, a very young girl whom the nuns have infected with their morbid fear of the world." Henrice gave a practiced sigh. "I was horrified to learn in her most recent letter that they have convinced her not to leave. Is this not so, Justine?"

"Oui," Justine murmured uncertainly.

Henrice picked up the slack. "We fear we have lost her forever, monsieur. She is expected to take her vows any day."

Monsieur De Valmy's reaction to this piece of news was a slight curl of his lip. "Such a waste of young flesh, *oui, mesdames?"*

He stood up abruptly. "I must have the cash in order to bribe those who might have word of your sister. It means nothing to me how you come by the funds. If you cannot beg or borrow, then you can whore in the streets for it." The last was offered with an inflection as cruel as a lash of a whip. "Or, as I warned you, you may lose Ondine. *Au revoir.*"

"I did not think matters could become worse," Henrice said when he was gone. "Foucants have sailed over bad patches before. *Tout de même,* but his suggestion is odious. As if we would whore among wool shearers and tin miners for our bread!"

"Whor—?" Justine could not complete the thought and fell to softly weeping.

Henrice gave her sister a hard look but could not scold her. De Valmy was more of a danger than Justine seemed to realize. She had not missed his spark of interest in their niece. He already held the fate of Madeleine's mother in his hands.

The light of a challenge accepted shone in Henrice's wide gray eyes. She had once gambled as often as her sister but she had never grown accustomed to losing gracefully. This time she had an ace up her sleeve in the form of Madeleine. It stood to reason that De Valmy would eventually learn they had lied about Madeleine. Before he did, she would have the *jeune fille* placed safely into the hands of Lord d'Arcy whose protection and money would solve all their problems.

"Now where did I put that brandy? Ah, *mais oui.*" She reached over and plucked several books from the shelf, plunged her hand into the empty space, and retrieved a dust-laden bottle of heavy brown glass. *"Tiens!* The very thing to perk up spirits."

Justine held out the teacups while Henrice poured two thimblefuls into each, and then both sisters sat in the gloom and sipped gratefully this savory reminder of their former lives.

As she drifted back to sleep there loomed just one tiny

speck on Henrice's sunny horizon. Madeleine would save them all when d'Arcy accepted her. Until then, she must not learn the danger her mother was in or she would surely go back to France to look for her.

Five

THE VIRTUE OF VIRTUE

*She said her name was Dorcas and that she was sixteen.
Sent by my host to valet me, she helped me undress without
a word.*

*In truth, I had no designs on the girl. I had retired in
exhaustion from the weekend house party's entertainment
which had left me spent, or so I thought. But Dorcas, that
lively minx with her bright button eyes and saucy smile,
had other plans.*

*Her fingers quickly divested me of my coat, waistcoat,
and cravat and then moved to the double rows of my
breeches buttons. She had me undone in a trice. The faint
stirring of the man below stairs upon release renewed my
attention to her.*

*With a soft exclamation of surprise, she took me boldly
in her hands. "Oh, m'lord, it's ever so lovely. So fit and
clean. Not crusty purple and veiny like some others."*

*Ever impressionable to female praise the arrogant fellow
stood right up and doffed his cap. "And look how well it
grows. Ain't bashful in the least, is he, my lord?"*

*I smiled ruefully as she looked up at me, reminded of
Pope's phrase that, at heart, every woman's a rake. Yet I
was less willing than nature would lead her to believe.*

"Are you breeched, Dorcas?"

She colored rosily, revealing for the first time her youth and immaturity. "I can be, my lord, for your consideration."

The brassy fellow wilted a little. Deflowering virgins was not my style. "Never mind, child. Get you to bed."

Instead of releasing me, she continued her stroking, a look of grateful relief on her face. "But you're achin', my lord. I can ease that achin', if you please. Sit there on the edge of the bed, my lord."

Charmed and curious, I complied. Smiling, she knelt before me. "So fresh and lively, it is. It deserves a kiss, my lord." Ever willing in the service of a female, my once expiring flesh came immediately to life at the touch of her lips. Encouraged, she took me in her mouth and enthusiastically applied herself to my rampaging member.

Conclusion: The English are wont to call this form of servicing the French Talent. Yet, as the supremely skilled creature kneeling between my spread legs was fresh down from Northumberland, her enthusiasm for the exercise has led me to conclude that an adjustment in geographical reference to the skill is necessary. Perhaps it should be deemed the Universal Talent.

Sebastian set his quill aside and blotted his freshly penned text with a satisfied smile as the room clock chimed the hour. Unfortunately, he mused, the results of his coming engagement would likely put an end for a time to his literary reminiscences.

Sebastian entered the British Museum with two purposes in mind. He had come to view an astounding acquisition, the Rosetta Stone brought back as plunder from Alexandria by English forces after their defeat of Bonaparte's army at the Nile two years earlier. He was also to report to General Leslie Armstrong.

Through Armstrong's offices, the Horse Guards found Sebastian's scientific studies of use from time to time, most recently to the army in Cairo in '01. He suspected he had been summoned for a part in heading off the efforts of Napoléon Bonaparte to expand his empire.

Sebastian spied the general just inside the doorway, his red uniform trimmed in expensive gold lace and buttons. There was a sense of majesty about the man who had once been considered among the most seasoned officers in His Majesty's colonial army. Armstrong had been Simon d'Arcy's friend and had stood second in the duel that ended his life.

"General," Sebastian offered coolly.

The man stared coldly back at the sartorially splendid young man in bottle-green tail coat, canary yellow waistcoat, buff breeches, hose, and slippers. A lifelong military man, Armstrong never quite recognized civilian clothes as normal attire. The man before him, whom he had not seen in some three years, was little more than a stranger.

"D'Arcy? Damme! It is! You've changed. Come the dandy, rot your eyes!"

"As you see," Sebastian returned with a calm smile. "How goes the war, General?"

The older man lowered his full head of snow-white hair at the mention of war. "Come walk with me, d'Arcy, and I will tell you."

For the next quarter hour they toured the long halls filled with the ruins of ancient cities without really bothering to look at them. The tour was but a formality so that they might discuss in private the real reason they were meeting. Sebastian surmised the seriousness of affairs not so much from the subjects under discussion as from the fact that the general spoke in a low tone instead of his usual parade-ground blare.

"Lost the advantage we gained in declaring war without warning last May," Armstrong said in disgust. "Bonaparte was distracted. Should have moved at once. Yet, nothing!" He paused, turning a grim face to the younger man. "That Corsican upstart means business this time. He will try to cross that damnable ditch given the slightest provocation!"

"Then we should offer him none," Sebastian remarked mildly.

"Damn it, d'Arcy! You sound like one of those placaters."

Sebastian shrugged off this hint at a lack of patriotism on his part. "Did you invite me here to chastise me for my political views?"

"No." The general made a sudden turn that forced Sebastian with him into an empty alcove where the newest in the ever-growing collection of Greek marbles was on display.

"Our blockade of the Channel is holding, but at a cost. Boney's threats keep our navy from defending our interests in other parts of the world. Yet there are weaknesses within the line. It must be partially lifted when our vessels water and victual."

"Unless you post a schedule well in advance, the lapses could hardly benefit a French invasion," Sebastian replied.

"Spies tell us that within twenty-four hours the Frogs are prepared to row across one hundred thousand men including artillery and cavalry."

Sebastian's skepticism showed clearly on his handsome face. "The time required to launch the number of craft needed to transport a hundred thousand men would take . . ." He paused for scant reflection. "Taking in the time needed to load men, cast off the requisite number of barges, getting them out of the basins." He smiled as he did the mathematics in his head. "It would require the better part of a week."

The general nodded. He stood in awe of Sebastian's intellectual powers but it would not do to swell the young pup's head. "We have men, professionals, working on the logistics of an invasion," he said blandly.

Sebastian approached the first marble statue. "As you know, my home in Kent lies along the Channel. On a clear day the French coast can be seen. 'Clear' is the key. Invaders are best served by calm and fog. Anyone with experience of the coast will tell you the chances of several successive days of calm on the Channel are unlikely but for midsummer. It is now nearly September. The merest squall would mean catastrophe for an invasion in which hundreds of transports must be rowed."

Armstrong smiled, having hooked his fish. "Then we may assume the French will not attempt an autumn crossing?"

"I would not presume to know the mind of Bonaparte, General, but I should think it unlikely."

"Yet there are those in high office who fear just such an eventuality." The general pulled thoughtfully at his lower lip. "Boney has boasted he will be in London four days after reaching our shores."

Armstrong measured his next words. "The most troublesome part is rumor. The countryside to the south has begun to panic. The handbills circulating from the coastal towns depict Boney as a bogeyman who eats children. And they don't stop there. The most fantastic schemes are being circulated. It is claimed the Frogs are building a bridge over the Channel. Others say they are digging a tunnel."

Sebastian smiled as he rounded the statue of Psyche. "These are not so much impossibilities as improbabilities. Some predict that the technology required for both endeavors lies in the not-too-distant future."

Armstrong subjected the chuckling man to a measuring glance. "It's also claimed they are preparing an air attack by balloon. A fleet of them will sweep over the Channel and rain terror from the skies." He averted his gaze from his companion. "I know, it is veritable silliness. Hysteria, that's what is it." He stole a glance as Sebastian's expression darkened.

"Again, in principle the idea is not folly." Sebastian couldn't in all conscience trivialize this theory. "But in practical terms, a balloon invasion from France is even less likely than one by sea. The prevailing air currents are against such a venture. Our own troops would have a better chance."

The general's eyes lit up. "How so?"

"Let me see, the number of balloons required to lift ten thousand troops. One hundred balloons carrying one hundred soldiers each . . . Yes, I suppose it could be done by hydrogen balloon. I'm not suggesting it be tried, however. The cost would be exorbitant."

"Yet hysteria is contagious," the general rejoined. "Many in Parliament are showing signs of the fever. I must have documented scientifically verifiable proof that such an invasion by the French is impossible." He laid a paternal hand on Sebastian's shoulder. "In addition, I wish you to calculate the exact detailed requirements to launch a counterattack."

Sebastian broke into laughter. "That is a job for a moonraker! Do me the kindness to think me made for better sport."

The general did not share his humor. "I am quite serious."

Sebastian frowned. "I hope this is not an order."

Armstrong removed his hand, taking with it the familiarity of friendship. "One can but beg a boon from a civilian, d'Arcy."

"So much the worse for me," Sebastian answered lightly, for he could see that the old soldier was in earnest.

He gazed contemplatively at the statue of Psyche. Something in the sensuous figure of the nude young girl wrought in marble brought to mind the memory of the little novitiate at Queen Anne's Gate the night before. At least he supposed that episode was real. The cerebral conflagration had, as usual, left him drained and uncertain of which experiences were real and which mere chimeras of his mind.

Turning away, he buried the thought. "Our army is scattered between duties in Ireland, India, and the colonies." He met the older man's gaze levelly. "I saw French troops in action in Egypt. Do not be deceived by the outcome. If Bonaparte ever makes good his first threat to reach our shores, his army, which numbers only fifty thousand, will make good his boast about London."

The general stiffened in defense of his army. "The government is attempting to rectify our lack of soldiery by exempting all volunteers to the militia from the *levée en masse.*"

"And?"

"The response has been gratifying if appalling. Every shop clerk and stable boy from Penzance to Dover has donned a uniform and declares himself ready to give his life for the cause." He harrumphed behind his fist. "As Lord Auckland has so aptly put it, if boasts and clothes are all that are needed to win the war, Napoléon is doomed."

The two shared a chuckle.

"You and I may see the humor of this ridiculous posturing, d'Arcy, but hearts and tempers run high. There are men on both sides who would like to see the conflict enjoined. London and Paris crawl with more spies than fleas. Even our best men may be among theirs, and vice versa. Trust no one."

"You are serious." Surprise inflected Sebastian's words.

"I am. England has enemies within enemies. The Choans, royalists, and republicans who hate one another would each like our help to spike Bonaparte's wheel, yet they've no love of the English, either."

"Then I suppose I must do my part."

"Well said, well said." He slapped the younger man on the back and shifted to lighter matters. "Still seeing those French courtesans, are you? I hear they keep strange company these days, Monsieur De Valmy for instance."

Sebastian turned a riveting stare on the man. He knew of De Valmy. His reputation was that of a royalist, black marketeer, and suspected blackmailer. However that may be, the Foucants owed him their lives. Who they chose as their friends was none of his business. "If this is your method of warning me about something, you'd best be direct."

Armstrong did not back down. "Men with wine in their bellies and fire in their loins can be devilishly indiscreet."

"I thank you for the warning, but the Foucants are the least politically ambitious souls on earth."

Sebastian's tone did not invite further discussion, but Armstrong was determined to make his position clear. "These are hard times. Old loyalties can divide even the most reasonable of men. Don't mistake your own."

"All that I share with women of like mind are carnal pleasures, if it is your business to know." Sebastian's face lost all animation. "And I think it is not."

The general skewered him with a glance that had sent lesser men to their deaths. At three score years, he was a roué of the old school, a man for whom women were quarry to be pursued to assuage his needs, feed his vanity, and secure his sense of power. Burdened by the indignities of unmerciful age, he was fast approaching the end of his physical dominance. That awareness fed his envy of the younger man.

"I hear you're penning a memoir. Bit of boasting, eh?"

"I am honored you find me worth spying upon, but surely my reputation has not yet matched that of my sire."

The General offered him a troubled frown. He and Simon d'Arcy had been friends from youth. Though Simon later became the worst of reprobates, he had once served his country with distinction as a member of the British Continental forces in the war against the rebelling American colonies. He could not say what war had done to Simon, but clearly the son had not forgiven the excesses of the father Simon had become.

"One day you may find better understanding for your father."

Sebastian ignored the remark. "I have other business, General, if you will excuse me."

"See that you keep your own counsel, d'Arcy," Armstrong called after him. "You will receive orders in a few days."

Sebastian left the museum without viewing the Rosetta Stone. The general's last remark had spoiled his appetite for anything cerebral. Keep his own counsel! As if he needed instruction on how to conduct his private affairs! As if he could not possibly teach that old reprobate a thing or two about the habits of a dedicated libertine!

Hard on the heels of his anger came the realization that it had nothing to do with Armstrong. It was a reaction to the mention of his father.

In a few short days since his return to London, all the memories he had buried during his sojourn on the Mediterranean seemed to be resurrecting themselves.

"Pall Mall," Sebastian called up to his driver, then climbed into his coach, flung himself into a corner, and closed his eyes with a sudden weariness. So be it. He would set the specters free.

There had never been any love between father and son. After his mother died when he was ten years old, they seldom met and spoke even less often. Then, the spring of Sebastian's sixteenth year, his father had found him trying to relieve a painful erection. Contrary to meting out the violent rage he had come to expect, his father had laughingly opened his own breeches and unself-consciously shown him how best to accomplish the matter.

Thinking his son's sexual maturity at last provided a link between them, he had dragged Sebastian from his studies at Eton to France where he took his reluctant son to a famed Parisian brothel.

Sebastian slumped lower onto the leather seat. The memories of his first week in Paris would always be tinged with feelings of anger and humiliation. His father had forced him repeatedly to "perform" with prostitutes while he watched and hurled instructions and criticisms. Galled by his son's disappointing showing, he had installed Sebastian in an apartment on the Rive Gauche with a discreet lady of the demimonde who was paid to instruct his son in all the variations of the amatory arts. No son of his would be allowed to be less than a satyr with women.

Sebastian smiled bitterly at those memories of his corrupted youth. Despite his father, he recalled the subsequent weeks in Paris fondly. It was not because of the discovery he had made about the pleasures to be had in a lady's embrace. It was because, for the first time in his life, he had found in his instructress a warmth and generosity and an acceptance of himself.

In the home of Madame Henrice Foucant, instruction in sexual matters had soon been superseded by discussions of books and the ideas of the great French writers—Montesquieu, Voltaire, and even the radical Rousseau. The two sisters were devoted to one another and, despite their occupation as courtesans, closer in many ways than any respectable family he had ever known. Who would have believed that they would prefer to share with a lusty youth in the full bloom of his powers chaste evenings playing the music of Handel and Mozart, he on violin and they with flute and pianoforte?

During their months together during the summer of 1789 he spent more time with Madame Henrice out of bed than in it, touring museums and making comparisons of literature and paintings, even smiling at the obscene graffiti of which the citizenry of Paris were so fond and facile. It was an enchanting world for a young man where riding lessons and physics lessons went hand in hand with attending the theater and discussions of snuffboxes, of the feeding habits of lap dogs, of the most fashionable color for silk. He continued to live chastely with Madame Henrice long after his father ceased paying the bills, yet the clouds of revolution were gathering in the city.

For carnal release, he soon found the world was full of accommodating women who required neither coin nor much coaxing to share their bodies with so handsome and virile a young man. Names and faces ran together in the sea of delectable female bodies. When the revolution came, he was expelled from France as a foreigner. He returned to England and school but found the celibacy of academics could not long contain him.

He loved women, found them intoxicating, rousing, mysterious, their characters an ever-changing mystery which constantly intrigued him. They in turn found him equally stimulating. He found nearly every woman he wanted was his for the taking. Perhaps, he thought moodily, that was why none held his attention for long. Only with the Foucants had his affection remained steady.

He sat up suddenly with the realization he had given more thought this day to the Foucants' little novitiate than to any lady he had seen since his return to town.

Armstrong's warning about De Valmy did not worry him. The Foucants had ably handled the man these past dozen years. But if the address he had visited last night was, in fact, their new residence, then much had occurred that they had not revealed to him in their letters. He would go by, perhaps this evening, to see for himself what the situation was. Armstrong's warning be damned!

In the meantime, what he had most need of at this very

moment was the attentions of a woman. He had recently heard about a new performer, a contortionist, at Madame Bordelaise's.

Two events spoiled his plans to visit the Foucant women that evening. The first was that he found the entertainment at Madame Bordelaise's so amenable that he stayed far into the evening. The second was that when he finally did tear himself away, he met on his street the alarming sight of smoke and flame, and the vigorous efforts of the fire brigade . . . on his behalf.

It seemed his newly hired cook had left a pan of sausages unattended. The resulting grease fire was rather quickly brought under control but not before it had done major damage to the kitchen, offices, and the servants' quarters on the ground floor, as well as filling the upper floors with a covering of soot and black smoke.

By the time he had sorted out his domestic problems, orders had come from Whitehall demanding his full attention.

London, September 1803

"What a hum!" Lord Bramwell Everleigh, Viscount Bainton, turned back from the window where he had been perusing the afternoon traffic through Curzon Square to aim his famous slanted smirk at his house guest. "You agree, of course."

"Hmm," Sebastian murmured politely, not looking up from the complex calculations he was noting on the lap desk perched on his knees.

"Cousin? Damme! Haven't heeded a word I say!"

Everleigh crossed over and snatched the quill from Sebastian's hand. Unfortunately, his cuff caught on the lip of the desk's crystal ink well as he moved away. It flipped out of its holder, splashing a stream of India-blue ink across Sebastian's calculations and down the right leg of Everleigh's buff breeches and silk-stockinged leg.

"Son of a whore!" Chagrin bursting from every thwarted inch of him, Everleigh crushed his cousin's plume in his fist. The calamus snapped, leaking ink into his palm which dripped like sooty tears through his fingers and onto the mirrored surface of his patent-leather slipper. Swearing more elaborately, he tossed the ruined stylus into the nearby cold hearth.

"That is—*was* my favorite quill," Sebastian remarked as he looked up at his cousin. "Is there something I've done to offend you, Bram?"

"Done little else since you arrived," Everleigh answered, quite red-faced by now. His attempts to mop up the spill with his handkerchief had succeeded instead in spreading the stain and spoiling his lace cuff. With a snort of disgust, he tossed the square after the quill before turning his anger to Sebastian. "Don't know why you accepted my invitation to share quarters. Make it clear you find me plaguey poor company."

"Not at all, Bram." Sebastian raked a hand through the shock of golden-brown hair on his brow. "If you object to my working as we converse, you should say so."

"What I object to is your snub!"

Indignation underscored Everleigh's words as he deposited himself, coattails lifted to prevent crushing, on the gold brocade settee opposite Sebastian's more comfortable chair. Extending his lean, muscular right leg in narcissistic display, he gave his ruined stocking one last glance of annoyance. Thoughts of the expense he would be put to in order to replace his ruined breeches and stockings further soured his mood. "Said to act as if this were your own domicile. Didn't expect you'd burrow away like a mole night and day."

"Very little space serves my needs."

Everleigh glanced about the bedroom which his cousin had furnished with pieces from his own fire-damaged residence. The paraphernalia littered about reflected his scientific bent. There was a highly polished brass telescope standing on a folding tripod by the window. Twin globes housed in ornately carved stands of Oriental design flanked the desk. One was of the earth; the other a star map. A sextant, compasses, a glass barometer in a mahogany stand, and an unknown instrument made of a glass sphere clamped to a calibrated rotating arm filled the surface of the huge desk. The otherwise sophisticated furnishings included a bed *en bateau* dressed in gold silk and white linens.

Everleigh wriggled an inquiring forefinger at the piece. "Looks damned confining. A bit of Italian frippery, what?"

Sebastian turned his attention to the bed shape made of acajou wood and ornamented with gilded medallions, ribbons, and pilasters. "It's a creation of the French brothers Jacob Desmalter and George Jacob. I'm told they derived their inspiration from the campaign beds of Napoléon."

"That garlic-eating Corsican upstart?" Everleigh leaned forward confidentially. "Bad form, buying French products when there's a war on. Unpatriotic!"

"Unlike filling one's cellar with smuggled French wines and champagne," Sebastian replied pleasantly.

Everleigh reddened, for he had been more than pleased by his cousin's gift of two cases of the best bordeaux he had ever tasted. "Don't change the subject, 'Bastian. Been avoiding me. Admit it."

"I begged your indulgence about last night," Sebastian answered. "I suffer from megrims. Sometimes a long walk and a stiff drink will dissolve them."

"Devil take your explanation! You refuse my every invitation. Yet, the very night I pop off to bed at an unfashionable hour, you slip out leaving me in a sound snore. Damn uncousinly, I say!"

Sebastian did not defend himself again. The embarrassing truth was that he could not adequately account for his hours after midnight. Not until he had stumbled back to Everleigh's residence just after dawn, stinking of whiskey with his garments at sixes and sevens, did he fully regain his faculties.

"If I partook of a bacchanalian evening, I cannot recall it." Sebastian smiled as he continued to sort his papers. "But I promise to include you in the next."

Everleigh's expression lightened. "Devil of it is, I begin to believe you. You don't know what you've done, do you?"

The annoyance in Bram's voice drew Sebastian's full interest at last. "What have I done?"

"Still won't admit it? Very well. I'll tell you what I've heard. You served a lieutenant of the 11th Light Dragoons badly last evening. Won't say the watch wouldn't have eventually interfered. But to land a facer on a decorated campaigner over a nunnery inmate? 'Bastian! It ain't done."

A strange feeling stirred the attic of Sebastian's memory. "Did you say nunnery?"

"The whore was dressed as a nun," Everleigh confirmed.

He leaned back and crossed his arms over his chest. "You'd better tell me in greater detail just what you've heard."

Everleigh nodded. "Had the full tale over a trencher of bacon and oysters at White's. 'Tis said you were passing in a hackney when a hue and cry erupted on the street before a brothel. Seems the lieutenant was taking exception to one of the inmates' departure *before* he'd paid his respects."

"Who was she?"

Everleigh cleared his throat. "A punchable wench." He used the cant phraseology for a novice whore about to be sold to her first man. "Can't think why her bawd thought to trick her out as a nun."

"Does rumor say why I attacked the lieutenant?"

Everleigh looked decidedly uncomfortable. "Deuce take it! The lieutenant had taken his riding crop to her. Said he'd have his worth out of her hide one way or the other. The girl's cries roused half the block."

"The lieutenant sounds a charming fellow."

Everleigh leaned forward and lightly touched his brooding cousin's knee. "What I want to know, Cousin, is what did you do with her?"

"I beg your pardon?" Sebastian drawled.

Everleigh straightened, an indignant curl playing at the edges of his lips. "Don't come the parson on me. I don't want her. Detest the chicken-breasted trade. Still, you'd better produce her. You were seen driving off with her."

"You've been bammed," Sebastian declared flatly. "I've no memory of the lieutenant nor a whore child."

"Best sweep your attic again, Cousin. Two very tidy cutthroats came calling this morning." He put the full weight of truth behind his next words. "Lieutenant Sherwood's seconds."

Sebastian did not so much as twitch an eyelid. "Go on."

Everleigh nodded. "Sherwood's men came here when they did not find you at your own residence. They were very eager to deliver Lieutenant Sherwood's challenge. Gave them short shrift. Said I didn't have your direction." He winked. "Once they left, I hied round to White's to have the tale confirmed."

"And?" Sebastian prompted.

"Wagers have been placed on a duel 'twixt you and Sherwood, as well as on whether you let the girl go or tucked her away for your own amusement."

When Sebastian did not respond, Everleigh heaved a

burdened sigh. "This makes your third challenge. Your chivalrous streak is commendable, desire to defend a female and all. Still, thought you'd learned your lesson when the Langley affair forced you abroad. We'd all heard the rumors that Langley beat his wife. Only you dared chastise him."

Sebastian surveyed his cousin coolly. "I merely advised Lord Langley to take his bullying tendencies out on someone able to defend against them."

"You said it before the full company at his club!" Everleigh countered. "He could do no less than challenge you."

Sebastian nodded with a small smile. "Exactly. My choice to make it a pugilist match. Thought he should have a taste of what he had been meting out."

"You beat him within an inch of his life! Langley ain't showed his face in Town since." Admiration and outrage mingled in Everleigh's words.

"I had a letter from Lady Langley not long after I left London. She said her family had taken her permanently back into their protection."

"Guess that makes you a hero all round."

Sebastian did not answer this. He had succumbed to Lady Langley's blandishments not out any real passion but out of sheer ennui. But the night of their first assignation when he had undressed her, he discovered bruises so plentiful that one beating could not explain them all. Shocked despite his own brutal childhood, he had made love to her as tenderly as he could in order not to shame her. Later he had sought out her abuser. Had he been motivated by altruism or had he merely been showing off? Two years later he did not have the answer.

"About Sherwood," Everleigh ventured after a moment. "Stand with you, goes without saying. Choice of weapons is yours but don't take him on with sabers. Member of the Dragoons. Neither with pistols. Can't afford for either of you to die. No, definitely not pistols. Unreliable. Leaves a hole, sometimes lead. Messy business. You once had a way with a rapier," he suggested hopefully.

"The Italian school of fencing with rapier and dagger. I trained while in Naples last spring."

"Right. Requires skill over brawn. Cunning over force. You might not die. Or kill him," he amended hastily.

Sebastian offered him a pointed glance. "Thank you for your concern, but I've no intention of facing Sherwood in a duel."

Everleigh met his cousin's gaze with seriousness. "It won't do, 'Bastian. Sherwood's honor has been impugned. Refuse to do the honorable, he'll have you on your marrow bones."

"I cannot imagine a contingency which would cause me to beg pardon on my knees," Sebastian said casually. "More than that, I see nothing in your tale to prove I'm the man guilty of insulting the Dragoon." He glanced at the decanter and glass on the table near his bed. "Care to share a drop of brandy? French, of course. You may do the honors."

Everleigh's expression brightened. The seriousness of their conversation made the brandy irresistible. "Glad to oblige."

As Everleigh poured, Sebastian glanced down at the ruined paper on his lap desk. "Have you ever attended an ascension?"

The non sequitur momentarily blind-sided Everleigh. "Ah, a *balloon* ascension. Can't say I have. Meant to. Covent Garden, see the aeronauts. Never quite found the time."

"It's an edifying experience." Sebastian closed his eyes to better enjoy the bouquet of his brandy. "I've been aloft, you know."

Everleigh's brow shot up. "Indeed not!"

"Made my first flight in '97 at Lourdes. Then again in

'99 in Ireland. Planned to cross the Irish Sea but the winds were against our efforts. An exhilarating experience. I nearly lost two toes to frostbite."

Everleigh's heavy frown brought his brows down against the bridge of his nose. "Don't know as it's wise to leave the earth. No wings to break one's fall."

Sebastian smiled at this simple illogic. "If men did not dare, there'd be no progress."

"Where's the progress in suspending men in a bladder of hot air?"

"The ascensions have made mapping the countryside easier and more accurate. If a mechanism for steering can be discovered, great distances will be crossed with a speed that is now otherwise impossible."

"Give me a carriage and four-in-hand and we'll see who covers the greater ground. Crack whip, you know."

"I refer to larger, heavier loads. One day every farmer may own his own balloon in which to ferry his hay or potatoes or even cattle to market."

"So then pigs *will* fly?"

As his cousin sputtered in laughter, Sebastian debated whether he should allude to his own efforts. "There are military applications, as well."

Everleigh's expression underwent a radical change. "I've heard rumors of Boney's intent to invade us. What do you know?"

"Nothing to alarm you," Sebastian lied.

Everleigh snorted derisively. "The Frogs have no standards. Why I've heard said that upstart Corsican promotes soldiers on merit. Commoner and aristocrat share the same rank, space, and table. Ridiculous!"

"It is thought by many that Napoléon commands the best disciplined army in the world."

Everleigh pondered the statement, then stared a moment into his brandy glass before he said, "What will you do about Sherwood?"

"Nothing."

"But his seconds—"

"Spoke to you." Sebastian snared his cousin's gaze with one of vivid blue. "I agreed to nothing. I'm leaving London on the morrow. Going down to Kent. The lieutenant's path and mine may never cross."

Everleigh doubted that possibility. "The family honor is at stake. You must stay and face the inevitable. We both know of men who refused a duel only to be set upon by hired thugs. Tar and feathers is another method of inducing shame. Then there was that quickly hushed-up business of a gelding last year." He paused to search his memory for the particulars. "Of course, the unfortunate fellow was not nobility. Merely a secretary said to have seduced his noble employer's wife."

"You make a poor job of entertaining your guests, Bram."

Everleigh tried a new tactic. "Sounds deuced dull, playing at science and numbers in the country. Hate math, myself. Wager only in tens to keep the figuring simple."

When this elicited no response he moved on to the next possible allurement. "There's to be a mill next month promises to be a beaut! 'Twixt the heavyweight champion Jem Belcher and Game Chicken Pearce. Stay for the Fancy."

"Thank you, no."

Everleigh frowned hard into his glass, searching for more sources of enticement. He suddenly lifted his head. "There's a new girl at Madame Bordelaise's. Performs such feats of nimbleness with a trapeze that—"

"I've already made her acquaintance," Sebastian remarked blandly. "Remarkable device, the trapeze."

Everleigh hung on tenaciously. "Got some choice morsel tucked away in your country residence? Some secret den of decadence, perhaps?"

"Sorry to disappoint, Bram, but I never entertain women

in Kent. I must keep distractions to a minimum when I work."

"That ain't the tale Eliott's telling." Everleigh's eyebrows began to twitch. "He says women make up the entire subject of your experimentation these days."

Sebastian sighed. "Eliott's mouth runs on wheels."

"So there is such a text! Eliott claims that not since Casanova has there been so bawdy a tale of adventures betwixt the sheets. Weren't going to tell me, were you?" His offense was genuine. "Showing your miserable script to all and sundry but not your kith and kin."

The polite knock at the bedroom door interrupted them.

"Beg pardon, m'lords," the Everleigh butler said as he entered with silver salver in hand. "These messages have just arrived for Lord Brecon."

Sebastian took the proffered envelopes. After a cursory glance at the contents of the first missive, he tore it up into small pieces, then rose to deposit them directly into the hearth. He then slit the second envelope and withdrew a single thin sheet of lavender paper.

"Egad! Smell the perfume from here!" Everleigh crowed. "Old flame fanning the embers of memory?"

"A most pleasant memory." A smile firmed the edges of Sebastian's lips. "Most pleasant." He looked up. "Sorry, Bram, but I must excuse myself. I'm going out, after all."

"Don't suppose she has a companion?"

"Isn't one mistress sufficient for your needs? Come to that, aren't you all but engaged?"

Everleigh's broad face reddened. "Nearly so. Lord Riverton's second daughter, Charlotte. Sweet child. Docile. Time I settled down. Thirty-one last August."

"How pleasant for you." Sebastian sighed. Since he had returned to London, he had discovered that nearly all his former acquaintances were leg-shackled. Marriage did not prevent them from making the usual rounds of their supper clubs, gaming dens, and mistresses' domiciles, but it did present a gulf between them and him.

He lifted the scented lavender sheet to his nose. For instance, they no longer received *billets-doux* at their homes containing invitations to dine from courtesans with a penchant for French perfume.

Everleigh cleared his throat. "About the other matter, Cousin?"

Sebastian shook his head. "Don't fret, Bram. Sherwood won't call me out even if all you say is true. Since he was so rash as to publish his intentions abroad, he is at this very moment having that fact explained to him at Horse Guards."

Everleigh's astonished gaze darted toward the little bits of paper piled in the hearth. When it arrived back at his younger cousin there was a new respect in that gaze. "What exactly is your connection there?"

As Sebastian smiled cherubically, mischief flashed between the thick tangles of his red-gold lashes. "Nothing official, Cousin. Nothing . . . official."

Six

After two weeks, Madeleine finally discovered the reason her aunts tolerated Mrs. Seldon. The woman was simply a genius with needle and thread. She stood facing the long glass, as amazed as was possible for someone who gazed at an image of herself.

Her figure remained slim but not painfully thin. Subtly rounded by liberal servings of cream and cheese and egg custard, she was now if not quite Aphrodite, then Circe. A high-waisted gown of sheer gray silk called London Mist carefully draped this new, more enticing form. The skirt fell in a column to the floor where it formed a short train in back. Silver-tasseled cords tied in a bow drew the gown tight beneath her breasts. The bodice itself was a mere band no more than four fingers deep, stiffened and embroidered with silver thread. Above its shallow depth her breasts swelled in remarkable display. If she attempted to so much as bend enough to adjust a stocking, she suspected she would spill out.

But it was not only her new form which astonished her. The face reflected back at her was a stranger's. Her hair had been trimmed to leave a dozen smoky tendrils curling about her face and neck. The crown had been drawn back and secured with a switch of curls decorated with a cluster of gray silk roses and silver leaves. Her lips were pinkened by crushed rose petals and her lashes darkened by a preparation of burnt cloves and cork and elderberry juice. She looked like someone else, someone regal, elegant, a gentlelady.

Her aunts had devised a remarkable beauty regimen for her. She had been made to sit daily in a hip bath comprised of equal parts milk and water with a concoction of whipped egg whites, olive oil, and honey masking her face. Her hair had been smeared with egg yolks, camphor, and glycerine and then wrapped in a hot towel. At night camomile-infused squares of linen were placed over her eyes while her hands were encased in gloves after being dipped in thickened milk boiled with almonds and sweet oil.

"This is most wasteful," she had repeatedly murmured through lips smeared by hog's lard. "Think of what I might have made with these ingredients. Soufflés. Custards. Desserts."

But her aunts would not be deterred. They had buffed and scrubbed and fretted and plucked until her heels were as pink and smooth as her now-healed palms and her dark brows winged away from her dark eyes at clean angles.

Madeleine brushed a curious hand softly over the fabric of her gossamer gown, so sheer that the slightest breeze disturbed its surface. Two layers of equally translucent fabric, a pair of long gloves, and pink silk stockings gartered at midthigh by satin ribbons comprised the remainder of her toilette. She was certain she could detect beneath the gown the shape of her legs and the pale tint of a garter. Certainly this could not be all.

She turned in question. "*Très bien.* Where is the rest?"

With an expression like granite, Mrs. Seldon rose heavily from her knees and moved to the box on the bed. She lifted from it a silk India shawl figured in pomegranates and finished with silver fringe. She draped the lovely piece in the crooks of Madeleine's elbows and stood back.

"Is there no velvet overskirt or brocade tunic?" Madeleine suggested hopefully.

Mrs. Seldon's face could have curdled milk. "The first

kick of fashion, that's the mam'zelles wanted. Straight out of *Le Beau Monde.* You'll not find better in the city." She held out bony fingers with red swollen tips. "Look till ye're blind, ye'll not pick 'em stitches out!"

Madeleine returned to an inspection of her image. "The gown is beautiful, but it's far too revealing. I can see— *C'est incroyable!* I can see *me."*

Mrs. Seldon snickered. "There's the point."

"The point?" Too often Mrs. Seldon's curious English phrasing went over her head. "I do not understand."

"Ye will! Tupped and stuffed properly, insight a week!"

Madeleine canted her head. "What is 'tupped and stuffed?' "

The woman's rheumy eyes glittered. "Why don't ye ask yer aunties? Ask 'em who's comin' to sample yer jam."

Something more malicious than usual in the woman's expression convinced Madeleine that further discussion would be fruitless. *"Bien,* I will!"

She gathered up her train of her gown to keep it from dragging on the floor as she stepped off the *modiste's* mat. She descended the narrow flight of stairs that led from her tiny bedroom on the second floor, wondering yet again why her aunts endured the detestable Mrs. Seldon, talented fingers or no.

As she reached the first-floor landing, she heard Justine's raised voice issue from the salon.

"Every penny? Gone?"

"Hush! Someone will hear you."

The tone of the exchange halted Madeleine. Like halls of the cloister during the Terror, the Foucant household hummed daily with a dozen little secrets and unexplained incidents. Her aunts were forever with their heads together over some matter. Yet they seldom spoke to her unless it concerned her appearance. On the rare occasions when they received callers, she was sent to her room as if she were an unruly toddler unfit to be in adult company. Unable to resist the opportunity to eavesdrop this once, she crept closer to the salon.

". . . was necessary," she heard Henrice say. "First impressions are everything. The mind must reel. The eye must pop! There can be no instant for reason or doubt. Remember *Maman*'s teachings. The impulse to possess is all!"

"But if tonight's *petite affaire* should come to naught?" Anxiety had not left Justine's tone.

"Impossible! She is too young to disobey and he is too virile to resist. You will see. Nature will decide for us before they do themselves."

"You have not prepared her and you promised you would."

"I changed my mind. Who can explain something so complex to one so utterly innocent? I asked her just yesterday as I was cleaning my jewels, 'Madeleine, do you not wish to own a diamond necklace like this one the duc de Luxembourg gave me in tribute?' Do you know what the girl answered? No, she says because she does not think diamonds are pretty. Not pretty? They lack color, says she. *Formidable!* What am I to do with such a backward girl?"

"Perhaps she needs time."

"We do not have time." Henrice's voice held that steely quality of final authority. "We must have a return on our investment, and soon. A promise of patronage will instantly open a dozen avenues which are temporarily closed to us. But think what such an alliance would mean? The Opera, Justine! A theater box at our disposal. Invitations again arriving by the score!"

"You are so certain he will like her. I pray you are . . ." Justine's wistful voice was momentarily drowned out by the sounds of a carriage on the street.

Madeleine pressed herself back into the shadow of the dark hall to digest what she had just heard. A man was coming? A gentleman, to judge by the concern in their voices. Someone to see her? To meet her? To offer patronage? Why did they never explain anything to her? Innocent she might be, but that did not make her an imbecile.

She had been most adamant about the fact that she did not wish a suitor. How dare they not even warn her? Suppose she detested this man on the spot? They could not make her like him. She would not like him!

The house was so quiet that she noticed the metallic clip of horseshoes on cobblestones had stopped. Moments later the doorbell jangled.

"He's here! He's here!" she heard Justine cry.

Madeleine scurried back up the stairs, but only as far as the first landing. Her heart beat so strongly that she felt it would burst if she did not learn something about this gentleman who seemed to hold her future in his hands.

"Lord d'Arcy!" She heard Henrice greet warmly as she opened the door. A lord? Could this be he?

"Bonsoir, Madame Henrice. Madame Justine," she heard a man intone in deep, sonorous syllables that raked a finger of familiarity along her spine. He sounded very like the Englishman she had met on the street several weeks earlier.

She leaned out curiously as he stepped into the hallway. She saw that he wore the new style of *chapeau* called a top hat which Justine reached out to take. Then, as if he suspected someone might be watching from above, he lifted his face for an instant toward the stairwell.

He was young and so vividly attractive as to be startling. Beneath a cap of thick curling golden-brown hair, his warm blue eyes slanting down at the outer corners were touched by lazy sensuality. His nose was bold, yet aesthetically pleasing. Lean cheeks and a firm chin framed a wide smile that scored his cheeks and pleated the upper edges to the corners of his eyes.

"Le beau idéal!" Madeleine murmured to herself, quite taken with the features of the gentleman's face. Perhaps

meeting him would not be so much a trial, after all. And, he spoke French.

He turned back at once to his hostesses. *"Qu'est-ce que c'est?* How it is possible that while others wither with age the pair of you shimmer with the dew of life?" Madeleine saw him reach out a hand to each sister. "You have divined the wizard Merlin's trick, surely, of living your lives backward?"

"Still the charmer, *mon cher,*" she heard Henrice say as he bent over her hand. "But, I own, I like it."

To Madeleine's amazement Justine cupped the back of his head briefly as he rose from saluting her hand. Holding him still, she placed a kiss on his cheek.

He must be a very good friend, she thought. When the gentleman kissed each of her aunts on the lips, they giggled like girls of eighteen as they spoke practically in unison.

"Naughty boy!"

"You don't deceive us with your flattery!"

"We are most put out with you."

"Three weeks we hear you are in London."

"Nothing!"

"We should slam the door to you, my lord."

Madeleine leaned forward for a final glimpse as he moved with the ladies into the salon. This time she noted other things about him, that he was tall and wore black tail coat and breeches trimmed in satin. Diamonds gleamed in the folds of his cravat and at his cuffs. He was quite wealthy, then.

"Mesdames, I can offer no defense. But what do I smell? *Gâteau chocolate?* My favorite!" His voice trailed away.

Madeleine leaned back against the wall. So this man was to be her suitor. She had seen him, felt the tug of magnetism in his beauty. And he spoke perfect French! At least she now knew what to expect.

Smiling, she turned and climbed back up the stairs to her room. Really, she did not understand at all this need for secrecy. Her aunts were quite silly.

Sebastian paused to consume the last bite of the deep fudge cake which he loved. He had steered the conversation through the shoals of polite topics for the last half hour, regaling the sisters with tales of Italy, but he was deeply disturbed by what he had come upon this night.

The Queen Anne's Gate address was the same one the little nun had shown him three weeks earlier. This narrow, decrepit house was a far remove from the lofty places where he had visited the Foucants over the years in both Paris and London.

He had smiled and played dumb when they blushingly apologized for their temporary quarters while their own homes underwent refurbishing. Though they laughed and smiled with the practiced abandon of old, he noted a new watchfulness in Henrice's gaze and that Justine looked a trifle drawn despite two bright spots of color on her cheeks. They were worried, an emotion he knew that was alien to either of them.

No two women had ever seemed more equipped to care for themselves and land comfortably on their dainty feet than the Foucant sisters. But something had spoiled their comfort. Was it the death of Ondine's protector? Or, Monsieur De Valmy?

Armstrong's warning came back to him. He had made a few inquiries, but De Valmy's true character lay in impenetrable shadow. No one would accuse him outright of any wrong, yet fear was palpable in all who mentioned his name. There were few he considered friends. Henrice and Justine made up the greater portion of them. They needed help and, he suspected, they had sent for him out of that need. Whatever their troubles, he would not abandon them.

"Even better than I remember." He set aside his fork and empty plate. "I won't ask for the recipe, for I should have my new cook, whoever that will be, prepare it every day."

"Such a shame about your house. Will it soon be restored? A gentleman needs his privacy, *mais non?*" Justine's bright gaze held his in suggestive inquiry.

"There are certain advantages to privacy . . . when one is not alone." That Justine leaned toward him to better display her lovely bosom set off by a deep square neckline and a diadem of rose diamonds did not escape his notice.

"Justine!" Henrice declared, ruffled by her sister's flirtatious manner with a young man she thought of as her own. "We are in need of fresh coffee."

Justine rose with a sulky pout. "Very well." She cast a last longing look at Sebastian. "Henrice prefers to have you all to herself. But me, I think you are enough for the pair of us, monsieur." She glanced pointedly at his groin. "Most certainly!"

He laughed appreciatively at her outrageous invitation, as empty as it was provocative.

"At last, *mon beau garçon,*" Henrice purred with a coquettish smile when her sister was gone. "*Vraiment!* You do not look at all well. Your mistress does not take sufficient care of you!"

"Alas, I am without a mistress at present."

"But that is terrible! A man of your appetites? How do you survive?"

He basked in her amorous gaze. "It's a trial I bear."

"Such a waste of a man of your superb talents."

It was a game they had played for years, long after either of them had considered the other a romantic partner. Perhaps, he thought, that was the reason this banter stirred him more deeply than the usual idle exchanges. The ban lent their flirtation an extra piquancy.

She clucked her tongue. "No mistress? No wife?" She

smiled as he shook his head. "La! What claims your time?"

"Little enough."

"Now you are being coy. Once you could not wait to explain to me your latest discoveries."

He sighed at more than decade-old memories of the sexual games they had once played, games where he was assigned the task of learning a new technique for each time they spent in bed. They had spun the game out for weeks. "Since you've always found my peccadillos charming, I'll tell of my latest literary effort."

"A book?"

"A memoir."

"Your memoirs? But you are so young." She lounged back in her chair, her gray gaze provocative. "What have you to tell?"

Sebastian laughed. "As you have oft pointed out, I am a man of considerable experience."

"You are writing a pillow book!" Henrice clapped her hands. *"Tant mieux!* How pleasant this must be for you. The research, I imagine, has been varied and plentiful?"

"I have attempted to make it such."

"You always were inventive, *mon beau cavalier."* She casually caressed his hand as it lay on the chair arm nearest her. "I will be very interested to read it. But you have not asked me why I invited you here tonight."

His tone again turned to banter. "You like my company?"

"Très bien. And because of this I wish to make you a gift."

"Will I like it?"

"Ah, that is for you to say."

"And if I say yes?"

"Why then, *mon beau garçon,* you will find yourself a little bit of paradise."

"This grows more interesting by the moment." He smiled in anticipation. "I think I will like this present."

Henrice moved her hand to his thigh. "But how can I be certain you will cherish this gift as she deserves?"

"She?"

Henrice saw the quick flash dart through his eyes and recognized it as one of hunger. He had always been impressionable to the merest carnal suggestion.

"You?" Sebastian questioned in a blasé drawl. So then this was the ploy, she would give herself to him in exchange for—

"My niece."

"Niece," he repeated. Not the little nun, surely? He had half thought he had dreamed her up, conjured her from the figments of his feverish imagination. "Why have I never heard of this niece before, madame?"

Henrice shrugged. "She is Ondine's child. When the Terror began we were forced to abandon her to God's care at the convent near St. Etienne. But now she is restored to us and naturally we want only the best for her."

Marriage! It was the first and the only thought that came into his head. Madame Henrice thought he might be induced to marry her little convent-bred niece. Never!

"We do not expect you to marry her," she said, as if his thoughts were written on his face. "I know your mind on these matters. I wish to make a gift of her to you as your mistress."

"Mistress." Sebastian chuckled. "You offer me a mistress, madame, sight unseen?"

She smiled wickedly. "I have seen *you,* monsieur. You are more than equal to the task. She is innocent, of course, and will require a light and skilled touch. Yet I trust you will bring her quickly to flower."

The carnal possibilities multiplied inside Sebastian's head. The little nun who had tempted him so chastely was being offered for his deflowering. It was too delicious to contemplate. But he was accustomed to outrageous invitations and little of his true feelings showed in his face. Not that Henrice's attentions were directed there. Her hand had slid up his thigh in a most impudent caress. "Does the girl know of this . . . arrangement?"

Henrice shrugged. "It is the French custom to make the arrangements first. It saves so many thwarted desires and broken hearts if a . . . suitable agreement cannot be reached."

"I see." Sebastian did, only too clearly. This arrangement was Henrice's way of pleasantly extracting money from him. Why had she not simply asked for his help? "Why me?"

She met his gaze coyly. "Any man may ruin a girl, *mon cher.* How many can bring her senses gently and completely to life?"

A brow lifted. "You think me capable of such a thing?"

"Oui. You are a true connoisseur. There are so few of us left. You have this and more, the intelligence not to bore."

"I think you are a flatterer, madame," he answered with a smile of a buyer who knows he is being sold a bill of goods.

"But of course!" Her fingernails left indentations as she dragged them up the fabric of his breeches. "Does the idea not appeal to you? To tutor a young girl's innocence, *c'est s'amuser beaucoup!* You are worldly enough not to crush her spirit but virile and experienced enough to know how to heighten her appetites. Lavish a few gifts on her, *mon cher,* show her the little pleasures as well as the large.

"I do not ask that you take her for long," she hurriedly added when she saw doubt begin to furrow his brow. "A man of your exacting taste will soon tire of her. Yet once she has known your patronage, she will be able to make a more permanent match elsewhere. Do this and you will have my favor forever."

Sebastian caught and stilled the hand that was stroking his rather obvious arousal. His body always had a say in these situations, but never the last word. "I am greatly flattered, madame. But I cannot take the innocence of a girl whose family is known to me. If she were married . . ." He gestured with the Gallic lift of a hand. "But a virgin? It is not done."

Henrice raked her nails against his groin. "You have my blessing in this matter. That should make things simpler."

"It does not. It smacks of incest, or at the very least gross indiscretion." He transferred her hand to her lap and leveled a candid gaze at her. "Have you considered what she will think of the fact that her seducer was once her aunt's pupil?"

Henrice sighed. "She need never know."

"Perhaps not. But there are equally dangerous pitfalls. She's young, led a cloistered life. If I do not frighten her to death, then she is certain to fall instantly and irrevocably in love with me." It was not a boast and they both knew it.

"Love!" She made a dismissive gesture. "We must all love, and lose and die, mon coeur. Perhaps, if you saw her—?"

"No."

Sebastian rose to his feet, convinced that if he did not leave this house immediately he would be very sorry. He suddenly wanted the little niece more than any man who did not intend to marry should want a gently bred virgin. He had not forgotten how she'd felt against him or the impression of her sweet, full lips beneath his palm. If he saw her and she was half as lovely as his preternatural gaze had rendered her, he would not be able to resist her. Every instinct for survival pushed him toward the door.

Henrice rose to her feet. "You disappoint me, Lord d'Arcy."

Sebastian offered her an apologetic smile. "Perhaps I

can do something. Give me a few days. I will find a decent fellow who'll be happy to oblige you. I regret that I have no more time now. I'm bound for Kent in the morning."

"But—!" Henrice caught herself on a rare note of agitation. "This promise of another suitor?"

He rubbed his chin. "My years away from London have left me ignorant of the intimate attachments of my friends. I shall write letters from the country and determine matters from there. I should have a candidate in a few weeks."

Weeks? Henrice willed away her panic as she approached him. *"Mon cher,* be reasonable . . ." She reached up to trail a finger across his lower lip. "A beautiful young girl waits upstairs for you. One word and she will go home with you this very night."

Close to the surface of Sebastian's mind was the thought that Henrice was offering him the ideal chance to realize his theory about the education of the Perfect Mistress. A chaste girl, convent-bred, yet of family stock which was sensuous, practical, and carnally rapacious. What could he not do with such a subject?

No, his first obligation was to himself. The second to his government. He had sworn to never keep a mistress again. Nor could he take up a project of mistress-training while pressing duty sent him south. Oh, but the temptation was strong!

He leaned down and quickly kissed Henrice's lips and then headed for the hallway. He picked up his top hat and cloak.

As he reached for the door handle, Henrice clutched his coat sleeve. *"Mon garçon,* please reconsider. For my sake."

Sebastian's features hardened with resolve. "Not if she were Aphrodite herself, madame, would I take your niece as my mistress!" That said, he turned and left.

In the echo of the closing door, Henrice heard a gasp. She glanced up sharply to find Madeleine standing in the half-shadow of the stairwell. *"Merde!"* she muttered under her breath.

"You expect me to become a—a courtesan?"

Madeleine could scarcely push the last word past her lips as she stood facing her two aunts. When she had not been sent for after half an hour she had crept downstairs once again, more curious than before. The end of the conversation she had come upon made her wish she had never set foot upon the stairs.

"You expect me to believe that my mother wishes me to become a courtesan?"

"I expect more restraint from you," Henrice returned with more poise than she felt. "You've suffered a shock. It is to be expected that you are upset, Yet—"

"Of course I'm upset! Why wasn't I told what you planned?"

"Pauvre petite," Justine cooed and put an arm about her waist. "You cannot comprehend it all. It is a new way of thinking for you. It brings into conflict your years at the convent. Naturally you must have time to sort out these things."

"When you were a child, it was thought best to spare you certain realities." Henrice's somber gaze rested on Madeleine's angry face. "You are no longer a child. I am sorry that you have learned of this reality in this manner. However, now that you have, we expect that you will take your place with pride among us."

"With pride?" Madeleine echoed. "How can I be proud of something in which I have had no part?"

"How naive you sound, Madeleine. Of course you had no part in it. These things are for your family to decide for you. The English fashion of women seeking their own protectors is vulgar and offensive. The family made an arrangement for me before my eighteenth birthday."

"Were you not insulted?"

"Quite the contrary. I met the gentleman at a ball. It was all very romantic. It was only after we were in love that *Maman* explained to me the circumstances under which I would be allowed to be a companion to this man."

"Did you not wish to marry him?" Madeleine asked, thinking of Audelia.

"Of course not!" Henrice said quickly. "Justine and I have lived better and with less strife than any married lady. From time to time circumstances require that we change partners but always we were more faithful than most wives. Your mother did not keep you in total ignorance. You must have some understanding of the situation."

"I never thought about it," Madeleine said coldly, but that was a lie. She had heard things, from Madame Céline and others. She knew her aunts, once as famed for their performances in the boudoir as on the stage, had taken lovers from most privileged courtiers in the court of Louis XVI. Poets wrote sonnets to them and balladeers sang about them. Handbills had carried the names of their latest *amours* and lists were kept by some curious personages of the duels that had been fought for their honor. Yet, despite her awareness, some childish place in Madeleine's mind refused to confront the unpleasant reality that her aunts were courtesans.

A feeling of dismal bitterness swept her. In every letter she had received, Henrice and Justine had promised that one day she, too, would be allowed to come and live in their privileged world. She had never given much thought to exactly what that would mean. She suspected that her mother wished her to wed. Was it possible that, instead, she had decided that her daughter should become a courtesan?

"Does my mother know what you were planning?"

Henrice wrestled her conscience to the ground and pinned it there with the point of expediency. Lord d'Arcy might change his mind at any moment and return. They must not be found quarreling. "Do you think we would act against her wishes?"

"You have told me so little," Madeleine said bitterly. "I think you lie about my mother."

Henrice's lips thinned. She had not meant for things to get so out of hand. Yet Madeleine's eavesdropping gave her little choice but to lay the full truth before her. "Since you insist on the truth, then you must swallow it whole. Ondine has done no more or less than Justine and I."

A mutinous anger suddenly replaced the wounded hurt in Madeleine's eyes. "I don't believe you." She turned to Justine. "What of my father? Mother told me herself that she was married. The ceremony was in a grotto church outside Versailles. She wore pink satin and my father wore blue and gold. The procession by candlelight . . ." She paused in trepidation to see her aunt drop her eyes. A chill sped through her. "I don't believe it! You want me to believe that none of the things my mother told me are true? That I had no father? That I—?"

"You had a father, *ma chère,*" Justine said softly. "A most handsome nobleman of the first rank. Had we remained in France you would have lived at court and been treated royally."

Madeleine pounced on this. "Who? Who was he?"

Justine glanced doubtfully at Henrice, who shook her head. "For your own sake we must not say."

"Must not or *can*not?" She shot Henrice a hostile glare.

"There is no need to be insulting," Henrice countered.

"Of course not," Madeleine answered sarcastically. "You tell me my mother is a whore and I a bastard!"

"Now you become offensive."

"Oh, you must have tricked her! My mother is the youngest." She turned the full scorn of her wounded pride on Henrice. "Did you deceive and sell her virtue just as you have tried to do with mine this night?"

"No one forced anyone." Disdain rippled through Henrice's voice. "Your mother took to the role of mistress naturally, as it was her birthright. She was at her most radiant when surrounded by suitors, like a flower seeking the sun."

"Henrice, perhaps, you should not—" Justine broke in.

"Not what?" Henrice demanded. "Not tell the truth? Why? Are we to be insulted while her dear mother is painted in watercolors of innocence?"

"How could you?" Madeleine felt like weeping. "Do you not value yourselves more highly?"

Henrice considered her niece's behavior to be beyond all bounds of propriety, yet she understood her reaction. "If you were sensible enough to pay attention in your spying, you will recall that I told Lord d'Arcy he needed only make your acquaintance this night. These things take time. He may yet agree to see you." That thought cheered her. *"Oui.* I expect he will return even tonight. If he does, it is most important that you are pleasant to him."

Madeleine folded her arms. "I will refuse him."

"It is not your choice. It is Lord d'Arcy's, and so far he has refused you."

She made it an accusation, though she knew well enough that it was not Madeleine's fault. If he had seen her, she was certain Sebastian could not have walked away. Even now with tears cresting in her dark eyes and her features pinched by shock and hurt, the girl was more arresting than either she or Justine had been at her age. She radiated a sensual elegance, a quality seldom achieved by ladies or harlots.

In her agitation the girl's breasts had risen from her bodice so that the upper crest of one deep pink aureole showed above the deep plunge of her neckline. If only d'Arcy would return at once! It was just the sort of unstudied detail to swamp even his considerable powers of reason.

"When Lord d'Arcy comes," she continued, drawing

strength from that hope, "I expect you to behave with grace."

"Why must I do this?" Madeleine's shock was beginning to wear off. Behind it came the fresh anger. "Why not take another lover yourself and spare me?"

A deep blush colored Henrice's alabaster skin. "Had we been allowed to remain in Paris, our lives should have been different. There society understands the rules of alliances such as ours. The English, they are so provincial."

"And the gentlemen stingy," Justine concurred. "A lady of exquisite taste can barely survive their lack of generosity."

Madeleine glanced about the salon in which they sat. Oriental carpets spread the floor. Gilded furnishings crowded every space. Tables were arrayed with crystal containers, silver dishes and porcelain pieces. She did not notice the shabbiness that had captured d'Arcy's eye. The ladies themselves decked in jewels and pomades and other frivolous bits of femininity did not seem to be sporting the trappings of indigence. "Perhaps you should cut back your expenses."

"Oh, we have, *ma chère*," Justine replied.

Madeleine eyed the huge square-cut emerald surrounded by diamonds balanced on her aunt's slender finger. "Perhaps you need less than you already have."

Justine's brow puckered. "You cannot think to suggest that I sell my baubles?"

"She does not," Henrice answered decisively. "Madeleine is being childish and spiteful. We will never pawn a single personal item! Our trinkets are all we have left of our former glory. They remind us of who we are. Without them we are nothing."

Madeleine did not know how to answer that heartfelt declaration of pride, it was so foreign to her.

"Ungrateful though you are, you are still a Foucant. Go to bed. In the morning you will have come to your senses."

The arrogance of that statement so infuriated Madeleine that she began to tremble. "And if I do not come to my senses?"

Henrice met her challenging glance. "Then you shall shut yourself up in a convent and away from your loving mother forever. Are you so selfish, Madeleine? I wonder."

Insulted to the soles of her feet, Madeleine turned without a word and left the room.

She banged her fist on the newel post as she climbed the stairs toward her room, pleased by the sensation of pain that spiked up her arm. At least she was still feeling something. When the rage wore off she was afraid she was going to be numb.

"I do not understand this new fashion for restraint among the young," Justine declared when Madeleine was out of sight. "It is so unattractive. Once, to live for *amour* was all."

Exhausted by the ordeal, Henrice eased herself with weariness onto a Recamier. "She will see sense in the morning."

"Do you think so? Myself, I do not. She is not one of us." Justine began to weep softly. "If only things were like before and we were home in France."

The doorbell rang.

Henrice popped up from her seat with an expectant look. *"Voilà!* Lord d'Arcy has changed his mind! I told you, he would not forsake me!"

She rushed down to the door and swung it open with a wide smile of greeting. The smile dried up. "Monsieur De Valmy."

At that same moment Madeleine, who had only reached the second-floor landing, paused and began descending again, prepared to tell Lord d'Arcy what her aunts would not, that she refused to become his mistress.

But the man standing in the hallway was a stranger. Dressed all in black with a mane of ebony hair and equally luxuriant mustaches, he possessed an arresting face as pale as it was mesmerizing.

"Monsieur De Valmy!" Justine cried as she rushed in.

"Why are you here, monsieur?" Henrice questioned less emotionally.

Madeleine saw his pleasant expression alter at Henrice's tone, be he spoke lightly. "Why, I've come to pay my respects to your guest." His black gaze moved between the sisters. "I understand you have been favored with the unexpected arrival of your niece, after all."

"Mrs. Seldon," Henrice said in an icy voice.

"A most remarkable woman." De Valmy's long mouth twitched. "With a remarkable thirst for the English gin."

Henrice said calmly, "Our niece has gone to bed."

His smile vanished. "Regrettable. I have news for her."

"Of Ondine? What is it?" Justine questioned.

De Valmy shrugged. "I should rather tell the child myself. If she is like most children she will be full of questions which only I can answer. I understand from Madame Seldon that she has grown into quite a precocious young lady."

Neither sister missed the implication. "Then you must return when we can provide hospitality," Henrice said stiffly. "Perhaps a dinner in your honor next week, monsieur? Perhaps by then we will have a donation for your cause."

"You understand me perfectly, Madame Henrice. How rare that is in a woman. I'm certain a few coins will go a long way toward helping Ondine. I will bid you *adieu*. Until *tomorrow* evening?"

"Tomorrow evening," Henrice murmured.

"Why did you do that?" Justine whispered angrily when De Valmy had left. "We have no money to give him. *Mon Dieu!* What shall we do?"

"I will think of something, I promise."

"You promise. You always promise!" Justine cried.

"This time I say you are wrong. Lord d'Arcy was offended by your proposition. You should simply have asked for his help."

Henrice stiffened. "I never accept charity."

"Non. But you would break little Madeleine's heart and trick Lord d'Arcy's coin from his purse. Always you must play the role of puppet mistress. You pull our strings and we must all dance. But this time, Lord d'Arcy snipped those strings. He won't be back, but De Valmy most certainly will! What will you do when he demands Madeleine's virtue in exchange for freeing Ondine? She will resist him. Debtor's prison, that's where we shall all end!"

Henrice eyed her stonily. "You are hysterical." She turned back toward the salon.

Madeleine leaned back against the bannister, her mind reeling from all she had heard this night. Who was this mysterious Monsieur De Valmy? What was his connection with her mother? Why were her aunts so anxious for money to give De Valmy unless—*"Maman* is in trouble!" she whispered.

She had suspected something was wrong from the first day she arrived. She curled her nails into her palms. Where was her mother? Why were her aunts keeping it a secret?

For the past hour she had been thinking that her aunts were totally selfish women ready to surrender her to the highest bidder in order to fund comfort for themselves. Now, her spying had produced a whole new set of reasons.

They were in debt to De Valmy, dangerous debt, the kind that could land them in prison. She pondered Henrice's impassioned declaration that, whatever the cost, they must hold on to the trappings of who and what they once were. Her family was composed of very proud, if eccentric, women. Perhaps the reason they had lied to her was that her mother was *already* in debtor's prison awaiting the funds to free her. Perhaps De Valmy had put her there. That would explain her aunts' terror of him.

She knew it would be useless to press her aunts for the truth. The truth would alter to suit their needs. Hard on the heels of that ungenerous thought was one that her aunts had, through a convoluted maze of reasoning she did not quite understand, been trying to shield her from De Valmy.

Instinct told her she could not appeal to him for the truth, either. One thing seemed clear. De Valmy wanted money in exchange for news about her mother. Very well, she would get it. But she would stand by as a sacrifice to her aunts' well-meaning but baffling stratagems.

She walked back upstairs feeling resolute. She had seen the marquis of Brecon. He was a ravishingly handsome man on whom her aunts seem to dote. She believed that they would not toss her to any passing libertine. He must be the best of the lot. Since it seemed he would not be coming back for her, she would have to find a way to go to him.

She wondered briefly what her life would be once she became a mistress. She was all the way to her room before she realized that she knew someone else who could supply her with an answer.

"Audelia!"

Seven

"And so, I have run away," Madeleine declared.

"I see." Audelia sipped a little of the tea she had poured for herself and her guest. "This *is* a dilemma."

Madeleine waited patiently for Audelia to digest all that she had shared with her. It had been easy enough to walk right out of her aunts' home at eight o'clock because they never roused before noon. But now that she had told her story she realized that she was facing a moment of truth. What a day ago was unthinkable had suddenly become not only necessary but essential. She needed advice on how to capture the amorous attentions of a rake!

"How serious you look!" Audelia exclaimed as she rearranged the satin comforter on her bed. "Perhaps it's the hour. I seldom rise before ten. But that's of no consequence compared to your troubles. How can I be of assistance to you?"

Madeleine smiled gratefully. "You must help me seek the protection of Lord d'Arcy in order to save my mother."

Audelia yawned. "But you aren't even certain your mother is in debtor's prison."

"This is true, but I know that my aunts must have money, and quickly, in order to save her from whatever trouble she is in. I thought of appealing to Lord d'Arcy directly, but I am afraid he will turn me down."

"Because he told your aunt that he would take no child

of her household? What makes you think he will change his mind once he learns who you are?"

"I will not tell him."

"You seem very eager to give yourself to him. I must wonder why." Audelia's expression turned arch. "But of course! I saw your Lord d'Arcy once. It was two years ago at a pugilistic display Richard and I attended."

"He is unobjectionable," Madeleine allowed softly.

"Unobjectionable? 'Sinfully handsome' would not be effusive praise in this instance." Audelia dipped her lashes over her eyes. "I found him quite daunting. Fiendish good looks but singularly remote. Could not imagine approaching him. Days later Richard told me he had been about to fight a duel the day we saw him. It was a boxing match, if you can imagine!"

Madeleine glanced up from contemplation of her own memory of his handsome face. "In France dueling is considered an art. What was the cause of this duel?"

Audelia's expression altered with thought. "I don't remember. The usual, I imagine. A woman. Lord d'Arcy won, but the scandal of the ordeal sent him abroad the very next day. I am surprised I had not learned of his return. He must be keeping very discreet company. He does have a reputation with the ladies. Too much so, if gossip be true."

"What sort of gossip?"

Audelia chuckled. "They say he beds women like cats catch mice. One simply has to cross his path to obtain his attention."

"Then it should be easy enough for me to attract him."

"Oh, that shan't be the trouble, pet." Audelia reached up to adjust one of the lace rags that had held her curls in place while she slept. "The trouble will come once you have him. Remember, cats eat mice. If he is anything at all like his father . . . well!"

"What is his father like?"

"*Was.* His father is dead. Struck through the heart by

the sword of a cuckolded husband." She reached up to make another adjustment. "It's said the late Lord d'Arcy took particular delight in debauching virtuous wives because wanton ones were no sport."

"I see." Madeleine sighed. "Yet his son told *Tante* Henrice that innocence does not appeal to him because a virgin would fall irrevocably in love with him."

"Don't believe him. What you heard was the clarion cry of a confirmed bachelor," Audelia answered with superior wisdom. "He does not want to be trapped into marriage, that is all. As for the rest, it's all a game. Men enjoy the sport of seduction."

"So then, I am to be the sport?"

"We were speaking of the father, of course. Yet I should think the present marquis's reputation speaks of the same power to charm. Richard says that a man who can have any woman he wants is not likely to be taken strongly with any one of them."

"That is a good thought." Madeleine forced herself to sound more cheerful. "You see, you help me. I am so ignorant. For instance, what does it mean to be tupped and stuffed?"

Audelia colored. "Wherever did you hear such language!"

"It is rude, *oui?* I suspected so."

"It is a vulgar term meaning a man has achieved intimate knowledge of a woman."

Madeleine frowned. So that was what Mrs. Seldon had been taunting her with the day Lord d'Arcy came to call. "So then, a mistress is one who gives her body to a man in return for money?"

"No, never money! A mistress is not a prostitute!" Audelia stoutly defended her position. "I would never sell my favors to any man, not even Richard. I could not. I do have my pride. But my Richard is so strong and gentlemanly and kind, and he loves me. Because I love him, too,

I give myself to him. For that honor, he bestows upon me this little house, a new gown every week. He has even promised that after the wedding I shall have my own carriage."

Madeleine did not quite see the distinction, but she supposed this was a new way of thinking and that she would come to it soon enough. "I am not at all certain that Lord d'Arcy will like me enough to give me a carriage."

"Are you not?" Audelia sized her up. "You are unusual looking, one might say continental with your short dark curls. Yet Lord d'Arcy is reputed to have very sophisticated tastes. You should more than suit."

Madeleine reached up to self-consciously touch her clipped hair. "Even if he is attracted, what is there to make him offer me a *carte blanche?* No, what is it the English say?"

"Slip on the shoulder," Audelia supplied.

"Vraiment! This slip on the shoulder, I must have it, and soon."

"That will require fast work. How do you propose to approach him?"

"I have a plan. Something Lord d'Arcy mentioned the night before sparked it. You will think me mad."

"So much the better!" Audelia leaned back and reached for her tea. Gazing at Madeleine's mischievous smile, she wondered how she could ever have thought this remarkable young woman with midnight-blue eyes was a nun. "Tell me and I promise to help you any way I can. Oh, but I do love stratagems!"

"Mon Dieu!" Stricken by remorse, Henrice dropped the note that had just been delivered and sank heavily into the nearest chair. *"Ma pauvre petite!* I drove her to this. Yet who could have guessed a Foucant—?" She struggled with strong emotion. "No, the girl has deserted us!"

"We should never have expected her to agree to our plan," Justine said between sobs into her handkerchief. "How will we explain this to Ondine?"

"To run back to St. Etienne's without telling us! To leave only a note!" Henrice's chin trembled with the effort to maintain her dignity. "It is beyond ill manners! It is cruel!"

Neither sister stirred when the doorbell jangled. They did not expect it to be Madeleine. Therefore the day could not get worse.

"There's a post from Lord d'Arcy," Mrs. Seldon said when she had made the journey from door to salon. "Which of ye wants it?"

Henrice held out her hand.

"Aren't you going to open it," Justine asked as her sister simply held on to it long after Mrs. Seldon left.

"Whatever it is, it's come too late to help us," she said bitterly. "Sebastian failed me. Madeleine has gone."

Justine snatched it up. "Then I will look." She tore it open and out floated a sheet of paper. *"Nom de Dieu!"* Her voice fell in hushed awe. "It's a draft for five hundred pounds!"

The sun shone warmly down from the mid-September sky. In a few days it would be autumn and the present warmth would be nipped by a chill. But for today, the countryside of Kent basked in the indolence of late-summer ripeness.

The coachman whipped up the horses, anxious, it seemed, to deliver his last passenger on this lonely stretch of countryside, the last before the constantly widening views of the coastline met the sea.

Madeleine did not blame him for wanting to be quit of his labor. She would not have minded walking the last mile or two in the sunshine if she had known where she

was going. Her only regret so far was the letter she had
posted to her aunts. In it she told them that she was returning to her convent school. What they could not suspect
was that she was willingly flying into the arms of the lover
they had once chosen for her.

She stared idly at the gentle landscape hemmed in by
hedgerows, where pastureland and harvested cornfields lay
side by side in patchwork patterns. Gradually the domestic
land gave way to bare-topped turfy down that smelled of
wild thyme and rock roses and which resounded with the
cries of gulls wheeling in the wind. Gradually the sky lost
its tame country air for a brighter smoky metallic surface
as they neared the Channel.

She had rehearsed her part over and over on the trip
down from London. She could not simply appear at Lord
d'Arcy's door with the request that he take her to be his
mistress. He would doubtless refuse if only because it was
not his idea. She had needed an excuse to gain entry into
his home and she was quite pleased with the one she had
devised. It gave her an excuse to linger for a week, more
than time enough for a man of the marquis's supposed
seductive powers to notice and claim her.

Audelia had been a dear, allowing her to stay overnight
with her and even loaning her clothes. Thinking of the
woman and her generosity, Madeleine wondered if she
would ever experience love, or did a mistress not allow
the finer feelings to enter into the arrangement? She suspected she should keep her heart locked up as she braved
Lord d'Arcy's den. But first, she had to tell a very convincing lie.

The manor house that came into view in the distance
as the coach skirted a line of oaks was as old as it was
imposing. The shale roof was a type she had never seen
before arriving in England. The walls were half timbered
with warm plaster festooned in ivy, the deep-red brick
house seemed warm and inviting, the windows flashing

welcome in the late-morning light. She knew at once that this was the country house of the marquis of Brecon.

Minutes later, the coachman pulled up at the head of the drive and allowed her to alight. Her heart beating rapidly, she picked up her bags. The portmanteau contained her clothing, most of it borrowed from Audelia. The string bag contained her only purchase, a copper-bottomed sauce pan. When she reached the door, she paused to withdraw from her pocket a long red ribbon with a note attached to one end by a bow. She slipped it over her head and adjusted the bow so that the letter hung down her front with the marquis of Brecon's name hanging face out.

Sebastian was busy at his laboratory table watching his test tube fill with the hydrogen arising from his latest attempt to design a chemical reaction that would produce the gas more quickly and cheaply.

His butler interrupted him. "Beg pardon, my lord. There's a female person come to see you."

Sebastian didn't glance up from his work. "Female? I'm expecting no females. Send her away, Horace."

"I tried, my lord, but she insists that she's made the journey from London expressly to do you a service."

"Service? I need no services done." He waved a hand in the direction of the door. "Send her away."

"My lord," the butler continued, looking pained by the necessity. "She claims to be a forfeiture sent you by a friend."

"A forfeiture?"

"The prize, is how she phrased it, my lord, won by you according to a bet made twixt you and another gentleman."

"This grows curiouser and curiouser." Yet Sebastian's attention remained focused on the apparatus before him. "I don't remember placing any bet for a woman. Did she say with whom?"

"The young person wears a—a note tied with a ribbon about her neck, my lord. She indicated that it was for you alone to open."

Sebastian's full attention was snared at last. He straightened up to look at his butler. "Did you say she bears a tag, like a birthday parcel?"

The man nodded solemnly. "Indeed, my lord."

Sebastian pondered the possibilities. "Haven't placed a bet in London in two years, Horace. Yet, 'tis true before I left for Italy, I amused myself by placing bets of the most ridiculous sort. In jest, I suppose it's possible that one of them included the attentions of a harlot. Perhaps the loser just learned of my return and is eager to have the debt off his conscience. Shan't know till I speak to her."

He lowered the flame beneath his vial, peering intently at the simmering liquid before continuing his thoughts. "I suppose you must send her in. No, better have her wait in the library." He favored his butler with a knowing smile. "Don't wish to unwrap so unique a gift among my pipets and bunsen burners."

Madeleine waited exactly two hours and twenty-five minutes in the marquis of Breton's library. She knew this because she had watched the time being measured out on the face of the small marble clock on the mantel. After the passage of the first twenty minutes, she took it into her head to peruse the library.

It was a huge room with bookcases, encased behind doors with lead-glass diamond panes, running along the length of the longer walls. The volumes were bound in leather jackets of Persian blue, winter green, Moroccan red, and saddle brown. At the far end of the room were three large windows hung in divided curtains of Chinese red festooned with pelmets of gold trimmed in matching braid. Matching windows also divided the bookcases along the outside wall, and at the far corner a pair of French doors led into the side garden. It was a splendid room, she decided, the finest room she could ever remember entering.

But its intimidating size would not keep her seated. She moved from shelf to shelf, searching out titles. There was Macpherson's *Ossian*. Schiller's *Wallenstein* in the original German stood beside Coleridge's 1800 translation. Works by Plato, Ovid, prodigious amounts of other Latin, Greek, and modern literature filled other shelves. There were books on architecture and volumes on medicine, mathematics, and chemistry. Always one with an eye for detail, she noted that many of the spines on the books were cracked and worn. This was not a library for show, but the working inventory of a remarkable mind.

After a half hour of browsing she turned to a study of the paintings. Hung high above the volumes were pictures of what she supposed were various deceased family members. Covering three centuries, there seemed little resemblance between them until one looked deeply into the faces, omitting the costumes and artistic flourishes of the various periods. Though some were handsome and others homely, the similarity of feature was pronounced. High foreheads, remarkably brilliant eyes, and thick, unruly shocks of wavy hair spanned centuries and sexes.

After tea was served and she refreshed herself, she strolled about inspecting the busts of historical figures and several remnants of ancient marbles placed about. The most arresting, being more than life-size, were the pair of young male and female torsos that flanked the green marble fireplace. It was impossible not to be impressed by the exquisite care with which each sculptor had etched the nude anatomy of living flesh into the cool white marble. Quite astonishing, and embarrassing, Madeleine decided after five minutes' reflection. She had never seen a man undraped before, be he marble or any other kind.

After a while she moved to one of the windows to gaze out. The sun was rising rapidly toward noon. If she were going to prepare her first meal this night, she would need to repair at once to the kitchen. Yet the park land drew her admiration. She had nearly forgotten during her weeks in smoky, noisy London how much she missed the countryside. If she were allowed to remain here, she would rise early and walk through the pastures each morning.

So engrossed was she in her perusal of the bucolic scene beyond that she did not realize when the fullness of her pelisse caught the edge of the large leather portfolio lying on the long library table, raking it off as she passed. Papers slid from inside and spread apart on the floor like the opening of a fan.

"Mon Dieu," she murmured in distress and stooped to pick them up before someone came in and saw what she had done. But in the act of bending over she froze, unable to believe what she was gazing upon.

It was an ink drawing of a fashionably dressed woman who sat on a low stone bench beneath a canopy of trees. She wore a wide low-brimmed hat of a decade earlier. There was a black ribbon about her throat and a foam of lace at her neckline and elbows. From above the waist it was the most conventional of portraits. But below her nipped-in bodice the picture altered so radically that she thought she must be mistaken. But no. There was no mistaking the gentleman on his knees before her. At first glance one might think he was making a formal declaration . . . until one looked at how the lady sat with her skirts hitched and one leg lifted and cocked at an angle that exposed the very center of herself.

She had never once in her life seen any lady, including herself, so disported, and she stared openmouthed. The gentleman in the illustration seemed likewise stricken with awe by the sight. His hands were clasped before him as he leaned forward, eyes wide and tongue aloll. It was some stunned seconds before her eyes recognized the script penned beneath the drawing. It read: "Homage at the Altar of Venus."

"Nom de Dieu!" Madeleine placed her hand over the scandalous sketch, and then after a second's reflection jerked it away.

"Perhaps it's allegorical," she murmured, looking for a purpose for the indecent rendering.

Cheeks flaming, she lifted the first sketch in hopes of finding a more tasteful example of such an allegory. Beneath it lay another, and all her doubts were vanquished.

Entitled "The Wanton Lark," the drawing depicted a pair of young lovers in flagrante delicto. Her dress draped about her waist, exposing both breasts and buttocks, the girl lay on the salon carpet with legs kicking the air. The man knelt between her legs, his breeches about his knees as he clutched his swollen organ in his fist at the apex of her thighs. They were each smiling in such appreciation for the other that there was no mistaking the lewd intentions of either.

Madeleine jumped to her feet, her body tormented by an onslaught of emotions too strong and awkward to be easily mastered. She pushed her hands into her cheeks, surprised to feel how hot they were. She should have been insulted to her very soul. She knew she should view the drawings as disgusting, despicable, indecent examples of sinfulness, a revolt of all that she had been taught. And yet . . .

Audelia, when pressed, had with much giggling and blushing explained the rudiments of coupling. Now she was faced with an exact, if crudely realized, pictorial example. She had come to offer herself in just such a manner to the marquis of Breton, had she not? Should she not know what that meant?

She glanced in alarm at the closed library doors and then at the floor where the pictures lay sprawling from the portfolio in abandoned display. This might be her only opportunity to gain such knowledge.

Five of the longest most excruciatingly enlightening minutes of her life passed as she studied the full sheaf of drawings. Heart hammering with the horror of being caught, she could not say she fully absorbed the details of any of them, apart from the enormous design of the gentlemen's appendages. And *gentlemen* they were, from the cut of their clothes to the design of their luxurious surroundings. "Gentlemen And Their Mistresses At Pretty Games," the text proclaimed on the final page.

When she could stand no more, she pushed the bawdy sketches back into their leather case and placed it on the edge of the library table from which it had fallen.

Some of the tension that haunted her body for the next half hour had dissipated by the time she heard footsteps outside the library door. She even managed to stand straight and composed when the door opened, and then she forgot herself and could have wept at the sight of the man approaching her.

He was dressed as one who had just come in from the stable with the collar of his cambric shirt open to midchest, his sleeves rolled up to the elbows, and a leather apron covering him from chest to midthigh. Heavy scarred boots shod his feet. If she had not seen him before, she would not have known him for a gentleman, let alone a marquis.

Unlike the night he came to visit her aunts, his hair was in disarray, sweeping his brow in untidy curling wisps of glossy gold and chestnut. Yet it was his singular features that made her stare when she knew she should not. The pleasing play of muscle and bone beneath faint stubble of golden whiskers on his chin as he smiled at her was simply riveting.

"Well, this is a pleasant break in my day." With languid eyes the color of one of *Tante* Justine's treasured baubles, her Persian aquamarine, he assessed her, taking in her sober traveling dress of dove-gray under a white-spotted India muslin pelisse edged in red and green paisley trim. Her head was covered in a small chip bonnet that tied under her chin with a small neat bow.

When his gaze came back to her face, he offered her a swift and intimate smile. "Is it true, you are mine?"

"Oui, monsieur."

"French. And a republican," he added in response to her use of the egalitarian term "monsieur" rather than the entitled "my lord." "Delightful."

He stepped back a step and crossed his arms. "So then, my beauty, unwrap yourself so that I may fully admire your charms."

The bold proposal did not shock her, yet she could admit to a certain surprise at his suggestion. Her thoughts ricocheted with breathless urgency to one of the drawings she had just viewed. The elegant young woman in a turban with her dress pulled up to her waist had been reclining on a carpet very similar to the one on which they stood. The fact that the drawing belonged to the very handsome man before her did not help in the least to deflate her sudden rise of nerves.

It occurred to her to wonder as she stripped off her gloves and then more slowly her pelisse if perhaps he seduced women on his library carpet. It took very little effort to send her thoughts hopscotching along. Had the ladies accepted the occurrence as naturally as the female in the drawing?

"Shy, pet?" His deeply disturbing voice arrested her wayward thoughts. He approached and lifted two long-fingered hands to the first button of her bodice. "Perhaps you require assistance."

His action sent her backpedaling even as he sauntered her. "I think you should read the note first, mon-

Her eyes, large, dark, and uncannily familiar, snared Sebastian's attention, but she looked away. He saw a blush bloom in her cheek and longed to brush a curious finger over its petal texture. "You do not seem the usual sort of doxy."

He said the words idly yet was delighted to see that they brought her chin up and her eyes, dark as midnight, back to his. An aquiline nose saved her face from mere prettiness while her mouth reminded him of the many sulky Raphaelite Madonnas he had viewed in Milan with lips that were full, pouting and impossibly sweet. Her sober gown and shy bonnet gave her the clichéd charm of quaint innocence. Yet he was certain she was far from innocent.

He removed his gaze from her face to the place where a letter hung by a red ribbon around her neck. He took appreciative notice of the thrust of her bosom upon which the note lay, feeling lighter in spirit with every passing moment.

She touched the letter. "You wish to read it, monsieur?"

"No." His gaze drifted back to hers. "I've no desire to know the name of the giver until I've determined whether or not I like the gift."

"You do not know what the gift is," Madeleine returned.

"I am rapidly forming an idea." A rake's smile played across that deceptively boyish mouth. "Will you not finish undressing for me?" He saw her gaze shift toward the doors. "No one will disturb us. Be assured that only I will delight in your display."

In a careless stream of sentences he had wiped from her mind any misconceptions she had brought with her about attracting the attentions of a rake. "You expect me to—to disrobe here?"

He reached out to cup her shoulders in his warm hands. "Have you a preference? The salon? The ballroom? The backstairs cupboard? I've played lady's maid in all of them."

Common sense made a great upsurge through her beleaguered senses. "The note, monsieur."

A shade of temper flashed in his eyes, yet he said, "Come, give me the card that we may hasten to the rest."

As he reached out to take the letter, Madeleine forced herself to remain still. Yet he did not remove the ribbon from her neck as she expected. The back of his fingers brushed the swell of her left breast as he took it. She supposed this was the approach libertines used with a certain class of females. She did not like it, but it did not matter. She was about to become one of those females. But not, she decided, without a little more effort on his part.

Sebastian slipped a finger under the wax-sealed edge of the letter still hanging about her neck and unfolded it. He spared the enclosed lines only the briefest of glances before looking up. "You have been sent to replace my dismissed chef?"

"Oui, monsieur."

He laughed softly and with a light touch brushed his palm deliberately over the swell of her right breast. "Are you certain *you* are not the dish of which I am to partake?"

Madeleine's pulse leaped as she dropped her gaze to a perusal of the floor. How easy it was to attract a man's amorous attention! Quite too easy.

"Have I offended you?" Though she was not looking at his face, she sensed a genuine interest behind his inquiry. "How clumsy of me. I apologize."

It did not sound like an apology to her. He was too amused. She lifted her gaze a little. "Monsieur, you will keep me, yes?"

"Oh, most certainly I shall keep you a while." He removed the ribbon from her neck. "Where would you like to be kept?"

This time her gaze made it all the way to his face. "Why, in the kitchen, monsieur."

"In the—? Ah, we shall keep up the charade a little longer, shall we?" He shrugged. "Very well. I'll have my butler show you the kitchen. It's about somewhere, as I recall."

Madeleine dipped to pick up her bags, but he reached out to catch her wrist.

"Don't bestir yourself. Horace will see to your luggage." He glanced about, expecting something other than the portmanteau and string bag at her feet. "Where is the rest?"

"That is it, monsieur."

He seemed to consider her reply as he placed a proprietary arm about her shoulders. "I suppose I should expect to be put to the cost of a gown or two. Quite right."

He curled a hand under her chin to lift it for his inspection. With his other he tugged loose the ribbon that kept her bonnet secured under her chin, then whisked it off.

She saw his gaze widen as he took in her cropped curls and her heart stumbled. "You are not my usual style, but no matter."

He cast her bonnet aside as he kept one caressing hand on her chin. With the other he lightly tousled her squashed dark ringlets. "One does not look a gift horse, or otherwise, in the mouth."

Madeleine gazed at him impassively. "You have a method of speaking, monsieur, which I do not understand."

"Don't worry over it, mademoiselle." The practiced sweep of his gaze over her seemed to strip all with it. "I'm certain when it comes to the language of love we shall find we speak in identical tongues and touches."

She blushed as he touched her chin with the curve of

his finger. "I think you mistake, monsieur, the intent of the letter."

"Not at all," he murmured as he leaned close to nuzzle her ear. When she balked, he drew back, but his arm held her firmly by his side. "It clearly states that you've been sent to see to whatever appetites I might have."

The audacity of his lie took her aback. She turned within his embrace. "I don't believe that is written there."

"Really?" There was a dangerous sparkle in his blue eyes. "Since the note was not addressed to you, I assume you did not take the liberty of reading it?" She choked on the truth that she had written it. "So then, I say it says your services have been engaged for my amusement. To what use I put you is to be determined by me."

For the first time it struck Madeleine that her plan might not succeed in the manner she had in mind. He was quite as devious as she! "I am an able chef, monsieur. Should you not at least try my fare?"

"But that is exactly my intention, sweeting." He coaxed her closer with his arm and bent his head to lay his lips on hers.

His kiss was surprisingly gentle, warm and soothing, its stinging devastation felt only as he lifted his mouth away.

"The first taste." He smiled into her suddenly bright gaze. "Are you still certain you wish to mess about with pots and pans when we could be doing this?"

"*Oui.*" Madeleine was amazed to hear the word come from herself.

"Very well." He released her, deciding to play the game out, for he was much diverted by the unexpected interruption in what had become a very dull week. The writer of the note had not signed it, a not uncommon occurrence in matters this delicate. The wrong note in the wrong hands could provoke disaster. But clearly no man sent so beautiful a woman to another for the express purpose of hiding her away in the heat and drudgery of a boiling kitchen.

He had no doubt that she would give up the charade within five minutes of entering that purgatory.

"So you truly wish to *cook* for me?" The word cook was struck by the hammer of his amusement.

"Yes, monsieur."

"Then you've been appraised of my culinary eccentricities?"

"Eccen— What, monsieur?"

"My special needs. My likes and dislikes."

"No, monsieur," she answered confidently, "but I should like to know them."

"Very well." He moved to pull back the chair tucked under the table set before the windows and indicated the seat. "You may wish to make note of them."

She looked at him suspiciously. "Are there so very many?"

"That depends on whether you have an especially good memory. But let us begin. You may tell me if you need to make mark of them." He cupped his hands behind his back and began to pace slowly. "Firstly, I never eat meat on a day that begins with T, that being Tuesday and Thursday in English. Conversely, I eat only meats on days beginning with the letter S. On Mondays, Wednesdays, and Fridays I consume only foods beginning with the letters M, W, and F respectively." He paused. "Are you with me so far?"

"Oui, monsieur."

"Clever girl. Then we go on." He paced to the far end of the magnificent room, calling over his shoulder as she followed, "I do not like milk or cheese, but will eat both together. I like my food piquant but not with onion, chives, or leeks."

That left garlic, shallots, and scallions, Madeleine quickly devised. "Is this all, monsieur?"

He turned abruptly to face her. "We just begin." He again indicated the chair at his desk, but again she shook her head. "I prefer pepper crushed, never milled, my salt ground fine as dust. My breads must be crusty but the center soft. Never toasted. I am partial to seafood but will ingest only those creatures which are served within an hour of their taking. I eat no rice, cabbage, or peas. I detest domestic fowl, puddings, cream sauces, sausages, ham, pies, garden vegetables colored green and orange, and hens' eggs." He lifted an eyebrow in inquiry. "Too much?"

Madeleine resolutely shook her head. She would have thought that a man with tastes so broad in other areas would not restrict himself so dramatically in the matter of gastronomic fare. She supposed she had little understanding of the real world.

"I expect my coffee—not tea—to be served hot, and so sweet it draws flies. I eat at ten A.M., two P.M., and eight P.M. with tea at four-*thirty,* not *four.* I expect at least five removes with every dinner and, of course, dessert. But mark you, I detest vanilla, peppermint, cinnamon, and most of all chocolate."

"Chocolate?" Madeleine echoed.

"Yes, is that a problem?"

"No, monsieur, I think everything will be fine," she answered with a small smile. She had heard him with her own ears tell her aunts that chocolate was his favorite flavor. This was all an elaborate lie! Very well, she would treat him in kind and be glad of it. "If that is all?"

Sebastian glanced sharply at her. She did not look in the least dismayed by his strange requests. "Ah, but this is Tuesday, the second Tuesday of the month. On this day, since it falls on an even number, this being the twelfth of the month, my needs might be called peculiar." He ignored the marked rise of her dark brows, for he was about to be even more outrageous than before. "On the second Tuesday of every month which falls on an even number I crave meat which lives on land but is not hoofed, which swims in the water but does not have fins, which moves through the air but does not have wings."

"All these together in one animal?" she questioned skeptically.

He nodded. "If you can manage it."

"I see." Madeleine suspected it would not do to look so satisfied. "I may need a small matter of time to adjust. I have not yet seen your provisions nor know your stock."

"Horace will acquaint you with the necessities." His smile made lacework out of her thoughts. "Unless you prefer to fulfill the debt in some other simpler fashion." He looked almost rueful despite the wickedness that frolicked in those oh-so-blue eyes. "There are appetites and appetites, mademoiselle."

Madeleine wondered that he bought her lie so easily when he was so recklessly inventive with his own. "I shall stick to the first part of the bargain, monsieur."

"You may begin your service with dinner. Afterward, we will assess whether you still prefer kitchen work to bedroom exercises." He jerked the bell cord which brought the butler so quickly Madeleine suspected he had been eavesdropping outside the library door. "Horace. Show, Mademoiselle . . . ?"

"Mignon," Madeleine supplied.

Sebastian bestowed a sweet smile upon her. "Show Mademoiselle Mignon to the kitchen, Horace."

"What is she planning to do?"

"I'm certain I don't know, my lord."

Master and butler were crossing the back lawn toward the pond in the distance. Horace looked quite thoroughly put out, which was rare for a man accustomed to running a household of up to forty servants in the marquis's family home in western Wales.

"The mademoiselle asked for a ball of twine and a broom handle. Then she took one of cook's meat forks from the kitchen and tied it to the handle. It was when she asked for the direction of the nearest pond of water that I thought I should bring the matter to your attention, my lord."

"I see." But Sebastian did not see at all. He had returned to his laboratory work, thinking a lot about the little French cook. She was a splendid little creature with saucy dark ringlets and equally dark eyes that were not quite blue or black or brown but some wondrous chimerical shade. He had been looking forward to their next encounter when his butler had found him dressing for dinner and fetched him out into his own park land.

They moved rapidly toward the pond shaded on one side by a sweep of trees and on the other by tall reeds. "How long ago was it you said she came this way?"

"Not above ten minutes, my lord."

Horace's sniff of disapproval was not for the person herself. "Do you suppose she plans to scoop up something from the pond for your dinner, my lord?"

"I don't know, but believe me I will find out." Sebastian paused within ten yards of the cane break that shielded the pond on this side. "I suppose I should have thought of it before. Perhaps she's been sent to poison me."

"You have such enemies, my lord?" Horace sounded unconvinced of the possibility.

"Not in the ordinary way," Sebastian replied. "But we are at war and I am making certain calculations for the military. Some spy may have gotten wind of that."

"She is French," Horace reminded his master, his tone conveying a very English suspicion of all things Gallic.

Sebastian's thoughts offered up another possibility: Bram's prediction that if he left Lieutenant Sherwood's challenge unanswered he would find another method with which to exact his revenge. The deceptive gift of a lovely girl might go a long way toward allying his suspicions until he was writhing in agony from a gut full of poison.

"What else has she done today, Horace?"

"Spent more than a hour in the woods, my lord, and came back with a basket full of roots and ferns and fungus."

"Fungus, did you say? My, my. The girl shows strange tendencies, doesn't she?"

"Most peculiar, my lord."

"Very well. You go back to the house. I'll handle this."

Madeleine had waited until she was certain she was out of sight of the house before quickly stripping off her shoes and stockings. She then tucked her skirt hem into the front of her waistband. The hitched-up skirts formed pantaloons that permitted her to move more freely. She knew she would not have much time. It was growing dark, but Lord d'Arcy had been adamant about the fact that he would not accept any water-bred meat whose freshness was more than an hour old.

She gasped as she stepped into the reedy pond, for despite the heat of the day, the water was quite cool. She waded a little out from the bank as the water swirled about her calves and then began moving toward the shady shallows where the croaking could be heard. So intent was she in her work that she did not notice the spy lurking behind the trees on shore.

Sebastian crept forward stealthily though he did have cause to wonder why he should be creeping about his own property like a poacher when the girl was the intruder. The reeds on the bank shielded him from view, but they also obscured his vision of what the young lady was doing. He was startled when the reeds suddenly shook and the water erupted in a splash.

"Aha! I have you, Monsieur la Grenouille!" came the cry from the other side.

Sebastian rose up on tiptoe and craned his neck to see

over the top of the reeds, but all he saw was the crown of her chip hat. What the devil was she doing capturing frogs?

Eight

The menu set before Sebastian was scripted in a fine hand in both English and French. The English version on the left side read:

Turnip Soup
Wild Watercress Salad with Shallot Mayonnaise
Sour-milk Battered Frog Legs with Garlic Butter
Grilled Mushrooms in Burgundy Wine
Fiddled Ferns in Cream Sauce
Pear Tart

He was amazed and delighted, and ever so suspicious of his new chef. He set the card aside at his place at the table and signaled to his footman. She thought she was clever, did she? Well, he would soon put an end to this masquerade and have a little fun besides. "Send in Mignon."

A few moments later Madeleine appeared in the servants' doorway. He noticed the dark tendrils escaping the white frilly cap which replaced the bonnet she had worn. Her face was flushed from the heat of the kitchen and a pearl of perspiration rode her upper lip. He could not resist wondering if she flushed so prettily in love's embrace. He would soon find out.

She now wore a dark-blue serge dress with white fichu and cuffs. The skirt was fuller and of heavier fabric than was popular among ladies of the day. Her hair was entirely covered by a white cap. It was the costume of a domestic. The white apron she wore over all gave her, he decided, the look of a shepherdess and quite flattered her narrow waist.

"Ah, Mignon. I have a bone to pick with you."

"So soon, monsieur?" Madeleine had deserted the kitchen reluctantly, for she had many dishes simmering at once and a staff openly hostile to her every effort. "But you have not yet tasted a dish."

"That is precisely the point. Come forward. Closer. I seldom bite."

Madeleine noticed as she approached him that he had changed to formal clothing for dinner: a dark-blue coat with silver buttons and waistcoat of dove gray. Beneath his cleanly shaven chin stood a double row of starched ruffles and the crisp white linen of his cravat. His curls had been brushed smooth, and her desire was strong to ruffle them with her hand. He really was quite beautiful, she thought.

"Did you forget my instruction?"

"Not at all, monsieur."

"You think not?" Sebastian made an elaborate production of picking up the menu and bring his monocle to his eye to read it though he had no need of the instrument. "It says here that you plan to feed me watercress and ferns. Green, madame! Green vegetables when I precisely said I do not eat green nor orange vegetables."

"Pardon, monsieur, but you said you do not eat green nor orange *garden* vegetables. Neither of these is from your garden. They are wild, as are the mushrooms."

"Ah, yes, the mushrooms," Sebastian murmured darkly, though silently he saluted her ingenuity. "We will let that pass for there are other transgressions. Mayonnaise? Admit you used eggs."

Madeleine kept her expression even. "Goose eggs, monsieur, not hen's eggs."

"Indeed?" He continued his perusal of the menu. "Here!" He tapped it with his monocle. "How do you explain the presence of garlic in the butter sauce?"

"I but follow your wishes, monsieur. You did not mention garlic when you said you do not eat onion, chives, nor leeks."

"The cream sauce? Deny it contains milk!"

"It contains cream, monsieur, which when left unstrained contains the curds for making cheese as well as the liquid of the milk, which you mentioned you will eat when combined. *Voilà!*"

"*Voilà,* indeed." Sebastian could scarcely contain his amusement behind his scowl. He had thought to disconcert her, but she had cleverly turned his every effort back on him. Such self-possession was rare in a woman of any class. It was singular in one so young and seemingly earnest. From where could she have sprung? He could not wait to hear her next explanation. "I give you credit for the above. But you cannot possibly have an answer for the last. Frogs?"

"You were most adamant of all about your meat choice," she replied calmly. "The instructions were for the second Tuesday of the month that falls on an even-numbered day. The beast must walk on land without hooves, swim without fins and move through the air without wings. The frog crawls on land, swims without fins, and leaps through the air without the aid of wings."

She folded her hands over her apron in a meek gesture, but he suspected that it was in mockery, for her cheeks were charmingly mantled in a blush of defiance. "I am but a poor French maid. I know of no other animal which answers your requirements. Have you in England, perhaps, a greater number who answer this description, my lord?"

The lapse into the more formal "my lord" gave him the final clue to her state of mind. She was playing a game with him, matching him wit for wit. Better yet, she had

neatly checkmated his effort to outwit her! That alone
made him decide to keep her even if her dishes turned out
to be inedible.

"Very well. Let me see what you have wrought."

"Oui, monsieur. The soup is first." Madeleine turned to
indicate to the footman to bring forth the first dish: a silver
tureen on an equally ornate platter.

Sebastian eyed the contents suspiciously when he lifted
the lid. "Turnip soup?" he questioned skeptically. "Roots
for broth, how quaint." Yet the aroma and velvety cream
texture the footman ladled into his bowl promised to be
heaven.

Instead of picking up his spoon, he leaned back in his
chair, his arms folded across his chest as he glanced up
with a quizzical expression. "You will taste it first, of
course."

"No, monsieur," she said a little slowly. "It is all for
you."

"But I insist."

"As you wish." She picked up the heavy silver spoon
and dipped it carefully into his bowl.

Sebastian watched in fascination as she dragged the
back of the spoon across the rim of the dish to keep it
from dripping before raising it to her lips where she sipped
a little from the side of the spoon. Her manners were remarkably refined, not those of a scullery maid nor even
country mouse. She was obviously French; her accent carried the inflection peculiar to one who had lived among
the royalty of the Bourbon court. Yet she would have been
a mere child when the revolution began. Was she a noble
orphan? Or was she merely a well-schooled harlot, fresh
from the brothels of Paris? How and why had she come
to England now? He meant to have answers for these questions before dawn.

"It requires a grinding of pepper and, if you prefer it
piquant, a touch of salt, monsieur," she pronounced.

"Let me see." He took the spoon from her hand, dipped into his bowl, and carried a spoonful to his mouth. The lovely flavor that filled his mouth made him close his eyes for an instant.

When he opened his eyes he saw this serious young woman with mysterious dark eyes studying him as if he were a plump leg of lamb which she could not decide how best to roast. He could not resist one more tease. He smacked his lips tentatively. "You are certain there is nothing else lacking?"

Her brows lifted in response to this possible criticism. "Lacking, monsieur? No, it is perfectly fine."

Sebastian finally loosed his smile. "I agree. It is perfect." He reached for his wineglass and held it out toward her. "I toast your efforts."

To his surprise she held up a hand in protest. "Please wait, monsieur. A premature toast may curdle the sauce."

" 'Tis a superstition I am unfamiliar with . . . but very well." He put his glass down.

Madeleine turned away before she remembered that, as a servant, she should have curtsied, but he was waving her away with a hand as she turned back to correct her error.

Sebastian consumed three bowls of turnip soup. He munched more contentedly than a cow in clover upon watercress salad with shallot mayonnaise. When the frogs legs arrived encased in a crisp golden lacework of batter gleaming with garlic butter, accompanied by assorted grilled mushrooms afloat in a clarified ruby-red wine sauce and moss-green tightly coiled fiddle ferns in cream sauce, he decided it was time to again send for her.

"Mademoiselle," he began in French this time, "I am to assume these dishes compose the entire meal? Good Lord!"

Madeleine bit her lip, embarrassed by the look of arrested disapproval in his face as he noted the dramatic change in her appearance. Her once-pristine apron contained a dozen colorful stains and her cap had wilted from the heat. A few strands of hair had escaped and clung to her damp cheeks and brow.

She ran the back of a hand across her damp brow. "I beg your pardon, monsieur, for my appearance."

Sebastian reined in his inclination to be sympathetic. "It is unusual."

Unusual! Madeleine thought resentfully. The day had been singular for its difficulties. She had been met with open hostility by the kitchen staff who felt she was usurping their place. She had waded through pools and tramped through woodlands in search of the near impossible requirements of the arrogant young nobleman before her. Unusual? Her position was *impossible!*

"I regret that time and circumstance did not permit the maintenance of the very highest standards, monsieur. I promise to do better in future."

"Are you fishing for compliments, Mignon?"

Pricked by his tone, she lifted her head and looked him directly in the eye. "No, monsieur."

"Good. Because you know that you are no less than a genius of ingenuity." He released a smile that was at once charming and seductive and amused.

"Merci, monsieur." The wash of relief that swept her tempted her to smile, but she held on doggedly to her defenses. "I am glad you find my small talents satisfactory."

"Satisfactory?" If she had used some other less preposterous word or seemed a little less impatient with his interference with her duties, he might have believed she was no more or less than she claimed. But there was something about her that spoke of a well-tuned sense of her worth.

She must, of course, be some friend's mistress. She was pretty, if in an unusual fashion, with luminous, faintly olive skin and eyes that held dark mystery and hints of secrets. Who would waste such beauty by sending her to toil so hard in a kitchen when she might have been sitting on his lap sharing his wine and food . . . and his bed? The note had given no clue. He suspected that there was some rare tale behind her purpose in coming here. Sooner or later, he would need to extract it from her.

"Come and sit with me, Mignon. I am tired of eating alone."

She looked at him in alarm. "I cannot, monsieur. I have a tart in the oven."

"I have servants. One of them shall watch the tart." He glanced at his footman. "See to it. Now," he said, rising from his seat at the end of the table. "I demand your company."

He walked right up to her and put his hand under her chin. He saw the look of mutiny enter her eyes. "Are you refusing to do my bidding?"

"Non, monsieur."

"In that case, let's retire upstairs." His fingers spread across her face, testing the softness of her skin. He noticed the perspiration trickling down the slender column of her neck and had felt the heat of her exertions rising from her cheeks where he touched her. There was a dab of flour on her chin and a smudge of soot from the stove's coal fire on her brow. Ordinarily such earthy marks of her humble station might have dissipated his interest. He was, after all, a creature of his age. In his circle of acquaintances even wanton ladies were pale, frail, cool-skinned creatures who did not flush or sweat or exert themselves anywhere but in bed. But with her, these marks of human frailty were added points of fascination. He did not stop to ask himself why. He merely experienced them as one does a sunset or flower.

"As delicious as your dinner is, Mignon, you are the more appetizing to me."

As she gazed into his amused blue eyes, Madeleine thought that perhaps her wits and bravery and self-possession would not be enough to save her from falling a little in love with him. But he must never know it!

Yet his kiss caught her utterly by surprise. Too astonished to struggle, she stood perfectly still.

Nothing of her nineteen years of convent existence had prepared her for the experienced touch of a worldly rakehell. Nuns had warned their charges against such men, debauched and profligate, sinners all with the appearance of angels but the souls of demons. She had prepared herself to submit to the expected pain and humiliation required to become his mistress. But it was to be a sacrifice for a greater cause, to save her mother and aunts. Why then did she feel only pleasant surprise in his warm, smooth lips traveling lightly over hers?

Audelia's warning that a man given everything he desires seldom values it weighed in along with the presence of the footmen to make her much too late pull away in protest.

Sebastian chuckled as she did so. Fully prepared for a struggle, he had not expected the shape of her smile to blossom under his mouth. An accomplished flirt would have made a token protest against his conduct . . . or would she? Perhaps, if she were as clever as this mademoiselle, she would only stare up at him in perfect silence as she did now, as if so unaccustomed to a man's kiss that she did not know quite how to behave.

The discreet cough of a footman brought him abruptly to his senses. Chagrin was a rare experience for him. He did not flush or stammer, but he did feel nettled by an annoying sense of having committed a faux pas nonetheless. He had always disdained gentlemen who seduced their inferiors, particularly members of their staff who looked to them for their livelihoods. Nor was he a man who delighted in an audience as he conducted his affairs. The midnight-eyed chit had quite bewitched him. She was truly as delectable as any dish ever set before him. "Come along, Mignon. You've earned a portion of your meal."

She cast a longing glance at the table laden with her day's efforts served in silver and porcelain dishes. She was, indeed, very hungry and very tired. "I would be happy to share your table, monsieur."

As he led her to a chair, one footman scurried to set the place for her while another filled the wineglass. She whipped off her apron and then allowed her host to seat her as her plate was served.

Sebastian reseated himself and relaxed in his high-backed chair, observing her with a smile. "Ladies first."

She looked at him across the crystal-and-silver-strewn table. "Do you think I would poison you, monsieur?"

The bold question took him momentarily aback. He had earlier considered the possibility. "*Would* you poison me, Mignon?"

"*Non, monsieur.* It would seem a waste of a handsome man, surely," she answered tartly.

Without daring to meet his gaze, she picked up her knife and fork. It amazed her that he did not speak as she carved a sliver of meat from one of the frog legs and brought it delicately to her mouth. Her teeth slipped like butter through the tender meat. As the flavors spread over her tongue, she could not keep back a smile of satisfaction.

Moving on, she tasted first a tender green coil of fern tip, and finally popped a plump mushroom button into her mouth. "Quite good," she announced with some pride.

Sebastian helped himself to a rather larger cut of frog leg. The pleasure of that first taste would always remain with him. His eyes widened, his taste buds sprang to life as his mouth watered in response to the burst of fresh flavors that filled his senses.

He had eaten many dishes in many countries prepared by the personal chefs of aristocrats renowned for their re-splendent tables. One taste of this dish was enough to convince him that Mignon was not a cook, she was a *chef de cuisine.*

"But this is magnificent!" he said even as he chewed, a breech of manners he seldom broached. "Eat up, mademoiselle. You have earned your keep this night."

Too hungry to demure again, Madeleine devoured her meal with relish.

Under the guise of consuming what was one of the best, certainly the most unusual meal of his life, Sebastian observed the strangely quiet woman across from him. She was really quite young, and though she appeared composed, he was certain she was frightened by her present circumstances. Yet there was more, something familiar that he could not put his finger on, some hint of *déjà vu* about her profile in candlelight.

Madeleine remained aware that her host watched her with disconcerting intensity as she lagged behind him in finishing her meal. He did not disturb her with question or conversation, merely drank steadily as she ate in silence. Finally, she thought perhaps it was impolite to continue eating when he was finished. She laid aside her silverware and wiped her lips on her napkin. Then she pushed her chair back, not looking directly at him. "Thank you, monsieur, I must return to the kitchen."

"Why are you really here, Mignon?"

She glanced across at him. "I do not understand you, monsieur."

"Oh, I think you do. You have proven by your choice of dishes that you have a fine and clever mind. Your obvious talent in the kitchen is unquestionable. You are pretty enough to grace a gentleman's arm as well as decorate his bed, yet you seem to prefer the heat and drudgery of my kitchen. Can that be so?"

Madeleine felt herself quite unexpectedly blossoming, wanting to please this singular male creature. Yet she knew she must not snare him only to lose him in a single night.

She rose from her chair. "Thank you for allowing me to share your meal, monsieur."

"Where are you going?" he demanded as she turned from the table.

"To my place."

Those words did not please Sebastian. Her place? She did not know her place. Certainly she did not behave as a servant nor was she a simpering maid. The only conceivable place he could think of for her was in his bed. Yet he resisted, for suddenly he realized that he did not want to force what was surely to be between them.

He raised his glass to her as she waited for dismissal. "Good night, Mignon. Sleep well."

Madeleine remembered to curtsy this time. "Thank you, monsieur. *Bonne nuit.*"

That husky whisper of farewell followed him up the stairs and into bed and into his dreams.

"The devil!" The ejaculation of surprised disgust followed a sound like a small explosion and then a crash and the sound of breaking glass. Alarmed, Madeleine pushed open the door to Lord d'Arcy's laboratory without knocking or waiting, as was the rule, for permission to enter.

Inside she found the marquis standing before his desk with hands on hips gazing at the pile of twisted metal and broken glass at his feet. "Monsieur, are you all right?" she asked in alarm.

Sebastian looked up with a scowl. "I was attempting to repeat an experiment by Humphry Davy. By using Volt's pile to decompose a substance, I had hoped to isolate the element sodium. Like a prize ass I forgot his reminder of how easily sodium in its pure form can be ignited." He held up a hand with blackened fingertips and a bloody slash on the palm to wipe the soot from his face. "Sorry if the explosion frightened you."

"Oh, but you're hurt!" She quickly set aside his dinner tray and grabbed the linen napkin.

"Watch for broken glass," he warned as she came near him. He reached out to steer her clear of the smashed apparatus.

Madeleine skirted the destroyed experiment and drew him over to one of the large windows that served his laboratory. "Sit here, monsieur," she directed.

He dutifully leaned a hip on the windowsill as she took his singed hand in hers and bent over it. "You are going to have blisters and you cut yourself," she announced after a quick survey. She looked up, nearly bumping heads with him. "I need water and bandages."

"The pump is there." He pointed to the end of his table. "And clean linen can be found in the drawer just above."

As she went about the task, his gaze followed her. For three days now, she had been a member of his household, and for three days when his mind was not focused on his work, Mignon always held the greater part of his thoughts. Her meals were a delight; varied, delicious, and quite inventive considering the limited fare provided by his country location. But it was not her cooking that made him think about her with such frequency. She constantly amazed him. Just now, for instance, he was impressed by her calm. She had not fainted at the sight of his blood nor rushed away for help.

She came back toward him, smiling as she carried a shallow basin of water she had drawn. "Put your hand in here, monsieur, so that I may wash away the grime." She placed the basin on the windowsill and took his hand in hers when he put it into the water. Using the napkin, she began to very gently clean his injuries.

He leaned in toward her as she bent over his hand. Rising from her soft dark curls were the scents of sunshine and autumn. She had been out walking again. He had noticed her passing his window every morning after breakfast was served and before she was needed to prepare his two P.M. dinner tray. She often walked the limits of his demesne, usually in her bonnet, but once, after a morning rain shower, with a bare head.

Not for the first time this week he found himself thinking that in every possible way, she possessed the attributes of his hypothesized Enlightened Independent Woman. But, no doubt, life would never give her the opportunities she would need to make a success of herself. She was too pretty not to marry. Some vicar's son or nobleman's secretary would wed her and waste her youth and beauty and intelligence because he could not appreciate it. If he were an ordinary man he would see only her slender, voluptuous body, her kissable pink lips, and want to possess her sweetness. If he were callow or cruel, he would want to subdue her intelligence and vivid spirit, afraid and jealous of what was clearly above him. In a few years, life would wear away the dappled blush now visible in her cheek. She would no longer be so vital that he could feel in this moment her living presence like an aura around him. Her eyes would no longer shine with the bright enthusiasm he waited for each time she appeared.

Emotion, dangerously similar to the kind that had several times recklessly set him against the men or mores of his own rank, swelled in his throat. He raised a hand to her bent head. He felt the desire to protect and save coursing through him, the same spur that had set him on the dueling ground against Meg's murderer and Lady Langley's abusive husband. This time he did not have to act when it was a matter of revenge. He *could* save her. Perhaps, in spite of common sense, he would try.

Against that altruism was an equally strong emotion. He wanted to touch her, to hold her bright intelligent tender beauty just once in his arms. His hand drifted away from her without that much-needed touch.

Madeleine was not unaware of the intensity of his scrutiny. For three days she had felt his presence often before he appeared. It was like being a mouse in a barn with a cat. The fear and elation of not knowing when he would continue the game Audelia had convinced her he could play so well was stretching her nerves to their limits. She had crossed his path as much as she could without being conspicuous. Yet, since that first day when he had kissed her with practiced ease, he had not touched her again. The days were passing. She had no way of knowing how her mother and aunts were faring against De Valmy. If she could not reengage this man's amorous attentions soon, she would have to find another way.

She looked up suddenly, focusing on his thin, noble mouth. *Kiss me!* she longed to shout. *Please make this easier for me.*

"I've finished the bandage," she said instead.

"Thank you," he answered, his eyes now on *her* mouth.

"I should go," she answered, but her hand was lifting to his cheek. Her damp fingers left water tracks on his face as she touched him. "Do you hurt much?"

"No." He closed his wounded hand over hers. "Thank . . . you."

He leaned toward her but she closed the distance.

Sebastian watched her close her eyes the better to absorb the inviting throb of his cool, dry lips against her own. The soft sigh she released in response heightened the emotion in his chest, one which was far more volatile than mere lust.

Pressing his advantage, he pulled her close with an arm about her waist and opened her unresisting lips with his. Her breath shivered over the tip of his tongue. She tasted of innocence, sweetness, and virtue. Recklessly, he filled her sweet mouth with the savage sweep of his tongue.

She jerked instinctively away from this intimate caress, her midnight-velvet eyes suddenly enormous in her face. "Why did you do that?"

The question surprised him. No woman had ever before asked him why he had kissed her. "Surely, as a woman, you understand my boldness is an ardent tribute to your beauty."

Madeleine knew that men and women pressed lips together, but she had not known that *tongues* were involved. Oh, her ignorance was deplorable!

She stepped back very carefully from his touch, as if it were cool deliberation and not maidenly shyness that dictated her actions. "I do not know with which women you keep company, monsieur. But, in France, a lady reserves the right to choose her partners."

Sebastian's brows shot up at this rebuke, as sophisticated as any ever served him by an accomplished courtesan. "You reserve that right, Mignon, to choose your lovers?"

If only he knew! He was her choice. But it would never do for him to know it. *"Oui, monsieur."* She stole a glance at him in hope she had not angered him. "Is that not the prerogative of even English ladies?"

He smiled charmingly. "English ladies, when they are induced to take lovers, are often unfashionably puritanical in their requirements of love. They wish to be seduced, thereby relieving their consciences of the responsibility for having succumbed to the act."

"Truly, monsieur? Then how can you ask me to act against the rules of your own society?"

"I would think no less of you. Indeed, I would think all the more of you. I am a man of sophisticated tastes. If you chose me as your lover I can promise you won't be disappointed." He held out a hand to her. "Come upstairs with me to my bed and let me show you how many ways I can pleasure you."

Madeleine stared at the hand he held out. Now things were suddenly moving too quickly. The bawdy drawings she had stolen glances of flashed through her mind. Fascinated and appalled, she wondered if he was referring to the inventive and sometimes seemingly impossible postures she had viewed. Could she possibly submit to do those things? The game! She must remember the rules of the game!

She placed a trembling hand in his. "You might think no less of me," she said slowly, seeking what would seem a worldly response, "but I should think so much less of you, monsieur. Even a stable boy is more respectful in his ardor."

Admiration polished his warm laugh as he pulled her closer. "I stand corrected, Mignon. You are, of course, accustomed to courtship. Am I gauche to suggest that we dispense this once with the formalities?" He touched her chin with the tip of a finger. "Or are you teasing me?"

Her serious gaze absorbed with aching clarity the beauty of his face by daylight. This man would be her first lover. Ruled strictly by instinct, she said, "If one achieved whatever one wanted anytime one wanted it, life would be excessively dull."

Sebastian's pulse quickened in delight. Here was a woman worthy of his efforts; strong, self-possessed, quick of wit, and spirited. A plot began to form in his mind.

He had not forgotten Peter Eliott's wager that he had not the ability to produce the Perfect Mistress. For lack of a subject he had not seriously indulged the possibility of ever collecting on it. Yet, Providence had set before him the raw materials in the form of this Mignon.

From the first she had touched him in a way that was new. He did not expect that she was a virgin, but he believed that she was still virtuous. He had pursued and been pursued by the most beautiful and talented of Europe's wantons. Yet he could not think of one other woman, be she lady or harlot, who would have hiked up her skirts as Mignon had done, not to satisfy his carnal appetite, but to put frog legs on his table!

With his guidance, she could learn how not to lose her

bright spirit's freedom to any man's tyranny, not even his own.

But he would not put the idea to her here in his laboratory where he had just blundered like a schoolboy. She deserved a better setting.

"Dine with me tonight, Mignon. Dress and come to my table as my honored guest."

"I will try," Madeleine answered cautiously as he leaned in to kiss her cheek. He was very assured of his devastating attractiveness. And she was not immune. Quite the contrary. Her knees were trembling.

Nine

THE WAGES OF GALLANTRY

The hay in the loft was fragrant and sweet. We had been riding across her husband's estate until a sudden summer squall forced us to seek shelter and find other means by which to entertain ourselves on that sultry summer afternoon.

Now she lay in utter abandon, her riding jacket forming a pillow for her head as I unfastened her blouse and unlaced her chemise. She quivered as a fork of lightning suddenly silvered the shadows of the loft, revealing the lush satin of her breasts. They were small, quite like a child's, but topped by the most remarkably large, long nipples I have ever seen.

"Am I not to your taste, my lord?" she asked with a sulky pout. "My husband will not look at them. I am too like a boy, says he."

"No boy ever tempted me to do this. Or this. And certainly not this." I tweaked one strawberry bud while licking the other until, having tasted my fill, I reached for her skirts.

"Oh! My lord! Dare we?"

Her question was said with all due protest of innocence but there was the gaze of the temptress in those slanted green eyes hanging on mine. That half-lidded look of desire women learn from repeated arousal.

"We have so little privacy," she continued even as she reached for the buttons of my breeches. *"I cannot possibly undress here. I should never get my stays retied or my hair redressed."* Her eyes suddenly widened with pleasure's anticipation when her hand slipped inside my waistband. *"Oh, dear! And someone is bound to suspect what we've done."*

It is a challenge a man must respond to. *"I will show you, my lady, a method equally satisfactory to your needs and mine."* Turning her gently onto her stomach, I flipped up the skirts of her habit and petticoats to expose the soft, full swelling of her ripely feminine hips. Pulling her gently to her knees, I entered her with all due enthusiasm from the rear.

Conclusion:

I have often wondered at the propriety of a society that allows women to swath their bodies in yards and yards of fabric yet leaves unsealed the very expanse of her femininity to the ministrations of every willing cock.

When we again lay side by side, neither her corset nor her curls had been dislodged in our mutual achievement of bliss.

It is to be remarked upon in passing that women who feel in any way slighted by Nature's bounty in the area of their bosoms are often made needlessly anxious by this occurrence. As if they have no understanding of their lover's true goal, they will fret or demand that the most lavish of praises be bestowed in compensation upon this part of their anatomy. The gentleman who neglects his duty in this instance will ultimately fail to garner the most profound ardor of his lady's desire. Neither must he be so odiously indiscreet as to make comparisons, analogies, or attempt to convince her that her *"lack"* is inapparent.

* * *

Sebastian laid his pen aside and picked up his wineglass. The bandage on his right hand had made the writing awkward but the sentiments had flowed smoothly enough. However well his memories were going, the evening ahead promised to be one of even better satisfaction than the lark he had penned while waiting to dress for supper.

Sebastian surveyed the remains of his supper in disgust. He had planned a grand evening with wine in abundance and Mignon's delicious food to be served them on the best linen and Sèvres china service. The crystal was Baccarat, the table silver part of his French mother's dowry made by a court jeweler to Louis XVI. He had ordered the last of the summer roses brought in from the garden. They now decorated the table amid silver-and-gold candelabra. The rest filled his bedroom where the bed linens were fresh and a new fire laid so that it would remain warm throughout the night. He had dressed with special care, with the addition of lace at his cuffs and a sapphire stickpin to his cravat. In all, one would think he was about to attend a formal evening in London instead of entertaining one little *domestique* in his country house.

It had startled him to realize that he had been a trifle nervous throughout the preparations, as if he had not often arranged tête-à-têtes with ladies that were to end in bed. Yet his anticipation had never been so high.

There was only one problem. He was eating alone.

Madeleine had appeared once from the depths of the kitchen. She had been damp and flushed from her culinary efforts, and still dressed in the drab domestic garb he was beginning to hate. She had come to apologize and say that the kitchen maid she had put in charge of the rotisserie had allowed the fire to flare up on the lamb she had been roasting for him. And it was most regrettable but equally obvious that she could not possibly abandon her meal to other hands.

So he had slumped in his chair and brooded and drank more liberally than usual because the blistered burns on his right hand ached and because he felt his pride and hospitality had been equally abused.

The removes as they came from the kitchen were a miracle of taste and presentation, but he scarcely noticed. He ate just enough to keep his hunger at bay.

He was not accustomed to being refused a lady's company, not when he had made his intentions clear. The thought that he was being defied pricked his pride to the quick although, in a more reasonable moment, he would have been the first to defend her. But he was feeling neither reasonable nor rational, and the less he felt of either the more he drank.

Madeleine was equally distressed over the events. Not until the dessert was ready to be served did she feel it safe to slip into her room to change. She suspected, despite a quick wash in her basin, she still smelled of the kitchen. To dispel the offensive aromas she rubbed her hair lightly with the abraded rind of a lemon and then pinned her damp curls up with a bandeau of yellow satin. Even after she chewed a mint leaf to sweeten her breath, she feared roasting lamb might still be the predominant fragrance surrounding her. In a last desperate attempt to remove the culinary scents, she rubbed a few blades of lemon grass from the herb garden between her hands and then tucked them into the cleft between her breasts before slipping into a gown of white muslin sprigged in yellow with a matching sash of yellow. It, the undergarments, even her bandeau, lace mittens, and slippers had been borrowed from Audelia. They all seemed to fit, but without a mirror she could not gauge her appearance.

Finally, she stepped into the dining room as silently as

a mouse and approached the imposing table and the nobleman who sat at its head.

Sebastian sat indolently in his chair with one leg thrown over the arm. An empty silver goblet hung from two fingers of his left hand. His posture did not alter a whit when she seemed to appear out of the dusk cast by the light of the candelabra between them. That did not mean he was unaffected by her presence. He said nothing for several long moments, simply surveyed her as if she were yet another in the string of the tempting dishes put before him this night for his consideration.

The simple gown she wore was sheer enough to reveal the soft contours of the enticing young body it veiled. The waistline was very high, supporting her breasts. The neckline low enough to offer a generous sample of that always enticing portion of female anatomy. Yet the most convincing power of her beauty was that without a single piece of jewelry or lace or fan or flower, she managed in this moment to cast into the shade the memory of every other woman he had ever wanted to seduce.

But she was late and he was a little drunk. He was not going to be easily swayed by her charming display. Or if he already was, he would not show it.

"Ah, the little chef appears at last," he said in a scathing tone. "Come forward, mademoiselle, and show me what the *domestique* considers fashionable this season."

The hard words hurt, but Madeleine was not totally surprised by them. She had known from their earlier encounter that he was peeved with her. She approached him slowly. "I beg a thousand pardons, monsieur. I have offended you by my tardiness."

"Offended me? 'Tis little enough trouble I've gone to." He indicated the table with a negligent wave of his goblet. "The flowers would have died in the hothouse as well as here. The china and silver care little whether or not they are used. And I . . . why, I've had the last hour and a half to recall the folly of my invitation."

He saw the color ebb in and out of her cheeks. "It is a lovely table, monsieur. I am honored by your thoughtfulness."

"Don't be! But do sit down. The meal must be cold but then *domestiques* are accustomed to eating the leavings of their betters, are they not?"

Madeleine's smile faltered. The deliberately demeaning words seemed unlike him. When she took the chair the footman rushed to pull out for her, her eyes never left Sebastian's face. When he waved the footmen out of the room with a snapped, "Leave us!," she wondered what was wrong. His voice and his demeanor lacked his usual finesse. Then he reached for the silver flagon to pour himself another glass of wine and she knew. He was quite intoxicated.

It did not show in his face or in his expression, which remained remarkably aloof. It was in his eyes, those glittering blue eyes that dipped in the corners. She had seen them sparkle with amusement, flash with surprise, kindle with desire. Now they glittered with self-indulgent umbrage. She knew then that she had lost the moment. There would be no seduction now, only recriminations and bitterness. This man who could have anyone no longer wanted her.

"What? Are you not drinking?" he asked when he noticed she sat with her hands in her lap. "Pass me your cup, Mignon."

He filled and handed it back to her without a word.

She examined the beautifully wrought piece of silver lined in gold. The base was beaded and grapevines had been stamped and hammered into the silver at the rim. "It's a very beautiful piece, monsieur."

He raised his cup with a smirk. "As are you, mademoiselle."

She looked away from him, her lips thinning. Despite the fact that his anger was her fault, she was finding humility a wearing emotion. Seeking to steady her nerves, she took a small sip of wine.

Sebastian saw the sudden look of disconcert that crossed her face as she lowered her goblet to peer into its depths. "What is wrong?"

She looked up with a slight frown between her delicately drawn brows. "You drink your wines too sweet, monsieur, and without bringing them to *chambre*."

He shrugged. "When I drink alone, I'm often too impatient to wait for the niceties to be observed."

"That is a horrible excuse," she replied before considering how it might sound.

"Perhaps," he answered more coolly than before. "Yet I suspect it is your French temperament that won't permit in others the eccentricity of taste which you claim by right of your heritage."

She was too disappointed by the evening's outcome to accept this final chiding with either distance or composure. Her gaze met his across the distance. "And you, monsieur, you bolt in minutes what it takes hours to prepare." She glanced at the table laden with the mostly untouched meal on which she had lavished such caring attention. "You English know nothing of savoring, of appreciation. One should take a spoon of sauce and roll it over the tongue until all its mysteries are discerned. But you, you do not care to learn if it contains basil or tarragon or chives. All the fine herbs I used with such care might as well have been clippings of grass!"

None of this was true, of course. Sebastian knew he could boast one of the most sophisticated palates in England. But his little chef's display of spirit once more humored and intrigued him. She had again completely forgotten her place, forgotten to be subservient with meek words and downcast eyes.

"If you think you can do better when it comes to choosing a wine, then prove it." This seemed to take her aback. She blinked twice. "Come, don't be shy. You've already said quite enough to land you on your ear outside my front door."

Madeleine realized that he was right. But she had been working very hard these last days to win his praise with her culinary efforts. Yet here he sat amid the remains, half drunk and not at all impressed.

He removed his leg from the chair arm, and though it was less vivid that usual, he smiled for the first time. "Come now, Mignon. Drink a little more of my atrocious wine and tell me why I displayed no taste in choosing it."

She smiled into her lap. "I am terrible to say such things to you."

"You are indeed!" He looked at her with growing warmth. "Drink, Mignon, and tell me what is wrong."

Madeleine picked up a second wine goblet at her place, this one made of crystal, and poured the contents of the silver one into it. Then, swirling the liquid slowly, she held it up to the candlelight. Frowning, she said, "It has not been properly filtered or decanted. The sediment is as thick as autumn leaves." She brought it to her lips for a small sip, grimacing this time as she did so. As she set it back on the table, she turned to him. "Monsieur, you were sold the lees doctored with a little sugar."

"The devil I was!" Sebastian frowned into his own wine, as if it could feel the insult. "I saw to the purchase myself not a month ago in Marseille."

"The reds travel well," she allowed, "though the whites often do not. If you bought good quality wine, then there should be nothing wrong with it." She lifted her gaze. "I think your butler is cheating you."

"Horace?" Sebastian's laughter echoed around the room. "But that is impossible. He's just come down with me from London. The wine came directly here."

"Then someone else in your household is responsible. Do you have a key to the cellar?"

"Of course."

"May I have it?'

"Why?"

"I wish to make a small demonstration. For that, I need to collect a few bottles from your cellar."

"I will come with you."

"That won't be necessary."

Her statement did not flatter his ego in the slightest, but Sebastian decided that if he pushed her, she might simply give up and go to bed. "Very well."

He fished the wine-cellar key from his pocket where he had deposited it after Horace had brought up the requested wines for the evening's meal. It was a large, ornate key on a heavy chain. "Here you are, my little chatelaine. Fetch your wines. But take the candelabrum with you to light your way."

She rose from her seat and came to collect the key. "I will ask a footman's help."

He frowned as he placed it in her outstretched hand. "You tell him if he is in any way impertinent he will answer to me."

She turned away before smiling. Without quite knowing how, the evening seemed suddenly to be back on course.

"The last wine is a Pinot noir, or black grape, from Bourgogne. Better than the last but not yet fully mature."

Madeleine poured a little from the bottle she held into the seventh and last of the crystal wineglasses arrayed on the dining-room table before Sebastian's chair. "In a year, better two, it will reach its peak."

It is you, Mignon, who are at your peak, Sebastian mused through a pleasant haze as he reached for his glass.

He had been right to send his footmen to bed so that he might be alone with her.

He took his time, watching her over the rim of his glass. He was filled with a strange excitement that he did not wish to analyze just yet. As she turned her face up to the light, a sudden predictable warmth flooded through him.

There was a touching earnestness and pride in her wine lesson. For the moment she was in charge, mistress to her pupil. He knew by the firmness of her cheeks that held her smile in check that the situation pleased her as much as it amused him.

"You will taste it, monsieur?" she prompted.

"Oh, yes, I will," he said in promise, more interested in a study of the delicate curve of her lip than in wine.

She had wit and brains, this wondrous little stranger whom fate had dropped into his lap. She spoke of wine with the confidence of a daughter of a Bourgogne vintner. How in heavens name had she come to be his prize in a forgotten bet made at White's? Not that it mattered. She was, without a doubt, the most valuable gift he had ever received.

After a moment she looked at him expectantly. "What do you think, monsieur?"

He dutifully sipped the wine. The richness of its red color was reflected in the flavor that blossomed on his tongue as he rolled it around in his mouth, seeking out the subtleties and nuances of its bouquet. Almost at once it was undercut by an astringent immaturity. She was right. That sharpness would fade in a year, or more likely two— just as the little chef had opined!—leaving him with a superior wine.

He put a trace of reserve in his voice to match her somber expression as he concurred with her assessment of the wine.

Madeleine nodded. "Now then, I ask you to taste the first bottle again."

He watched the play of candlelight and shadow along her profile as she again poured for him. A touch of the exotic lay in her cheekbones, he decided. The results of a distant infusion of the Moor, perhaps? His fingers moved restlessly on the stem of his glass. He really was showing an unusual amount of self-restraint in not simply snatching her into his lap.

She had provided him with thin slices of bread and cucumber in order to cleanse his palate between tastings. He reached and plucked a round of cucumber. He could feel the effects of the wine in his blood. She poured only one dainty teaspoon of wine into her own glass. Regrettably, she was remaining sober.

He lifted the glass she had filled and took a large gulp. Grimacing, he spewed the mouthful back into the glass. It was coarse and so sour his mouth puckered. "It tastes as if it was strained through an unwashed peasant's smock!"

"This is likely the product of the Hungarian Tokay grape in a very bad year. The grapes were rotten and immature when harvested after too much rain." She crossed her arms with a significant look at him. "This is the wine you drank with my very fine food tonight."

Sebastian did not bristle at her trick. She had made her point very effectively. But it did not interest him nearly as much as the thrust of her breasts nestled in the cradle made by her crossed arms. Who would have thought so slender a girl would have such a lush bosom? He wanted nothing more than to open her bodice and suckle each sweet peak.

He set the wine aside. "Why did I not notice the difference before?"

"You have been tricked, monsieur." She pointed to two of the bottles. "You will observe you opened two bottles tonight. The bottles are exactly the same." She reached into her apron pocket and pulled out two corks. "If you will look at these you will notice a difference between the one I pulled from the good bottle and the one I found on the sideboard that is from the wine at dinner." She held them out. "You see?"

"Not really," he murmured. "Hold them closer."

As she bent toward him, he inhaled the scent of her skin and found the unexpected scent of lemon in his nostrils. That fragrance was mixed with the more subtle one which he had come to recognize as the tantalizing scent of her own body.

He took her hands in his, pretending to study the corks, but he was really more interested in the shape of her slender fingers and imagining how they would feel on his skin. He looked up at her, letting his flagrantly aroused gaze slip with supple warmth over her face.

She smiled back. "The right one is a new cork," she pointed out. "The edges are not stained as deeply as the other one. I am certain you were served good wine first. But after a few glasses, it is not uncommon for the diner not to notice the exchange, unless one has trained the nose."

"Trained nose." Sebastian smiled at the picture the word conjured in his mind. He had known many women trained in many ways but their noses were not part of their arsenal of talents. There were things he longed to teach her, talents that would make her mistress to his mastery.

He lazily caressed her tender inner wrists with his thumbs, divining her pulse. It was rapid but no match for his own. "Who trained your nose, Mignon?"

"Madame Céline, the former duchess d'Aixligy."

He looked up sharply. "Of the Aixligy vineyards?"

"You know them, monsieur?"

"I knew one of them. The heir and I passed a few pleasant hours in Paris together the summer of '90." His expression hinted at the pleasures pursued but she did not rise to his provocation. The duc d'Aixligy heir had died before the year was out at the hands of a Parisian mob, as had several other of his Gallic aristocratic friends. Yet, this was not the time for such memories. "You are of their household?"

"No, monsieur. From '91 until '95 Madame Céline sought shelter in the convent where I was reared. She brought with her the best of her wine cellar. She said she could not bear the thought of the rabble toasting the deaths of her family and friends with her wine. Rather the cloister should bathe in it."

The mention of a convent did not escape Sebastian's notice, but he left it for the moment. "Did you bathe in it?"

His heavy-lidded gaze traveled significantly down over her, absorbing the details of her slender voluptuousness before slowly rising to look into her night-shrouded eyes. "Are there wine-stained toes hidden in your slippers?"

Madeleine laughed. "No, monsieur."

No, monsieur. How perfectly respectful. No doubt she would protest loudly if he pulled her into his welcoming lap.

But Madeleine would not have protested. She was too secretly pleased to have succeeded in charming him from his anger. But now that he was looking at her as he had in his laboratory, she was suddenly shy. She wanted to please him, to make him want to make her his mistress, but she did not know if she would survive if he did.

She longed to push back the rich brown lock of hair that fell in a loop across his brow, casting a shadow over his perfect features. Looking at him, she forgot her stratagems and plans. She saw only the beguiling man with his lopsided smile. She felt inexplicably the urge to touch, just touch him, but forced her thoughts in other directions. "The lesson is finished, monsieur. I have proved that someone preserves the bottles you empty, then refills them with cheap wine."

He again rubbed a lazy thumb over her pulse. "How did you happen to suspect that?"

"I have seen it done, monsieur. Madame Céline used the trick to save good wine. They were put in cheap vats with false tops which contained sour wine. When the kegs were tapped to access their value by first the Republican and later the Napoléon armies, they were passed over as only good as altar wine."

"You've had a most unusual education," he said thoughtfully. "But now that I know the depth of your experience in deception, how do I know that you didn't switch these bottles in order to blame my staff?"

She regarded him quizzically. "Why would I do that, monsieur?"

"To impress me," he suggested gently. "To worm your way into my good graces."

He saw astonishment lift her features. "Why should I do that, monsieur?"

He cocked a world-wise brow. Women more beautiful and certainly more sophisticated than the little convent-bred miss before him had devised elaborate schemes to engage his attention.

He stood up abruptly and placed his hands on her arms. She seemed to vibrate before him, her silhouette picked out by a corona of silver light. "You are very beautiful. Have many men told you so?"

Madeleine shook her head.

"Then you must come from a place where the men have no eyes or no tongues."

Sebastian enfolded her in a gentle embrace. She did not pull away. He bent his head and buried his face in her neck. The intoxicating fragrance of her, lemon mixed with mint, the feel of her body through their clothing, even the rhythm of her heart held him in thrall. He wanted her. Simply and without any need for lies or artificial declarations.

Madeleine held her breath. This was the moment she had been waiting for, for him to make his desire for her known. He would take her now and, in the morning, she would be his mistress. She should feel relieved, joyous, triumphant. But there was a hard little knot of fear forming in her stomach. It felt like she had swallowed a lump of ice. When he lifted his lips from her neck, she saw her destiny in those eyes of vivid blue. She shivered and wondered what would be left of her when he was done with her.

Sebastian's smile was achingly gentle as he looked at her. She was clearly fascinated by him. Her bosom was moving with inviting distraction beneath the shallow neckline. He was not so vain that he mistook every women's glance as one of provocation, but he knew how she often studied him when she thought he was unaware of his scrutiny. That frisson of awareness had also kept the blood humming in his veins. She was the last thought he took to bed and the first he awakened to. In the laboratory this afternoon her touch had been a tender one . . . and she had kissed him. Tonight he would take the lady herself into his bed and it would be she he would awaken to tomorrow morning.

If she were amenable, he might even take her first here, pressing the warmth of her hips into the hard table. No, too soon for that kind of rough play. He wanted the luxury to enjoy at leisure what promised to be the new and rare experience of her.

He suffered no other moment of indecision. With his fingertips he traced a slow path across her flushed skin and then along the edge of her lower lip. "I don't believe that you are the timid sort, are you?" He pressed a silencing finger into the tender surface of her lips. "Don't answer. Let me show you."

His moved his hand slowly if confidently from her face to her bodice, where he dragged his fingers in bold defiance down over the full swell of her left breast. He felt her tremble at his intimate touch. "You see how easy it is? You like my touch and I like touching you. It is as natural as that, isn't it?"

His hand cupped her breast, his thumb seeking beneath the thin muslin the nub of her nipple. "Ah, there it is. And so hard!" Between half-closed lashes spangled by the candlelight, his eyes burned flame blue. "You are very responsive, sweeting. How nice for both of us."

Fascinated more than frightened, Madeleine allowed him to draw concentric circles about her nipple until he again reached the center which he lightly pinched. A sweet burst of pleasure rose into her throat and escaped at a soft moan.

"Yes, you like it." Sebastian watched her lids flutter in token resistance and then close as he touched her face, cupping her cheek in one hand. His fingers slid into her curls above her left temple as he swayed into her. "I'm going to make us both very happy, Mignon."

It took a moment for Madeleine to realize that he was holding on to her as much for support as out of carnal interest as he nuzzled her neck.

Laughing a little in relief, she braced her hands on his chest to push him away. "You are inebriated, monsieur."

"Only by you," he murmured. "You intoxicate me." He leaned back from her, but one arm was locked about her waist to prevent either of them from straying far. "Don't be alarmed. I may be a trifle foxed, but I won't disappoint you." His questing fingers twined into her curls. "So soft, like a child's curls. You are so sweet. And you smell delicious. You smell good enough to eat."

He did not wait to gauge her reaction to this gallantry. He bent his head and caught her lips in the embrace of his.

His mouth was warmer than Madeleine expected from his earlier kisses. The hot intensity of his breath was like the interior of an oven. Strangely, her body reacted with a swift sudden tension that swept her from crown to toes. This was no gallant's salute, but a thorough melding of lips in an erotic massage that made her hands curl into the fabric of his shirt. So then, it would not be a fate worse than death. Oh, thank goodness!

When he finally raised his head, they stared at each other for a long, silent time. Eyes half closed with drunken revelry, he began to chuckle. "Come to bed with me, Mignon."

She looked at him and heard her own voice as a distant husky whisper. *"Oui, monsieur."*

Ten

"Monsieur?" Madeleine whispered uncertainly after an interval in which he simply leaned his cheek against hers in perfect stillness. "I agreed, monsieur."

Sebastian laughed under his breath. "I know you did. But there's no need to rush." He lifted his face from hers. "You're trembling. Are you so very anxious then?"

Her face was solemn. "I want to please you."

His smile could have melted plaster saints. "You already do. In so many ways. I can't begin to tell you."

Madeleine did not pull away from the hand that slid with defining purpose from her waist down over the fullness of her hips. The suspense of waiting seemed worse than anything he might do to her, after all.

"Do you like the way that I touch you?" he asked lightly.

"Oui."

The hand on her derrière, its heat impressing her skin through the light veiling of her gown, gathered and cupped her, pulling her into his hips. "And this? Does this please you?"

"Oui." But it was a less certain response. So this was what a man's body felt like, she thought in a rush of surprise. He was heavier, harder, firmer than she. Yet the strange knot that pressed upon her low down did not seem in size even remotely related to the appendages sketched in the pictures she'd seen. But then she did not understand

the anatomy of men. Perhaps there was something . . . more.

His lips nibbled her cheek and then her eyelids, feathery tickling sensations that made her smile. "You taste like mint and lemons, my little chef. Are you certain you did not sprout outside my door?"

As she lifted her head in embarrassed laughter, he caught her smile with his mouth. His lips opened on hers and his tongue touched hers with a lick of slick heat that made her gasp.

He lifted his mouth. "Why do you jump when I taste you? Have you not been kissed many times, Mignon?"

She looked stricken by the inquiry. Had she made a mistake already? Yet her native honesty supplied the answer. "No."

"A pity." He smoothed fingers over her soft, full mouth. "You deserve kissing, Mignon. Lots and lots of kisses."

With his pulse faintly throbbing, Sebastian again laid his lips very softly to hers. The passion was stripped away, only the salute of precious consideration remained. And it burned brightest of all, for she lifted her arms to embrace him.

Innocent, he thought. How amazing. Of course, he knew her inexperience with kissing was no indication of virtue. He had been amazed to learn during his research how many men well versed in mistress-keeping disliked passionate kisses. Some found it unnecessarily or disconcertingly intimate, others faintly disgusting. One paid a whore for the pleasure found between her thighs. One's mistress required more tangible signs of affection while many husbands did not wish to arouse their wives in so unseemly a fashion. This was the logic.

What a waste, he thought absently. Leaving a woman like Mignon unkissed was like making love to her through a hole in a blanket; the goal of one's quest might be achieved, but a good deal of the pleasure in lying with a woman went unfulfilled. He explored her mouth a little more, just to be certain that he was right. Then he smiled, the impression of it pressed upon her closed lips.

"Come here," he said, as he pulled her gently toward the chair she had abandoned. Seating himself, he pulled her down into his lap.

"Now then," he said, as he anchored her with one arm about her waist. "I'm going to teach you the fine points of kissing, Mignon. Would you like that?"

Madeleine looked into his face, made more handsome by the play of candlelight and shadow and felt her heart stumble. "I wish to learn whatever you wish to teach me."

His smile was a gift of praise so bright that she looked away. He cupped her face very gently to shepherd it back to his. "Come, sweeting. Do not be afraid. We both seek the same goal: pleasure. I want to give you that."

He leaned in so that his lips were only an inch from hers. "Put your arms about my neck, Mignon. Not so tightly. That's right. Lean your shoulder into mine. Now take a deep breath. Another. Slowly . . . slowly. That's better."

He laid his lips for an instant against hers. "See how nicely you fit in my arms? Now, kiss me. Welcome my mouth with yours."

Closing her eyes against her own shyness, Madeleine pressed her firm lips onto the satin contours of his. The warmth was the same as before but something seemed wrong. He was not kissing her back. His lips remained unmoving under hers. Frowning behind closed lids, she slanted her head to one side to better fit her mouth to his. Still, there was no response. She reached a hand to his cheek, her palm unconsciously urging a pucker from him as she pulled his face closer to hers. He obliged. His lips firmed under hers and then parted.

It was a very small difference, she marveled, but oh so powerful in its effect. His breath invaded her, the impressions of wine and warmth and his own unique essence mingling.

After only a moment Sebastian drew back, his gaze recording the flushed curve of her cheek and then the dreamy currents of her dark eyes. "Now then, did you like that?"

She nodded.

"What did you like about it? Don't be shy. Tell me."

She gave it a moment's thought. "Your taste. There's the wine, monsieur. And something else more subtle." Her brow pleated in thought. "Almost like ginger spice."

He chuckled. Leave it to his little chef to compare him to a condiment! "Is that good?"

"Oui." A shy smile curved her lips. "Gingerbread has been my favorite treat since childhood. I like it still hot because it is moist and sweet and pungent with spice."

"That is how I want you," he said warmly, "hot and moist and sweetly filling my senses." The incredulous expression on her face astonished him. Then he remembered his suspicion that her previous lover had not taught her to desire and certainly not to express that desire. He meant to do both.

His embrace gentled as he slid a hand down her spine urging her closer until her breasts were pressed lightly against the contours of his shirtfront. "Taste your fill of me, Mignon."

Madeleine leaned into him as he bent toward her, feeling more confident than before. This time she was not startled when his tongue slipped through his lips and slid along the seam between hers. She shivered but did not pull away as his hands urged her closer. He did it a second and then a third time, long slow wet swipes that made her stomach quiver and her heart stutter.

Fingers touched her cheek and then his thumb was at the corner of her mouth, dragging gently until her lips naturally parted. His thumb moved the center of her lower lip and dragged it down, revealing the vulnerable inner surface.

"Good," he murmured as his tongue traced the liquid-drenched lining. Very carefully, he set his teeth in that succulent fullness, sweeter than any fruit.

A shivery sigh escaped Madeleine at his intimate caress. How had he even thought of it?

Pleased with her response, Sebastian continued to use his fingers to ply their kisses, to alter the shape of her mouth to fit his, and finally to forage and find her shy tongue. He rubbed its texture as she shivered again. She quickly came alive under his touch, her untutored passion revealed in the unthinking massage of her hand over his heart as they traded kisses. Smiling, he pulled her lower lip into his mouth and sucked it until she gasped with each tug. When he released her, he was rewarded for his lesson. She playfully gave the tip of his sensitive finger a lick.

His arousal was instantaneous and so powerfully derived he groaned softly. He had known she would be special. He was beginning to think she might be indelibly unique.

"Give me your tongue, sweeting." Smiling, he teasingly brushed her lips with his own. "Open to me, Mignon. Let me taste the first of your many mysteries."

With only a brief hesitation Madeleine did as he asked and darted her tongue swiftly against his lips.

"Again," he whispered.

This time she swept the moist, hot tip over the contours of his parted lips. "Yes, sweeting. Take all the time you need. Seek all the mystery of me as I shall of you." He smoothed a hand lazily up and down her spine. "We have all night."

Yes, Madeleine thought in relief, for the sensations inside her were so new and strange that she needed time to become accustomed to them. This business of coupling was more pleasant than she had been led to expect. He was like a fine wine; bracing, bold yet subtly favored, and even more intoxicating. She wondered if it were possible to become drunk from his kisses. Her heart was hammering a little thickly and her thoughts were spinning in the most delightful fashion. If this was a measure of the pleasure of coupling, she suddenly understood why women abandoned their senses to it. Or was it a secret only this man knew? Sighing in curiosity, she turned more fully into him as her mouth opened in invitation.

Holding his own desire in abatement, Sebastian met her tongue with the tip of his. The shiver of surprise that shook her filled his arms. His mouth fastened on hers, no longer teasing but demanding a deeper response. One hand moved to her hair, gently gripping a handful of curls as the other found her hip and rolled her lower body toward his.

Surprised by his sudden aggressive gesture, Madeleine whimpered and struggled . . . but only for a moment. Something was happening to her as his mouth plied hers with nibbles and licks and variations of pressure so skillful that her lips seemed to swell and become even more sensitive. Something flared inside her, and moved outward to encompass her whole body. Inexplicably she no longer wanted to separate from him. Instead of pushing, she was pulling him closer.

When he lifted his head to inquire, "Do you like it?" she answered with complete honesty, *"Oui, monsieur."*

"Sebastian." He touched his open mouth to hers, chuckling. "We are going to be lovers, Mignon. When we are alone like this, call me by my Christian name."

"Very well," she answered in a small voice. "Sebastian."

Her accented speech caused his name to sound more erotic and seductive than any aphrodisiac he had ever sampled. "Say it again," he whispered as his lips barely grazed hers.

"Sebastian," she murmured in a fluted caress of his lips.

"Sebastian?" she whispered when he again lifted his head.

"Yes, Mignon?"

"I like kissing you."

"I like kissing you, too, convent brat," he murmured.

A sound from the rooms below startled them, but he caught her across the hips when she would have risen from his lap. "No one would dare bother us," he assured her.

But his assurance could not outweigh her conscience. Madeleine avoided his next kiss. "Won't they guess what we are doing?" she whispered.

Sebastian saw the trepidation in her eyes and rejected the casual denial. It would be too cruel a blow for her if one of the servants maliciously hinted to her what they knew or suspected. "My staff does not gossip. They will treat you with respect due your position."

What position is that? Madeleine wanted to ask, but she kept silent. What place had a mistress in a gentleman's household?

Had so many other women sat here like this and accepted his expert kisses as his clever hands roamed their willing bodies? Were the servants inured to the parade of women in his life?

Aware of the tenor of her thoughts, Sebastian propped her drooping chin up with a finger. "Do you think I would do anything to deliberately hurt you?"

She gazed into his eyes and saw in those deep-blue depths not only desire but an honesty of character that was uniquely his own. She believed he would try to protect her. She did not know if he could succeed. What more could she expect? She was going to be his mistress. "I want to be with you, mons— Sebastian. If you still want me."

"I can't think of anything I've ever wanted more," he answered in complete honesty and kissed her swiftly and deeply.

When satisfied that he had rekindled her senses, he

shifted her off his lap and stood up. "Come, sweeting. We will go where we can lock the world away."

"Shall I undress you? Or will you undress for me?"

Madeleine met his gaze across the width of the firelit room. Her courage had lasted all the way up to this moment. With her hand wrapped securely in his, she had allowed him to lead her to his bedchamber and even turn the key in the lock. But now, with the enormity of what lay ahead expressed in his words *shall I undress you,* she wondered if she could do this.

"Do you care for brandy?" Sebastian spoke softly, casually, but his deceptively mild gaze was taking in her every expression. She was afraid as she had not been below. He needed to guide her back to that moment.

He moved toward a crystal decanter and the glass beside it. "Would you care to join me? I usually have a brandy before bed." He saw her eyes widen as they darted to the four-poster and he could have kicked himself for the clumsy reference to the bed. She was not accustomed to being handled. He wanted to ask how many men she had lain with, but that would be equally indelicate under the circumstances. However, he was rapidly forming an opinion. She'd had one far-too-fastidious ineffectual lover, perhaps worse than no lover at all. Who had sent her to him? Eliott? Trevor? Some other nod-cock dandy with whom he had once struck up a casual game of cards that ended in a wager he could not even remember?

He poured a light splash in the glass and then lifted and offered it to her. "To warm you."

She shook her head, a tight little shake of denial that did not bode well. Her eyes were the only source of animation in her shadowed face, their brightness in the darkness revealed by the flickering hearth flames. She was clutching the front of her dress to her bosom as if it was a holy relic.

Afraid she would bolt altogether, he did not approach her. He glanced at the bed, decided that it would be a definite mistake to position himself there, and turned to sit in the wing chair by the fire.

He saw her gaze dart about his room. It was a large chamber with stuccoed compartmented walls and an ornate ceiling, and white-veined black marble fireplace. The bed, draped with silk damask of dull gold, dominated it. It had been built more than two centuries earlier in the expected but never realized visitation of the Virgin Queen. He had never had a virgin, queenly or otherwise, in that bed. Mignon, he suspected, would be as close as he ever came. " 'Tis a pleasant room, is it not?"

Madeleine swung back as if he had sneaked up on her. He had not moved, but still lounged in his chair with his cravat loosened and his long, muscled legs stretched out before him.

"Monsieur?"

They were back to "monsieur." Definitely a bad sign.

Sebastian set the untouched brandy aside. He held a hand out to her. "Come here, Mignon."

Madeleine forced herself to move forward but there was roaring in her ears like the ocean as the tide moves in. She would not die, she told herself. Nearly every woman came to this moment. She thought about Audelia and her aunts. She could not bear to think about her mother, not here, not now, not when she was about to do what she was about to do.

She paused just out of his reach. "You will be kind, mon— Sebastian?"

Her trepidation touched him. Was he being a bully? Did she feel she had no choice? "I will be more than kind, Mignon. I will be very good to you . . . if you will let me."

He did not lean forward the extra inch it would have

taken to capture her wrist. He turned his palm up in offering. "Will you let me?"

She took his hand and let him pull her closer until she stood between his spread knees. Then he reached up very carefully and took her by the waist to lower her onto his left knee.

Gratitude filled him as she nestled in his lap. He pulled her head down on his shoulder and wrapped his arms around her, holding her against her fears and his need. But he knew it was only a ruse. The delicious weight of her against his groin was going to make letting her go impossible. The smell of her filled his nostrils, the lemon fragrance of her hair and the warmer, richer tones of her body. He was going to love every inch of her, but first, she needed to regain her self-confidence.

"Do you know what I do when I'm alone at night, when I am very tired yet very restless?"

"No," she said in a small voice.

"I smoke a cigar. Have you ever tasted tobacco, Mignon?"

She shook her head on his shoulder.

He smoothed a warm hand down her arm while surreptitiously urging her hip against his groin. "Would you care to try it?"

Her head popped up from his shoulder. "A cigar?" Her eyes were dark as midnight water.

"No, perhaps you wouldn't like it." He smiled at her with a secret humor. "But you might like my brandy." He reached for the glass and held it up to her lips.

She took a sip and then he snatched the glass away and leaned forward to catch her mouth in the embrace of his before she had time to swallow. He tasted the burning impression of brandy on her lips as he teased her with his tongue. As she softened against him, he kissed her thoroughly and deeply, drawing away her reluctance as he fed her hunger.

Madeleine felt a place opening somewhere inside her, the same place his kisses had found before. Everywhere his mouth touched, a new sensation registered in her body. She did not understand what was happening, but she certainly liked it.

When he lifted his head, she answered his smile with her own.

"Now, it's your turn," he said, and took a sip. Holding the swallow in his mouth, he again kissed her. Madeleine responded with all the enthusiasm of her delighted senses. Gradually, she understood the rhythm he was teaching her. Her hand began to stroke his hair in accompaniment as he fondled her tongue with his. Finally, she took over the game, retreating and foraging into his mouth with an eagerness that made his hands tighten painfully on her waist. Low down, in the center of her being, a new ache began. Quite unconsciously, she moved restlessly on his lap.

Sebastian understood the source of that restlessness. His mouth moved lower, his teeth lightly grazing the cords of her arched neck as his hand found the shape of her breast. The hand in her curls moved downward in a slow, molding caress that learned the texture of her skin, so fine at her temples and cheekbones that it scarcely seemed real. He traced the shape of her delicate bones. He discovered the pulse trembling under her chin and lower down in the hollow of her throat. Then with deliberate slowness his hands slid even lower down and found her breast.

She gasped softly as his fingers lightly squeezed her. "Do you like the way I touch you?"

She did not answer, but she moved against him, unconsciously arching her breast into his hand as he tugged at her nipple through the fabric of her gown. *Oh, yes, you like it, sweeting. Just wait. I've so many other ways to pleasure you.*

His hands moved to her back as he kissed her, unfas-

tening her buttons with astonishing speed, and then he
slipped the fabric off her shoulders.

Lost in the wonder of his kiss, Madeleine did not realize
what he was doing until she felt the chill of the evening
against her skin. She shifted away from him, opening her
eyes. He was smiling but he was not looking at her face.

"You are simply . . . exquisite," Sebastian murmured as
he stared at the perfectly formed globes bobbing against
the translucence of her chemise. It was cut so deeply that
one pink areola peaked enticingly above the neckline. He
touched a questing finger to the lush pink-brown velvet.
"Sweet."

His action freed Madeleine's momentary awe. She
grabbed his hand. "Please—!"

He frowned. What prize ass, he again wondered angrily,
had taken her virginity without ever seeking to appreciate
her highly sensual nature? He did not stop to think about
his sudden anger at her early betrayal. But he did intend
to thoroughly erase it from her mind. After tonight, when
she thought back to her first happiness, it would be this
night, the night he had brought her fully alive.

His fingers curled over her hand holding his, capturing
it, and then he directed it back to her breast where he
carefully uncurled her fingers against her own skin. "You
are beautiful, Mignon. The things you feel when I touch
you are your body's way of saying that you like me." He
took her forefinger between two of his and slipped it under
the edge of her chemise, making her touch herself with a
light stroke.

"Look how your flesh buds at the touch," he murmured,
and kissed her brow. He directed her finger to the pearled
nipple again. "Isn't it pleasant to touch and be touched?
I want that pleasure, too, of touching you and winning
your response." He replaced her finger with his own,
scooping the nipple free of her chemise so that it rested
proudly against the pale gleam of her satiny skin. "Oh,

yes, you do like me." He traced tiny circles about her nipple. "You do like me, don't you, Mignon?"

"Oui," she whispered a little desperately. A hard shiver ran along her spine as her breast blossomed under the refined luxury of his experienced hand.

He smiled, suspecting how hard it must be for her to confront her passion for the first time. It was not, after all, as if she were in love and giving herself unthinkingly into her beloved's embrace.

It crossed his mind, only fleetingly, that if she had been in love with him, then in showing her the power of her own passion he might win her heart forever tonight. But he was not the sort of man any woman should love. He was a man who could best appreciate her passion without taking her heart. And that, in reality, was a better bargain than she might have made. He would be careful not to lie to her or say in passion things she might misinterpret. He did not want to dupe her, only pleasure her. Someone else could mine the prize of her heart.

"In a little while, I will show you how to touch me so that you will know how well my body likes you. But first . . ." He bent his head and took her blossoming flesh into his mouth.

The sharp sweet stab of pleasure took Madeleine by surprise. She arched against him, offering herself when she had thought she would not. As he suckled her, tears gathered beneath her lashes. Her hands flexed in his hair. She thought she must hurt him, but if she did, he showed no sign of it. His mouth was fastened on her and his tongue stroked her taut nipple until her breast seemed to swell with the unbearable pleasure and her tears escaped. When his head moved, seeking her other breast, she leaned back against his cradling arm, half swooning with the sweet ache of it. Her whole body ached in a way she had no words for.

Without realizing it, she drove her hips harder against

his, innocently pressing his hardened flesh in a rhythm her body instinctively provided. She heard him groan softly but thought that he like she was responding to the hot, wet rhythm of his mouth.

You are so nearly ready, Sebastian mused in exultation. *I know your body weeps for mine and you shall have me, Mignon, I promise.*

His lips moved from her breast, his tongue trailing up her breastbone to her neck and face, leaving a warm wet slick of desire on her skin. He found her ear and thrust the tip of his tongue into it, hearing her sigh in satisfaction.

"You know what comes next, don't you?" he whispered. "You find my kisses pleasing. So much more so will be my pleasuring of the rest of you."

Madeleine wanted to say something, anything, that would put her on a more even footing with him. But words failed before the beauty of his passion. She could only stare at this man who ignited her senses to madness. Then even that was too much and she hid her burning cheeks against his, wondering if all rakes so easily turned women into the deaf and dumb creature she had become.

He scooped one arm under her knees and lifted her easily as he stood and then carried her to the bed.

He followed her down onto the mattress, half covering her body with his own. One kiss turned into many, until she was kneading his shoulders with passion and he was breathing harshly with desire. "A moment, sweeting," he whispered.

He lifted himself quickly off her. He was accustomed to shedding his clothing with economy. His shirt flowed with his cravat to the floor and then his shoes and stockings followed. Finally, he worked the buttons of his breeches free and shoved them down his thighs.

He looked up at her gasp to see her sit up abruptly, too amazed by his blatant display to spare a thought for her own half-undressed state. "The drawings did not lie!" she exclaimed.

"Drawings?" Sebastian questioned. Then it struck him that perhaps her ineffectual lover had never shown himself to her. "You've never seen an undressed man before?"

"Only in pictures," she replied.

He smiled ruefully. "I had not thought of that." He lifted his arms, determined to brazen it out. "Well, what is your opinion, sweeting?"

Madeleine's bemused gaze moved reluctantly from his groin up to his face. "It is a remarkable achievement, monsieur."

Laughter shook his body, luring her startled gaze back to his arousal. "You have a way with words that is original." He put a knee on the bed, bringing the object of her interest much closer. "Would you like to touch me?"

Madeleine drew back with a quick shake of her head.

"Don't be afraid. I promised to show you how a woman knows a man likes her. This is the proof." He picked up one of her hands clasped protectively over her naked breasts and brought it to his groin, curling her fingers over his erection. A hard shudder took him at her touch and she gasped in response.

"It is alive!" she said in dumb surprise.

"It is part of me. A most unruly and impudent part, Mignon, but one best formed to please you." He moved her hand back and forth along its length. "Do you feel how it grows when you touch me? This is good. The longer and harder it becomes, the better able I am to please you."

Madeleine looked up into his face. So then, the pictures did not lie. He would now expect her to pull her dress up to her waist and open her thighs. She trembled, her shivering hand making his flesh throb and jump. "I do not know if I can . . ."

"You can," he said confidently. "Just let me help you

undress. You are crushing your pretty gown beyond redemption."

He never understood why a woman could be persuaded out of every bit of her clothing if she thought she was saving it from destruction. He lifted the muslin over her head only to find that he could not completely remove it as long as she held his erection.

"I never thought I'd ask a lady to release me in such a moment," he said, as he pried her hand loose. "You may have full rein as soon as I— Ah, that's better." He cast her gown to the floor and sent her chemise after it.

"Now," he said, as he moved fully onto the bed and stretched out beside her. "Where were we? Ah, yes, you were lying so." He pulled her down beside him. "And your sweet little hand was . . ." He placed it on his hip beside his groin. "Do to me as you will, Mignon. I am your obedient servant."

For a long moment, her hand lay inert beside his erection. He closed his eyes and propped his hands behind his head, determined to be patient. But his body was throbbing and his arousal was painfully apparent. He sighed gratefully when her hand finally moved and her fingers tentatively encompassed him.

Madeleine rose up on an elbow, the better to view his body. Stretched out before her, the long, sleek turns of his muscle-bound body were deftly sculpted by the firelight. Deep shadows sailed along his ribs and into the swallow concave valley of his belly. Below, his erection arched out of his body so arrogantly she now understood the overeager pride with which the artist had rendered his characters' appendages. So this was a man. It made her smile.

His chest was smooth with small flat nipples showing chocolate brown in the gloom. He had taken such delight in suckling her, she wondered what he would taste like and if she would enjoy the experience as much as he had.

Sebastian groaned as she leaned into him, the soft impression of her breast prodding his arm. He gritted his teeth as her hot little tongue grazed his chest and then his left nipple. It came instantly to life, tightened by the cool effect of her moisture in the night air. His belly quivered as her hand instinctively tightened on his erection. She pulled it gently, as if trying to stretch it. He set his teeth in his lower lip with a moan.

She stopped. "Did I hurt you?"

"No!" he muttered. "I like—it."

Her hand slipped up and down his shaft again and he closed his eyes, wondering how he had come to deserve this sweet torture. Was this the same girl he had not ten minutes ago wondered how he would coax into bed? She was not as ignorant as he had supposed. She was a wanton as surely as he himself.

As she continued touching him, his body's responses grew almost unbearable. Wherever her kisses fell on his chest, he felt his skin catch fire. The slightest friction of her skin on his made his erection rear in exaggerated reaction. For reasons that defied explanation the drag of her tongue on his skin seemed to strip away and bare his nerve endings, offering exquisite abrasion. He set his teeth in his lower lip, half afraid he would not be able to control the moment if he did not stop her. Her inexperienced handling was the most rousing he had never known.

Then the explanation materialized. He could hear the fire hissing and spitting as clearly as if it were held to his ear. The wet rush of the wind through the trees outside keened in his ear as if there were no thick walls buttressing the sound. He turned to Mignon. He could hear the sweet sip of her breath as it slid in and out between her lips. He watched as an aura spread out about her face in a bright prismatic chroma. A brainstorm! He never before made love when caught in its thrall.

Suddenly he could stand no more. He reared up and pushed her back in the bedding.

Madeleine fell back as he straddled her. When she reached for him, he captured both her wrists and pinned them to the bed above her head.

"Now," he said deep in his throat, "it's my turn."

He dipped his head and kissed her hard, his tongue plunging again and again into her mouth, demanding a surrender of protest she had not even thought to launch.

Her heart hammered her ribs in breathless confusion as his mouth left hers and moved down the front of her body. He paused to torment one breast in the hot velvet hollow of his mouth. She arched against the bed as he suckled deeply on the other, bringing her just to the border of pain but then relenting.

A wild, indescribable sweetness snaked through her as he moved even lower, her wrists still caught in the manacles of his fingers as he nudged her thighs apart with his knees. Swept by the sensations he offered her, far more overwhelming than his physical dominance, she surrendered to the pleasure of his control.

The laps of his tongue on her skin agitated the sensations rippling through Sebastian. The room buzzed with sounds and smells, but he closed his eyes, consumed with her smells and her sounds, and her textures. She was all velvet and cream beneath his questing mouth, warm and sweet in places, musky and wet in others. With his fingers he learned the difference between the sheer silk of her breasts and the creamy surface of her thighs. With his tongue he absorbed the unexpected green-lemon scent of her cleft and the sweet pungency of her sex. She squirmed so deliciously under him that he ground his hips on the bedding to relieve his aching. He did not want to disappoint her but he was bursting.

When he finally released her wrists, she lay perfectly still. Very carefully he reached down and found the center of her, a wet and warm pouting of flesh so soft he could scarcely believe he touched a real woman. Her gasp as his hand slid over her shivered over his nerves. Her whimper as he made her open a little to admit a finger reverberated against his bones.

"Hush," he whispered. He tasted her and she sobbed, her head thrashing back and forth on the coverlet. *"Non! Non! Par grâce!"*

Too much, experience told him. She was much too ready and he was too close to release to endure the onslaught of raw pleasure he wanted to unleash for her. He crawled slowly back up her body, his hands gentle as he dragged his damp skin along hers, giving her the feel and heat and silent assurance of his body's presence. He was trembling so hard with need he knew he would not be able to bring her to release this time. No, better to be selfish and quick. Then when he had brought himself back to a level of sanity that he could manage, he would start again and pleasure her as she deserved.

He bent quickly over her to kiss her back into relative calmness and then he said, "I'll be as slow as I can, Mignon. But you must know what you've done to my good intentions."

Madeleine opened her eyes. Mired into total submission by the feelings running rampant through her, she could see little more than his imposing dark form bending over her. Every nerve in her body was stretched so taut she could hardly speak. "Can you not be quick?"

An explosive chuckle shook him. The capacity to surprise always seemed to be hers. The laughter helped. It backed his body off the precipice the critical degree required to allow him to lift himself with measured control into position between her parted thighs. He slid into her tight wet warmth so far, and no further. He pushed against the unexpected narrowing and heard her gasp. When he pushed harder, she cried out and squirmed in resistance.

"Mignon!" he whispered accusingly through gritted teeth. "You are a virgin!"

She knew his opinion of virgins. She did not think about how he might know the difference. *"Non,"* she murmured miserably and turned her face to hide it in the bedding.

Sebastian told himself he should stop, but his body was not listening. His hips drove again and again against her resisting flesh. Nothing could stop him now. The fragile barrier of her maidenhood certainly would not.

He raised up on his knees and lifted her hips to his. Then he bent forward and kissed her long and deep. "I'm sorry, sweeting. I must hurt you a little." Damnation! He hoped it would only be a little.

He pressed a heavy kiss onto her mouth as his hand found and plied her gently low down. Then his body arched up on hers as he plunged in hard and swift.

The sharp cry of pain broke from her as at the same moment he felt himself break through the barrier of her virginity. He welcomed the pain of her nails digging into his shoulders, hoping it assuaged a little of her own misery. He heard her sob from a long way off, though her mouth was right by his ear.

His supra-aroused senses were centered at their joining, and it required the whole force of his will to lie still upon her. She was so tight that he did not have to move. His body was pulsing inside her, seeking to fill and expand that very narrow center of her womanhood. He could hear her blood moving in her veins, the very essence of her life. And it seemed the most precious sound in the world. His body shook with the effort not to take her with the violent need he feared would do her damage.

In the end it was she who began moving restlessly under him. Guided by pure instinct, she stroked his back as she pushed her hips inexpertly into his and then she sighed and whispered, "Please, help me."

That was all the encouragement he required. He surged up on his elbows and moved fractionally deeper into her. "More pain?" he murmured anxiously when she gasped.

"No!" It was a ragged whisper. "Do that—again."

Sebastian knew his expression must have been a grin of heartfelt chagrin. "Again and again and again, just for you, sweeting."

Madeleine felt wild and frantic and faintly frightening sensations building inside her. His thrusts came quicker, invaded deeper and harder into her. Strangely, her aching body welcomed him. Low down the pounding rhythm seemed just what she required. Her hands flexed on his shoulders, wanting to pull and tug and help, yet accepting the power of the man arching over her. The moment of release surprised her. She cried out in delighted incomprehension at the rhythmic fluttering convulsions echoed in the shuddering of her entire body.

Sebastian gritted his teeth, gratefully determined to maintain the rhythm until she subsided against the bedding. Then he gave up to the shooting forth of release. His cry was loud and sharp, embarrassing him in its helpless surrender to something utterly new.

And he knew in that moment of spending that he had failed, failed utterly to keep apart from her. For an instant, he no longer existed alone in the world. In this moment, in this place, in her, he was a part of something greater than himself.

He lay over her a long time, holding on tightly until their hearts began to slow and breaths to even out. And then he rolled over and pulled her with him. His hands slipped along the satin and velvet plush of her skin as he settled her against him, a hand scooping her hips into his. For once he was silent, at a loss as to how he might compliment the woman who had pleasured him. What he wanted to say he dared not even think.

Madeleine smiled in the darkness and stroked his face. So then, this was what men and women did together. She did not wonder at their eagerness, or their embarrassment. She had never felt more fragile, or happier. She had been

right to choose this man. He was as good as his beauty
would seem to make him. He had been kind and gentle,
and considerate of her. She was going to like being his
mistress.

Eleven

Madeleine sat on the horsehair blue brocade sofa in the library. She had been summoned here by Lord d'Arcy, who had yet to appear. What did a woman say to the handsome rake she had bedded the night before!

She had awakened in Lord d'Arcy's bed just before dawn to find herself alone. She waited, hoping he would return. But when the first rays of the sun stretched resolute fingers of rose into the umber sky, she realized that he might not. She told herself that he had most likely thought of an experiment he wished to conduct or had had a great insight he wished to capture on paper. She had learned many things about him in the short time she had been here. One of them was that he often lost track of time when something of surpassing importance held his attention; as *she* had in the deepest hours of the night.

She closed her eyes for a moment, allowing herself the memory of the night before.

Though she had no previous experience in such matters, she was certain Sebastian d'Arcy made love as if he had personally invented the art: easily, gracefully, with an intuitive sense of how to please. They had made love a second time without a word between them. She had simply followed his example, kiss for delicious kiss, touch for touch, embrace for embrace, learning from him how to vary the pressure and movements until her breath was lost and her lips throbbed.

The sensations he had invoked had not been convincingly conveyed by either Audelia or the pictures she had viewed. The utterly consuming need to touch and be touched, the susceptibility of her skin to the brush of his hands or the rasp of his sprouting beard, the pressure of his breath on her breasts and thighs that made her want to weep with inexpressible need; none of these miracles had even been hinted at by physical explanations of the act. And the miracle of possession! He had not rushed toward fulfillment the second time, but had stayed tumescent within her for what seemed like hours, sometimes barely moving, until she had lost consciousness of the boundaries of their bodies as they melded perfectly into one being.

Madeleine opened her eyes with a tiny shake of her head. Was this the expertise that every rake held at his command or was Sebastian d'Arcy's brand of loving singular? Intuitively, she suspected that no other man would ever make her feel this achy need to touch and be touched. It remained with her now, even after a truly difficult morning.

Disappointed by his absence yet still confident, she had left his bed to dress for the day's work. She had not met any of the servants on the back stairs as she crept to her room, though certain doors had opened a crack behind her as she moved along the corridors. When she arrived in the kitchen after changing, she was in time to catch the end of Horace's announcement that Lord Brecon would turn out without references anyone found tampering with or stealing his wine.

The staff's sullen, defiant glances had all been for her. She was not liked. She had known that from the first. Now she was an enemy. She had reported their thievery. Even Horace's face was chill with censure as he murmured a greeting.

As she prepared Lord d'Arcy's breakfast tray she suspected that the incessant whispering behind her back was about her. She had tried not to look distressed when Horace announced that he would be carrying up his lordship's tray to the laboratory, which was her usual duty. It was his lordship's specific instruction, he had added with a pointed glance at her.

"It's the richest milk curdles the quickest!" the elder kitchen maid had jeered.

The snickers that greeted the statement confirmed the worst: *They all knew.* Every one of them knew she had spent the night in the master's bed!

Madeleine supposed she should have expected that they would figure it out and not like her for it. There were already many strikes against her. She was young and pretty, a stranger and a foreigner. Now she had won their master's interest. The convent had not been so idyllic a place that she had not experienced jealousy. What she was not prepared for was treachery.

After the butler left with the tray, she had been repeatedly jostled by the kitchen maids. Once, they had made her splash boiling water on her shoe. Luckily she had been wearing sturdy work boots and not thin slippers, but she doubted they had taken that into account.

Madeleine raised her eyes to the closed double doors as the sound of footsteps sounded in the hallway beyond. She did not know what to think of herself. She seemed like a stranger inside her own skin. And yet she did not, despite the servants' hostility and her own embarrassment, regret a moment of the night before.

On the other side of the door Sebastian paused with a hand on the latch. He knew his many failings better than anyone else. The one thing he had not suspected, until just before dawn, was that he was a coward.

Mignon had been a virgin. And it had never occurred to him to inquire! He was a profligate. He'd had women beyond counting in every conceivable way and positions.

He was accomplished in many of the refinements of love-making . . . but he had never before taken a virgin.

He had allowed his desire to mask the obvious signs of her virginity because he did not want to believe that she was untouched and, therefore, off-limits by his personal code of conduct. He felt like a fool and an idiot, and the worst kind of cad. Yet he was a self-confessed libertine who applied the masculine prerogative to be urgent and aggressive and, to a certain degree, unscrupulous in carnal needs. He could accept the responsibility of taking her innocence. That did not explain the guilt of knowingly taking her a second time. He had deliberately set out to show her the depths of her capacity for passion. And that might seal her doom.

His hand flexed on the latch. Oh, how she had flowered for him, blissfully, deliciously, completely. And when she had wept on his shoulder in helpless need, he had taught her how to control the intensity of the feelings he had skillfully aroused in her. And then he had taken her higher, made her gasp and weep again and then smile.

When she fell into exhausted trusting slumber against him, his conscience kept him awake until it finally drove him from the room. He had deliberately awakened her sensuality and now he must pay the price.

When the door suddenly opened and Lord d'Arcy appeared, Madeleine scarcely had time to rise to her feet. One moment the room had been as still as a church on Monday morning. Now it seemed filled with the physical force of its owner. The sunlight was brighter, the bouquet of roses more vividly colored, the air fresher. The warmth rushed through her as she hurried toward him in greeting. "Monsieur!"

She smiled a little foolishly as she hugged his waist. "I have missed you, mon— Sebastian," she whispered softly.

When he did not embrace her back, she released him, embarrassed by her forwardness. He was smiling his oh-

so-attractive smile but there was a wariness in his blue
eyes that worried her. "How are you, Mignon?"

She smiled convincingly. "I am well, monsieur."

Sebastian searched her face and found it perfectly composed. "Good." *And lucky for you,* he mused darkly to
himself.

He swung away from her almost immediately and began
pacing. He had not known what to expect upon entering
this room. He had been prepared for any kind of a scene.
After all, he had—coward!—crept away before daylight to
sit in his laboratory and pull his thoughts together. She'd
had to face the reality of awakening in his bed alone.

Another woman would have behaved shyly when faced
with her seducer. Another woman would have thrown herself into his arms in relief or rage or shame. Even the
least accomplished wanton would have smiled and praised
him with flattery, tried to reestablish her mastery by se-
ducing him with kisses, or hidden her face in his jacket
and wept for her lost virtue—his desertion. Mignon had
done none of these things. He had taken possession of her
in the most intimate way a man could know a woman and
yet she remained more of an enigma than ever.

He was a gallant lover. He knew his *amours* expected
to be greeted with a kiss and embrace that hinted at a
little of the passion that had carried them to paradise the
night before. The inclination was there. But, with Mignon,
he knew better. He could not embrace her affectionately
and place a light teasing kiss on her lips. He was very
much afraid he would pull her down beside him on the
rug and make them both a lot happier than either of them
were at the moment.

He did not want so much to take her to bed as to carry
her away from everything and everyone forever. The desire
to protect a woman was not a new feeling to him, but this
longing to possess her utterly was. He did not miss the
look of anticipation in her expression. She thought herself

half in love with him. It was natural, it was expected, it was the worst mistake she could make.

He wet his lips with a quick swipe of his tongue. He was uncomfortable with playing so great a role in another person's life. Yet she now was his responsibility, because he had not been able to deny himself the pleasure of bedding her. "I suppose you have a position waiting for you when you return to London?"

The question took Madeleine off guard. He had not even touched her. She bit her lip in disappointment. How could he be so calm, so indifferent, after the night before? Could he not see in her face how badly she needed his arms around her and the assurance of his kiss? Had she been too enthusiastic in her responses to him? Was he tired of her already? "No, monsieur."

He paused in his pacing. "Did you say no?"

She was gazing at him with absolute attention. *"Oui, monsieur.* No."

"May I inquire what you expect to do when your week is up and you must return to London?"

Madeleine took a quick breath. "Must I go back, monsieur?"

This Sebastian had not expected. She seemed so conventional a girl until she spoke. "You wish to remain here?"

This time Madeleine exhaled and inhaled before answering. "I would like, monsieur, to remain with you."

Sebastian glanced sharply at her. "You realize what you are saying?"

"I am asking to remain in your—employ."

"My employ." He canted his head to one side. "You have no family, no friends in England?" He waited for confirmation which she gave by a quick nod, and he believed her. No friend or relative would have allowed so pretty and innocent a young woman to enter a bachelor's household. "I don't suppose you will now tell me how you happened to become involved in this bet?"

"No, monsieur."

He chuckled. How well she could shut him out without the slightest bit of discomfort or the least impenitence. If he were not looking at her eyes, he would have thought her perfectly at ease. But in those dark depths he saw the vulnerability she was trying so hard to deny, gallant spirit that she was. That glance was more effective with him than any number of tears would have been. Her courageous spirit needed guarding and protecting until she could do it herself.

His expression softened. "You must realize that your sex is a strike against your desire to make yourself a success as a chef."

He was not surprised that she did not speak. He was becoming accustomed to her silences that were as effective against an opponent as any battery of words. "Allow me to press a few realities on you. You won't find a position in a house where there's a wife to be jealous of your beauty. 'Tis no idle flattery. You must have looked in a mirror a time or two."

"Oui, monsieur. I am passable."

"Passable? A heifer with a bow is passable at the village fair." He scanned her critically. "You are flagrantly exotic. With the right clothes and a little tutoring, you could become a Dark Incomparable."

She looked at him with equal interest. "This is good?"

"This is good. But it will prove a downfall to your dreams of finding decent employment. No widow will have use for a chef of your prodigious talents, either. If you find employment at all, it will likely be in the employ of a bachelor, such as myself."

"I see, monsieur. This is not so good, no?"

Sebastian felt his face heat in answer to the speculative lift of her eyebrow, but he was prepared to brazen it out.

He came toward her slowly, a subtle threat implicit in the act. "He probably won't appreciate your finer qualities, nor your talents in the kitchen. He will find you a delectable morsel all the same. If you refuse him, he will turn you off without a reference and make certain that it is whispered about that you are the uncooperative sort. That will close even more doors to you." He paused only inches away this time. "Do you follow me?"

"I believe so, monsieur." Madeleine held back her elation, for she suspected where this conversation was leading, and it was exactly where she hoped it would go. "You do not paint a pretty picture of your sex." Irony gave a lilt to her reply. "If I will find no suitable employment in London, then I must look elsewhere."

"Without an extraordinary stroke of luck, you'll find no situation. If there is a husband, brother, uncle, or son above the age of sixteen beneath the roof, you may be certain you will be constantly pressed by amorous attention. In the end you may well end up seduced and abandoned." He searched her face for signs of her thoughts. Something bright sparkled in her dark eyes. "You would not like that, would you?"

"No, monsieur."

Definitely, there was laughter in her voice. It disconcerted him. "So then, what do you propose to do?"

"I think, monsieur, that you have a better understanding of these things than I. So I ask, what do you recommend?"

He could have kissed her in gratitude for that opening. "I propose that you might stay here, for a time, but we must come to a new arrangement."

He paused to see if she was put off by the idea of conditions. It did not seem so. She was still watching him as closely as a browning meringue. "I am a scientist. I research ideas, develop hypotheses, test those hypotheses, and then generalize theories from the results." Afraid of misleading her, he chose the words carefully. But how to explain without making his proposition sound like the typical *carte blanche* a gentleman offered a woman he wished to bed exclusively? "I hypothesize that it is possible for a woman, a single woman, to lead a full and independent life, much as a man may."

Madeleine frowned. "If she is not wealthy, how will she earn a living?"

"Through self-reliance." He picked up the thick sheaf of papers on the desk and looked at it. "I should like to test this hypothesis. Until now, I have not found a suitable medium."

He turned to face her fully. She stood so proudly and resolutely before him. He ached to hold her and tell her how precious he had found her gift of herself the night before. He wanted to explain that what he was about to offer her was being done in an effort to save her from himself as well as every other man who would ever want to place her under the bondage of his authority. But he knew he must not. It would negate the experiment before it began.

"I believe that you are the subject I have been searching for, Mignon."

"I see." Madeleine's expression masked her feelings. "How would you teach me to become independent?"

"My methods will seem unorthodox to you. My teachings may go against all you have learned in your convent. Some measures may even seem ruthless or immoral to you. I am not capricious or self-serving in this. Great thinkers, men such as your countryman Voltaire, believe that for progress to continue the world requires a new code of ethics."

" 'C'est une des superstitions de l'esprit humain d'avoir imaginé que la virginité pouvait être un vertu,' " Madeleine quoted.

His eyes widened. "Yes, Voltaire did say that the virtue of virginity is but a superstition. Where did you learn that?"

"In your library, monsieur. I come here every morning to read while waiting for my bread to rise." If possible, he looked even more astonished. "It was perhaps an error on my part?"

"No, not at all. But why that passage, Mignon?"

"You wish me to become your mistress, *oui?*" She nodded, her face perfectly composed. "I accept."

"You accept." Something had just occurred which Sebastian was certain he had missed. "You wish to be my mistress?"

"*Oui.* In return for certain considerations from you I will allow no other man to lie with me. I understand these usual considerations are things like a house and furnishings and new gowns. I wish a small allowance instead."

"You wish?" More than a little astonished to have had the matter taken out of his hands by the solemn young woman before him, curiosity prompted Sebastian to ask, "Why?"

"*C'est mon affaire.*"

Sebastian's temper flared in annoyance. "It damn well will be *my* business if it's my money you spend!"

Madeleine wondered suddenly if perhaps she had made a mistake in her frankness, but the fact that he had not one kind word to offer her after the night before had swamped her rational nature with indignation. Well, pure chance had armed her to offer him cold, unemotional reason for reason. "I found something else in your library, monsieur."

She pointed to the papers he held. "This manuscript, I think now it must be yours. In it, the writer says that an independent woman allows no man to have a say in the private matters of her life. She accepts that which she desires and spurns the rest. I quote, 'No man should ever have a monopoly of a woman's affections, for it will plant in even the best of men the seeds of tyranny. It is not money but principles which should rule her choice.' Did you not pen this, monsieur?"

For a moment Sebastian was speechless. She sounded as prim as a parson's daughter as she recited his own inflammatory words. "And if I did?" he challenged.

"I but follow your dictates by example. *Enfin, monsieur.* You may share my bed but not my privacy."

An urbane and sophisticated man by any standard, Sebastian suddenly felt gauche and clumsy. She had taken charge of an awkward moment and turned it into one where he was the one seeking his bearings. *She had read his manuscript!* Why had he not thought to offer it to her? God help all mankind when he was done polishing her natural inclinations.

"Did you, by any chance, deliberately choose me as your tutor?" Vanity, nothing altruistic, prompted his question.

Madeleine knew it was not the moment to turn away from being bold. He paid closest attention to her when she was saying something he did not expect. "I have observed, monsieur, that you are a man of taste, intelligence, good habits, and many attractive physical qualities." She looked up at him, feeling a sudden ache in her middle. Why did he not caress her? She needed it so badly. "Monsieur Voltaire would despair of me. But I believe you will quickly alter my lamentable ignorance."

He stared at her in amazement. "I suppose I should be flattered that I meet your requirements." Mischief danced in his blue gaze. "But how do you know you have chosen wisely?"

Madeleine considered the question. "You were very kind to me last night, monsieur. *Enfin,* I can make no criticism of your performance since I have no other experience with which to compare it."

"I suppose I asked for that," Sebastian murmured to himself. He moved away from the desk. "Let us be clear. I don't intend only to be your teacher in bed. That is the least of my concerns." *Liar,* his conscience taunted, but he needed to retain a modicum of objectivity. "You could leave for London today and offer yourself to any gentleman you come across. You would find you are a little wiser in the ways of men and richer for the bother." He ignored the pucker of hurt that altered her expression at his callousness. Guilt was a new experience for him, but he was quickly learning to recognize the signs. "If you remain with me, however, I'll require your dedication to learning principles as radical as they are potentially liberating."

He placed a hand on her shoulder much as a father would a child. The comparison would not hold. As he looked deeply into her dark eyes, which seemed to be the color of blue plums this morning, lust pulsed to life within him. Quick and compelling, as urgently as a stream at spring thaw, the depth of his desire surprised him. The little virgin had chosen him as her debaucher! So help him, he would not disappoint her.

"Can you do this, Mignon?"

She held his gaze. *"Oui, monsieur."*

He removed his hand, afraid that it would turn caressing. "Then, I must warn you against something." He met her wary gaze with hooded reserve. "Do not fall in love with me."

The words hung in the air for several seconds, as much a challenge as a threat, and they both knew it.

"I am no better than the villains I will train you to guard against," he went on in a reasonable tone. "In fact, I may be worse because I am proposing to protect and help you while offering to be your lover. Unless a maiden is forced she usually will retain an affection for her first lover. So then, I must warn you, I am not capable of the feeling most people would call love. Do you understand?"

Madeleine struggled with a disappointment that had no name, and yet her face glowed with an inner excitement whose cause he could not guess. It was too late. She was already a little in love with him. But she would never ever tell him so. "I do not understand all you say, monsieur. But I will learn."

He gazed longingly at her, and wondered how he would feel when she gave herself to someone besides himself. He knew how dangerous it was to contemplate that future. Yet, because he did care more than he wanted to, he was going to teach her how to protect herself from men like himself. In the process she might well become the greatest courtesan London had ever seen. "I am giving you a choice. You needn't come to my bed again until you feel you can do so out of curiosity and not affection."

That very fine resolve warred with more primitive instincts that urged him to sweep her up and carry her back to bed. He trembled with the urge to bury himself so deeply in her that when his body exploded in release, it would shatter both of them. And then when they were sated and breathless he would tell her that he had not meant any of the things he had just said. He wanted her exclusively for himself. Madness! Perhaps, if he just kissed her?

Madeleine could guess none of his thoughts. Looking up into his handsome face, she saw only unhappiness and a new restraint. As much as he seemed to want to, she knew he would not kiss her. Behind those vivid blue eyes were shadows of doubt. Did he doubt her, or himself?

"Very well, monsieur," she chose her words carefully. "I do not wish to seem rude, but about the allowance?"

Sebastian smiled, relieved that they seemed past a dangerous moment. "Not at all." He backed away from her under the pretext of laying his manuscript aside. "If you have read my treatise, then you know a successful mistress must be a good businesswoman. I suppose you have a figure in mind?"

She did not. "I will accept your decision."

"Five hundred pounds a year. How is that?"

Her expression of surprise betrayed her. She had not expected more than a quarter of that amount. Yet she knew she should not say so. "Is that what you pay your current mistress?"

"I have no mistress at present." He saw relief skim her expression. Was she worried about competition? Or was it more personal? Despite all reason, he hoped it was the latter. "If I did, I might be inclined to be even more generous to her."

Madeleine gathered from his expression that this was a test, though the purpose of it eluded her. "You seem to require very little for your money, monsieur, since I am not required to share your bed. May I not earn the money in some other way?"

Intrigued as always by the workings of her mind, he said, "What would you suggest?"

"Perhaps I could continue to prepare your meals."

"No, you will be too busy for that, I regret to say."

"Then, may I not help with your work?"

"How could you help me?"

"You are a scientist with many experiments in progress. I write as well as speak and read French, English, and Latin. Monsieur Horace says you often spend half your nights transcribing the day's notes. Could I not help do this?"

Sebastian stared at her. How quickly she had managed to push her nose into, it seemed, every corner of his life. In five short days she had reordered his household. By the end of the week, she would no doubt be explaining his own experiments to him. She seemed to be too good to be true.

"Very well, as long as it does not interfere with our lessons."

Madeleine smiled. "There is one other thing, monsieur."

"Why am I surprised?"

"When the lessons are complete, I should like you to write a letter of introduction for me."

He smiled. "To what purpose, Mignon?"

"If I must make my way in the world, I will need an entrée into society."

He laughed. "When I am done with you, all of London will know of your existence."

She regarded him skeptically. "You are very certain of your abilities, monsieur."

He brushed his thumb across her lips. "Kiss me, Mignon, to seal the bargain."

She did so, a kiss as light and brief as a butterfly's passing. He caught himself leaning into her beguiling softness and pulled back. If only she knew how enticing she was without a single word of his instruction to guide her. When he finished with her, London's rakes would need to guard their hearts and purses very carefully or she would soon own them all.

Madeleine had set off for the village right after lunch. The sun was still high in the midafternoon sky as she reached the summit of the furze-covered hill and looked down into the village of Hythe nestled at the base of the harbor channel. Beyond the village, the Channel shone sea blue in the fall light.

In her pocket was a bank draft for the extraordinary amount of one hundred and twenty-five pounds. She had come to town to send the greater portion of it to her aunts.

She had given the matter considerable thought and decided to pen only the simplest of notes to her aunts. It read, in French:

Dear *Tantes* Henrice and Justine:
      I am well and safe. A small miracle! I have found a position of employment. Enclosed is my first quar-

terly stipend. Use as you see fit. Give my love to
Maman.

                                        Madeleine

She was not yet ready to tell them where she was and
why. But this money might mean her mother's salvation.

She was aware of the curious stares she attracted as she
entered the cobblestone street of the village. The narrow
lanes were hemmed in by ancient houses whose walls were
buckled and bellowed by age. No one spoke as she made
her way to the bank. The man behind the desk took her
note from Lord d'Arcy with a lift of his eyebrows and the
tightening of his lips, but he wrote her a draft for one
hundred pounds and gave her the difference in five-pound
notes.

"Where will I find the mail?"

"At the coaching inn," the cashier replied, but he did
not expound on that statement or even look at her again.

Madeleine left the bank with the distinct feeling that she
was disliked in the village. Because of this, she did not
ask anyone on the street for directions, she simply walked
along the lanes winding through the village until she saw
at the far end of town the sign for the coaching station.

She kept her eyes down as she entered the general room
of the station. It was low-ceilinged and heavily beamed.
Thick smoke had gathered and hung in a bluish mist just
above her head. She glanced surreptitiously at the group
of men, one in a makeshift uniform, whose pipes were the
source of the smoke, but she did not meet any gaze directly as she passed their table toward the clerk.

"I wish to post a letter to London," she said to the
red-faced man behind the counter.

Instead of taking the missive she held out, he subjected
her to a thorough searching glance. "What sort of talk is
that you're speaking?"

"English, monsieur."

"French!" He fairly shouted the word, drawing the quick feral attention of the other men present.

He snatched her missive. "What's a French whore doing in Hythe?"

Madeleine held her astonishment in check, though she wondered why every Englishman she approached suspected her of being in that despicable profession. "I am employed at Lord d'Arcy's home."

He thrust his head toward her over the counter, his lipless mouth drawn back in a lewd grin. "You be Lord d'Arcy's doxy, ain't you? Heard he had a new one down from London."

Madeleine held her ground. "I am Lord d'Arcy's *chef de cuisine.*"

His expression soured. "Is that a fancy word for tart?"

"It means I cook for him."

"Then how come I ain't never seen you in town afore? The d'Arcy cooks all come to Hythe to do their marketing. You ain't been here afore. I'd've marked you."

"I am new." She pointed to the letter he held squashed in his fist. "How much to post it?"

He looked down at her letter and then held it up as he shouted to the ring of men watching them. "You hear what I said? She's a Frog."

The mention of her nationality sobered instantly the half-dozen smirking faces staring at her. Before they had been interested only in her trim ankles and narrow waist. That carnal interest was discarded by the announcement that one of their dreaded enemy was among them.

The man in a red coat swaggered over to her, his narrow face framed by greasy ropes of dark hair. "What's a French doxy doin' in Hythe?" He put out his hand as if to tug her bonnet. "Here, let's have that off so we can have a look at you, lovey."

She swung away from him back to the clerk. "I have a letter to post to London. Will you take care of it?"

"You ain't gon' do it, Jake!" said the man whose red jacket bore the stripes of a sergeant. "Could be a Froggie trick! Could be she's spyin' on us. That note could be a spy's message."

Madeleine turned quickly. "It is a letter to my aunts!"

The soldier stopped just short of touching her again as he jabbed a dirty finger at her chest. "How do we know your aunts ain't spies, same as you? How do we know you didn't come ashore during the fog last evening? The broadsheets say to be on the look out for suspicious folk. The countryside's crawlin' with French spies."

The sergeant grabbed her arm in a brutal grip. "I think you are a spy. I think you came to spy out the harbor and now you done it, you're sending your spyin' messages to accomplices. Spy!"

Madeleine took a halting step backward each time he uttered the word spy, but he held her arm as his spittle flecked her cheek on the last word. His companions' faces grew more threatening as they surged forward. She told herself they could not do anything to her. She was under Lord d'Arcy's protection, but the dirty sweat-streaked faces of the men forming a circle around her tried that belief.

She swallowed her pride and her fear, knowing that the two together could only make things worse. She looked down at the calloused hand on her upper arm and then at its owner, the soldier who had done most of the speaking. "Who are you?"

"I'm Wheal, head of the local militia," he boasted.

"We're patriots, we are!" shouted another.

A third man lifted a wickedly curving grappling hook from the floor by his chair and brandished it before her. "Going to thrash Nappy ifin' he dares show his Froggie face on our coast!"

" 'Twas your like we've been warned to watch out for," the uniformed man said.

"I am no spy. I am in service to Lord d'Arcy." Madeleine

backed up several steps, looking about for someone to corroborate her statement. "Go and ask at Brecon Manor."

"We don't need to bother his lordship. Grab her, boys, we'll take her to Hastings to the magistrate!"

"I don't really believe that will be necessary."

Madeleine swung her head toward the door at the sound of a man's voice and saw the d'Arcy butler Horace standing in the doorway.

"Monsieur Horace," she greeted, relief warming her words.

The butler gave her a scant nod. "Mademoiselle Mignon."

"You know her?" asked Wheal.

Horace gazed impassively at the man. "I do. Miss Mignon is his lordship's new chef."

The men grumbled among themselves, but fell back.

"Why didn't she say so in the first place," one of them muttered.

Madeleine thought it best not to contradict them, but she could not leave her letter unposted. She looked at Horace. "If you would be kind enough to wait a moment, I will walk back to the house with you."

The man offered her the sketchiest of nods. She thought he did not look pleased to have been her rescuer. No one in Lord d'Arcy's house liked her much, but at least he had come to her assistance.

She turned back to the coaching master. "I wish to mail my letter."

He looked at the crumpled note he had placed on the counter. "We don't carry French correspondence." He smirked. "The address is in French."

Madeleine glanced at her missive and then reached out to smooth out the crimps made by his fist. "It is written in English," she replied as she pointed at her script.

He squinted but did not really look at it. "Looks like French to me. Can't read it."

Madeleine bit her lip. The money had to get to her aunts!

"Perhaps if it bore his lordship's mark, it might be franked to London where someone who reads French can interpret it," Horace offered from the doorway.

The man behind the counter gave him a sullen look. "Suppose that might work. Won't guarantee it."

Horace came forward and added his signature to Madeleine's letter and then, using the seal he carried on his key chain, embossed her missive with the marquis's crest.

"These are tense times, mademoiselle. I would not, if I were you, venture from the grounds of his lordship's home again without a companion," Horace offered coolly when they had gained the street. "Kent folks don't much like foreigners."

"That is an understatement, Monsieur Horace," Madeleine replied. She suspected he might have added that he did not much like foreigners, either.

"Who were you writing in London, miss?" Horace inquired as he handed her up into the ponycart parked just outside the coaching inn doorway. "His lordship said you had no people in England."

With that simple statement Madeleine knew that it was no mere coincidence that he had been in Hythe. He was following her. But why? She did not look up at him. "Did you not remark the name when you franked the note in his lordship's stead?"

He did not reply, but both of them knew he did not need to. Her smile of triumph did not last past her next thought. If he told Lord d'Arcy what he had seen and heard, her troubles might not be over.

It was only a matter of moments before anxiety began nibbling at her happiness like mice at a piece of cheese. How would Lord d'Arcy respond if he learned she was the Foucant niece? Would he be angry? Disappointed? Insulted? What if he did not want her for his mistress?

Each possibility stole another morsel of her happiness until all that was left were a few miserly crumbs of fear and trepidation. He must want her! She would do whatever he wanted of her, if only he would keep her.

Twelve

October 1803

"Oh! I see it! I do!"

Madeleine's hand tightened on the brass-and-wood cylinder as she pressed her right eye to the end of the telescope. Through its bright lens the distinct triangular shape of a white sail wavered.

"What sort of ship is it?" Sebastian stood just behind her. She felt his hand touch her lower back.

Madeleine squinted, trying to force a sharper picture of the sheeting that flew before the identical gray-blue of ocean and sky. "I cannot tell."

"Look again. 'Tis essential that you learn to recognize vessels if you are going to live so near the coast."

She tried to concentrate, but it was becoming more difficult with every second. His hand was now slowly smoothing up and down the small of her back. During her very first lesson nearly three weeks ago, he had told her that she must learn how to tolerate a man's touch. Whenever they were alone, he touched her in some manner. She could not label the touches seductive, for they were never intimate or forced. Yet, whether he played idly in her curls or toyed with the ribbon tied about her neck, or simply stroked the tips of her fingers as they discussed other matters, his touches were never as casual as they seemed and were impossible to ignore. She moved restlessly now under his hand.

The telescope moved a fraction and the sail disappeared from the horizon of her view.

A hand reached around and over her shoulder, realigning the telescope. "Concentrate." The command was spoken right into her ear.

She bit her lip. Whenever she responded to his touch, he chastised her, yet she suspected her reaction secretly pleased him. Why else would he end every lesson with the same pompous admonishment, *Don't fall in love with me.*

"How many masts are there?"

"One." She squinted harder. "No, two. Uh, one."

His hand moved to the indentation of her waist which he lightly clasped. "Square rigged?"

"Oui, and three sails on the bowsprit. Oh, I recognize it. It's a schooner." She turned her head to look back at him for confirmation. He was so close she scraped her cheek on his chin, so close his breath fanned her face, so close his eyes made the sea seem dull and drab by comparison.

She saw those eyes flare with acknowledgment of their proximity. Her gaze came to rest on his lips, inches away. He had not kissed her since the morning they had sealed their bargain. She held her breath, hoping that this time he would ease this inexplicable hunger that tortured her each time they were close.

His hand on her waist tightened to draw her back toward him. At the last moment, he propelled her sideways until she was facing the chart pinned on the wall beside the open window. "Which is the correct silhouette?"

Half blind with disappointment, she chose one at random.

"That's a cutter, with one mast. Schooners have two." He gave her waist a squeeze and then took a step back, allowing her to turn around.

Embarrassed and faintly disappointed that he was no

longer touching her, she offered him a bright false smile. "I am hopeless, monsieur."

He shrugged. "At least you can identify what you see even if you have not yet mastered the terms." He reached out to cap the end of the telescope. "You chose the correct silhouette. That was the Aldebaran, one of our coastal cutters on its daily watch through these waters. England spends as much time guarding her coast against smugglers, as she does against the French. Fortunately we are more successful with the French."

Matching his nonchalance, she said, "Fortunate, too, for your wine cellar, monsieur."

He had completely revamped his wine cellar within a fortnight of her discovery. She had no idea how much it had cost him, or who supplied him with new wines, but every night the wines served at dinner were impeccable. Unfortunately, now that she had risen from the kitchen to a guest room on the second floor the meals were plain English fare of boiled meat, potatoes, and cabbage.

Sebastian's expression was blank as he leaned back against the top of his desk and lifted one leg for anchorage. "Come and look at what I have for you." He pointed to a shallow walnut box he had brought in with him at the beginning of the lesson. He flipped open the lid. Lying nestled in black velvet were half a dozen exquisite pieces of jewelry.

She knew he was watching her face for her reaction, so she smiled and nodded. "Very nice, monsieur."

He reached out and hooked a long strand of pearls with his forefinger and lifted them. "Tell me, are they real or paste?"

She took the three-foot rope of pearls and held them up to the window. The daylight revealed their pale ivory luster with just a hint of opaline iridescence. "They are lovely."

"But are they real?"

She took a section of the rope and brought it to her

mouth, running the pearls lightly over her teeth as *Tante* Henrice had taught her to do as a child. There was no roughness to the pearls' surface. She lowered them and shook her head. "No, monsieur, they are not real."

He smiled as he accepted them back. "Clever girl. You are right. They are too smooth, too perfectly round to be real. They are paste, made from pearl dust and glue. Now look at these." He offered her several unset stones from his pocket. "Which are real and which are not?"

Madeleine gazed at the carbuncle and cut rubies and sapphires winking in her palm. One by one she held them up to the window, turning them this way and that to allow the light to pass through them. She set them aside into two piles. When she was done she went to the bookshelf and chose a heavy volume. Without a glance at her teacher, she came back and slammed the book spine end down like a mallet over one pile of stones. All but one shattered. She picked up the sapphire and placed it in the second pile. When she looked up, Sebastian was smiling at her in bemusement.

"Effective if potentially hazardous to my library." He dusted off the book and set it aside. "But there is a more effective method." He pulled from his pocket what appeared to be a monocle. "Look at them through this and tell me what you see."

Madeleine took the eyepiece and, picking up a sapphire, held it to the light as she squinted through the lens. The gem appeared several sizes larger than before. In its depths she saw shadows. "I see tiny shapes like needles and something like smoke in this stone." She looked back at him, "It is defective, no?"

"No. Those imperfections are called feathers and silk and are proof of a natural stone." He picked up another blue stone. "Look at this one."

Madeleine cocked her head to one side as she moved

the stone back and forth before the lens. "This contains swirls and bubbles."

"That is because it is glass. It is worthless, though quite pretty."

He tossed it back into the box. "Not everything of beauty is valuable." His smile was sweet, cynical, heart-breaking. "A smart—and educated—woman will not be fooled."

Madeleine shrugged. "Is it not rude to subject a gift to such rigorous scrutiny?"

His expression turned faintly amused. "Have you considered why a man would give a woman such rubbish? He hopes to steal from her what he wants her to think he is purchasing."

"Is all affection so mercantile?" she murmured in distaste.

"You are after independence, Mignon. It is a commodity that must be purchased. Gemstones are more valuable than currency. Banks and even regimes rise and fall. But jewels and gold are acceptable barter the world over."

She gazed at him with doubt. "To be independent, I must be mercenary."

"Exactly. You want your independence, don't you?"

"Oui," she whispered in a spurt of anger. She very much wanted to be free of this hunger for him.

"Now, as a reward for your perspicacity you may choose something from the box."

Madeleine eyed the jewelry with some reluctance. This lesson of ruthless self-interest had been drilled into her in every way possible these last weeks, but she still found it repellent. She did not want his jewelry, she wanted his laughter, his teasing, and his affection. If he had offered it to her as a symbol of friendship, she would have treasured even one of the paste stones. But she knew he would not do that. This was simply a reward for a lesson learned. Her days were filled with lessons and lessons and more lessons. She now knew all the pieces in his silver service, how to properly fill a gentleman's pipe, how to address the English aristocracy, to whom and when to curtsy, and even enough politics not to insult a Whig or Tory. The philosophical foundation of his theory of the resocialization of women was pulled from a dozen scholars from Aristotle to Rousseau. She had read treatises until her head ached and her mind wandered.

Yet, as she gazed into the treasury of jewels spread for her consideration, she would have traded them all for an hour in the arms of the man standing beside her.

Because he was growing tense, she chose from among the very elaborate settings a small diamond hair ornament in the shape of a butterfly.

Sebastian stared at her a moment, trying to decide if she was being canny, or thoughtlessly foolish. "Why so small a piece?"

She shrugged, not wanting to answer with the truth. "It is small enough to cause no comment when I arrive in London. Something grander would make people wonder how I came by it. I do not wish to seem so well set up that the gentlemen will feel they cannot afford me. Nor do I wish to offend the wives by wearing better jewelry than they themselves own. It is unseemly, *oui?*"

If she had changed into a spaniel before his eyes he could not, she suspected, have looked more surprised. It lasted only a fraction of a second, and then he was again in command of himself. "You are full of surprises, Mignon. You may keep the piece. It was my mother's."

Madeleine gazed at the delicate piece, closed her hand over it a moment, and then put it back. *"Merci,* monsieur, but no."

His smile hardened. "Changed your mind for a richer piece?"

She looked up into his blue gaze and saw clearly that he was offended. "It belonged to your mother. I think you must have loved her a little, despite what you say about your absent heart. I could not take from you anything so precious unless you chose especially to give it to me."

She saw that she had managed to surprise him again, but he did not respond to her implication. "Then choose something else."

"Perhaps another time," she answered, and turned away before he saw all too clearly what she really desired from him.

"Are you a spy, Mignon?" he asked politely.

She never knew what Horace had told him about her trip to Hythe. He never mentioned the incident to her. But the question was asked, every day, in some manner. She answered him according to her mood, whimsically, foolishly, silently. One of his first lessons had been about conversing with men. He said that most men do not desire women to be intelligent, only entertaining.

She lifted a gaze of sweet appeal to him. "What could I possibly want of you, monsieur?"

Sebastian turned his head to look out the library window, as if his deep blue eyes did not need the aid of the telescope to pick out the tiny sliver of sail riding the swells in the far distance. "Have you finished Richardson?"

The abrupt change of subject did not deceive her. The twenty volumes of *The History of Clarissa Harlowe* had bored her to tears. *"Oui, monsieur.* I cannot imagine a woman writing such a sad story. In my ignorant opinion, the rake Rob Lovelace underestimated the power of love. He did not believe in it and the woman Clarissa did not trust it."

"Which do you suppose is the greater fault?" When he reached for her hand, it took every ounce of her self-possession not to pull away. "Can I assume that you don't feel yourself ruined by your single lapse of virtue?"

For a moment Madeleine was unable to speak, suffocated by desire and the fear to act on it. His tone was deceptively cool, yet in his eyes was a faint mocking challenge, and she knew she would never tell him how she really felt. Never. Yet, to her surprise, he turned away first.

"Do you dance, Mignon?" he asked in that deep fine voice she had grown to like better than any music she had ever heard.

She wanted to refuse him, but the thought of doing something other than studying tempted her. "A little, monsieur."

He turned back to her, his expression once again charming. "You have a curious habit of underestimating your abilities, Mignon. Let's find out, shall we?"

He took her by the hand and led her out of the library, across the hall and into a small room she had never before entered. It was on the east side of the house and therefore in shadow this afternoon. The curtains were drawn, adding to the gloom, but she could see the faint dusty colors of pale blues and pinks and creams of the furnishings. An easel stood near the pair of closed windows and a pianoforte stood in the far corner.

After closing the door, he released her hand and went straight over to the piano. He opened the top and then sat down, positioning his hands on the keys. Only then did he look up at her. "Now then, show me the steps you know, Mignon." He began to play a minuet softly.

"I did not know that gentlemen played the piano, aside from musicians, of course," she said.

Sebastian laughed. "You consider musicians less than men?"

"No, I did not mean that. It is only that at the convent, the mastery of a musical instrument was considered a lady's accomplishment."

"And are you accomplished?"

"Not nearly so well as you. No, don't stop," she said when he lifted his fingers from the keys in midmeasure.

"If I continue to play, then you must dance. Agreed?"

Familiar with the repartee he expected, she answered, "If you continue to play, then perhaps I will feel more like dancing."

He smiled in approval. "As mademoiselle wishes."

She watched as he bent gracefully over the keyboard, his hands gliding effortlessly over the ivory and ebony keys as quite beautiful music poured forth. He was a lord, a marquis, young, sinfully handsome, outrageously charming, intelligent, rich, talented—and spoiled. There seemed nothing he could not bring to hand by the exertion of his will. No wonder he did not want her to fall in love with him. It would be so predictable and doubtless boring for him to have yet another woman prostrate at his feet.

After listening to a few bars, she gathered up a corner of her skirt and swung away so that she could no longer see his face. She would not be predictable. She would not!

Sebastian watched her from the corner of his eye. She moved as lightly as a feather caught on a whimsical breeze. Desire mingled with speculation as his fingers skimmed over the keys with the tender thoroughness he longed to use on her body.

For three weeks he had held them in suspense, taunting her but daring her to resist the tug between them. He told himself it was because he was half certain she was a spy.

Horace had bungled badly when he had followed her to Hythe. He'd not thought to read the name and address on the letter she had posted to London. Her assertion that she was merely paying back rent was ridiculous. Yet, he had no reason to doubt her. Why, then, did he?

Was it because he could not look at her without needing an excuse to protect himself from his feelings? For three weeks he had waited for her to come of her own volition to his bed. For three long lonely weeks he had slept alone. He was going to have to do something, to protect them both. Perhaps he should ride up to London in the morning.

It would not take long. Two days and he could return here a new man, a satiated man, a man capable of resisting her.

When the piece was done, he looked down at his still hands. He knew he should leave right this minute. If he rode hard he could be in London before morning. He looked up to where she stood with her skirts still swaying. "Come here."

Madeleine obediently approached him, and he rose from the stool and held out his hand to her. She smiled disarmingly. "I like dancing."

Sebastian wondered if she realized how effortlessly she moved her body to the rhythm of the music. "But now we are going to practice a different lesson. Give me your hand. We will begin with the customary greeting when gentlemen and ladies meet. The hand salute."

He took her unresisting hand in his and turned it palm down so that the curving tips of her fingers balanced over the cupping edges of his. "Now when you meet a gentleman who's gained your acquaintance through the proper channels of an introduction, you will offer your hand like this." His voice took on the lecturing tone she had come to detest. "The fingers should droop naturally from your wrist like wisteria blossoms from the branch." He moved their joined hands up and down a little. "So far so good, yes?"

"Oui," Madeleine murmured, and smiled in spite of herself.

"Very well. The gentleman will gently draw your hand to his lips as he bends to it." He followed his words with actions. Yet when his lips were within an inch of her fingertips he suddenly straightened again.

"You see, the most polite of address has been paid you."

Madeleine frowned. "Is that it? But it is not a kiss at all."

"Very good. It most certainly is *not* a kiss. It is a salutation, a mere token of respect. It makes a man appear equally gallant to the sickly and the obese, the favored and the poxed. Ah, now you laugh. Good."

Madeleine was laughing, but more at the mischief in his sky-blue eyes than for the instruction he offered.

"Now we will proceed to the next. Attend the difference."

Again he lifted her hand and bent his head over it. But this time she felt the distinct sensation of warm lips brush her skin for an instant.

He straightened and smiled. "What is the difference, Mignon?"

"You kissed my hand, of course."

"Ah, I actually touched you. It is not done unless the lady is wearing gloves."

Madeleine's frown returned. "I don't understand."

"Don't you?" He moved closer, but his expression was guarded. "The difference is contact. Once a man is allowed to touch a lady's bare skin he is likely to believe that she is inviting him to take other liberties."

Madeleine laughed in disbelief. "You are joking, of course."

"What apple cart did you fall from, child?"

"Don't call me child," Madeleine said in annoyance. "I may be ignorant of many things, but I am not a child."

"No." Sebastian's gaze wandered to the modest neckline of her muslin dress. "You are not. My apologies, mademoiselle. So, we go on. The next salutes are those you must under no circumstances tolerate from any man in public. If he has not already paid you the proper courtship in the form of flowers, perfume, and jewelry, you may deny them in private. Even then, if you do not like him, you should scorn these intimacies altogether."

He met her eyes again. "Men always pursue the woman who refuses them. Courtesan or would-be wife, the more she refuses, the more she will be pursued. Never sell yourself short. Take much and offer little.

"Never allow a new gentleman in your circle of acquaintances to do this." He pressed his mouth firmly and lingeringly to the tips of her fingers.

"Or this." His lips parted and she felt the damp heat of his mouth against her fingers.

"And never this." He caught her center finger between his teeth and licked the tip.

He let her go even as she jerked her hand back.

"You see? It is very simple for a man of skill and daring to turn the most unobjectionable of exercises into an occasion for misconduct, particularly when the woman is unwary or inexperienced."

"Do *you* practice such ungallantries?" she asked as she slowly rubbed her tingling fingers against the folds of her skirt.

"As often as possible. But only on those who are easily impressed." Amusement tugged his mouth. "Are you easily impressed, Mignon?"

She shrugged, determined to match his nonchalance. "I shouldn't think so. I liked the first salute. The second was even better. But the last . . . I did not like it so much."

"Did it make you uncomfortable?"

Madeleine's brows lifted. "It made my stomach jump."

He looked inordinately pleased. "Now we shall move on to the next salutation, one which is favored by your countrymen."

Madeleine was taken aback when he suddenly reached for her and drew her in by the shoulders. Before she understood his purpose, he bent his head and pushed his right cheek against her own. Just as swiftly he pressed his left to her left and then he straightened. *"Voilà!* This you are familiar with, of course."

"Of course," Madeleine lied. She had seen aristocratic ladies occasionally greet one another in the cloister halls in this manner but never among the nuns.

"Beware of strangers who claim kinship with you.

Would-be cousins and uncles take the worst liberties." This time he did not grip her by the shoulders but brought his hands up slowly to cup her face. Madeleine trembled as those vivid blue eyes fastened on hers. His thumbs were tucked under the arch of her chin, the fingers setting in fan-shape display along either side of her face from jaw to the bridge of each cheek.

"Now then, pay very close attention." There was no sentimentality in his gaze. He looked as if he were about to show her how to lift a man's head with one slash of a saber. "Never allow a man who is not your lover to ever kiss you like this."

He bent his head to her, averting his mouth at the last moment from hers to ply her right cheek with the satin plush of his dry lips. His mouth lingered, moving in a slow leisurely circle that seemed to measure the contour and texture of her skin.

"Or this." He found the crest of her left cheek and applied the same concentrated attention to its surface.

"Never this." This time when he touched her cheek, the moist heat of licked lips left a heated trail on her skin.

"Sweet," he murmured low in his throat as he repeated the action on the other side.

Her cheeks burned with the impression of his forbidden kiss when he lifted his face a little away from hers. He smiled into her round-eyed stare of midnight blue.

"And never *ever* this," he whispered softly as he turned her face away from his. An instant later she felt his lips on her ear. He puffed the most gentle of breaths into it, then applied the astonishing lick of his tongue in its very center. The decadent caress set off a quiver of feeling so strong it buckled her knees.

She reached out to grip his shoulders, whether to push him away or hold herself upright she could not tell. She tried to think of something rational to say, something that would not sound like hysterical embarrassment, but noth-

4 BESTSELLING HISTORICAL ROMANCES BY YOUR FAVORITE AUTHORS CAN BE YOURS, FREE!

Kensington Choice, our newest book club now brings you historical romances by your favorite bestselling authors including Janelle Taylor, Shannon Drake, Rosanne Bittner, Jo Beverley, and Georgina Gentry, just to name a few! Each book is filled with passion, adventure and the excitement of bygone times!

To introduce you to this great new club which is part of Zebra Home Subscription Service, we'd like to send you your first 4 bestselling historical romances, absolutely free!   And once you get these 4 free books to savor at home, we'll rush you the next 4 brand-new books at the lowest prices available, as soon as they are published.

The way the club works is that after your initial FREE shipment, you will get our 4 newest bestselling historical romances delivered to your doorstep each month at the preferred subscriber's rate of only $4.20 per book, a savings of up to $7.16 per month (since these titles sell in bookstores for $4.99-$5.99)! All books are sent on a 10-day free examination basis and there is no minimum number of books to buy. (A postage and handling charge of $1.50 is added to each shipment.) Plus as a regular subscriber, you'll receive our FREE monthly newsletter, *Zebra/Pinnacle Romance News*, which features author profiles, contests, subscriber benefits, book previews and more!

 So start today by returning the FREE BOOK CERTIFICATE provided. We'll send you 4 FREE BOOKS with no further obligation: A FREE gift offering you hours of reading pleasure with no obligation...how can you lose?

We have 4 FREE BOOKS for you as your introduction to KENSINGTON CHOICE! To get your FREE BOOKS, worth up to $23.96, mail the card below.

FREE BOOK CERTIFICATE

Yes! Please send me 4 Kensington Choice (the best of Zebra and Pinnacle Books) Historical Romances without cost or obligation (worth up to $23.96). As a Kensington Choice subscriber, I will then receive 4 brand-new romances to preview each month for 10 days FREE. I can return any books I decide not to keep and owe nothing. The publisher's prices for Kensington Choice romances range from $4.99-$5.99, but as a preferred subscriber I will get these books for only $4.20 per book or $16.80 for all four titles. There is no minimum number of books to buy and I may cancel my subscription at any time. A $1.50 postage and handling charge is added to each shipment. No matter what I decide to do, my first 4 books are mine to keep, absolutely FREE!

Name _____

Address _____ Apt. _____

City _____ State _____ Zip _____

Telephone (_____) _____

Signature _____

(If under 18, parent or guardian must sign)

Subscription subject to acceptance. Terms and prices subject to change.

KC0296

ing could get past the alarming sensations he chased round and round the whorl of her ear with his tongue.

"Only the most profligate of libertines would press a lady in this manner," he whispered an instant before he took the soft bud of her lobe between his teeth.

"Oh, please!" she whispered, bending back even as he bent toward her. The feelings he roused affected every sensitive spot on her body. One of his hands left her cheek and found her waist to offer a counterbalance to their embrace as he nibbled her lobe and then began to suck it ever so gently.

Finally, his lips left her ear and moved back to her cheek, leaving a slick path over her skin. He licked the edges of her lashes until they were spiky with his moisture. He touched his tongue to the tip of her nose and then slipped it up its slope to her brow. He tilted up her face and sucked each of her cheeks delicately and then kissed her chin.

Why did he not kiss her lips, she wondered, near weeping with anticipation. Everywhere he touched her she felt a new point of happiness. Yet she was no longer pulled in against him. The only contact of their bodies was wherever his lips fell and his hands moved to shape and alter the incline of her head to his purpose. Her fingers dug into the fabric of his coat at the shoulder seams. His coat would be hopelessly crushed, she thought inconsequentially. Surely he would kiss her. Certainly he must kiss her!

With her breath coming very quickly between her parted lips, Madeleine raised her mouth.

She saw his eyes flare in recognition of her silent offer. She saw the slant of self-satisfaction lift a corner of his beautiful mouth. She did not care that he knew what she wanted, or how badly. If only he would give it to her, kiss her so that she would not die from the ache of wanting it.

But he straightened up and away from her, leaving her mouth untouched.

Trembling from thwarted passion, Madeleine briefly closed her eyes. When she opened them, it was to find him standing several feet away, regarding her with amused tolerance and a *soupçon* of sympathy. "Have you learned something today?"

Yes, she thought wildly, *that he could crack and melt her bones without the aid of heat.* So this was the skill of a master rakehell. No wonder women succumbed. She longed to strike him, to launch half a dozen of his thickest volumes at his head, to pummel him with her fists—to run weeping in embarrassment from the room. She did not move.

"Any man who dares to so insult you deserves to be slapped."

Her mouth was so dry she could only manage, *"Oui."*

His expression quickened. "Yet you do not act."

"Do—? Oh." She blushed, realizing that her feelings must be all too accurately expressed in her face. *"Merci,* but I do not need to practice this."

"But perhaps *I* need the lesson." Sebastian subjected her to a long cool appraising glance as he approached. No woman who had ever been on the receiving end of that glance had ever remained indifferent to it. The women responded as if it were either the vilest of insults or the most intriguing opening gambit of a seduction. He wondered which route Mignon would take. "You have just allowed me unconscionable liberties."

"Unconsca—chu—?" The word stuck in the roof of her mouth.

"Unconscionable." He reached and touched a forefinger to her lips to still her effort. "It means indefensible, sweeting. I have insulted you." He spread his arms in invitation. "Punish me, Mignon."

"No, I couldn't—"

His expression suddenly altered, a frigid chilling reproach where moments before there had been fire. He gripped her hard with both hands, his fingers digging into her shoulders without any attempt to mediate the pressure. "Then I shall assume I have the right to strip you here and now and take what I want."

He thrust his face, hard with new and urgent emotions, into hers. "Because I do want you, Mignon. I want you very badly."

Confused by his sudden change, she twisted out of his grasp. "Please don't!" she said on a gasp of girlish laughter. Ashamed of her silly response, she offered him a tentative smile of reconciliation. "I don't like this game."

He returned that smile but it was unlike any she had ever seen on his face. "Don't touch you? Are you not a whore in the making?" His voice held the lacerating snap of a whip. "Have you not asked for what I so badly wish to give you?"

As he reached for the top of her bodice, astonishment held her motionless until his fingers dug into the cleft between her breasts. She tried to wrench away and she heard the fabric shred as he jerked it downward. He grabbed her by the waist with his free hand and drew her close. "Come then, Mignon, undress for me."

She began to struggle in earnest, but he was much too strong for her. She heard her gown tear again and felt the cool air on her exposed skin.

"No! Please! Stop!" But he did not stop. He was reaching for her breasts, pushing his hand inside her chemise. Truly frightened, she swung out with her right hand with all the force at her command. The impact snapped his head around as the sharp crack of contact seemed to reverberate through the room.

She reeled away as he released her and gathered the remnants of her bodice over her breasts with shaking hands. When he did not immediately come after her, the suspense of not knowing why made her turn around. He stood where he had released her.

The sight of the deepening red mark on his pale cheek, struck her conscience. "I'm . . . sorry!" she whispered in genuine distress. "I didn't mean—"

"Of course you did." Grinning like a boy who had won a prize ribbon, he reached up and rubbed his flaming cheek. "Lord, sweeting! You require a great deal of provocation."

She halted her backward retreat as understanding came quickly to rescue her conscience. Fury replacing fright. "But that was horrible of you!"

"Yes, it was." She saw that perversely he was enjoying himself. "But my actions were a common response for an aroused man in my position who has decided he must have a woman in your position."

He advanced on her slowly, making her dance on the knife edge between fear and embarrassment. "You let me go much too far. If this were any other than an exercise, you would now be there." He indicated the floor. "On your back with me planted between your thighs." His expression turned teasing—tender and faintly amused. "To prevent that, you must stop a man much sooner than you did."

Madeleine stared at him as if he had grown fangs and a spiked tail. "You are . . . outrageous . . . despicable . . . horrible!"

"But I'm right. I am right!" She noted that he was breathing no deeper than usual while her own lungs burned with exertion. She met his eyes bravely and saw the old familiar smile in them. "Remember the lesson. Now, come here."

Bruised and confused by the last moments, she turned angrily away. At the beginning of the lesson his touch had been so welcoming, so enticing. She had not wanted to hurt him in return for the pleasure he had given her. She had thought he would be tender, would kiss her, make love to her again. Fool! He had deliberately used her feelings against her!

All the pleasure of the minutes before had evaporated. She choked on a sob, feeling used and humiliated, and very uncertain of what she had done wrong.

He came up behind her, but did not attempt to touch her. Yet she felt his presence along every nerve ending of her spine. Feeling much too vulnerable, she whipped around, a chilled look on her face.

"Ah," Sebastian said on a long breath of satisfaction, following all too accurately the complicated and tortured thoughts reflected in her expression. "You feel I have wronged you. You feel wooed and then abused by a suitor. That was your mistake."

He took a deliberate step back. "I warned you. Don't look to me for that. Any man with life between his legs can supply the answer to the question my harmless kisses roused in you. You are here to learn how to attract and hook and use for your gain the attentions of wealthy men who can give you the life you desire. Keep love and finer feelings out of it or they will ruin you."

His words struck the final blow to her three-week-old daydream. "I hate you."

He laughed, rich, insulting laughter that made her want to strike him again. "How childish you sound. You must conquer that tendency, also."

He reached out to catch the single tear trailing down her cheek on his fingertip, snaring it even as she averted her face. He studied the limpid drop on the point of his finger before destroying it with a stroke of his thumb.

His gaze came back to her with a leveling weight. "Men can be notoriously short with women who cry each time they are not given their way. The impatient and unimaginative often resort to beatings in an attempt to alter that behavior."

The silence was galvanized by his very stillness. Madeleine saw that his thoughts had turned inward. "My first mistress died at the hands of another lover. He did not understand her reluctance to perform certain, shall we say *tricks?* for his amusement. When he grew tired of her, he did not want any other man to have her. He conceived the notion that she had found a new lover, and he beat her severely. She died as a result. Do you wish to be beaten, Mignon?"

The gently spoken inquiry made the hair on her arms lift. The man she thought she knew had vanished behind some invisible but distorting glass. All trace of humanity had left his face. A cold cruel calculating mockery of his features froze her blood. "What happened to her murderer?"

"I called him out and killed him," he answered lightly.

She did not doubt that he was telling the truth. It answered a question she had not known how to ask before. How could he have done what he had just done? Because he was capable of much more.

"Never touch me in violence again," she said in a slow but steely cadence, "or I will leave."

He nodded shortly, the mask fading away. "Much better. To succeed as a mistress, you must act like a duchess. Duchesses never cry. They pout, they demand, they emote with great feeling, but they do not admit to their private hurts."

He took her hand, ignoring the token resistance she made and brought it to his lips with both hands to kiss it warmly. "I do not apologize, but I beg your pardon. I told you some of my lessons would be hard ones. You may well hate me when we are done. But, Mignon, you will know what it takes to get on in this world you have chosen. Now go and wash your face."

Madeleine met his gaze with resolve. To be dismissed like an errant child was the final humiliation. It burned in her throat like acid. "You make your point most effectively, monsieur. Now go to the devil!"

* * *

Sebastian glanced at his pocket watch. She was fifteen minutes late. His dinner was cooling. He repocketed the watch, noting the nervous shifting of the footmen. He debated whether he should go up after her. If he did, it would make things more difficult between them. She had not come to his laboratory after the incident in the music room. He supposed that was his fault, too. It was all his fault.

After he had cooled down, he realized that he had been very angry with her. She had only to look at him to make him want her. She had only to smile and he wanted to bask in it like a puppy frolicking in a pool of sunlight. He wanted all of her, in his library, in the ballroom, whenever and wherever they were together he wanted to make love to her. She wanted it, too. Her feelings for him were there in glorious detail in her dark eyes. He had wanted desperately to warn her off, to back her away. Now he had done it.

He doubted he would ever forget the shocked look on her face after she had slapped him. If he had turned on her like a rabid dog she could not have been more hurt, frightened, and offended.

Sebastian reached for his wineglass, amazed that he should be so filled with self-loathing. His damnable temper. His damnable father's temper. It had overtaken him.

He rose suddenly from his chair on this thought. Was she hiding because he had hurt her? Perhaps he had unknowingly wrenched her arm, or bruised her.

He was halfway to the dining-room doors when they suddenly opened.

She wore the old-fashioned gown she had worn those days when she had cooked for him, plain and dark and full-skirted with long sleeves. It was a servant's gown. Her expression was perfectly composed, but he knew it was meant to be a rebuff, an expression of her contempt for his authority over her. His lips twitched in admiration. It was very daring of her, considering the afternoon's events, but it eased his anxiety. If she was still capable of this measure of challenge he could not have badly wounded her.

"Mignon, how kind of you to join me." He pulled out her chair instead of waiting for one of the footmen to do it. "Wine for mademoiselle."

Madeleine noticed in passing that he had dressed in black velvet and satin, as if for a ball. She wondered if he had an engagement this evening, but she did not ask for fear of seeming too interested in him. Instead, she watched in guarded surprise as champagne foamed and filled her glass. Finally, she looked at him in inquiry. He was watching her with calm amusement.

"You are wondering why I am being kind to you after I treated you so ill this morning."

Madeleine had to pry her lips apart. *"Oui."*

He leaned back in his chair. "It is the way of some men. We are quick to anger and just as quick to forget that anger in the face of beauty." He leaned forward and set a small velvet box on the table beside her right hand. "A gift. A token of my esteem."

Madeleine withdrew her hand from its vicinity. "I cannot be bought, monsieur."

He smiled, his eyes spangled by candlelight. "I promised I would deal with you honestly. Life is not easy for any woman in this world. You will always be at the mercy of someone stronger until you have amassed sufficient wealth and power of your own. Now open the box and see if what it contains is not a pleasant investment for your future."

Madeleine thought about several possible responses, including hurling the box at his head. She suspected that he would think less of her for the childishness of her display, so she reached for the box, found the spring that held it shut, and released it.

Nestled in the black velvet interior was an inch-and-a-half-wide bracelet of pavé diamonds. The gold clasp was worked into the shape of a butterfly with yellow diamond wings and sapphire eyes. It was the most beautiful thing she had ever seen.

"This, too, was my mother's."

She glanced up at him without expression. "Did your father give it to her?"

Madeleine saw something new enter his expression! Anger, cold, intelligent, incisive anger. It made a rigid mask of his beauty, freezing out of it all human feeling. "Yes, an engagement gift like the hair brooch. I understand he once called her his *petit papillon*."

She watched him with a wary gaze. "They must have been very much in love."

"I do not know why she married him." His voice was curiously flat. "I do know that before she died, he gave her clothes and jewels to his whores. The butterflies were all he left her. No doubt they weren't flashy enough for harlots." His smile was as chilling as it was false. "So you see, you must never mistake generosity for love, nor love for constancy. Aren't you going to try it on?"

"Perhaps . . . later." She closed the box and put it in her lap.

The gift had become another lesson in the venality of men. She wondered if he was as bad as he thought he was. Or better yet, why she should doubt it.

"You are still angry with me."

She stared into the flames of the candelabra. "It is not the lesson that angered me, monsieur. It is the method you chose." She turned to him, her emotions mastered. "You might have warned me before you illustrated it."

"I might have. But would it have been as effective?" He said after a short silence, "Now you will always remember what happened and be on guard forever afterward, won't you?"

"Oui. But I will never like you for the lesson."

He held her hostile gaze where flames danced the dark depths. "Pupils never like their teachers until the lesson bears fruit. Another day, I will teach you how to protect yourself more rigorously. But not, I think, now."

The first hint of humor edged into her expression. "But I should like most vigorously to learn how to defend myself against you."

"I'm certain you would. But you might attack this lesson more aggressively than I am prepared to withstand. You will have your chance to pay me back, I promise."

Madeleine smiled a smile that was only partially reserved. "Most assuredly I look forward to the moment, monsieur."

He lifted his glass in salute. "Friends, Mignon?"

Madeleine lifted her glass slowly, her gaze speculatively on his. "To *la revanche,* monsieur."

"Touché, mademoiselle. To the rematch."

Thirteen

. . . *the marchesa gazed down the length of her flushed naked body into my face framed by her lush thighs. Sinuously, she disentangled herself and gently positioned me by her side. With a delicate finger she traced first the line of my cheek and then the curve of my lower lip gleaming with her body's moisture.*

"You have a very talented mouth, caro, *equally adept at conversation in half a dozen languages as well as the sweet, silent expressions of desire." Her finger drifted lower until she plowed one delicate finger in the black curls nestled above her cleft. "Will you not continue your facile dialogue with my body?"*

"Gladly, cara.*"*

"Dolcemento, mio cicisbeo," she murmured as I turned toward her and once more dipped my head to nibble at her.

As I licked her lavishly anointed femininity, she settled into a sprawling recline of open thighs that took better advantage of my salutation of that orifice with lips and tongue and fingers. It was to be expected that . . .

"C'est incroyable!"

Her cheeks flaming as if they had been brushed by nettles, Madeleine let the page of the ribald text drift from her trembling hand back onto the tabletop. For several long seconds she sat perfectly still, feeling hot and cold by turns, thoroughly shaken by what she had just read by mistake.

She had been set the morning task of reading Lord d'Arcy's theories on the management of money. Horace had informed her that the text was lying on the long table in the library. What she found were two identically bound manuscripts lying side by side. Random chance had set her hand on the wrong one. But once opened, she could not tear her eyes away from the amorous episodes unfolding on the paper before her. The hour designated for dull study had become instead a titillating perusal of acts of erotic revelry.

She licked her lips but it did not help. Her tongue was as dry as the rest of her mouth. To think that men and women did such things, and that someone—who?—had written about it.

More than half certain she already knew the author, she reached for the other manuscript to compare the handwriting to the first. The bold script was unmistakable. Lord d'Arcy had written them both.

She closed the texts and pushed both a little away as she rose from her chair. "So then, this is how a London rake misspends his leisure," she murmured. He collected salacious drawings and penned tales of his bedroom cavorts.

She moved slowly to the window. Beyond the distant line of trees the Channel gleamed like a snail track in the bright morning light. She concentrated her thoughts on the vista of the lovely day but they would not remain fixed there.

It had been more than three weeks since the night she had given herself quaking in fear and anticipation, to Sebastian d'Arcy. As the days passed it had come to seem nearly impossible that she had actually lain naked in his arms. His manner, almost fraternal since that night, had only added to her confusion. At times she felt, all reason aside, that their lovemaking had not occurred. But now, after reading that stirring text that affected her body in recognizable ways, the experience was impossible to deny.

She shifted her shoulders, discomforted by a lingering tightness deep down. The delicious sensations, as wondrous as they were unsettling, would not leave her. She suddenly realized why. They were irrevocably bound up in thoughts of Sebastian d'Arcy. Along with her shock lay an extraordinary curiosity to know if the tales were true. And if Lord d'Arcy could be so easily moved to rapacious desire by the great variety of women he wrote about, why did he spurn her? Was it because she was not as knowledgeable, as adventurous, as attractive as other women?

She took each point and examined it. How could she be as adventurous when no one had ever explained to her that any of the postures she had read about were possible? As for adventurous, he had challenged her not to seek his bed again until she could do so out of curiosity instead of affection. Well, her curiosity was now piqued! As for beauty, she did not know how to compare herself to the women whose nether anatomies were better detailed than their faces.

Still facing the window, she ran a questing hand over her breasts, finding a certain satisfaction in their full weight, better certainly than the lady in the hayloft who had been so reticent about her meager endowments. Her hand continued to trail over her hip, lush enough for the handfuls of flesh he seemed to so enjoy kneading during coupling. Her hand paused in embarrassment just short of where she ached low down. She bit her lip. She could not begin to know if she was adequate there, though the feelings stirring her womb were strong enough to make her want to squirm.

The moments had been so confusing, the pain and then the shattering bliss of being touched there. He had grunted and groaned like a man in agony but then whispered his delight in her. But perhaps she had missed something. If only she could do it again, and pay attention this time. He had agreed to teach her when she was ready. Well, most certainly now she was!

But what if he no longer had interest in touching her in the ways depicted in his text? What if she approached him and he refused her?

"Non! I will not allow that!"

"Will not allow what, sweeting?"

Madeleine turned back from the window so quickly her skirts tangled about her legs. Sebastian stood a few feet away, dressed for riding in a brown jacket, form-fitting buckskins, and boots.

He moved closer. "I hope you are not refusing to see me?"

"No, monsieur." The fiery sting of surging blood enveloped her as she took a guilty sidestep away from the table. Had he been standing there long? Oh, what difference did it make that her face was red and her heart was leaping like a hare crossing an open field? He might surmise any reason for her reaction to his sudden presence, but he could not, thank *le bon Dieu!* read her thoughts.

Sebastian did not need to read her thoughts. The reason for her discomfort was plainly stamped on her flushed face. She must have read at least a little of the manuscript he had planted as a tender trap. "Are you feeling well, Mignon?"

"Oui." He watched her try to master the high note of anxiety in her voice. "Of course."

"I only ask because you look a trifle . . . flushed." He did not hide his amusement. "One might almost say feverish."

She took a hasty step back as he lifted a hand to her brow. "I am fine, but really. I was thinking very hard that is all."

Thinking or feeling, convent brat? he mused behind a bland expression. She was shocked, that much was clear. He swung an arm in the direction of the table. "These feverish thoughts, do they concern your lesson?"

He felt almost sorry for her as she turned a stricken gaze on the two identical covers. "I—well, perhaps. All those numbers, because I am not very good, they make my head ache."

"Really? I was quite impressed with the way you corrected the arithmetic errors in my lab notes these last weeks."

Madeleine subjected him to one of her silences.

His smile widened. So, she was not going to admit to having perused his erotic text. That was encouraging. If she had been insulted or outraged he had no doubt she would have confronted him. What he saw in her suspiciously wide dark eyes was delicious and guilty curiosity. So much the better.

He walked over to the long table and picked up one of the texts. He heard her swift intake of breath and looked back over his shoulder. "Is something wrong, Mignon?"

"No, monsieur."

He picked up the leather portfolio. While seeming to examine the contents, he studied her in swift sidelong glances. Agitation quickly pinkened her cheeks. The dew of excitement beaded on her upper lip. Her hands were trembling as they hung by her sides. Best of all a strange excitement lurked in her eyes. She did not know which text he held. He was not going to enlighten her.

He looked up, his tone brisk. "Go and get your pelisse. I've had a lunch packed for us. We're going on a field trip."

Madeleine spent a moment studying the carpet's floral design in order to marshall her composure. "Where are we going?"

"Do you have other plans?"

She could not miss the twinkle that danced in his eyes when she looked up. "No, monsieur."

"No, *Sebastian*," he corrected. "Then I will meet you in the front hall in a quarter of an hour." He held out the leather folder. "Shall I bring your lesson along? Perhaps, on the way, you'd care to demonstrate for me what you've learned."

Her scarlet response almost made him laugh aloud. *It's only the beginning, sweeting.*

When she was gone, he chuckled as he glanced again at the erotic scribbling he held, then lifted his gaze toward the door through which she had exited. Had she thought of him while she read? Had she put herself, as he now did, in his partner's place? Flushed and shocked, covered in sheen of dampness and desire, had she writhed here in this quiet library in secret delight? Was she wondering what it would be like to be so thoroughly ravished? Very dangerous thoughts. The exact thoughts he wanted her to have.

It had come to him during the restless night that he was expending far too much effort in resisting her allure. Weighing his actions he could but conclude that he had behaved badly yesterday. The lesson had nothing to do with teaching her to be on guard against a rake's blandishments. He did not doubt that she had hesitated to rebuff him precisely for the same reasons he had sought to humiliate her. She wanted him. And he, heaven be merciful, wanted her.

He had believed that as a scientist he had to remain objective and dispassionate in order to properly evaluate his findings. Now he began to suspect that he had made an error in reasoning. By forbidding the natural course of seduction, he was allowing it to take on far too much importance in his overall training. Between two and two forty-five A.M. he had worked it out. This kind of self-denial was alien to him. By going against his own nature he was distorting his research. In denying his attraction, he had allowed it to become the ruling motivation behind every word, glance, and touch between them. They were two young healthy attractive people. Of course they wanted each other. It was natural lust, nothing more. By three A.M. he had faced that fact and formed a plan.

He would finish her education with only one change in his curriculum. He was going to teach her to glory in her beauty, to revel in the natural charms nature had given her. When he was done she would be a wholly sensual being, as certain of her sexual allurement as she was of the power to use it.

This little deception of the manuscripts was only the first in his campaign to free her from the constraints of modesty and virginal reluctance. If her desire for him arose through her own thoughts, then she would not feel she had been seduced or taken advantage of when they came together again. This time she would have to believe herself to be the seducer.

The day was bright, the sky a rare vivid blue background for dozens of white-cloud hillocks as they rode in a country carriage driven by Sebastian across the North Downs. Madeleine welcomed the warmth of the mid-October sun, for it was a distraction to her nervous anticipation. The idea had come to her while she was changing. She was going to seduce Sebastian d'Arcy.

Since she was committed to becoming a mistress, she was going to make certain she learned her sexual repertoire from him. But it was a daunting goal, and one best begun away from the prying eyes of his servants. Perhaps once she had lain with him again she would no longer mind the sniggering, smirking, and hostile glances she had met at every turn at the marquis's residence these last weeks. Just as the servants knew she had graced his bed once, they also knew she had not been there a second time. Well, that was about to change.

She was vividly aware of Sebastian's presence beside her. She could feel his confidence like a breeze against her skin. Their shoulders brushed together and his leg swung against her skirts whenever the cart hit a rut. The faint essence of his body warmed by the sun undercut the salty scent of the coastal air. She longed to lean against his shoulder, to tuck her arm in his, but she felt it was much too soon to touch him. "England is a beautiful land."

"It's autumn," he replied as they reached the shadow of one of the turf-topped chalk ridges that made up the Downs. "Do you know what that means in England?"

Madeleine shook her head.

"It means that the days of fine weather will rapidly deteriorate. In a week or two the sky will more often than not be gray, and dampness will lie like a sodden quilt upon the land." He pointed in the direction of the Channel, hidden for a moment as they rode tucked between the hills. "The seas will swell and fret. The tides will run more roughly. The wind will whistle at night and the skies will brew up a rain or two a week."

"It sounds most unpleasant," she replied, wondering why he should render so drab a picture of the place he called home.

"It's even more unpleasant for those who would go to sea. Sudden squalls play havoc with shipping."

Sebastian stole a sidelong glance at her as they entered the grassy lane between two tall hedgerows which cut off the view of the surrounding hop-fields, wondering what she would do if he slipped an arm around her waist. "A French sloop was skirting the shore last evening. I hear that after nightfall they put in west of Hythe and gave the local fishermen a fright. It's surmised they were meeting someone. What do you think?"

Madeleine looked at his profile, shaded and shadowed against the brilliant sky, and felt a wistful pang of desire. He turned his head and gave her a lazy teasing smile. His eyes were the cerulean of the sky. Sunshine polished his skin a pale gold as the wind ruffled his hair. If she but lifted her hand to his lean cheek . . .

"Have you no theory, sweeting?"

Madeleine blinked. He was waiting for her reply. What, she wondered dazedly, was the question? "I may be French, but that does not make me the Corsican's confidante."

"So then, Boney is no compatriot of yours?" His expression was faintly ironic. Lord, if only she would give him some sign that she welcomed his touch. "If you are not part of the advance to the invasion, then I suppose I may relax."

Madeleine switched her parasol from her right shoulder to her left so that it blocked her view of him. His daily reminders that their countries were at war disturbed her more than she wanted to admit. If he truly did not trust her, then why did he allow her to remain? Oh, but she knew the answer. She felt it in every throb of her pulse, in every baiting glance between them. He was not indifferent, only cautious.

Sebastian wondered at his clumsy conversation. It was not like him to rouse the enmity of a woman he wished to bed. Perhaps it was because he knew that if he did not hold Mignon at arm's distance a little longer he would end up ravishing her. Or perhaps it was because he liked sparring with her. He was never bored in her company and that in itself was a refreshing change. He had only to gaze into Mignon's solemn face to feel instantly aroused both intellectually and physically. Willing women were more plentiful than anything else in his life. This woman he wanted to know, inside and out.

The realization came as a distinct shock. For once in

his life, physical attributes came second in his estimation of a woman. Instinct told him to be wary. Desire told him to be bold. Practicality made him patient.

As the ground gradually rose toward a flat plain, Madeleine saw in the distance at the top of the gentle slope a broad tableland that was filled with people. Men and women were milling about what appeared to be a maroon-and-silver lake which undulated on the grass like waves on the water.

The scene could have been a gathering for a fair, except that there were no booths nor banners nor jugglers nor musicians. Yet the joyous atmosphere of an outing gained in intensity as they neared. Some men unloaded casks from drays and others unloaded what appeared to heavy coils of sailing ropes. Still others carried heavy tubing. In their wakes followed laughing children and barking dogs.

Sebastian halted the cart a good distance from the gathering. "Why don't we go and see what the excitement's about."

He promptly alit and turned to help her down. As his hands found her waist, their gazes met. For an instant she saw in his eyes a heat that had been missing for nearly a month. His smile seemed to answer her thoughts and then her feet touched the ground.

He swung the wicker basket containing their meal from his right hand to his left in order to offer her an arm as they crossed a low open bridge that spanned a stream no wider than a footpath. He lifted his hand with a cry of greeting.

A man in a heavy twill jacket and thick leather boots looked up, doffed his cap, and came quickly over the ground to meet them.

"Mornin', m'lord. M'lady. Grand weather for a sail aloft."

"I wish we were ready," Sebastian answered. "But today's exercise is only a test, Tobias."

The man nodded. "Still, if ye like, ye could take the lady up for a look round while we're checking the lines."

Sebastian turned a mischievous expression to Madeleine. "What a good idea, Tobias. Mademoiselle Mignon is quite fearless. Mademoiselle, allow me to present Captain Tobias Wickum. Captain Wickum is considered one of the foremost aeronauts in Britain. He has no less than fifty ascensions to his credit."

He saw the sudden smile she turned on the captain as she held out her hand. "What a pleasure to meet you, Captain Wickum. I once saw an ascension at the Tuileries. Never have I forgotten the bravery of the aeronauts. You are a hero, Captain!"

"I thank you, m'lady," Tobias replied. "That's high praise. High praise, indeed. I hope today's small demonstration will give you a taste for the experience. Be glad to take you aloft any time."

"Really, monsieur?" She turned a questioning glance on Sebastian. "Is this possible?"

His gaze flicked between the old man beaming as he pumped her hand a little too vigorously and Mignon's own shining expression. The wind had whipped color high in her cheeks. All his plans aside, he was suddenly and simply proud to be in the company of so fetching a young woman. "I suppose something could be arranged."

Tobias touched his cap. "I'll just be getting back. 'Twill take a while to fill her properly. M'lord."

Sebastian nodded and waved him on. "Take your time, Tobias. For our purposes today, we favor skill over speed."

When he was gone, Sebastian turned a knowing expression on Madeleine. "You've made your first male conquest."

She shrugged. "That wasn't my intent. I expressed a heartfelt sentiment."

"The best kind," he concurred smoothly as he took her arm to direct her toward the cliff and the sea. "Tobias will be recounting the story of your meeting in every grog shop from here to Dover. But, tell me, when did you see this ascension in Paris?" He bent a knowing glance on her. "One hears Napoléon finds ballooning of peak interest these days."

A frown of annoyance puckered her brow as she paced beside him. "I was four years old. It was one of Monsieur Blanchard's flights."

"How interesting. Then you know that Jean-Pierre Blanchard was the first to cross the Channel by balloon? He flew from Dover to Guisnes in two hours in 1784."

"That is the year in which I was born, monsieur."

"Really. So young? I've imagined you to be several years older. Perhaps it is the result of your vast experience of the world."

Madeleine turned her face from his, uncertain why he continued to bait her. She noticed men laying ropes out in a crisscross pattern on the ground. "What are they doing?"

"Setting up a flight to test the modifications of my balloon."

She spun about, halting him in his tracks. "Your balloon?"

He gazed into her upturned face. "You sound surprised. Any man with capital or the wherewithal to raise it can own a balloon. Of course, that does not necessarily mean he can find someone to build it for him."

"But you have found Tobias," she answered, wondering what he would do if she laid a hand on his firm cheek.

"Actually, the design is my own." Lord, how could she look at him like that and not expect to be kissed!

"You design balloons? Why?" If only he would touch her she would go willingly into his arms even here where dozens of strangers could see them.

"Because someone must," he answered fatuously and took her by the arm to steer her in the direction they had been heading. If he did not get her into seclusion soon, he was going to embarrass them both. "Let's eat our lunch while we discuss your fill of balloons. The ascension is hours away yet."

A hundred yards away from the ballooners he found a sheltered spot in the shadow of a stone outcropping that faced the sea. He took a blanket from the basket and spread it out on the tough grasses and then subsided in lithe grace upon it. "Aren't you going to join me?"

Madeleine turned back from her contemplation of the Channel to see he held out his hand to her. *Oui,* she thought recklessly, *I will join with you in every way you care to show me.*

She knelt on the blanket beside him and reached up to untie the ribbon that held her bonnet. She lifted it from her hair and shifted fingers through her curls to bring them to life.

Sebastian watched her through slitted lids. She had no idea how tempting she was, how he longed to sift his own fingers through her sable curls, how he longed to pull her close with a handful of those curls, to tip her face up to kiss her soft, plump lips. He leaned back on his elbows and stretched his long legs out.

As he watched her unbutton her pelisse, he decided that he would prefer to push her hands aside and slide each button free himself and then slowly peel it down her arms. He considered how he would kiss her throat, softly at first, then more intently, sucking her tender skin until he left a ring of love bites there for her to remember him by.

Mignon made him want to possess, to own, to label and brand and claim. He shut his eyes, feeling the answering need in his body take steely shape.

"The Montgolfier brothers originally used fifty-pound parcels of dry straw to fill their balloons with hot air," he said suddenly behind closed eyes. "For more intense heating, several bales of wool were interspersed with the straw."

"The hotter the air the better, *non?* "

He opened his eyes to find her watching him with quiet absorption. *She really listens,* he thought. Then he noticed that she had removed her pelisse and that an extraordinary expanse of her lush bosom was revealed by the gaping neckline of her gown. He became alert and watchful at the same time. When had she unhooked the back of her gown?

Her gaze left his for a moment traveling, to his unexpected delight, down his torso to his groin. "The balloon is flaccid as long as the air is cold. But when it is filled with heated air it expands greatly and rises, *oui?* " she suggested softly.

She was flirting with him! His erection stirred as he gazed at her beneath hooded eyes. "You've been reading again."

A smile teased her mouth. "I enjoy understanding how things work, monsieur." Her wandering gaze came coyly back to his and he felt his belly quiver. "One is not so afraid if one understands, *oui?* "

They both knew they were no longer talking of ballooning. The thought sent a tingling quiver of anticipation down his spine. "I applaud your reasoning. I do not want you to be afraid of any experience."

Madeleine blushed at his phrasing, and then his hand found her wrist and gently squeezed it. "Tell me more about your balloon, monsieur."

"We are by experimentation attempting to eliminate many of the obstacles to regulating balloon flight." Leaning up on one elbow, he slid a hand up her arm to the edge of her cap sleeve. "There are many practical problems. For instance, the small difference in density between hot and cold air. Normal air weighs about seventy-five pounds per one thousand cubic feet. Hot air weighs fifty-eight. Montgolfier's hot air balloons could rise but only so high, a distinct limitation."

He caught the lower edge of her sleeve between two fingers and tugged until it slid down her arm. "Then there is the need to continually feed the fire to stay afloat."

"How so, monsieur?" She leaned forward, braced by her arm, and her open neckline slipped down her bosom and caught on the crest of a nipple, revealing the full curves of her left breast.

Sebastian's slow, lazy smile lit up her middle. "The weight of the fuel greatly limits the cargo and number of passengers which may go aloft."

His fingers left her arm to skim the edge of her fallen neckline. He saw the blush that trailed his fingers' path and felt the globe of her breast tremble to his touch. "Fire is quite dangerous. If the wind tilts the gondola it may shift and fall apart, or worse, ignite the balloon."

Madeleine caught her breath as his thumb traced the shape of her nipple hidden beneath the tuck of fabric. "But there are now hydrogen balloons."

"Exactly." He reached into her neckline and cupped her breast. As she moaned he sat up swiftly and encircled her shoulders to pull her against his chest as he gently squeezed the fully mounded flesh. "Hydrogen gas is much lighter than hot air and so more buoyant and reliable." His hand tested the weight of the mound and found it compelling. "Once the balloon is filled and plugged, it will remain inflated for a very long time, thus great distances may be crossed over long periods of time."

Madeleine laid her feverish face in the crook of his neck and shoulder and sighed as his fingers closed over the aching bud of her nipple. She could not believe she was being so brazen, but she thought she would die if he suddenly drew back from her. "Once the balloon is filled there is no need for additional fuel?"

"Not once it's properly inflated." He nuzzled her ear with his lips. "So then the balloon itself becomes the source of the weight problem. The first balloons were made of waxed paper or heavy silk coated with caoutchouc, a crude rubber. But they did not always seal well. A sudden deflation in the midst of a trip can be embarrassing, if not calamitous."

His hand roamed freely inside her bodice, learning the different textures of her skin from delicate silk and creamy satin to finest velvet. "We are testing a much finer coated silk today, more like skin."

"Then the ride will be smoother and more certain?" she whispered, and gasped softly as he lifted her up onto his lap.

"The ride, sweeting, depends on the nature of the elements involved."

He lifted her again with an arm about her waist and quickly pulled the fabric of her skirts out from under her hips so that her bare backside lay against the stretched buckskin of his breeches. "It can be a smooth ascent, an easy gliding, then a gentle descent into the safety of the ground." He pressed his hips intimately to her naked bottom. "Other times it's a tumultuous ride with great shocks and buffets, shifts of quick risings and sudden plummets. That can be quite exhilarating."

He turned her face to his with a hand at her chin. The lazy amusement in his blue eyes was backed by fire. "Which, do you think, you would prefer?"

Madeleine looped her arm about his neck and gazed at him through passion-misted eyes. "The second sounds interesting but most dangerous, mon— Sebastian."

"Do you not like danger, Mignon?" He lifted a finger to touch her lips which were slightly parted from her effort to control her breathing. "Some of the greatest pleasures a man . . . or woman . . . can enjoy make the heart beat quickly."

His finger stroked along her lower lip as he bent his head to kiss her neck. The hand at her waist rose to cup from beneath a breast. "For instance, touching you makes

my heart beat faster." He lifted his lips from her neck.
"Does my touching affect you in the same way?"

Madeleine gazed at the sensual line of his mouth which
she wanted so badly pressed against her own. "I admit
nothing. An independent woman never reveals her feelings,
only her desires."

He leaned in closer to her so that his breath fanned her
parted lips, both of them oblivious to the men working
diligently nearby. "What do you desire, Mignon? Is it
me?"

Madeleine drew as far away as his bracing arm would
permit. Still gazing into his seductive blue eyes, she felt
as if she stood naked before him. Left no other defense,
she hid behind her wit. "You are a very attractive man
and I am a green girl whose experience with rakes is scant.
Of course I am drawn to you. You try so very hard to
make it easy for me."

His hand moved again, down over her stomach into her
lap. He pushed against her, forcing her legs slightly apart.
"Suppose I make it even easier?"

His hand delved into the warm, damp softness between
her thighs, rubbing the fabric of her gown back and forth
against her until she gasped with every motion. All the
while his challenging gaze never left hers. "Soft and
warm. Sweet, Mignon. How will you answer now?"

Her voice grew husky from his tantalizing rhythm and
its answering hot rush of drenching sensation. "You make
it . . . very difficult . . . to resist you, monsieur."

"I intend to make it impossible!" He kissed her hard.

Madeleine closed her eyes, telling herself that this was
what she wanted and marveling at how easily it had been
accomplished. But she was not an experienced wanton. She
could not completely close out the distant sounds of
strangers. Her passion was too new and tender to survive
the fear of discovery.

She leaned her head weakly against his shoulder when

he lifted his head to catch his breath. "Please, if some-one—"

"Shhh!" Sebastian did not want her to complete the thought. He knew the very instant she had started thinking and where her thoughts had gone and what they had done to her sweetly aroused desire. He did not think they would be disturbed. Even if they were, it would be worth it to him. But, he suspected, she would not yet understand the demands of a passion that held all else in contempt.

His hand left her lap and came to lift her face to his. He kissed her gently, holding her lips to his even when she would have pulled away. After a moment she melted against him, her lips pliant and clinging once more. He kissed her thoroughly, blending their mouths together in kiss after kiss until sweet longing coursed through her. He did not want her to lose the pleasure she had so quickly come to but could not yet fully have. He had waited long celibate difficult weeks for this moment. He would save it for them both.

"Do you trust me, Mignon?" he whispered when he had dragged his lips to her ear.

"I suppose I must," she answered with a shaky smile.

"Then I promise you, you will have your balloon ride this very afternoon. I promise!"

Madeleine wondered what he meant even as he lifted her back onto the blanket beside him. She stared in confusion as he delved into the picnic basket and began laying out their meal of bread and cold fowl, mustard, India pickles, and cheese. How could he contemplate eating when her lips and breasts and loins throbbed with thwarted desire?

She pushed her sleeve back up her arm and rearranged her loose bodice. When he noticed her actions, he said, "Turn around and let me hook you." He did so with remarkable skill. She did not linger over the question of where and how he had learned it.

Then he leaned back on one elbow and drew in a leg and ate with the gusto of a man who had accomplished a full day's satisfying labor.

Less enthusiastically, she picked at the cheese and bread, leaving the rest untouched. Really, men were incomprehensible.

. . . . .

Fourteen

"You see the casks there, m'lady?" Captain Wickum
was pointing out the fine points of an ascension to his
audience of one. "They contain a mixture of iron and zinc
shavings, water and sulfuric acid. The gas is produced by
the action of the water and the sulfuric acid acting upon
the metals. By means of the tubing laid out by the workers
they are joined to the central cask. The central cask is
open at the bottom and stands in a copper vat of water.
By passing through the central cask, the gas is cleansed
of impurities. The cleaned gas then passes into the neck
of the balloon via the nozzle being held aloft by the frame-
work. See how it's working?"

Madeleine did. The great envelope of maroon-and-silver
silk had begun filling with hydrogen, which ruffled its
silky contours as it began to bulge and sway in the wind.
Now she understood why there were so many people
about. By using padded poles and manipulating the network of ropes trailing from the balloon, they were prodding and supporting the thousand of yards of delicate silk
to help ensure its even inflation.

"It is so much more enormous than Monsieur Blanchard's," she said in admiration as the balloon belled to fill
the sky.

"That is because it is meant to carry fifty men."

Madeleine turned to see that Sebastian had returned
from his monitoring of the hydrogen-making apparatus.

"When fully inflated, the balloon will be more than 260 feet long." He traced the outline of the envelope with a hand to the sky.

"Why such a large balloon, monsieur?"

He grinned. "To carry soldiers, Mignon."

"Soldiers?" she echoed. "Who would want to do that?"

He stared at her, but he could not see any sign that she was other than serious. "The American colonial Benjamin Franklin predicted two decades ago, after witnessing an ascension in Paris, that balloons would become the fighting machines of the future. Rumor has it Napoléon is equally impressed. What do you think?"

Madeleine gazed up at the brilliant billowing silk slowly rising into the blue ether. "I think it would be a shame to make an instrument of death out of something so beautiful."

"That is not a very scientific answer, Mignon. That is a woman's answer."

She smiled faintly. "Am I not a woman, monsieur?"

He smiled down into her upturned face. *"Oui, mademoiselle,* you are most definitely a woman."

Captain Wickum grinned at the pair. "Don't suppose your lordship would like to take the lady on a tour of the gondola before it goes up?"

Sebastian's gaze never left Madeleine's face as he said, "What a good idea. How long do you propose to keep her aloft?"

"Oh, an hour, maybe more, depending on the wind. No need to fill her completely on account of she won't be making a voyage. Still she'll need stay aloft long enough to test her seams for strain under the weight we've allotted her."

"You intend to use trail ropes to keep her tethered?" Sebastian inquired as a wicked idea formed in his mind.

"Yes, m'lord. We sank an eight-foot anchor ring and are using the heaviest naval cordage." The older man's thoughts had followed his lordship's with alacrity. "It should be perfectly safe, m'lord. I'll just check on our progress."

"Why do men always label vessels 'she?' " Madeleine questioned as the captain walked away.

"It's a man nature to think of as female anything willing to accommodate him in its interior." Sebastian's grin was pure mischief. "Especially if it's equally unpredictable and temperamental. Or perhaps it has to do with how a vessel responds to a man's touch." He touched the brim of her bonnet under the pretext of straightening it and saw her lips part as if he had touched her instead. "When the vessel maneuvers well, he thinks of it as a lady. When it behaves badly, he's reminded of a willful vixen." His voice lowered half an octave. "When he's riding snug inside her and lulled by her movements beneath him, he cannot help but characterize her as a wanton."

Madeleine's voice took on a hushed quality as she said, "I don't know that I like the comparison, being a woman myself."

"I like your being a woman," he answered as his fingers moved to refasten the top button of her pelisse. When he was done, his fingers rested for a moment on her collarbones. "And very soon I'm going to show you how very glad I am that you are."

He caught her by the wrist. "Come now, quickly, if you want a ride."

Madeleine had been slightly dispirited ever since lunch, once she realized that it was not possible for her to fully seduce him with so many other people about. Her thwarted passions and anxiety over her boldness coupled with her lack of appetite had combined to put her in a sulky mood. So she resisted the tug on her arm. "Where are we going?"

Sebastian turned back to her with laughter. "I promised

you a ride. You said you trusted me. Don't balk, Mignon. You may never have another chance."

She was not yet certain of what he had in mind but she allowed him to pull her along in his wake.

Once they had skirted the people working frantically with poles and lines in the enormous shadow cast by the billowing fragile envelope of silk, she saw the balloon's gondola on the far side of the field. It was placed slightly on the down side of the rise, out of sight unless one had walked all the way around the balloon to the far side. It was shaped like a hull of a sloop but flat-bottomed without a keel. There was a gangplank from the grass up to its slightly elevated deck. Sebastian crossed it confidently, drawing Madeleine with him without pause.

He leaped down on the deck four feet below and then turned to lift her by the waist down beside him. The interior was built like a ship with sandbags hanging from the railing and several dozen waist-high barrels lashed into place fore and aft. "What are these for?" Madeleine asked as he approached the first set.

"Each barrel represents roughly a man's weight," Sebastian said as he released the ropes holding the gangplank in place. "We are testing the effects of stress on the lifting power of the envelope today."

"Why the straw on the floor?" she asked as the thick layer of dried grasses dragged at her skirt.

"A precaution merely," he answered as he watched the gangplank slip smoothly away. "The hay will act as a cushion should a barrel break free. A twelve-stone barrel bouncing freely could easily punch a good-size hole in the hull. A man would be less likely to do similar damage."

"I see," Madeleine said carefully. "And the gondola's shape? I have never seen anything but reed baskets."

"It was borrowed from an original design by Meusnier. Since Channel crossings are foreseen, if the balloon should fail to reach land this shipshape hull will float."

Madeleine's eyes widened in astonishment. Sebastian watched the shadow of the balloon pass overhead and then the sun emerge from beneath the edge of the silk ellipse.

There was the barest sensation of movement beneath her feet, but Madeleine scarcely noticed, for Sebastian was coming toward her with his arms outstretched. The gondola dragged a few inches, the wind tugging on the balloon she surmised, and then a slight free swing . . . and then nothing.

"I suppose we should go back," she said softly as he reached out to snag her bonnet ribbon with a forefinger.

"In due time and after a fashion." Sebastian pulled the ribbon free and tossed her bonnet in the straw.

Madeleine glanced quickly left and right, but she could not see anyone beyond the edge of the rail. Still, she felt compelled to say when he began unbuttoning her pelisse, "Someone might see us."

"Who do you suppose, other than a hooked-beak booby, has vision so keen?"

It occurred to Madeleine to wonder what had happened to the cheerful voices that had filled the afternoon air. She glanced again toward the railing. "I just think I should . . ." She turned to elude his arms and ran to the railing.

At first she saw nothing. The dizzying line of the horizon fell far below her expectation. As her gaze descended in desperate search of it, an equally disorienting sensation of heaviness began to invade her mind. By the time the two combined in understanding she saw that the ground had dropped precipitously away from her. In fact, it was far below her and receding with dizzying speed.

"Mon Dieu!"

She spun about and found Sebastian had come up behind her. "The world, it's gone!" she cried in fright.

"Not quite," he informed her. "Any second now we shall—!" The abrupt halt in their ascension snatched the floor out from beneath their feet and he caught her as her knees crumpled. "Yes, the trail ropes have caught," he mused aloud with a chuckle. "Presently, we shall know whether we are fixed like a kite in the sky or—"

The gondola swung wildly for a moment as he held on to her, but he could not keep his feet and they tumbled together into the straw-strewn floor. "—or in for a more memorable adventure than even I had planned," he finished breathlessly.

Madeleine struck at him with her fists. "You did this deliberately!"

He looked up at her from his sprawl, laughing and not bothering to dodge her halfhearted blows. "You did seem to want to be alone with me. I've simply provided the opportunity. *Ouch!* That's my nose!"

"You should have told . . . *ooh!*"

Madeleine's voice drifted off as the floor beneath them swung once more in a left-sided arch and her stomach took off for the opposite point on the pendulum. She flung herself, facedown and spread-eagle, into the straw beside him.

Then the vessel suddenly straightened and stilled and hung, humming lines and all, in the taut stillness of the autumn sky.

Though she believed she was paralyzed by fear, Madeleine moved first. She pushed herself upright on her knees and scrambled away from Sebastian. "Stay back!" she cried as he sat up, presenting a rakish charm with straw clinging seductively to his hair and clothing. "Don't touch me!"

"Now, Mignon, how can we make each other happy if we don't touch?" he asked in maddening reason.

He climbed to his feet and dusted off his jacket. "But, before the preliminaries, I think I should inform the ground crew that we are well." He walked over to the side of the gondola and leaned out so far Madeleine thought he might tumble head-first over the side. Then she saw his arm moving back and forth in a wide sweep. He was signaling.

She stood up slowly, testing the reliability of the treacherous ground beneath her feet. It seemed steady now but vibrated with a force not unlike that of a ship at sea. There was no rise and fall, but the tension of forces working against one another was unmistakable.

Sebastian turned back in time to see the gathering panic in her face and then she launched herself at him. She pressed her full length into him, seeking to become part of him. *"Mon Dieu! Mon Dieu!* I want to go down!"

Having felt much the same during the initial seconds of his own first ascension, Sebastian gathered her close. "Hush, Mignon. It will be all right." He kissed the crown of her trembling head. "Don't you want to see what so few people have ever seen? The view is quite spectacular."

She buried her face even deeper in his jacket front. "Don't . . . won't . . . can't" were the only words he could pick out of her mumblings.

He told himself that he only needed to hold her until she collected herself and that she would again be rational. That she really should enjoy the gorgeous afternoon. That if she looked southeast, as he was doing over the top of her burrowed head, she would see her homeland in the form of the coastal towns of Calais and Boulogne-sur-Mer.

But she was rubbing herself against him so enticingly. Her little body squirmed so sensuously the long-denied emotions of sexual desire and sweet longing coursing through him were overpowering cold reason. It was dangerous, but he knew they had to have each other, or they would both explode.

He caught her tightly to him, molding her hips to his as he ground himself slowly against her. She moaned, but whether from desire or fright he could not yet be certain. He stroked her from shoulder to thigh, luxuriating in the incredible feel of her beneath her gown. And then he was lowering her down onto the straw-covered floor of the sloop, lifting her skirts away so that her heated skin, satin smooth and pulsing with life, was exposed to his touch.

He held her to her knees before him as he stroked her bare hips and bottom. How soft she was and yet how firm, a perfect fit against him. He wanted to tell her how he had been waiting for her. But he said nothing because words carried weight, and promises, even unintentionally given, would be impossible lies.

His hands lifted to stroke her face, to calm and reassure her as his words must not.

His fingers were gentle. Madeleine felt in the shape of muscle and bone and warm skin the strong gentle reality of the man before her. And then he was kissing her.

She arched under his caresses as he pressed her back into the clean straw, meeting the subtle pressure of his hand with her body. Her hands found his shirt and pulled it out of his waistband and then they slid under up his chest, rubbing, soothing, pressing and skimming over his skin. His belly quivered at her delicate touch. This was not like the first time when she had been thinking and waiting, afraid and uncertain. This time she was a woman who knew exactly what she sought. When she touched him lower down, brushing his arousal with the back of her hand, a groan of pleasure was wrung from him. At his response, she tightened her arms to bring him closer than before.

Sebastian had promised himself that he would not rush her, would let her set the pace but waves of urgent sensation rippled through him as she lifted his shirt and pressed an openmouthed kiss over his left nipple. Her hot little tongue licked him and then drew a circle on his chest. The intensity of desire tightened painfully in his groin.

"Lord, sweeting, wait!"

He caught her hands with one of his own, as with his other he molded her body to his. He lifted her up to unfasten her gown and then he stripped it down her arms. And then he laid her back in the straw and took one hard-budded nipple in his mouth. She arched up under him and he threw a leg across her thighs to hold her as he suckled her with a need to match her own.

Glorious sensation streaked through Madeleine. She pulled a hand free of his grasp and brought it to her mouth, biting a knuckle to keep from crying out her pleasure.

Sebastian lifted his head and smiled. "No, sweeting. Don't hide from me." He took her hand from her mouth. "I want you to cry for me, beg for me." He kissed the teeth marks embedded in her skin. "Let me know how I please you."

Madeleine gave up control to him as he kissed her. His tongue plunged in and out of her mouth in a sinuous rhythm as old as time. Everywhere he touched her became a flashpoint of sensation. She was melting. His velvet-rough tongue licked at her lips, her eyelids, her ears, her breasts; a flickering sleek wet flame over her skin until she was writhing in need.

His mouth sent new and vibrant messages deep down into her body. She did murmur then, whimpered as he tugged at her so sweetly.

The wild hunger was building inside her. The deep clamorous need tensed sensitive nerves and delicate muscles that made her body shift and undulate beneath the heavier weight of his. She did not know when or how he had undressed but he was suddenly warm skin against hers, the firm walls of his chest pressing the softer mounds of her bosom.

Then he was sliding down her, his mouth leaving a hot wet trail that turned instantly cold in the high altitude. She began to shiver, wanting to tell him to stop. He *must* stop before she shivered to death. But he was moving lower, over her breasts and below, past her waist and the indentation of her belly button, over the slight swell of her abdomen. Fingers touched her fleece and then parted her.

"Oh!"

His fingers found her first, the pulsing weeping center that begged a touch she could not quite ask for. And then his lips followed and she cried out at the exquisite sensation, no longer afraid of a pleasure too great to hold inside her.

Sebastian rose up quickly to stroke her face. "You love it, don't you?" he whispered against her mouth. "You are made for this. Let me show you," he whispered, and kissed her cheek. His hand slid down once more to the juncture of her thighs. "Open to me and let me please you as you deserve. That's right." His fingers slid in a little. "Oh, Mignon, feel how badly you need me there. Let me reward that need." He snaked down her body once more, wedging his shoulders between the sprawl of her thighs, their skins never breaking contact.

He seemed to possess a perfect knowledge of her, of what she needed and where and how much. A light touch here, a stronger touch there, the rhythm of fingers and tongue surpassing even the descriptions of joy she had read.

Sebastian smoothed her fretfulness with hands splayed over the silkiness of her belly. Then he framed her hips with his hands, lifting her for his mouth. He heard her cries of release in gratitude. He wanted only her pleasure, her happiness, for her to sing his praises in this most flattering of songs. He stayed with her until her body stopped quivering and her cries turned to gasps and then to sobs. He felt drunk with the power he possessed to please her. She was made for this, made for him.

Finally, he moved up over her, shedding his breeches as he did so. He emerged hot and heavy throbbing against her belly. As he lifted himself and gently parted her thighs, he smiled into her eyes. And she smiled back.

Armed with the knowledge that he had been waiting for

this moment to come again, ever since he had foolishly left her in his bed that first night, he took his time. He smoothed a hand over her silky skin, first her belly, then an admiring caress for each of her breasts.

"You're so lovely," he whispered, surprised he had been moved to speech. Yet, how soft she was and how real. More real than any other woman he had ever touched. And he would be grateful to his last breath that she had chosen him to be her lover.

He frowned at that thought, wondering from whence it had come, and at such a moment. Cads lied, seducers dissembled, practiced libertines omitted.

He entered her slowly, sighing as her wet swollen warmth opened for him. She arched beneath him and he cupped her from beneath to brace her hips as he pressed strongly into her. He heard her gasp and hoped he did not hurt her. She was so narrow and so hot. Before he could inquire, she arched under him again, this time setting her heels in the straw, and he felt himself sink deep within her.

He began moving in and out of her, lifting her higher and higher with each thrust until her cries matched his groans and then blended in perfect harmony, drowning out every other consideration in the world.

Neither of them spoke a word for a long time, There was no need.

He remained in her for as long as he could, unwilling to separate even a few inches. Something had occurred which he dared not think about.

Finally, he stirred, the rough drag of his cheek abrading her love-swollen skin. "I suppose we should signal again." But he did not move.

Madeleine curved a hand about his cheek, and he leaned forward to kiss her, sucking her lower lip with the same strong urgency he had her breasts. And then his fingers moved to the markings he had left like a ring of strawberries along her neck. His mark. How strange that need to brand her with his touch.

When his gaze met hers he was suddenly for the first time in many years, doubtful of a woman's response to his loving. "Are you all right?" he asked gently.

She slowly shook her head but she was smiling. She touched his face carefully, for it seemed to her he was so taut he might shatter like spun sugar. "Have you ever made love in a balloon before?"

His face was so serious he could have been in pain. "I've *never* made love quite like this before."

She nodded and touched his mouth reverently. "I think I believe you."

The balloon test had been declared a success. Major Wickum had stayed behind to see to the deflation and storage of it. Despite the nobleman's reputation, no one watching Lord d'Arcy and his lady companion drive away guessed that the pair had spent their afternoon entangled on the floor of a hydrogen balloon, the world's first aeronautic lovers.

"However distasteful you may find it, wars stimulate the endeavors of science," Sebastian said crisply, making a point in his argument. "Your countrymen have made it of necessity an art."

Madeleine bridled under this declaration. "Do you mean to say you think the French are more bloodthirsty than the English?"

Sebastian gave the pony his head over a particularly rough patch of ground as they journeyed homeward.

"Let us examine that possibility. The famous chemist Lavoisier helped both the American and French revolutions by his improvement in the manufacture of gunpowder. The French Revolution repaid his efforts by lopping off his head with the guillotine as a profiteer." His smile was ironic. "But the French are generous people. A year later, they rescinded their actions and made him a national hero. I'm certain that, wherever he is, Lavoisier has forgiven them their moment of pique."

Madeleine sniffed. "I don't know that I can believe you."

"I'll admit that other scientists fare better in France." He proceeded to cite several names, elaborating on the accomplishments of each.

"You seem to know a great deal about the French techniques of warfare," she observed suspiciously. "What is your interest?"

He smiled charmingly. "I am a scientist, too."

"And half French?" she suggested tartly.

He glanced at her sharply. "Who told you that?"

"I don't remember. Someone on the staff mentioned that your mother was French. It was after the incident."

The fact that she looked away quickened his interest. "What incident?"

Madeleine considered how to answer. After the incredibly blissful afternoon she had spent making love among the clouds, she felt close enough to reveal to him almost, but not quite, everything. "I am not liked by your English staff, monsieur. Because I am French I am much whispered about. Some say I've come to England to do mischief."

Sebastian did not miss the careful wording that someone else might have mistaken for her lack of facility with English. "This caused an incident?"

"The morning after my arrival, one of your upstairs maids received word that her seaman son had died during a French shelling of the English blockade. She took great exception to a Frenchwoman's presence in the house. Monsieur Horace was kind enough to remind the staff that your own mother was a French lady."

Sebastian suspected he was not hearing the whole tale. "Why wasn't I told?"

Madeleine shrugged. "A small thing, really." At the time she had been afraid to tell him that she was the cause of the altercation. The woman, wielding a butcher's knife, had been disarmed by two of the footmen, but not until Madeleine had grabbed a boiling pot and threatened to douse her. If she had remained helpless she very much doubted anyone would have come to her aid until blood had been drawn. Still, the woman's grief was real, as was her loss. She needed her job and Sebastian would have had no choice but to dismiss her as an example of a servant who had dared attack another member of his staff. "Tell me more of these scientific discoveries, Sebastian. Your country's perhaps?"

"Another time. We're home."

Madeleine looked up. They had arrived back at Sebastian's residence more quickly than she had expected. As they entered the gates, she spied a horse on the drive. The animal wore the ornate full-dress housings of officer's mount.

Halting the cart suddenly, Sebastian murmured, "It would seem I have company." And not to his liking, for he recognized that livery as that of the Royal Horse Guards. Whitehall had come to him. They must be desperate.

He flicked the reins, sending the pony cart past the front door and around toward the servants' entrance.

When he had reined in, he turned to Madeleine. "I am going to ask a personal favor of you, Mignon. I want you to enter the house by the servants' door and go straight to your room and stay there until I come for you." He smiled at her in a way that said he would have touched her had they not been sitting before a dozen windows through which they might be glimpsed. "It may be late."

Madeleine nodded, understanding that for whatever reason, he did not wish her to be seen. "I will wait."

Sebastian climbed down, saying more loudly, "The Royal Institution of London, established by Count Rumford before he left England for France, hosts an excellent series of lectures both philosophical and scientific. I should be happy to escort you to one, if you like, when next we're in London."

He made the astounding invitation seem matter-of-fact. *As if he expects that I will be with him in London,* she mused as he helped her down. *I wonder why.*

He stepped away briskly as a footman came out to take command of the cart and headed toward the front of his house.

Madeleine did not look at the footman nor at the maid she passed in the kitchen hallway. Nor did she glance at the upstairs maid she met on the backstairs. She went straight up to her room, stripped off her bonnet, pelisse and boots, and fell across her bed and instantly to sleep.

Sebastian entered his salon with a quick angry stride. It did not temper his mood to find a major of the Royal Horse Guards dressed in the full regimental uniform of brilliant red laced coatee, crested helmet, and gilt-and-laced *sabretache* sampling his brandy. The entire county of Kent must have been aware of him traveling through its borders in the broad daylight.

"Why did you not simply carry a banner writ large with the words: 'Whitehall requires Lord d'Arcy! Take notice!' Damnation! I hate incompetence."

"Perhaps that is why General Armstrong thought to include me in the major's entourage," a woman's lilting voice said from the depths of a settee turned at right angles away from Sebastian. She then rose to show herself.

Sebastian's years of boudoir contretemps held him in good stead. "Lady Elizabeth, a delight!" he greeted with just the right degree of warmth to suggest the nature of their former acquaintance.

She dimpled prettily. Her gown was scantily cut for an

October evening and her pale hair had been arranged with the suggestion that it had just been ruffled, or needed to be, by a masculine hand. "That is more like it, Sebastian. I began to think your powers of discernment were failing. Once you boasted you could tell within an hour when I had been in a room."

That was before his senses had been filled to brimming with the haunting taste and smell of Mignon, Sebastian mused ruefully. Lord! Her fragrance lingered on his skin like an expensive perfume. Self-preservation kept him from approaching the lady before him, lest she catch the telltale scent of the afternoon's lovemaking.

He put up his hands in defense when she would have approached him. "You will excuse me a moment, Lady Elizabeth. I have been in the fields all day with my laboratory assistants and smell of—well, smell."

Her eyes widened slightly in distaste. "By all means see to your ablutions, Sebastian. The major and I have shared a most comfortable journey down. I imagine we shall find a method of entertaining ourselves until you've returned." She favored the handsome young officer with a particularly intimate smile meant to rouse Sebastian's jealousy.

The fact that he had never been jealous did not enter into it. He had once been careful to mark all rivals, but, in Elizabeth's case, he felt not the slightest twinge of interest in her bed partners, be it the major or any other man.

He glanced at the major. "I assume you have a message for me?"

Without a word the young man opened his *sabretache* and withdrew an envelope sealed with the emblem of the Horse Guards.

Sebastian took it and smiled. "I imagine I will be some little time deciphering it. You will excuse me if I am late for dinner. I will have my butler see to your needs." He bowed in Lady Elizabeth's general direction before withdrawing.

It was nearly midnight when Madeleine heard footsteps outside her door. She had eaten alone in her room but she was not unaware that Sebastian had dined in company that included a very beautiful lady from London. The house was abuzz with the news of the new arrivals.

She tried not to think about what the lady's presence might mean. She tried not to attach any significance to the fact that Sebastian had not stopped by to at least reassure her. She tried and failed not to resent being sent a tray in her room as though she were too young or gauche or inferior to share the table with his noble guests. She *did* resent it, and she hated without even seeing her the woman who had spent the evening basking in Sebastian's company.

She had not gotten ready for bed, remembering his promise to come to her room, regardless of the hour. But she was glad she had slept a little and then washed and changed into her last neat gown. Each time she closed her eyes she felt again the sway of the gondola beneath her and the sensation of Sebastian surged over and in her.

Her door suddenly opened without a knock, which surprised her almost as much as seeing Sebastian enter in full evening dress. That did not perk up her spirits.

"I am sorry but— You're not abed," he said in amazement when he realized she was sitting by her cold hearth in the glow of a single candle. "Where is your fire?" he demanded.

"I'm not a guest but a servant in your home, monsieur," she reminded him in a perfectly friendly voice. "The maids do not rekindle it after dark."

"They will——" Sebastian broke off that statement as he came across the room toward her. They would not. He had come to do something that four short hours ago he would not have thought possible. He had come to send her away.

He did not say anything for a moment, simply stood above her watching the candlelight play over the planes and curves of her face. He had known more beautiful, more voluptuous, more skilled and certainly more ribald women. But there was something singular about Mignon. "I don't even know your last name."

Madeleine nearly told him. She had decided as she sat in the room waiting that it was time her masquerade ended. He deserved to know who she was and how and why she had deceived him, but the scent of lilacs stopped her.

"She must be a beautiful woman."

Sebastian started. "Who?"

"The woman who smells of lilacs." She could not be certain for it was too dark, but she thought his countenance darkened in a blush.

"Beth always wore too much perfume."

Beth. Not Lady Elizabeth. Not even Elizabeth.

Sebastian debated how much of the truth to tell her. Elizabeth's presence in his home was a ruse. As the woman herself had explained at dinner, the thought was that any spy would assume General Dighton's profligate wife had come to Kent under military escort to renew relations with an old lover, perhaps even initiate a *ménage à trois*. In truth, she had come as cover for the major who had brought him very disturbing orders. The major would be gone in the morning while Elizabeth would remain a few days. But she would not be sharing his bed. He had been ordered across the Channel for a very delicate and perilous enterprise. Down on the coast a ship was waiting for him at this very moment. Of this he could tell Mignon nothing, nothing at all.

He squatted down before her and took her hands in his. "You're cold," he said in accusation. He did not wait for her to answer but leaned forward and scooped her up from the chair into his arms. He carried her to the bed and sat down on the mattress with her still in his lap, and pulled the counterpane up over them both.

"I thought you'd never come," Madeleine said as she hugged him.

The first misgivings about touching came as she settled with a sigh against him. Contrarily he nestled her more closely to his chest, tucking her curly head under his chin. "Now listen to me, Mignon, and don't interrupt me with fractious comments. You've been a good and clever student. Our delightful afternoon convinces me that you're ready for the next step." Keep the moment light, he reminded himself, but it was so hard when he knew he might be holding her for the very last time. "Therefore, I'm going to reward you with a trip to London."

He felt her body tense against him, but she said nothing. "I'm arranging to rent a small house in Belgrave Square for you. I'll also write introductions for you to several friends. I'll say you are a distant relation on my mother's side, which accounts for your being French. It is off-season in London. Only those who are not fox hunters will be in town, which is excellent as it will give you time to become adjusted before the crush begins around Christmas."

He went on a little more sharply. "You will, of course, need clothing. You are to have a generous allowance at Madame Helène's. You will find she is the most skilled dress maker in London. Your innocence is your greatest weapon. Dress as a young lady in her first Season."

He looked down hoping to glimpse her expression, but her face remained tucked to his chest. "Lady Elizabeth has graciously offered to arrange several social outings for you. My cousin Bram can be counted on to act as your escort. He is a solid reliable sort, engaged to be married shortly. He'll be happy to squire you about, but you are not to attempt your first liaison with him. Is that understood?"

She did not even twitch a finger. "I've grown very fond of you, Mignon. But we agreed at the outset that a relationship between us is impractical. The point of the experiment is to see if it can be acted upon. You must make this next step, for yourself as well as for the sake of my scientific curiosity. I will come to see you in London—"

"When?"

"Once you're settled. I would not for the world wish to queer your path. The too-pointed attentions of a rake such as myself might discourage your more reluctant admirers."

He steeled himself for a last bit of jaded wisdom. "Remember what I've said about your choice of lovers. They should be men of whom you are fond but hold no strong affection. Romance is for the entrenched. Be prudent, careful, and discreet. Within a year London will be yours. Then you may take to bed whomever you wish. Have you any questions?"

"Oui." Madeleine was surprised by the sound of her own voice. She thought there must be too many tears in her throat to allow for sound. "Is Lady Elizabeth your former mistress?"

"Nothing quite so formal." Sebastian was usually more tactful when answering one woman's questions about another, but he knew he must drive a wedge between them.

The afternoon had been perfect, too perfect. He had learned that he was capable of falling in love, as his reason defined that emotion. The realization did not please him. The fact that he could love did not negate the possibility that in loving he could still destroy.

So then, he would finish the tutelage he had begun with this last lesson: that the truest pleasures involved the strictest discipline. The purifying refinement of every genuine voluptuary lay in the piquant torture of loss. Through suffering she would learn self-control over her emotions.

"There is a last matter which we, well, we have not covered. It is in regard to *les redingotes d'Angleterre.* A device, sweeting, which a gentleman wears to keep a woman from coming to bed with child."

"You have never before mentioned such a thing," Madeleine whispered.

"An abysmal oversight," he agreed and one he fervently hoped would not come back to haunt either of them. "But as there is no time to explain its use sufficiently, I ask you to appeal to Lady Elizabeth for explanation. She's a sophisticated and discreet woman of the world. When she returns to London at the end of the week she can be counted to advise you in this and other matters."

"I won't require the pity of your mistress," Madeleine said proudly as she raised up from him. So, Lady Elizabeth was staying on here . . . with him. That would explain why she was no longer needed. She did not look at him, for she knew she would shame herself with tears. "When am I to leave?"

"In the morning."

She did turn to him then. "So soon?"

He lifted a hand to touch her face but did not. "Yes."

There were so many things he wished he could say. But he knew it would be cruel to make promises he did not believe he knew how to keep, nor even if he would be around to make the effort.

Madeleine stopped her mind utterly from thinking about the coming morning. She reached up and curled an arm about his neck. "Stay with me tonight."

Sebastian felt that much maligned organ, his heart, split like an overripe fruit. "No. I am expected elsewhere this night."

She snatched her hand away. "In Lady Elizabeth's bed?"

He set his jaw and lied. "Yes."

Fifteen

"Who do you suppose she is, this Mademoiselle Mignon?"

"Can you not guess, *ma soeur?* Lord d'Arcy's new mistress, of course."

Henrice and Justine Foucant peered curiously through the window of the hired hackney up at the simple four-story Georgian-style brick house on Belgrave Square. The invitation to this house had come just after nightfall the day before. Henrice had been in favor of ignoring it, but Justine had had one of her dreams during thè night, brought on by a migraine. In it she had been told that her future lay behind the door of this address.

"I hope your aching head is not in error of good judgment," Henrice pronounced ominously.

"C'est impossible! My head pains always presage good luck."

Justine reached up to adjust her newest purchase, a chip bonnet with an autumn gold plume which curved flirtatiously above her brow. It complemented, not surprisingly, the golden-brown velvet tunic she wore over a white long-sleeved muslin gown in concession to the cooling breezes of October. Henrice wore a tucked silk bonnet with matching purple velvet spenser, trimmed in gold tassels, as were her embroidered bag and slippers. The Foucant women were in full battle dress to meet an enemy, a female rival for the affections of Sebastian d'Arcy, marquis of Brecon.

They waited for the driver to ring the bell and then alit and mounted the steps to the door which was opened by the d'Arcy butler.

"Monsieur Horace!" Henrice greeted in a mixture of surprise and vexation. "But what are you doing here?"

Horace bowed formally. "Madame. And . . . Madame. A pleasure as always." But there was a doubtful frown on his normally placid face. "I am on loan, as it were. Were you expected?"

"We were summoned," Henrice answered sharply, "by the marquis's own hand. There is a person, a Mademoiselle Mignon in residence here, *mais oui?*"

"Yes, madame." He moved back to allow the French-women to enter. "If you will wait in the salon," he indicated the room, "I shall inform the mademoiselle that you are arrived."

The house was deceptively small from the outside. The sumptuous salon they entered boasted stuccoed walls painted a soft green and topped by fine corniced scroll-work of papier-mâché which divided them into compartments. The chimney was of carved statuary marble depicting Aphrodite's birth on a clam shell and flanked by half columns of pale-pink marble. The ceiling was medallioned and the rugs were Flemish. The furnishings were a fine collection of Chippendale. A few of the Adam-designed pieces were instantly recognizable to Henrice's sharp eyes as having once graced Lord d'Arcy's own home. Whoever the *fille de joie* was, it was clear she had snatched not only the marquis's interest but also his pursestrings. And how quickly!

"This should have been Madeleine's house," Henrice said with barely contained anger. "Now it is wasted on this—this Mignon creature! Sebastian was never so senti-mental before. Look there on that table. That is the Greek bust I gave him for his twenty-fifth birthday!" She set her jaw, thoroughly put out with her young man. "You can be certain this *petite amie* is far more clever than the usual sort. Of course, she is French!" she ended as if that fact gave some consolation.

"Why should Lord d'Arcy wish us to be kind to his mistress?" Justine questioned in pique.

"Because we are now in his debt." Henrice looked cross. "I told you we should have sent his money right back. We do not need his pity."

"But then we would not have been able to appease Monsieur de Valmy. He was most agitated over Madeleine's departure."

Henrice shrugged. "Another deserter of my affections. I shan't forgive either of them, ever!"

"That is a circumstance greatly to be pitied."

The two sisters rose abruptly to their feet at the sound of the lady addressing them in perfect French.

Mademoiselle Mignon stood before the door which had opened and closed so silently that neither of them heard it. She wore a fine silk muslin frock embroidered in leaves. A deep bertha collar edged in lace covered her bosom. A *cherusse* with rows of pleated ruffles framed her face from cheek to chin. Her mink-dark curls had been brushed up and tied with a deep-green velvet ribbon to match the sash under her bosom. Only those ringlets closest to her face hung free.

There was something familiar about the elegant young lady, but it was not until she came within ten feet of them that the Foucant sisters blurted out in chorus, "Madeleine!"

"I was told to expect visitors today. I was not told whom." Madeleine was glad her voice did not crack for she had feared she would not be able to carry the moment off once Horace told her who was below. "Horace tells me Lord d'Arcy invited you here."

"Oui, but he did not mention you," Justine said with a smile of delight. "But what are you doing here, *ma petite?*

Do you know this Mademoiselle Mignon? Neither Henrice nor I have yet met her. Which is why—"

"Enough chatter, Justine," Henrice interrupted coolly. "Madeleine has something she wishes to tell us."

Madeleine clutched her hands, then released them at once. "I am Mademoiselle Mignon."

Henrice was almost too stunned to quite believe the implication behind her niece's announcement. She glanced at the doors. "Is this Lord d'Arcy's residence?"

Justine turned to her sister with a frown. "Lord d'Arcy's residence? But how can this be?" She glanced back at Madeleine. "Have you met Lord d'Arcy?"

"I think they have more than met," Henrice said smoothly, her gaze discerning as she observed Madeleine's defiant gaze and flushed cheeks. "You have taken a lover, Madeleine. It is Lord d'Arcy, *oui?*"

Madeleine inclined her head briefly.

"Madeleine!" Justine cried in mixed dismay and delight. "You have truly taken Lord d'Arcy as your lover? *Félicitations, ma chère!*" She hurried over and swept her niece up in an enveloping embrace, murmured French congratulatory expressions usually reserved for the newly married bride.

Henrice briefly closed her eyes as if a pain had unexpectedly struck her. In a way it had.

She had been prepared to give her niece to Sebastian. She had convinced herself that it was the wisest and best match in England for the pair of them, and she was right. But she had not considered up to this very second how she would feel when she learned that her niece, young enough to be her own daughter, took that splendid young man into her bed. He had had dozens of paramours since he left her sheets for the last time nearly ten years earlier. But not one of his lovers, even those she knew, had ever caused her a moment's jealousy. Yet the piquant sense of loss brought by Madeleine's admission, struck her sharply. Time moved on, the world turned, years advanced. Young lovers chose younger mistresses. *C'est la vie.*

She opened her eyes and loosed a self-satisfied smile. "You see, Madeleine? I knew you were meant to be one of us. But how and when did you acquire the sense to realize it?"

Madeleine met her aunt's critical gaze with perfect calm. The dangerous moment, the one she had been trying to prepare for ever since she returned to London three days ago, had passed. She was not as shaken by the wake of confrontation with her relatives as she had expected. Perhaps it was because she had so exhausted herself with fits of tears during the last three days that she had no real capacity left for shock or shame or even anger. "After due consideration of the alternatives, I decided to pursue your suggestion. But I preferred to do so in my own way."

"You ran away like a naughty ill-bred child!"

Madeleine's smile deepened. "You will admit, however, that I succeeded, for I presume you received my bank draft?"

"We did! Such a treat." Justine touched the brim of her bonnet. "Do you approve?"

"Very nice," Madeleine answered, but she was watching Henrice, who glanced about the room.

"Lord d'Arcy has been most generous to you. Does he know who you really are?"

"Non. I presented myself to him at his country house in Kent as Mignon, *chef de cuisine."*

"And your excellent skills won him for you!" Justine declared. "I knew it! The quickest way to a man's purse strings is not always through his breeches."

Henrice saw Madeleine flinch, but her overall mantle of calm remained in place. "Why do you suppose he invited us here to meet a stranger?"

Madeleine wet her lips. "Lord d'Arcy has sent me to London to meet his social circle. He told me he was writing letters of introduction to a variety of his acquaintances in order to help me settle in town. I suspect you were among the number. Horace tells me there was even an announcement in today's *Gazette*. According to Lord d'Arcy's wishes, I am being introduced as having some slight claim as a relation to him through his French mother's side of the family. His cousin Lord Everleigh left his card before now. I am expecting him this evening. And there will be . . . others."

"They believe that they are meeting a d'Arcy relative, not a Foucant, *oui?*"

Madeleine nodded. "I'm glad you understand."

"Enfin, I do not." Justine eased onto one of the matching horsehair-stuffed settees upholstered in robin's-egg-blue brocade. "Is our name not sufficient?"

"Apparently not, for Madeleine and Lord d'Arcy's purposes," Henrice replied censoriously. "What exactly *is* his plan for you?"

Madeleine curtsied gracefully. "You are the first to meet Lord d'Arcy's newest experiment. I am to be the prototype of the Independent Woman."

"The what?"

"I believe he once called the position that of Enlightened Mistress."

"His mistress?" Justine added for clarification.

Madeleine shook her head. *"Non.* The experiment, in order to succeed, depends upon my ability to gain and maintain an independence free from any particular gentleman's protection." She added after a bracing breath, "Most particularly Lord d'Arcy's."

"Ma foi!" Justine murmured faintly. "Why should you wish to escape the marquis's protection?"

"I have heard of this theory," Henrice said slowly as she shifted on the settee. "But it was several years ago and I thought the marquis had given it up as *une absurdité.*"

"He has written a scientific paper on it," Madeleine said in defense. "I am committed to helping him prove his theory."

"Then you are a fool." Henrice rose. "Let us go, Justine, it is perfectly obvious that our niece does not require our help."

"But do not scowl so at the child, Henrice," Justine admonished, distressed that the battle of wills between her sister and niece had so quickly resumed. "Madeleine is family." She gazed enviously about the room. "And she has done well."

"Vraiment?" Henrice's face was tight with affront. "What service can we be to you, little niece?"

"Tell me about *Maman,*" Madeleine answered promptly. "Is she safely back with you?"

"No." Henrice snapped the word with finality.

"Where is she?"

"What do you care? The Foucant name is not good enough for you. Your aunts are not respectable enough for you. You have a house, a protector, and London will soon be at your feet. Do not worry about us. We will care for your mother."

Madeleine recoiled as if she had been slapped. "It is you who are unfair. Never am I told anything useful about my mother. For all I know she could be in debtor's prison or dead." She met her aunt's daunting gaze defiantly but inside she shrank a little. "Oh, I do not want to fight!" she whispered in despair.

She came and knelt at her aunt's feet, taking her hand in hers to bring it to her cheek. "Please, I beg you, *Tante* Henrice. Tell me where my mother is."

"If you do not tell her, I shall," Justine exclaimed as tears rolled from her eyes. "And you know how terrible I am at the telling of any tale."

Henrice nodded stiffly. *"Très bien.* If Madeleine wishes to learn of her mother's foolishness, then she will hear of it." She indicated the settee. "Sit, *ma fille.* It will take some minutes' telling."

Madeleine was suddenly feeling a weak and dizzy sensation in the pit of her stomach. She did not want to know everything so quickly. A day and a half ago, she would not have thought it was possible to be happier than she was. Now, she doubted it was possible to be much more miserable. Her mother was still absent while the man she loved had sent her away so that he could lie in the arms of another woman.

She rose and, without seeming to touch the floor, moved to the bell rope and pulled. "Allow me to see to your refreshment and then you may tell me everything." So, at last, she would learn the truth.

Five minutes later the Foucant ladies were sipping chocolate. "In short, your mother has returned to France. Word came to her about news of a certain family friend who had been thought lost during the revolution. She wanted to learn the truth. We expect her back any day. And that, my little niece, is all."

But Henrice's short recitation on her mother's whereabouts left conspicuous gaps in Madeleine's understanding. "All this time I thought perhaps *Maman* was in debtor's prison and she did not want me to know of her shame."

"You may be certain no Foucant will ever darken the door of debtor's prison," Henrice snapped.

"Why did *Maman* not ask me to meet her in Paris instead of requesting I come to England?"

"She did not know she would be returning to France when she wrote you," Henrice explained between sips of English tea. "It all happened so quickly. There was no time to write and prevent your journey."

"So you say." Madeleine nibbled a corner of a Scottish shortbread cookie to give herself time to think. It tasted like ashes in her mouth but she had not had an appetite for three days. "Why did *Maman* seek the services of Monsieur De Valmy to help her across the Channel?"

"Because she was convinced that it was the only way she could gain passage to France. Monsieur De Valmy has certain connections which London's French émigré society finds of use from time to time."

"What sort of connections?"

Henrice fixed a stern eye upon her. "Not all of us have *la bonne chance* of an English marquis's protection. We are foreigners and the English have again declared war upon our homeland. It makes a certain secrecy necessary. Monsieur De Valmy's services were necessary."

Temper showed for the first time in Madeleine's expression. "I am sick to death of hearing of this war. It is all the English speak about, Lord d'Arcy included."

The sisters exchanged glances. "Will Lord d'Arcy be coming to London soon?"

Madeleine shook her head, not about to be led away from the subject uppermost in her mind. "Who is this person my mother wants so desperately to find?"

Henrice shook her head. "We must not speak of it."

"Tell her, Henrice," Justine whispered.

Henrice's gray eyes shuttered over. "Your father."

"My fa—?" Madeleine glanced in disbelief from one sister to the other. "My father lives? Who is he?"

"He is a son of the blood royale," Justine whispered.

The words did not make sense to Madeleine. "But you said I was the result of a—a liaison."

"You are the love child of a very important man," Henrice said quietly. "In France we do these things differently from the English. There are court records of your birth and parentage, baptism certificates, papal documents of your existence. For your sake and your mother's, we have never spoken on this subject since we left Paris. There are people who would, for their own selfish purposes, wish to make use of such knowledge. Perhaps, one day . . ." Her Gallic shrug expressed a wealth of unuttered hopes and resignations.

Madeleine struggled toward comprehension. "Even if it's true, how can it matter? The king is dead and the Bourbons routed. Napoléon rules the Consulate."

"Not all aristocrats are dead," Justine whispered, as if the walls could be concealing a spy or two.

"If by the grace of *le bon Dieu,* the Bourbons return to the throne," Henrice continued, "you might have claim to certain inheritances—"

"And a title," Justine added softly.

Silence stretched between them as Madeleine stared into the depths of her cup. "Is my father so great a man?"

Henrice inclined her head. *"Oui."*

Madeleine's head throbbed with the thready aching of heartbreak compounded by these new and unexpected revelations. The required adjustments of the last two days were nearly too much for her. Yet one thing was utterly clear. "I think it is time I met this Monsieur De Valmy." She was mildly surprised when Henrice did not contradict her. "You have no objections, Aunt?"

Henrice sighed. "It is purest folly. De Valmy will not be more candid with you, he will simply lie and take your money."

"But if I can help Mam—"

"No one can help Ondine but herself."

"Monsieur De Valmy is a very bad man," Justine said softly. "And you are a very pretty young woman."

Those softly spoken words held more of a threat than Madeleine would have guessed.

"You are under Lord d'Arcy's care for now," Henrice pointed out. "It's a position you will forfeit if De Valmy learns your true identity."

Madeleine had suspected ever since she had overhead her aunts' conversation with De Valmy the day she ran away that Lord d'Arcy's formidable protection was the real reason her aunts had sought to place her in his bed. Yet she had decided only this morning not to remain on Sebastian's guilty conscience any longer than necessary. That meant seeking the amorous attention of another man.

Her hand crept up to stroke the concealing ruff about her throat. She did not need to gaze into her mirror to recall the feel of Sebastian's lovemaking. Until the love bites healed, until her heart healed a little, she could do nothing.

But she had listened to his theories and those lessons brought a certain ruthlessness now to her decision. Until she could bring herself to find a protector, she would at least shelter those she cared about. "The house is mine for as long as I wish. Unless you have made preferable arrangements, I would like it if you both moved in here with me."

Justine clapped her hands. "We shall be delighted, won't we, Henrice?"

"That is very generous of you, *ma fille,*" Henrice answered pleasantly, aware of the concession she made for all their sakes. "But what will Lord d'Arcy think of such an arrangement?"

"If he doesn't like it, he can come to London and tell me so," Madeleine retorted. "Until then, I shall treat his promises as binding. He invited you to visit me, and as I am unchaperoned, the company of two ladies should insult no one."

"We are not the best chaperones perhaps, for a young lady," Justine suggested gently.

"Do either of you know Lady Elizabeth Dighton?"

Henrice's brows rose. "I do."

"Lord d'Arcy thought she should make a good confidante," Madeleine said meaningfully.

Henrice laughed with genuine mirth. "That English *chienne!* It is well known she is on intimate terms with the greater number of noblemen, bachelors, and husbands in London."

Including Sebastian, Madeleine silently added. "If the marquis felt her friendship would do my reputation no harm, then your company certainly should not." She paused, going pink for the first time this day. "Do either of you know how one accomplishes the use of *les redingotes d'Angleterre?*"

"Madeleine!" Justine covered her mouth with a hand as she blushed a deep berry shade.

Henrice smiled. "Sebastian is a very sensible young man. In due time."

"Where is Lord d'Arcy?" Justine questioned in perfect ignorance of Madeleine's veiled references to her unhappiness.

Madeleine looked stricken. "He is—away."

"But you've only—?"

Henrice shot her sister a quelling glance, comprehending what her sister did not. "We should be pleased to move in immediately."

Madeleine offered her aunt a grateful glance. *"Merci.* You must excuse my rudeness, but I am still fatigued from my journey. I have done nothing but stand for fittings since I arrived. Now I must rest, since I am to expect Lord Everleigh this evening."

"But of course. We will show ourselves out." Henrice rose to her feet. "Come along, Justine. There are many things we must attend to if we are to move quickly. *Adieu.* Until tomorrow."

Madeleine smiled. "Until tomorrow. About De Valmy?"

"Leave him to me," Henrice pronounced.

"What do you suppose is going on?" Justine demanded as they climbed back into their cab. "Sebastian's absent and Madeleine looks almost ill."

Henrice shrugged. "A lovers' quarrel. You do remember them?"

"Of course!" Justine's eyes lit up. "I especially remember the *réconciliations*. Once a Prussian officer in Von Schill's Hussars . . ."

Henrice turned a deaf ear to her sister's reminiscence as she pondered the more pertinent situation of her niece. It seemed impossible that Sebastian could have tired of the girl so quickly. There lingered in Madeleine's face the flushed contentment of love's first experience. But there had also been the telltale violet bruising of recent tears beneath her lovely eyes. It seemed obvious that things had come to an abrupt and stormy parting between them. It was the way of youth, of course, whose feelings were so unpredictably volatile. But no man, not even as generous a soul as Lord Sebastian d'Arcy, would offer to set up an ex-lover in so grand a house as a mere punctuation to a brief affair! She was beginning to think that too much affection rather than too little had sent Sebastian fleeing Madeleine's arms.

That thought pleased Henrice. For a man who claimed he had no heart, Sebastian had a curious habit of taking on the role of knight errant for women, no matter how humble the female concerned.

She knew why Sebastian was a defender of women, the more helpless the better. Therefore, as long as he thought Madeleine was bereft in the world, a waif in need of his protection, he would not, no matter how it seemed to Madeleine at the moment, abandon her. That did not mean he wished to become entangled with her himself. Hence this nonsensical business of the Independent Mistress.

Had Sebastian really been foolish enough to suggest Madeleine find another lover so soon? *Mon Dieu!* Only infatuation would explain an action so bizarre.

Henrice's busy mind continued in calculation. One other

thing was equally certain: her little niece bore all the marks of a young woman in love.

"Do you think he has deserted her for good?" Justine asked at the end of her revelry.

"Impossible! He has every intention of making use of the house he has marked as his own. Has he not already placed some of his belongings in it?"

"Mais oui! Why did that not occur to me?"

Henrice did not answer that. "As for Madeleine! *Pfft!* Love had never had a better face for its expression. First we will move in, then I shall set about reordering the lives of the young lovers. We should have been allowed to settle the terms of their liaison first. It saves so much bother later on. For instance, I must learn if Madeleine holds the deed to her house."

"It is a very nice little house," Justine answered. "Easily large enough for four discreet ladies."

"Exactly. But if the marquis thinks to make it his love nest, we may soon find ourselves back out in the cold."

"Ah! Then perhaps we might suggest to Madeleine that he, to keep us from under foot, expend a small stipend to house her family."

"You expect a great deal from Madeleine's affections. Remember, he's her first lover. She won't want to press him for anything more than the chance to share the air he breathes. Madeleine is maturing nicely. There is new steel in her spine. She will not take well to being maneuvered."

"I think you must be speaking to yourself. Certainly I have never tried to take advantage."

Henrice subsided into silence. No, Justine had always left the unpleasantries of life to someone else. As usual, the burden was hers.

Bramwell Everleigh had never been more glad in his life that he was related to Sebastian d'Arcy on the paternal side of the family branch. The reason for this sudden delight was the young lady sitting across from him.

She wore a cream Empire frock veiled in Brussels lace. A matching length of lace, embroidered with tiny pearls, completely encircled her long slender throat. Below it, however, her satin bodice revealed the breadth of her luscious bosom. He lacked Sebastian's splendid frame, magnetic beauty, and confident sexuality but he shared a cousinly appreciation for a beautiful woman. From the froth of midnight dark curls piled high on her crown to the toes of her blue satin slippers, Mademoiselle Mignon was delicious enough to eat with a spoon.

"It is most kind of you to visit me Lord Everleigh," Madeleine said as she poured a sherry for him. "A gentleman in your position must lead a very busy life."

"Not at all! Never too busy to extend to a family member the honor of my company. Sebastian's letter was most pointed in the favor required." He reddened slightly. "Sorry. I can't imagine why I said such a thing. No way to address a lady." He looked at the fire blazing away in the hearth as if it would provide an explanation. It must be her eyes. They were absolutely the most riveting he had ever gazed into.

"But we are more like cousins, are we not?" Madeleine inquired as she passed the sherry to him.

Everleigh looked back, his composure restored. "Only after the marriage custom, mademoiselle." He cocked a flirtatious brow at her. "We ain't blood kin."

Madeleine smiled back. "Ah, Cousin Bramwell, I am a simple French girl. These distinctions are lost on me." She reached for her own poured glass of sherry. "You must call me Mignon when we are *en famille, oui,* Cousin Bramwell?"

"Cousin Mignon. Sounds much nicer when you say it. Cousin, that is." He lifted his glass in brief salute and took a large swallow.

Under the sweep of her lashes Madeleine sized up the young Englishman. He was tall and thicker than Sebastian, dressed in dark-blue evening coat, white satin waistcoat, cream breeches, and black slippers. His hair was more auburn than Sebastian's with wide whiskers that extended down toward his chin. His features were pleasant but less defined than his cousin's, with eyes of a softer blue hue. An attractive man who for reasons she could not quite understand was gazing at her like the basset hound kept in Sebastian's stables.

"Can't imagine why Sebastian hasn't mentioned you before," Everleigh ventured after a second sip.

"It is because he did not know of my existence until recently," Madeleine answered, determined to add no careless lies to the deception. "His mother married and moved to England long before I was born, of course. There was no reason why he should know I existed until I approached him."

"Of course. And Uncle Simon wasn't the sort to allow his wife to travel with him. But then I suppose you know that?"

"In truth, I know every little about the d'Arcy family."

Everleigh nodded. "Can't say I'm surprised. 'Bastian wouldn't be out to tell tales on his own. The way his father behaved toward the end. By Jove! It was outside enough!"

"The late marquis was a man of great temper?" Madeleine prompted, for Audelia's hints about Sebastian's father had prompted her curiosity. Here at last was someone who could shed a little light on the family history Sebastian would not speak of.

"Temper? Distemper is a better word. Don't ask me to reveal the particulars. Too indelicate for innocent ears."

"One hears so little," Madeleine mused aloud. "I suppose it is an old story." She leaned a little toward him, drawing his eye to her bosom. "He was, perhaps, unkind to his lady wife?"

"He was an old reprobate!" Everleigh stared at her décolletage a fraction longer than was strictly polite. "Won't say it ain't a man's prerogative to—to, well, entertain himself. A man must have his clubs and his hobbies." But he did not quite meet her eye.

Madeleine nodded. "Also in France, there is the *mariage de monde*. Once a lady has produced the male heir, many husbands and wives lead discreet if separate lives."

"You don't say?" Everleigh's interest was primed. "I've always heard the Frogs—sorry, the French had a way with libertine tendencies far surpassing our own."

Madeleine gracefully rearranged her gossamer skirts over her slim legs. "It is all very much an agreed-upon arrangement." She cudgeled her memory for tidbits of her conversations with Madame Céline. "Every fashionable woman has an official lover and every man an official mistress. If someone else catches the eye . . . *Enfin!* These *petits indiscrétions* will occur, even in England *oui?*"

Everleigh found himself agreeing a little too heartily as he gazed at the silhouetted shadow of her slim legs. Not many women dared wear gowns so sheer. Yet the French were notorious for their knack for veiled provocation. For instance, if the freshly sprouted rumors about Mademoiselle Mignon were true, then she was Sebastian's new mistress and not his cousin at all. Eliott was certain she was the Ideal Mistress he had wagered against Sebastian producing before the end of the next Season. He was human enough to hope that—his fiancée and mistress aside—rumor did not lie. If so, he would pursue the lovely Mignon himself, if 'Bastian allowed it. However, there was something of surpassing sweetness about the lady before him that made him reluctant to think of her as Haymarket ware.

"Of course, there are limits, standards in England," he went on in defense of his own rather straightlaced thinking. "Ladies do not take lovers as a matter of course. While the standards of men rightly differ, the late marquis sundered all rules of propriety!"

"In what way?" At his jerk of surprise, Madeleine quickly lowered her gaze. "No, you wish to be discreet and I would never but never compromise your honor." She lifted a softened expression to him. "I should be desolate if I encouraged your confidence in any way that discomforted you. *Non,* we shall leave it for another, someone not so involved with niceties, to tell me this troublesome family history."

"I suppose you will hear of it, in any eventuality," Everleigh temporized. "And it would be better if it came from family rather than a stranger." He added gruffly, "Rumor cuts up one's character rather more than the truth."

Madeleine found it remarkable that Sebastian's advice about how best to extract information from a man was correct. By appealing simultaneously to his sense of right and his protective instincts, she had won this concession from Lord Everleigh. Remarkable. "How kind you are to spare me rumor. Yes? Tell me all."

"Simon d'Arcy, Sebastian's father, always was a devil with the ladies. Long before he wed Marguerite he was said to be ever ready to cover anything in a skirt." His face caught fire. "Damme! Didn't mean that! Well, yes, the devil, I did! You're French, so you will understand plain speaking, am I right?"

Madeleine merely shrugged in answer to his inanity.

"Still, my mother claimed he loved Marguerite and that all was well until after he came back from the rebellion in the American colonies. The family claims the war changed him. Since he was born the year his father was posted abroad, Sebastian never knew him until after the war. By then, it was too late. Beat the boy, not that many fathers don't. But he never had a kind word for his son. Marguerite's health failed soon after he returned and Se-

bastian's father had a prodigious appetite for women."
Again his eyes slid away. "Kept two or three women at a
time. Finally brought one of his tarts in to act as mistress
of his household. Presided over his table, entertained his
friends while Sebastian was banished to public school and
his wife to her bedchamber. The *ton* will turn a blind eye
to most doings, but Simon d'Arcy spit in their eye. Probably was a blessing when she died. He forked over his life
in a duel over another man's wife. Devil of it, Sebastian
seems to have inherited his father's proclivities, for dueling
that is."

"What duels?"

"Didn't Sebastian tell you?"

"He is a most circumspect man," Madeleine replied.

"Tight as a clam," Everleigh agreed. "Can't say as if
anyone really knows him. Though I believe this last business sobered him up a bit. Glad to hear it. He can't just
leave England for two years in the backwash of one duel
and then turn up in town and promptly land himself in the
broth of another such scandal. Suppose that's why he's remained in Kent."

Madeleine did not follow half of what he said, but the
gist of it was filtering through. "Cousin Sebastian has
fought many duels, yes?"

"Too many for an Englishman. Every one of them's
been for a woman's honor, give him that. The first over
his lost mistress. The second was in defense of a pum-
meled wife. This last, you won't credit it. He stormed a
brothel to save a virgin harlot from the temper of a member of the Light Dragoons."

Somehow that did not surprise Madeleine. Sebastian
was a passionate man. Whatever he believed in, he
would follow with action. "Has he been in love many
times, then?"

" 'Bastian? Love?" Everleigh shook his head. "Doubt
he knows the meaning of the term. No, our cousin has

staggering success with women. Likes women, all women, but love don't enter into it. There, I've been indiscreet enough on our first meeting. Don't know why I went on about it all." He looked at her as if he were coming out of a daydream. "There's something about you makes a man feel at his ease."

"I will accept that as a high compliment."

"So you should. Wish Meg . . ." He rose abruptly to his feet. "Must be going. I should write 'Bastian and tell him Captain Sherwood's been posted in Ireland." He chuckled. "Hope I haven't bored you with my rambling. You'll be asking me to leave and not come back."

"To the contrary, Cousin Bram. You have been most entertaining, not to mention enlightening. Will you not care to stay for supper?" The look of astonishment that registered on his face warned her that she had transgressed. "I have made a *faux pas*. What is it?"

"In London, unmarried ladies don't invite gentlemen to dine, unchaperoned."

"I see." She touched his sleeve lightly. "I must keep you near so you may save me from these embarrassments. Please come another time when the Foucant ladies have joined my household. Lord d'Arcy extended the invitation as I am in need, as you say, of chaperones."

"I don't know about—well, I suppose they are old enough to provide a certain sense of propriety. I accept your invitation to return. Can't think when I've had a more delightful chat."

"And you, Cousin Bramwell, are far too gallant not to turn every lady's head when you choose."

"In that case, would you care to join me for a musical evening tomorrow night? Sebastian says you should get out a bit before he returns to town. Charmed to squire you about, if you'd like."

Madeleine held out her hand to him. "I'd be most grateful, Cousin." She noticed that he saluted her hand by kissing the air a fraction above her skin. Very proper. Sebastian would have approved, she thought, and felt a tiny spasm of loss.

Sixteen

December 10, 1803

"This cannot be possible!" Madeleine looked up from the household ledger of bills to the d'Arcy butler. "How is it that my small household incurs such expenses? Two hundred pounds in one month? I could not consume so much in a year."

Horace pursed his lips. "Mademoiselle is often not at home, but the mademoiselle's guests entertain frequently."

"The Foucant ladies' little card parties could not possibly require such expense."

Horace dipped a finger into the ledger to point out a few items. *"Pâté aux truffles,* Dom Pérignon, and oyster suppers, mademoiselle. A foreign menu is expensive." He shrugged. "The Foucants have, one might say, exacting tastes."

Madeleine tapped the ledger impatiently with her hand. "I do not care what the arrangement is, I cannot, I will not pass these bills to your employer's solicitor. Can we delay them a while?"

Horace smiled for the first time. "On the marquis's word alone, Mademoiselle may delay the bills nearly indefinitely."

She looked up hopefully. "Have you heard from him, Horace?"

After nearly a month Horace understood the ubiquitous

"he" and "hims" always referred to Lord d'Arcy. It was as if the mademoiselle could not bring herself to utter his name. "Lord d'Arcy has not been in touch since we returned to town," he said, as he had nearly every day since coming to London with her.

Madeleine turned her face away. "Very well. I will speak with the ladies. But I must go out this morning for a final fitting. Tell Cook not to set my place at lunch. Lord Everleigh will be my escort this evening. Please have his favorite brandy waiting."

"Very good, mademoiselle. About your guests? They are planning another small evening in."

Madeleine looked up with a mutinous smile. "Then they must eat cake and ale like the rest of us. If they should question the fare, send them to me."

Horace smiled. He did not always understand the thinking of the little French mademoiselle, but he understood why his master had been so fascinated with her. In fact, he had grave reservations about his lordship's continued absence from London unless he had been sincere in his statement that he wished to see the mademoiselle securely off into another gentleman's care. If so, his plan was going apace.

The house on Belgrade Square was filled practically to the rafters with hothouse flowers. These tokens of esteem distressed the cook who complained constantly of hayfever. As for Lord Everleigh, that young blood had scarcely missed a day's attendance upon Mademoiselle Madeleine in these last weeks.

"Lady Elizabeth left her card this morning. Again."

Madeleine lifted her shoulders in annoyance. The woman had called twice a week for two months, but Madeleine could not bring herself to entertain a rival for Sebastian's affections. She simply could not! "I am permanently out to her."

"Very good, mademoiselle," he murmured. "Also, you

asked that I remind you that Viscount Priestley and Mister Hollister are expected for tea."

"Thank you, Horace. Inform Madame Henrice that I will require her as chaperone."

"Very good, mademoiselle." He then bowed out.

Madeleine closed her ledger, briefly rubbed her temples, then rose and went to the window. The glass panes were etched in the corners by the lacework of hoarfrost. Beyond her yard, the square was deserted; even the evergreen vegetation looked stiff and chilled. The December nights had turned frosty, though everyone assured her that there would be a few more mild days before winter set in.

She blew softly against the chill pane, obscuring her reflection with a condensed breath. She lifted a finger to draw swirls on the pane. The warm October days in Kent were long gone. All that lay before her was the business of constructing a life. But she felt as frozen inside as the yews outside her window.

CHOOSE

She looked at the word written in the condensation. She had chosen, but it was not to be. He had warned her against it. Perhaps it was in part because he had warned her that she had fallen desperately and hopelessly in love with Sebastian d'Arcy.

Already the weeks had begun to blur the memory of him, and that was what frightened her most of all. When she closed her eyes and willed herself back to the moment in the gondola when his body had arched hard and heavy and powerfully over hers, she could scarcely recall it. It was as if she had been unable to think or even breathe when he had made love to her. But the wonder remained that at his hands' ravishment had not been a fate worse than death. It had been bliss.

The memory caused a sudden painful wrenching inside her. She doubled her fist and pressed it to the glass, bowing her head to it as she did so. *"Mon Dieu!"* she whispered in insight. So this, then, was the temptation of the flesh. It did not seem right that she should have so brief a taste of it only to have it snatched away.

Where was Sebastian? Why would he not respond to any of the letters she had posted to Kent? Was it possible that he was truly finished with her?

Jealousy flared as she thought about him dispensing his sensual charm upon whichever female happened to catch his lusty eye. To judge by his memoirs, he was remarkably democratic in his choice of lovers. Whether chambermaid or duchess, English or Moor, all that he required was a refined dedication to voluptuous carnal pleasure. Perhaps she had been too tame, too inexperienced to more fully engage his attention. Perhaps that was why he was refusing to see her until she had taken another lover.

She had been very disappointed when she returned to London to learn that Audelia was absent from town. At least then she would have had one friend near her own age with whom to confide and converse. But she learned through Lord Everleigh that Richard Baltry's wedding had taken place in October and that he and his bride were on an extended honeymoon in Scotland until after the New Year. Audelia, she supposed, had fled town so as not to be reminded of Richard. She could not blame Audelia. She felt the same resentful pain of jealousy when she imagined Sebastian lying in Lady Elizabeth's lilac-scented embrace. This then was part of the life of a mistress. How sad and how lonely.

That is how this life is, Madame Céline had once said. *To the lucky few it offers a few magnificent moments to hold against a lifetime of a thousand small struggles and horrors.*

Madeleine straightened up, struck by that realistic appraisal of life. Had she had her magnificent moment? Even if she never saw Sebastian again, she was luckier than most. She had had her magnificent moment in the arms of a remarkably talented lover. She must not try to bargain with fate for more.

She turned from the window. She had gentlemen guests to prepare to entertain. Sebastian's predictions had come true, to a point. She had become a fascination for the *ton* who inhabited London on these bleak days. She had lost count of callers and gifts and tokens that came her way. Invitations piled up though she appeared to be reluctant to be drawn into the fashionable life. Lord Everleigh was her one constant companion. But she knew even that must not continue. It was time she moved to fix the attentions of one of her many other admirers.

Perhaps tonight—despite her heart's longing—she would meet someone new at the soirée and she would capture the dashing blade's heart, and he would sweep her off in a whirlwind of romance. Then Sebastian d'Arcy would be free of his responsibility for her and she would be free to forget him . . . or at least she would pretend so well that not even her heart would know the truth.

It was a pleasant evening's entertainment. Beneath the roof of Comstock House, a musical soirée was well under way. There had been an operatic performance by an Italian tenor newly arrived in town, followed by renditions of Mozart and Handel by one of London's lesser known harp-sichordists. A trio from the orchestra of the Opera House had made their debut before the host signaled a break in the entertainment which would allow the guests to refresh themselves. Several of the gentlemen chose to retire to the smoking room while others gathered about the punch bowl to assuage their thirst with the highly alcoholic "rack."

The ladies for the most part clustered in groups of threes and fours to carry on conversations about who was wearing what, who had arrived with whom, and who was seen glancing longingly at whom.

Madeleine, who had long ago grown tired of the sameness of the functions she attended, had the supreme satisfaction of being the focal point of the more aggressive dandies who for whatever reason found themselves unfashionably stranded in town on this dismal night. She was certain her gown was half the reason. Made of cloth of gold tissue that floated about her like one of Salome's veils, it boasted the highest waist and skimpiest-cut bodice in the room. Its severe cut with short train was all that kept it from being a scandal. Her dark curls were bound up bandeau-style and her only ornament was the diamond bracelet Sebastian had given her.

She feigned a politeness she did not feel for these young men. Handsome, wealthy, and arrogant in the extreme, they ogled her as if she were a kitty of gold guineas to be won by the better player. Clearly, they cared more about who among them would win her rather than in seeking to engage her affections directly. Suddenly, her decision to find a protector tonight resolved into a more simple desire only to escape.

She found Lord Everleigh to be amazingly industrious in his part as escort. She had to do no more than make eye contact with him across the short distance of the anterior hallway where he was chatting with their hosts and he came to her, adroitly shouldering aside her assembly of would-be beaus.

"You look all but smothered," he murmured under his breath, then turned to her audience. "Claireborn, Mademoiselle Mignon is in need of raffia. Shelley, do see about a bit of lobster for the lady. St. James, a pillow, if you please. Southerby, my lady's wrap for the chill in the air. Has anyone the wit to discover a strawberry tart?" The young men, thus charged, scattered like leaves in every direction

"You handled them very well," Madeleine said in amused admiration.

"Was a bit of a bully in school," Everleigh answered proudly. "Serves me well, even now. Plaguey poor company, the lot. Wait until the Season begins. Then there'll be company and parties worth your effort."

Madeleine gave him a strange look. In the last two months she had attended no less than four functions a week. While Everleigh constantly complained of the lack of events, due to the fact it was the off-season, she could not imagine a more hectic schedule. Even so, she was utterly and completely bored.

She turned to him and put a hand on his arm in urgency. "Take me home, Cousin Bramwell. Please."

Everleigh glanced down at the slender hand resting on his jacket and then at her face, and what Madeleine saw in his expression surprised her. No man had ever looked at her quite like that, with his heart in his eyes.

Bram is a solid, reliable sort, engaged to be married shortly. He'll be happy to squire you about, but you are not to attempt your first liaison with him. Is that understood?

Sebastian's admonishment came back to her like a splash of cold water, but she was too unhappy to turn her back on the appeal in those eyes. The affection she felt for Bramwell Everleigh was genuine, but she knew it could never be confused with love. So then, why should she deny herself the only happiness to come her way in weeks? Why not a brief liaison with a man who held her in high regard, who did not consider her an experiment or a piece or prize to be won and used for sport? Lord d'Arcy could not have everything his way.

She squeezed his arm. "Take me home, Bram."

She did not miss the slight widening of his eyes at her use of his pet name and then the smile of joy that stretched his mouth. "My honor, Mignon."

The most exciting thing that had occurred all day was

the wash of snowflakes that greeted her as Lord Everleigh escorted her from the Comstock house to his carriage.

"A demned sight early for this sort of thing," Everleigh muttered. "Two weeks into December. Not likely to bode well for the winter ahead."

Madeleine shivered beneath her silk cloak trimmed in velvet. "I fear I am not prepared for the winter," she said softly.

"Gad! You're trembling." Everleigh gallantly swung his evening cape of wool from his shoulders and placed it lightly about hers.

When she had stepped up into the coach, she moved to the far end of the seat and smiled brightly as he climbed in. "Do sit beside me, Cousin Bramwell. I will keep your cloak, but only if you will share it with me."

Madeleine could scarcely believe she had uttered the words, but he stepped right up and moved beside her. "You must think me unforgivably gauche," she murmured, hoping the semidarkness of the blinkered coach lights hid her guilty blush.

He turned to her. "What I think is that you're a very unusual sort of lady. A cut above, Cousin Mignon, a cut above."

"Thank you, Cousin Bramwell." Conscience-stricken, she deliberately cast a shadow on the proceedings. "One hopes you've had word of our dear cousin?"

Bram looked uncomfortable. "Sorry, no. I even strolled to Whitehall the other afternoon to see General Armstrong. Said 'Bastian's in his demned Kent laboratory concocting only heaven knows what sort of foulness for the government. Thought I might ride down on a weekend. Would you care to come?"

Madeleine shook her head. "I do not wish to disturb him, particularly after he's been so kind to me."

"No kindness as I see it, looking after a mother's kinswoman."

"You are most gallant, Bram." She paused. This was the moment to insert a bit of the truth. "But I have heard the rumors circulating about me. They say I am not a relation at all but the marquis's *petite amie* and that you have been chosen to stand guard over his interests until he returns."

Bram looked shocked, as though he had not heard the rumors himself. " 'Tis jealous lies, that's all. You being a distant kin, practically related to me, by marriage anyway."

"But the ladies also talk and shy from me."

"The old hen clutch? Let them cluck, I say!"

Madeleine laughed softly at his jollity. "You are good for me, Bram. When I am with you I forget a little . . ." She let her voice trail off, as if he knew what she meant when, in fact, she had made certain no one knew the source of her heartache. "It disturbs me that a good and kind man's name is being bandied about because of me."

"Nothing of the kind. Idlers will always talk. But what can they say when 'Bastian's not even in town to squire you around?"

"That dreadful duty has, alas, fallen to you."

"Dreadful? Demned stroke of luck, say I. Did you glance about the affair tonight? Ain't a fellow under sixty wasn't pea green with envy that you entered on my arm. 'Bastian must be off his pins, to let you out of his sight."

She sighed and glanced out of the window. "I think I must tell you something, Bram, since you have been so extraordinarily kind." She closed her eyes in shame for her own coquetry. "I am living on Lord d'Arcy's largess. I have no other means. But I cannot in good conscience continue to do so."

"Don't know what else you can do. Where's the problem? 'Bastian don't mind spending his blunt."

Madeleine turned back to him, her expression appealing. "You have a mistress, do you not?"

"I—well." He sounded as if he had swallowed a crumb and it had gone down incorrectly.

"Tell me, Bram." She touched his gloved hand as it rested on his knee. "Is it a fate worse than death for a young woman?"

"Is it?" He leaned away, angling his back to the door as if he needed the distance for judgment's sake. "You can't be thinking—? My *dear!* Never let the thought cross your mind again! Why, 'Bastian— No, *I* would never allow you to so lower yourself."

Her pulse jumped at his heartfelt declaration. "You are a very good man, but even good men keep mistresses. Why should the life to which you subject your *petite amie* be impossible for me? Are you not kind to her? Do you not pay her bills, keep her fed and housed? Is she not grateful for your many kindnesses? I am practical in the extreme. I have no name to speak of, no connections, certainly no dowry. My youth and little beauty has but one value and that will not purchase me an English husband."

Flustered and embarrassed, Everleigh could not suppress the knowledge that he had expressed sentiments all too similar when pressing his advantage with the young dancer whom he now kept. But that a lady, a family connection, should speak of taking up the life of a light o' love made him object most strongly.

"I cannot, I say, cannot believe that you are talking such fustian! I'll not have you toss yourself to the wolves of London! You have no idea, no idea, what such a life would lead to. If 'Bastian's put a limit on your allowance, then I shall take it up. Couldn't do other. Too dashed fond of you!"

Madeleine was not entirely surprised by the arm he suddenly flung about her shoulders to pull her close. She had seen the speculation in his expression even as he spoke. The gallant and the seducer in him were at war.

"Dash it! Mignon. If 'Bastian has thrown you over, I'll not stint on pressing my suit."

Madeleine shut her eyes and let him kiss her, mostly

because she felt it was time she had some other experience with which to compare his cousin's kiss.

It was a disappointing lesson.

It was not that Bramwell didn't kiss well. Yet, even after the well-executed and thoroughly polished kiss of an experienced London toff, she felt nothing . . . except a fathomless longing for the man she could not have.

"Don't know why I did that," Everleigh murmured, more shaken than he expected. "I mean, I do. But it'll cause a contretemps. Matters to put right. Consequences to be dealt with." He smiled at her, a little surprised at his own thoughts. "Didn't think I'd get the chance, for all that. Not with 'Bastian in the picture."

Madeleine gazed at him with sympathy, and suddenly put her gloved hand to his cheek. "I am sorry," she whispered, but the words seemed inadequate. *Je me trompe.* Tears threatened her because she suspected he would be the kindest man she approached in London.

Everleigh did not pretend to misunderstand. "It's my damned cousin, isn't it?"

She looked away. Oh, why had she blundered so badly? Silence would have bought her a lover. "I don't think I am ready, after all, to step so boldly into that world of which we spoke." She took a deep breath. "Of course I will understand that you may no longer wish to call."

"I should hope you're not turning me off for my bold behavior?"

Something in his voice stopped her from answering sincerely. Instead, she laughed. "You are more bold than most but less bothersome than any of the rest."

Everleigh leaned back against the cushions, folded his arms across his chest and smiled, his pride restored. "You've remarkable pluck for a Frog."

"And you, Cousin Bramwell, are a remarkably good flirt for an English Goddamn!"

They were still laughing over the moment when his carriage pulled up before her residence. The blaze of lights coming through the open drapes lent a theatrical bent to the falling snow.

"Would seem your chaperones are entertaining late this night."

Madeleine's mouth tightened. She had asked her aunts to keep their soirées more private, and here her house was lit up like a Guy Fawkes bonfire. She stepped down in the slushy street, shedding Everleigh's cloak as she did so. Even as she gained the first steps, a pair of young men in military uniform exited her door, leaving it swung wide.

"Hello, darlin'!" the first one cried when he spied her.

"Come on in," said his partner, offering her an exaggerated bow as he swept a hand toward the doorway. "Might be tempted back, if you'll sit a round with me at the faro table. Won't mind losing to you, or winning your favor, either, right?"

"Clear off!" Everleigh said in a commanding voice.

The two young officers, clearly drunk, glanced up as if in expectation that a general stood on the steps below. "You heard me. And in future, you will address the marquis of Brecon's kin with respect! Clear off now before I call the watch."

One officer squinted at the man dressed as a civilian, then smiled. "She's yours, is she? Should keep better watch of her. Might get swept up in the winnings."

He flicked two fingers at his brow and then sauntered off arm-in-arm with his equally drunk companion.

"You must do something about this," Everleigh warned as he helped Madeleine through the door. "Always thought 'Bastian's idea of housing the Foucants with you was a poor one. You should know they have a reputation."

"I have heard," Madeleine returned lightly. "But then, who am I to quibble?"

Frowning, he took her by the arm. "Never say such a thing again, Mignon. I know desperation. You are alone in the world. It is to be expected that you might make an error in judgment." He smiled suddenly and roguishly. "I can only thank the fates that you made it with me. Friends. Agreed?"

Madeleine looked down at the hand he held out to her and then, smiling, took it. "Agreed. *Merci.*"

"Then I think you should consider a weekend in the country. Winter's coming on. The *ton* goes to ground until after Christmas. Then London will be right jolly again."

"Oh, I think not . . ." Madeleine began, only to have her attention drawn away by the sound of footsteps descending the main stairway.

"Perhaps I, as a fellow countryman, can persuade the mademoiselle," said a voice that she had been dreading hearing for nearly three months.

She turned to look up into the saturnine features bent in singular intensity upon her. "Monsieur De Valmy," she intoned without enthusiasm.

"De Valmy," Bram said with great reserve. "What are you doing here?"

The abrupt tone did not discomfort the Frenchman. He merely smiled at Madeleine as if they were old friends instead of the merest of acquaintances. "I was hoping for just such an eventuality. Now that I have found you at home at last, Mademoiselle Mignon, will you do me the honor of a private moment of your time?"

A sudden shrill cry from above followed by raucous laughter turned all their attentions to the party above stairs. Madeleine glanced down at Everleigh. "Cousin Bramwell, may I impose on you to inquire of my guests if the gaming is about to end? I would be most grateful if that is so."

"Certainly, Cousin Mignon." Everleigh emphasized the familial relation as he surveyed De Valmy. "I shall be back down in a jot."

As he mounted the stairs, Madeleine gave De Valmy a

brief glance. "This way, monsieur." She indicated the salon to her left.

He was very dark, she noticed as they moved into the room. Black clothing and black stock aside, there was a darkness in his black eyes that seemed to eat up the light, so that even in the glare of a dozen tapers, she felt as if he had thrown a shadow over the room by entering it.

He was tall and thin and the still watchfulness in him made him seem predatory. Thanks to her aunts' diligent intervention they had met but twice before in the briefest of exchanges. Because De Valmy's circle and Everleigh's were far apart, they had never met outside this house. Yet her aunts could not refuse him entrance when he alone was their connection to Ondine. While her aunts continued to treat him with courtesy, he continued to spin stories of vague sightings of Ondine. True or not, they all agreed that he had to be tolerated until Ondine reappeared or sent word herself.

She moved to the fireplace and held out her hands to the flame. The snow was excuse enough for him to believe that he alone did not chill her but she suspected he knew the truth.

"Yes, monsieur? What is it you have to say to me?"

When he did not speak at once, she turned to glance at him. He stood behind a wing chair with a slight smile on his severe handsome face. She suspected he was a man of infinite patience. He would wait for days, weeks, months, perhaps years for what he desired. No wonder her aunts feared him.

"I am simply attempting to decide how best to broach the subject, mademoiselle . . ." He made a small gesture with his hands. "It is most strange, but I have never heard a surname attached to you."

"*Oui.* An eccentricity of mine," Madeleine replied, having perfected the answer weeks ago.

"*Teins.* A clever device among the English who care so

very much for the pedigree, *oui?* But no matter." He stepped past the chair and approached her. "Still, you remind me of someone. I shall remember. I always do."

Madeleine lifted her chin in defiance. "Please state your business, monsieur. The hour is late and I am very tired."

"Of course. I regret that the matter concerns certain debts incurred by your household."

Madeleine shrugged, looking down at the fire. "I cannot imagine to what you refer, Monsieur De Valmy. I have incurred no debts of any kind with you."

"Perhaps I phrase myself badly." How polite he sounded, but he now stood too near. "The debts were incurred by members of your household. The Foucants, to be precise."

Fear knifed into Madeleine's stomach. He must know who she was. "They are in debt to you? In what way?"

"They have incurred certain gaming debts." When she looked up at him, he bowed sardonically and handed her a piece of paper. *Tante* Justine's signature flourish could not be mistaken. Beside it was penned the amount of five thousand guineas.

Madeleine refused to allow her face to show her dismay as she handed it back. "I think it rather indelicate of you to reveal a lady's private debt of honor to one it does not concern."

His thin lips stretched out in a mirthless smile. "It does not concern you that there is gambling nightly beneath your roof? Are you not responsible for all that occurs here?"

"I do not keep a record of my guests' guests," she answered glibly as she tried to keep her pulse from trampling her nerve.

"Perhaps you should, mademoiselle. For instance, there are certain women who come to your home who are known to borrow from family, friends, even lovers in order to fund their insatiable passion for deep play." She jumped when he touched her shoulder with one long finger, but he did not pursue her when she sidestepped away from his handling.

She looked up at him in defense, unwilling to be caught off guard a second time. "Is that all, monsieur?"

His eyes glittered in the firelight. "I tell you this because there are gentlemen present as well who are more than willing to accept a lady's favors in lieu of money owed." His smirk left no doubt as to the kind of favors exchanged.

"Lord d'Arcy may not care to have a residence to which he holds the mortgage turned into a high-class brothel." His gaze lowered to the deep cleavage revealed by her gown. "Or is this his intent?"

Madeleine refused to turn away. "You are impertinent, monsieur. I do not care to further our acquaintance!" She turned abruptly and walked briskly away.

She did not expect to reach the doorway undetained. Her heart beat so strongly, her hands trembled as she passed through the doorway into the safety of the hall. She assumed she appeared perfectly composed until she saw the arrested look on Everleigh's face as he came down the steps toward her.

De Valmy appeared in the doorway behind her, whispered, *"Au revoir, mademoiselle,"* and headed for the front door.

"What was that?" Everleigh demanded when he reached her. "Did that fellow insult you?"

"Not deeply," she murmured, knowing she would have to tell Everleigh something, for he had seen the distraught look on her face. "He seems to have heard those rumors we discussed earlier."

"The devil he has!" Everleigh's face flushed in anger. "I'll just sort him out!"

Madeleine put a restraining hand on his arm when he would have followed De Valmy out the door. "Do not, Cousin Bramwell. It will only encourage rumor if it is heard that you must defend me. And think what Lord d'Arcy would do if word reached him?"

"A duel," Everleigh said under his breath. "Very well, if you are satisfied."

She reacted with a shiver. "My honor, Cousin, can suffer no damage from a man who has no honor."

Everleigh smiled at her. "Well said! You think like a man, little cousin, so you do!"

She removed her hand after a quick squeeze. "You spoil me with flattery, Cousin."

An hour later, when the guests were all gone and the house was empty and dark and silent, Madeleine stood a moment at her window watching the light snow. The lacework patterns falling out of the night-black sky made her wonder where Sebastian was and then just as abruptly made her hope that he was as lonely and cold and miserable as she.

"I hate him!" she murmured against the frosty pane. "I truly hate him!"

Sebastian stood on the cliffs above the churning sea, wearing a cavalry mantle and busby of Napoléon's Mounted Guides. Despite the swirling sheets of rain, he watched for the telltale flash of a lantern at sea that would tell him the ship he waited for had reached the French coast. In the interim months he had grown a mustache and sideburns and added a fake plaited pigtail with red ribbon to his slicked-back hair. His knowledge of gutter French had improved immeasurably by fraternization with the citizens of the Iron Coast, as the French called the impregnable shore that faced England's southern coast across the Channel.

Information was plentiful. The trouble was, most of it was less than useless. The Choauns were moving much more slowly than Whitehall had hoped. The plotters were said to be delaying in expectation that the Comte d'Artois, younger brother of Louis XVI, would join them in Paris, ready to replace Napoléon when he was toppled. But, the devil of it was, none seemed to know exactly where the Comte was, or what his plans were.

After two months of plying the coast to sketch and count and measure, he was fairly certain that Napoléon's field of balloons in Boulogne Forest was no serious threat to England. At the rate of ten men per balloon, he would need to launch a thousand oiled silk craft to bring a sizable troop across the Strait of Dover. It was not practical.

So then, the war would progress in the more traditional ways, with intrigue and treachery and shell and musket balls, and rifle fire and saber rattles and diplomacy and political coups though the outcome was still far from certain. After this night, he would be free to return to his laboratory and his memoirs, and a certain empty peace. Perhaps he would even consider taking a mistress again, if only for the comfort of reliable companionship.

Much to his surprise, he had grown accustomed to having Mignon under his roof. Perhaps, if he found a discreet widow, willing to idle away her hours . . .

A sudden flicker of lightning kindled the sky to silver gray, revealing not only the foaming of breaking waves on the rocks below, but, he knew, the vulnerable outline of himself sitting like a statue on horseback. It was foolish to continue waiting. The seas were impossible. The wind lashed like an icy whip across his face. No right-minded captain would have set out this night. It would be snowing farther north, perhaps in London.

He closed his eyes as thunder cannonaded overhead, causing his horse to shiver and paw the ground, and willed himself to London . . . and to Madeleine.

Many times these last weeks he had tortured himself with the look in her eyes as he had left her to go, so she thought, to another woman's arms and bed. Had he been right to be so severe with her, to hurt her so badly? But he had thought then that her pain of wanting and waiting for him to return—or for the impossible—would be worse. She must not wait for what could not be.

It was kinder this way. No doubt she was at this very moment dancing happily in some lucky man's arms, smiling at him, her plum-blue eyes sparkling.

The flash, when it came, was so far out at sea that Sebastian did not at first credit it. The lightning flickered uncertainly on the backs of the waves before it came again, a single golden flash of warm light on the cold steel sea.

He watched for the next quarter hour as that sturdy ship came ever closer to shore. The game, of course, was to greet the conspirators coming ashore and ship out at the same time. They were not expecting him and they would not take kindly to his piggybacking onto their clandestine landing, which they believed was known only to other royalists. It really was amazing, he reflected, what gold could buy even from the most ardent supporter of any cause. Regrettably, he'd had to kill a man, an officer in the Mounted Guards tonight in Biville. By morning, he would have no place to hide.

As he watched, the wind died down and the sea flattened out a bit. The occasional flash of light between sky and sea betrayed the launching of boats over the side. They were, it seemed, as desperate as he to reach their homeland.

When the rocks behind him suddenly came alive with the sounds of men, he knew this was his moment of truth. He had to make it down to the edge of the cliff and over the side to meet the first boat that came upon the shore. As they landed he would exchange places in one of the boats and row back to the ship. It was a gamble no sane man would have made.

The horse under him fretted as the thunder rumbled again but he urged her forward, toward the very edge of the cliff that hung suspended in the night. He slipped from the saddle with only a light jingle from the muffled harness. Enough.

"Halte!" someone cried. A sentry? A military guard? A royalist sympathizer? He knew it did not matter. Any and all would kill him if they could.

He did not obey the command as his assailant must have known he would not. He slipped and slithered over wet stones, scrambling blindly across the short distance to the lip of the cliff.

"Halte!" again came the coarse cry in French.

No lanterns were needed when the sky suddenly split with two jagged forks of lightning. His head and shoulders were clearly visible against the glare of the sky in the second before he slipped below the horizon of the cliff.

From the right he saw two musket flashes. He ducked and breathed a sigh of relief as the sky closed over in darkness and thunder shook the pebbles free beneath his feet. He had escaped.

But it occurred to him as he climbed down the treacherous rock face that he must have struck his right arm on a rock as he dove for cover because there was now a dull ache there just below the shoulder. By the time the surge of the sea lapped at his ankles the arm had become numb from supporting his weight on the climb down. It would be a cold and murderous row to the ship, he decided, with a bruised arm weakening his efforts.

He heard men whispering at his back as he descended and turned as someone opened a lantern. He looked into the face of the *émigré* noble Armand de Polignac, a royalist of known fanatical persuasion.

"Things go apace," he said jauntily, using the agreed-upon password to the Frenchman's surprise.

"They go with God," the Frenchman answered with a Gallic shrug.

After tossing his rain-soaked fur busby away, Sebastian

clambered into the boat, oared by two English seaman, and fell heavily against a seat board. The stab of pain astonished him as it twisted all the way up his arm from the elbow to deep in his shoulder. He realized that his right side felt sticky with an oozing warmth that was not rain or seawater. The marksman on the cliff above had not missed, after all.

As he lay faceup in the boat's bottom, the first crystal flakes touched his face, stinging him with cold. But he was no longer thinking of winter and London. He was remembering an autumn afternoon in Kent, with a bright maroon sky and a slanting sun, the commingling fragrances of warm sweet hay and heated sex, and the woman whose hold over him had grown stronger the longer they were apart.

Strange, he was not sentimental. He was not the kind of man to feel guilty for having taught a virgin the power of her sensuality. No, the mistake he had made was in thinking that by taking her he would exorcise his desire for her. It was a good theory. It should have been proven out. He must have overlooked something in his calculations. But what?

Suddenly, he knew. "Mignon."

Seventeen

"We must keep in future a very strict budget," Madeleine concluded. "I must approve of all purchases. And there will be absolutely no more gaming beneath this roof. Agreed?"

Henrice's lips thinned. "I am not accustomed to being on a leash, little niece."

Justine made a moue. "For myself, I am desolate that you would deny your shut-in relatives the small consolation of entertaining a small gathering of friends."

"Is that how you would describe that party of revelers last evening?" Madeleine responded, touched to the quick by their antagonistic replies. "Two of your guests, English officers, accosted me on my own doorstep."

"But of course, a mistake," Henrice replied tersely.

"They are young, *chérie,* and so handsome in their uniforms. You cannot blame them for conducting a small flirtation, *oui?*" Justine added.

Madeleine eyed her unrepentant aunts across the breakfast table. Though both were dressed in fashionable dishabille, neither of them looked refreshed by having stayed abed until noon. She suspected the reason was the amount of champagne they had consumed the night before. "Your guests waste our wine, our money, and threaten our reputations."

Henrice raised an imperious eyebrow. "When, *ma petite,*

did the house and the money become yours? And whose reputation do we speak of, exactly?"

Madeleine bit back the angry words that rose to mind. Her head ached from another almost sleepless night where even dreams held no refuge. She was determined not to turn the discussion into a confrontation. But it was very hard. Her aunts seemed to believe they lived in a serendipitous world without consequences. She knew better. She did not yet know exactly what form it would take but there had been an implicit threat in Monsieur De Valmy's actions the night before.

"We must trim expenses, that is all I am saying. Lord d'Arcy's largess is not inexhaustible. The responsibility is mine. Therefore the decisions must be mine."

Henrice drained her cup. "I refuse to be dictated to by a child."

Furious to be pushed into a corner by her aunt's words, she nevertheless knew it was a declaration she must counter or she would lose control once and for all. "I perfectly understand. I do not wish either of you to be unhappy." She lifted her gaze, looking at one and then the other. "If you feel restricted, I won't be offended if you decide to return to your own abode." Sadness peeked through her resolve as she added, "But I should like very much to have my family with me just now."

She held her breath as Henrice elegantly dabbed at her mouth and then refolded her napkin. "I suppose," Henrice began in a theatrical drawl, "we could scale back our card parties to twice a week. The cachet of exclusivity would benefit us, Justine."

"No more card parties," Madeleine said flatly, but her stomach doubled into a fist as she met her aunt's formidable gray stare. "No more gambling. Is that quite understood?"

"You are growing to be quite the little martinet," Henrice said as she rose from her place. "It is most unbecoming in a woman!" She turned away after signaling Justine to follow her.

"Please wait, *Tante* Justine," Madeleine said quickly.

With a reluctant shrug, Justine eased into her chair. "I think, little niece, that there is more to this than you are telling," she said when Henrice had left the room.

"Monsieur De Valmy showed me a paper last evening," Madeleine began, and saw her aunt flush from cheek to bosom. "*Tante,* how could you become indebted to such a man?"

Justine shrugged. "It is not uncommon for a guest to share the bank when one plays faro, for everyone knows the bank usually wins. *Enfin,* because we were short of funds, the monsieur offered to put up the full expense of it." A tiny frown formed between her brows. "I do not know how I came to lose so much when I was clearly winning at the beginning of the evening. But this is of no moment." Her expression cleared. "The monsieur is most accommodating. *En tout cas,* he hinted in a note that came on my chocolate tray this morning, that he would be willing to settle the debt in return for our company for a weekend at a small party in the country. A very select company of handsome men and beautiful women made merry with music and laughter and a masquerade ball. *C'est s'amuser beaucoup!*"

"If Monsieur De Valmy has a part in it, I suspect a great deal," Madeleine murmured darkly. "Certainly, you will refuse?"

"But we are all invited." Justine's lashes swept down flirtatiously. "I believe, *ma petite,* that if you were to agree, the monsieur would be even happier."

"No, I do not like him," Madeleine answered.

"You are being gauche. Of course I have accepted for you. If not for Henrice and myself, you would never have this lovely house with gorgeous clothes and more admirers than you can count. In return we ask only this small favor."

Madeleine focused on her breakfast plate. "Monsieur De Valmy made odious suggestions to me last night. He hinted that gaming debts could be paid off by granting certain favors." She glanced up. "What does he want?"

Justine shrugged elaborately. "What every man wants. A little feminine company, a smile, a pat, a few kisses perhaps. Trifles."

Madeleine stared. "I cannot believe you expect me to be—nice to him for the sake of your profligate gambling habits."

Justine's bright eyes fixed on Madeleine. "I cannot believe that you are behaving as a thankless brat who should be grateful she's not been asked to do worse!"

Madeleine could not quite credit her ears. Her *tante* Justine was the last person she expected to turn on her. "Please try to understand, it is not you I am refusing. It is Monsieur De Valmy. I do not like the way he looks at me."

"Ah! So that is it." Justine's eyes narrowed with a hint of malice. "You have grown very arrogant, little niece. These clumsy English noblemen have swelled your head with dreams of glorious conquest. But women like us who live by their wits and beauty cannot afford to be too scrupulous in their choice of companions. Or is it that you feel you have already found your fortune in Lord d'Arcy?" Two bright spots of color appeared on her cheeks. "I would not count so much upon that! He is as faithless as he is beautiful. There is scarcely an acknowledged beauty in London he has not taken at least once." She lifted her chin in triumph. "Ask your *tante* Henrice!"

Madeleine raised her eyes, and in them was an expression that made her aunt pale.

Justine rose quickly, tipping her teacup so that a brown stain appeared on the linen. *"Ma foi!* Do not listen to me! I babble when I am angry. *Pardon!* I must pack." She turned and fled the room as if the hounds of hell nipped her heels.

Madeleine remained seated as her aunt's words tolled in her head.

She had not needed her aunt's reminder that Sebastian d'Arcy was a self-confessed rake and profligate. Had she not read his memoirs? Had he not warned her again and again not to count on him? He had made her his lover but he would never make her his mistress. His advice had been not to confuse her emotions with the necessities of gaining a situation.

She suspected he would be contemptuous of her aborted attempt to seduce Bramwell Everleigh. Was it so important that she felt no passion for him? That was better. But her frightened response to her lack of desire, even her bungled confrontation with her aunts, seemed to indicate that she was holding on to exactly the kind of foolish daydreams Sebastian had warned would ruin her.

"So then, I will go to the country for the weekend," she murmured. She would see how the sophisticated conducted their *amours* and then she would follow suit. Someone had to rid her of the haunting whisper of Sebastian's low seductive voice, erase the memory of his mesmerizing blue eyes, blot out the feel of his hands on her skin. But it would not be Monsieur De Valmy. It would not!

As Sebastian left the house on Belgrade Square he wanted to hurl epithets at his coachman and kick the spokes out of his carriage. Instead, knowing his fury was dangerous to one of his temperament, he waved them off and strode down the street in long angry strides.

"De Valmy!" he spat.

He had spied the man's profile in a passing coach as he neared the square where he had rented a house for Mignon but thought nothing of it. Now he knew that more than likely Mignon had been in that coach as well. If duty had not required him to report first at Whitehall upon his arrival back in London, he would have intercepted her and prevented this.

He had been detained on the coast by a fever brought on by the shot he had been given in the arm and exacerbated by the thorough chilling he had received while waiting for the ship. Still shaky from the fever and loss of blood, he had come up to London only this morning. But the pain in his arm and the shivers of his lingering illness were nothing compared to the rage seething through him.

"The little fool!" How could Mignon have blundered so badly?

The maid who answered the door at Belgrade Square had told him that her mistress was off for a weekend in the country with Monsieur De Valmy and the Mesdames Foucant. The only thing the ever-so-helpful little wench did not seem to know was who was hosting the country weekend and where the country house was located.

"Somewhere south along the coast, your lordship," she had said proudly.

"Somewhere south!" Sebastian muttered. That narrowed it down to several hundred miles of shoreline.

Yet he suspected their destination lay between Brighton and Dover. Armstrong was more strongly suspicious than ever that the Foucants were agents for De Valmy. The general's grim recitation of the number and names of guests who regularly visited the house on Belgrade Square under the auspices of gambling had given Sebastian pause, especially since it was his coin which had unwittingly funded the enterprise that had grown up without his knowledge. They included officers in His Majesty's army, French émigrés with rabid political leanings, and minor politicians both Tory and Whig. In short, Whitehall suspected nothing less than a spy ring was operating in Belgrade Square.

Rumor in intelligence circles said that De Valmy was

inexorably bound up in the plot to overthrow Napoléon. Whether he was royalist or republican or even Huguenot was still much in doubt. But one thing seemed clear. England could not afford to shield a spymaster they could not control. Whitehall wanted De Valmy compromised and eliminated from the game of political chess the Europeans were playing with Napoléon. Because of his ties with the Foucants, Sebastian had been charged by Armstrong, not over an hour ago, with engineering De Valmy's fall. The trap had been set before he left the offices of the Horse Guard.

Sebastian paused under the streetlamp, feeling the heat of indignation press in at his eyeballs. If he did not find her first, that trap might also catch Mignon.

Even if De Valmy was doing business with the Foucants, that did not explain why he had been taken up by Mignon. Certainly she must have heard something of De Valmy's unsavory reputation. What could have possessed her to take him so far into her confidence that she would agree to go away with him? Despite his frequently voiced doubts about her loyalty, he had never really believed that Mignon was a spy. But there were others less likely to delve into her character. If she were caught with De Valmy, she might be forced to pay the price of her ignorance.

He had no doubts why De Valmy had approached Mignon. She was young, beautiful, and French, devoid of family and with no protector. He could well imagine the Frenchman, pretending a special kinship with her as a fellow countryman. No doubt he had traded on her insecurities to gain her confidence. Were they yet lovers?

That thought wrenched another string of obscenities from him. Where was Bram while all of this was going on?

"Poor little slut!" he murmured viciously under his breath. He would not have sent a poxed jade into De Valmy's clutches. He squelched the feeling that by abandoning Mignon at the outset of her venture into the world of libertines and courtesans he might have done just that.

He glanced around to find that his driver, who had been following at a discreet distance, had pulled up beside him. He turned and wrenched open the carriage door. "Home!" he cried, then got in and flung himself into a corner.

Mignon was not his responsibility, he reminded himself. He had only promised to help her begin the life of a mistress. If truth be known, she had betrayed him by not using the tools he had painstakingly sought to teach her. No, he was behaving in a perfectly reasonable fashion, as would any man who wanted very badly what must be forbidden to him. He was sulking.

So why did he feel this devilishly annoying sensation of having let her down?

He had schooled her well in the faults and needs, weaknesses and conceits of men. But she seemed to have forgotten to be wary of men who would lie about their influence in order to impress her. She was too young, too trusting, too innocent to take on and best De Valmy. He would have to save her. But first he had to find out where she was.

"Bram will know!"

But when his driver halted the carriage a few minutes later, Sebastian looked out in surprise to find himself before his own home. Belatedly he realized that he had given this direction to his driver instead of Bram's house. He leaned out to correct his error when he decided that there was the possibility that Horace might know where Mignon was headed.

"Evening, Horace," he greeted his startled butler as he strode in past him into the foyer.

"A very good evening, sir— my lord!" Horace lifted his candle higher as he closed the door. "I scarce did recognize you, my lord, with your new mustaches and coif."

Sebastian smiled and flicked the pigtail over his shoulder. "A disguise, Horace, for a dilettante."

"Alas, you've sustained an injury, my lord."

"Hunting accident," Sebastian lied as he patted his sling.

"Of course." Horace knew a politic lie when he heard it. "Your lordship's journey was a success, I trust."

Sebastian nodded and glanced absently around. "I see the renovations are complete."

"As of the end of last month, my lord." Horace began lighting the branch of candles that stood on the entry table. "You've been away some while, my lord. We had feared for your safety, particularly the young lady, my lord."

Sebastian swung suddenly around. "Where is she, Horace?"

" 'Ere Oiy am!"

Sebastian glanced up the main stairway with soaring heart in the direction from which the light feminine voice had come. But Mignon was not there. A girl in nightrail and bare feet who could not have been more than thirteen stood looking down at him. "Oiy been waitin' like anythin' for ye to return!"

She flew down the steps and flung herself into his startled arms. She felt as frail as a newly hatched chick as she locked her thin arms about his waist. Beneath a red-gold fleece her face was liberally sprinkled with gingery freckles. "Oiy knew ye'd come back. Oiy promise t' do ye proud. I've been a good-natured wench, Oiy 'ave. Scrubbin' with the best. Ask Mister 'Orace if Oiy ain't!"

Thunderstruck, Sebastian appealed to his butler. "Who is she?"

Horace lowered his eyes. "I thought perhaps you knew, my lord. You presented her on the doorstep last September about four of the clock one morning. You were in high dudgeon, my lord. I believe, you mentioned something about an officer of the Life Guards whom you wished to horsewhip."

Sebastian glanced down at the would-be harlot. So Bram's tale about Lieutenant Sherwood was true. "The very devil!"

"As you say, my lord." Horace gave the girl a distinctly sharp glance as she continued to hug the marquis. "You said to find the child some useful work. Mrs. Hodge made her a tweeny."

"Why haven't you mentioned the girl these last months?"

Horace coughed discreetly. "As you have not, my lord, I thought you felt the matter satisfactorily settled."

Sebastian did not know whether to be amused, gratified, or just annoyed that his butler seemed so in tune to his thoughts and feelings. He smiled briefly at the girl. "Go up to bed now—er, child. And continue working hard," he added with a gentle push.

As she scurried away, Sebastian turned a grim face on Horace. "As you know me so well, why the devil did you allow Mademoiselle Mignon to leave town with a rotter like De Valmy?"

Horace looked decidedly uncomfortable. "I did not know Mister De Valmy was involved, my lord. You did not, however, charge me with restricting the lady's travel."

"An oversight," Sebastian murmured, but the truth was, he had been too eager to see her gone from his life to consider how many ways she might possibly come into danger. "Why did Lord Everleigh not stop her?"

"Your lordship's cousin is up in Derbyshire. Lord Everleigh asked me to make his excuses should you return before him. His fiancée's family had requested his presence at their family estate for an extended period."

Sebastian smiled grimly. "The girl's family must have heard of his attentions to Mademoiselle Mignon. I don't suppose you know where she went?"

Horace smiled at last. "Indeed I do, my lord. A weekend at Locksley House, where Lord and Lady Howard are holding a masquerade ball tomorrow night. I retained your invitation on the chance . . ."

Sebastian smiled for the first time that day, though the Howards were notorious for their parties, which were no more than excuses for trysts. "I doubt I pay you enough, Horace."

Horace beamed. "Indeed you do, my lord."

The crowd at Locksley House was small by the standards of most country parties, her aunts told her, numbering only two dozen who were actually staying at the house. But to Madeleine the boisterous crowd of merrymakers seemed a larger crush than at any party she had yet attended. Perhaps that was because they were all crowded under one roof, owing to the inclement weather. Lord and Lady Howard, their hosts, seemed to encourage all sorts of raucous play, from billiards to cards to charades of dubious context.

The champagne had flowed freely from the moment of their arrival and couples had seemed to change partners every hour. She was certain that several of the husbands and wives she had been introduced to when she arrived in the afternoon had not been in the same pairings by evening. After dinner there had been much secret smiling and dropped gazes, furtive touching and fading away into the shadowy edges of the rooms.

If she was not certain before, she knew so now: it was a weekend of assignations for wealthy libertines. All the men were well dressed and full of smug confidence while all the ladies were beautifully gowned and coiffed with roaming eyes and inviting smiles lurking behind the flash and flutter of their fans. Tonight, an additional hundred and fifty guests had been invited for the ball meant to launch the Christmas season.

Henrice and Justine, gowned and groomed to perfection,

had floated among the gathering with ease while Madeleine hung back, ever alert for the mysteriously absent Monsieur De Valmy. During the journey down, he had scarcely glanced at her, as if her presence were all he required, not her attention nor, thank goodness, her interest. When he did not reappear after dinner, the evening had passed without incident, if she discounted the adoration of a young baron something-or-other, who had followed her about during the evening like a puppy looking for an owner.

By the morning, Madeleine begun to relax. Along with the rest of the guests who drifted out from their rooms beginning at ten-thirty, she stopped at the sideboard in the dining room for an informal breakfast of broiled kidneys, steak, ham, eggs, pheasant, scones, toast, jams, and tarts.

When she had filled her plate, she caught the eye of two ladies.

"Do come sit with us, mademoiselle," encouraged the women she'd had a pleasant if short exchange with the evening before.

"Thank you," Madeleine replied as she took a chair beside them.

"We were just commenting on your success with the baron last evening," the dark-haired lady said, and exchanged pleased glances with her redheaded companion. "At four and twenty, he has just come into his majority."

"A living of twenty thousand a year," commented the redhead. "He is ripe for the picking!"

"We are all but strangers," Madeleine said carefully before biting into a scone.

"Ginger hair in men often means fire in the belly," the redhead observed with a salacious smile.

"He is such a delicious morsel," continued the brunette, "I could swallow him whole!"

The redhead accorded her a sly glance. "According to rumor, you already have!"

As the two women giggled indelicately loud, Madeleine

glanced away. But they did not seem to notice her embarrassment. Their conversation continued as they began comparing the proportions and relative merits of several other gentlemen's genitalia. Madeleine did not know whether to be more shocked that they spoke so openly of such things or that they claimed the experience required to have an opinion about so many men. Was this how she would be in a few years, jaded, bored, reduced to thinking of men in terms of their prowess in bed, or the coins in their purses?

The brunette glanced again at Madeleine. "Tell us about Monsieur De Valmy. One hears he is rather unconventional in his tastes."

"Or better yet, tell us about the marquis of Brecon," challenged the redhead. Her voice held a shade of envy and spite. "Too bad he is not here. Rumor says he is a man vastly equipped to please in both the purse and the breeches! And tell us, have you found his legendary proportions bold enough to please?"

"I beg your pardon, you must have me confused with someone else." As their avid faces remained trained on her, Madeleine rose and moved away.

"The offensive little tart!" exclaimed one of the women. "Who does she think she is fooling?"

"To hear her, one would think she did not spread her legs but to wash between them!"

Madeleine ignored the ribald laughter and curious glances of the rest of the company as she passed out of the room, her meal left uneaten. She had suspected the true reason for her being invited here. Now it was plain. She was expected to provide entertainment to such gentlemen as required it. She tried to shut out the panic behind such a realization but she could not. De Valmy had brought her here for his delectation or perhaps that of someone he chose to impress.

She could not look to her aunts for protection. She had

the feeling, despite their smiling faces, that they were more afraid of him than she was. Why else would they have insisted on sharing a bedroom with her? But they would not be able to watch her every second.

Nor could she simply run away, which she had no doubt she could accomplish despite the snow and cold. But if she did, De Valmy's wrath would then fall on her aunts and perhaps even her mother. She must seem content if not pleased to be here.

Retiring to the library, she found it blessedly empty. After a quick survey of the shelves, she plucked out a novel, discovered an out-of-the-way nook behind a curtained alcove and, despite the chill, curled up on the windowseat to apply herself to the text. At least alone she was not subjected to constant ogling. During the masquerade tonight she would find someone willing to drive her back to London. If that meant cuddling the young baron, she would. Better his than De Valmy's touch.

The guests for the masquerade began arriving in late afternoon, everyone expecting to change into costume once they arrived. The gentlemen for the most part did not appear until well into the late afternoon, having been on an expedition despite the cold to observe the progress of the Martello gun towers being erected in anticipation of Napoléon's invasion. And so the talk had turned to war and the politics of war until the bell rang to announce that it was time to dress.

Madeleine walked through an empty hallway toward the steps that led down to the ballroom level. She had deliberately waited until most of the others were finished powdering and primping and scolding maids they thought were too clumsy or slow or ignorant to know which pieces of their costume went where.

There had been any number of shepherdesses in farthingales and enormous broad-brimmed hats and little crooked staffs but their bodices were cut so low as to reveal all but their nipples. In one case, a woman dressed as an Egyptian deity sailed past in a gilded headdress rather like a ram's head that obscured all of her face but her wickedly smiling mouth. Her pleated linen dress, held up by tiny straps, left completely free breasts whose nipples had been rouged with carmine. There were Marie Antoinette gowns with center panels removed to reveal silk-clad legs with fancy beribboned garters. Others wore medieval cone-shaped hennins with veils that hid their face but gowns cut so deep as to make a mockery of the masks. Still others wore fanciful gowns more suited to a Turkish harem that revealed a flash of thigh or turn of breast. In common was the emphasis on titillating the amorous eye of a male.

Madeleine wore the beautiful gown Mrs. Seldon had made for her months ago when everything in her life had seemed possible.

"You must not wear the chemises," Justine had admonished her. "It spoils the gown. Off, off with them! Do you want to put a damper on the evening?"

Madeleine moved slowly from the stairs to the entrance of the ballroom draped in the merest silhouette of sheer gray silk beneath which her silk-stockinged legs undulated like shadows when she moved. She told herself that she had done things more courageous or daring than enter this ball under a mere drape of silk, for instance crossing France on foot, bargaining with smugglers, and dissembling her way in the marquis's home. But each of those decisions had been her own and endangered no one but herself.

With her aunts' help her hair had been arranged to leave a dozen smoky tendrils curling about her face and neck while the crown had been drawn back and secured as before with a switch of curls decorated with a cluster of gray silk roses and silver leaves. Beneath her mask her lips were darkened by crushed rose petals. Lady Harold had provided masks for those, like Madeleine, who had not brought their own. Hers was a simple black velvet one that amply covered her eyes and nose.

As she stepped into the room she was acutely aware of every shift and sound and sensation. The silver-tasseled cords of her bodice swung gently beneath her bosom as she moved, like silent bells pealing out her passage. Gradually she began to understand the allure of a masked ball. She felt like someone different, someone stronger and more courageous than herself. She was for the moment someone more invincible and less afraid than the mere mortal Madeleine Foucant.

She felt strangely emboldened behind her mask even though her body had never been more revealed. She could tell by the puzzled stares and whispered comments that followed her progress into the room that no one recognized her. Yet as she passed one of the mirrored panels of the ballroom she did not at first recognize herself. And then she smiled. The play around her was all quite risqué. The crowd was rapidly growing drunk though it was hours yet before the late supper that was planned. The orchestra was playing a tune appropriate for the more libertine couples who wished to try their balance and footwork in the bold new dance from Austria called the waltz.

Madeleine turned away from the men and women twirling round and round in one another's arms. It was quite embarrassing, rather like watching strangers kiss.

After a few minutes, Madeleine noticed that De Valmy was among the gentlemen lounging at the edge of the dance floor. He was not in costume but retained his severe black attire. He carried a mask on a stick but he did not hold it up to his face, as if he preferred everyone to know who he was.

When he turned suddenly and spotted her, the glittering glance he gave her made her heart jump. She did not think he yet recognized her but she could not take the chance.

She turned and moved hastily toward the nearest exit.

It led into the solarium which she had not been in before. The room was lit by Chinese lanterns but they did not illuminate the dark corners so that when she trod on a foot in the path, she cried out in as much surprise as the owner.

The couple, who occupied a stone bench, broke apart. The man's shirt was hanging open and the lady's bodice was completely unlaced. *"Pardon, monsieur, madame,"* she whispered though she was absolutely certain they were not married to each other.

She seemed the only one discomforted by the interruption. They smiled at her with bright feverish eyes, then turned away if she were of no more importance than the passing of a butterfly on the wing. She saw the gentleman's hand reach up and caress the lady's naked breast. Before she had the presence of mind to turn her back, he looked back at her and winked.

She turned rapidly away in the opposite direction of the ballroom, wanting just a moment to restore her nerve. A few seconds later, she heard footsteps behind her and darted into the shelter of a large overhanging palm, afraid De Valmy had followed her after all.

The distinct clink of boot heels neared and then she saw a shadow appear on the solarium floor before her. The sharp silhouette of a regimental shako and the unique shape of a pelisse hanging from his right shoulder betrayed his costume as that of a soldier. His shadow lengthened on the flagstones as he moved toward her.

She watched in trepidation as he passed. Yet, this was not De Valmy. The stranger wore the signature sky-blue dolman, fur-lined pelisse and overalls of a French hussar. Considering the fact that the masquerade's host was a British officer, and that the gathering was rabidly opposed to Napoléon, it seemed a daring if not outright foolhardy costume.

Suffused with a tingling excitement that someone else besides herself shared at least a fleeting contempt for the evening, she stepped suddenly from the shadow as he passed.

"*Halte,* Monsieur Hussar," she called softly after him.

He turned sharply on his heel. Something familiar in the set of his shoulders drew her eye, yet she would swear she had not seen him earlier in the day. As the lantern light fell across him she saw that this was not an approximation but a genuine uniform of the most flamboyant regiment of the French Army.

Excitement laced through her as she noted the sky-blue color. The wide black leather inseams and red striped overalls, the braided dolman and fur-edged pelisse, and red sash were all items with which she as a Frenchwoman was familiar. Who was he?

He wore a narrow mask beneath the brim of his shako, hiding his eyes, but a devilishly attractive smile lifted the silky mustache slashed across his upper lip. A plaited piece of brown hair hung by his right cheek, bound by a tiny red ribbon. It was this last telling detail that made her smile. French hussars were notoriously vain.

For a long moment he continued to regard her as though it was no surprise to him that she had stopped him. He was not as tall as De Valmy, but even in the stillness there was a dramatic vitality to his broad shoulders and long, muscular legs. It was only when she noticed her own shadow stretched out between them like a plea that she saw clearly and in great detail the shape of her calves, thighs, garters, and hips through the sheer veil of her gown. Backlit to his advantage, she could hardly have been more naked. And that, most probably, was why he was staring.

"Would mademoiselle care to dance?" he asked in perfect courtly French.

"I do not know this German waltz," she answered in French.

He approached her slowly, his left arm extended, palm up. "Then you must permit me to teach you, for your countrywomen swear by the delight to be had in it."

Madeleine did not doubt that the delight came from the lascivious pleasure of partners being held in one another's arms.

Yet this compelling stranger seemed far removed from the tawdriness of the weekend. It was not until his firm warm hand closed over her silk gloved one that she realized she had held it out to him.

As he drew her toward him, Madeleine experienced the sudden heady feeling that he knew how inexplicably attracted she was to him. She told herself that it was because he reminded her of home, because the uniform was just the sort of bold gesture she longed to make to the company inside those ballroom doors.

He slipped his left arm about her waist and she gasped as the heat of his hand branded the small of her back through the thin fabric. "Mademoiselle wears so little I feared she should be cold," he whispered in French, "but she is not. I am deeply honored."

The self-congratulatory bit of flattery made her laugh. "Are you always so certain of your effect on the ladies?" she asked, and lifted her hand in expectation that he would take it as she had seen the other dancers do.

"Mademoiselle will excuse the awkwardness but . . ." He released her to lift the edge of the pelisse slung over his right shoulder.

"You are hurt!" she exclaimed when she saw his sling.

His smile drew her attention to the shapeliness of lips half-hidden beneath his mustache. Something haunting in that firm curve of lower lip. Why would Sebastian's memory not leave her! "There is a war on, mademoiselle, and I am this country's enemy."

Madeleine caught her breath and then released it. "Not mine, I think," she answered deliberately.

She felt that behind his mask his eyes were leveled on hers. "No, never yours, I begin to believe. Then, for tonight, you will keep my secret?"

"Oui." The small word made her feel like a conspirator of great daring. "So, Monsieur Hussar, how is this dance accomplished?"

His chuckle moved warmly along her spine with bittersweet surprise. She must be a little mad, for it seemed everything and nothing at all reminded her of Sebastian d'Arcy. She moved unconsciously toward him, as if he might protect her from her own thoughts.

"Mademoiselle must put her right hand in my left, yes. And lay her left on my right shoulder." He nodded when she had done so. "As I cannot embrace you as I would like, you must hold on tightly, mademoiselle, and match my steps with yours. Are you ready?"

He moved slowly at first, humming softly in accented time to the music to help her find the rhythm. Madeleine curled her hand tightly about his neck as he picked up the rhythm, turning her ever more quickly until his boot heels rang on the flagstone and her slippers whispered in answer. Her heart began to beat a little more quickly. Her fingers clasped his more and more tightly. She stumbled only once, falling against the arm under his pelisse, and she saw his slight grimace.

"Oh, I've hurt you!"

He released her and placed his hand on her waist. "In German villages the men hold their partners about the waist while the women lay their arms about their partners' necks. It would make it easier and safer for us."

It was Madeleine's turn to laugh. "Easier, *oui,* Monsieur Hussar, but safer, I doubt."

Yet she raised her arms to his shoulders as he slipped his arm behind her back. They moved then as one, in and out of the light cast by the lanterns, amid the deep green and inky black shadows of foliage of the solarium.

When the music came to an end, Madeleine was breathless with surprise and something more. For a moment of blissful peace she stared up at him; her arms lay lightly circling his neck and his arm strongly supporting her back.

"Do you play these games often, mademoiselle?" he inquired in a voice it took no effort to realize was teasing.

"Never before, Monsieur Hussar," she answered equally lightly.

His face was in shadow but something in the darkness altered as the faint gleam of his teeth could be seen. "How can I believe that, mademoiselle, when you play at love so well?"

"Do I? I did not know," she answered simply. One hand slid down his front, her fingers curving into his lace belt. "It is only that . . ."

"Oui, mon coeur?" he whispered huskily as he bent to her.

"I feel as if I know you." She did not know why she said that.

"And do you want to know me better?"

"I don't— Perhaps." His lips were only inches from hers. *"Oui,* perhaps."

"That is a qualified yes." How reasonable his voice sounded when she was so anxious she could not draw an easy breath. "A night of love requires no great commitment, mademoiselle."

"A night—? *Mais oui.* I remember." How could she have forgotten! Everyone present was expecting to find a dalliance this night. Her hand tightened on the belt lying diagonally across his chest. "Oh, Monsieur Hussar, if you will take me away from here tonight, I will be most grateful."

"How grateful is *most,* mademoiselle?"

She leaned into him until the soft weight of her breasts

spread upon his chest. Her voice quavered. "How grateful do you require, Monsieur Hussar?"

He laughed, his warm breath gusting against her cheek. "I almost believe you are as innocent as you seem."

"But I am, monsieur. I am. Please, you must understand I am here under duress. I did not know what sort of party this was."

"But for consideration you are willing to be spirited away."

"Oui." Was she not behaving in the exact manner which she had been taught was appropriate for a woman with hopes of gaining wealth and influence through men who were attracted to her? Yes, she was, and she needed this man's help and protection.

When he reached the last little distance to lay his lips on hers, she moved to meet him.

The warm, searching mouth on hers was not a disappointment this time. Her pulses leapt in joy as her arms tightened on his shoulders. When his lips parted on hers, stroking hers open, she quickly and naturally supplied the shy touch of her tongue. His sigh of approval spilled into her mouth and the world of dark sensuality opened once more behind her closed lids. There was life after Sebastian d'Arcy!

When he finally dragged his mouth from hers, he was no longer smiling. "You surpass my expectations, Mignon. *Félicitations.*"

Eighteen

That deep calmly amused voice could only belong to
one man.

"Sebastian?" she whispered incredulously.

He put a finger to her lips and drew her with him to
the far end of the solarium where the sounds of the revelry
and the light of the lanterns did not reach. Finally, there
was only the whisper of the wind outside and the white
splash of moonlight streamed coldly through the glass panels of the solarium. He reached up and snatched off his
mask.

Straining in hope and anxiety, Madeleine sought hints
of recognition in the masculine face turned toward her. But
his features were silvered by moonlight and obscured by
the black velvet slash of shako brim, dense glossy mustache, and angled shadows of the night. Then he smiled
again, a sensual self-assured smile of confidence, and she
knew.

She did not break the silence he had imposed even as
he pulled her to him as if they were still in the dance and
spun her around so that she was pressed against one of
the Greek columns that supported the rotunda ceiling.

He unhooked the strap that held his shako in place and
tossed it away. He unbuckled his pelisse, letting it slide to
the floor. Then he reached up with his left hand to catch
her face in the branch of his fingers. "First this," he whispered against her mouth.

He kissed her as softly as if he had never touched his mouth to hers before. She tasted the music of desire in him as the dizzying pace of the waltz they partnered now moved inside her. She pressed the contours of her body to his, breasts to the rough texture of his woolen dolman, her stomach cradling the first stirring of his arousal, her legs brushing against his heavy thighs in invitation.

The hunger in him came with an unexpected swiftness as he suddenly pulled her closer. His kisses became wilder, a heady heated tangle of lips and tongues.

She lifted hands to embrace his face, letting the party and the night and the world drift away. All she needed was him and the delicious sensation of his wanton mouth pressing and licking and sucking at hers until it seemed she would find her release through the persuasion of his kiss alone.

She felt his hand glide over her body. It was like making love to a familiar stranger. The sensations were different, the rasp of beard, the silky brush of mustache on her skin, and yet the taste and touch of him was blessedly the same.

Her hands went to his trousers but she could not find the placket. He laughed softly. "Let me." He unhooked his dolman with his left hand and then the tabs that hid the buttons of his overalls. She heard him swear under his breath at his released suspenders and then tackled with one hand the double row of buttons.

She tried to help, and his choked chuckles of frustration roused hers. Giggling like children, they struggled together to free him from the impossible complications of his uniform. Finally, he was undone enough so that she could push the heavy military trousers from his hips. The light furring of his buttocks tickled her palms as she shoved the wool down to his thighs and then she felt him arch hot and hard and free against her.

"My turn," he murmured as he caught her mouth with his.

Never releasing her, he slipped his wounded arm from the sling to use both hands as he gathered the sheer silk of her skirts. When she was bare to the waist, his hands slid underneath to caress and knead the warm naked skin of her hips and bottom.

She felt his knee press strongly to part her legs and then he bent slightly as he lifted her with his good arm. She surged up on tiptoe as he found the center of her and then he tucked his hips and arched upward, sliding into the incredibly welcoming warmth.

Madeleine caught her breath on an exclamation of joy. No one must hear them or they would be discovered. But he urged her higher against the column, his greater height demanding the angle. She hooked her arms around his shoulders and lifted herself, her silk-clad thighs closing over his narrow, naked loins.

Yes, mercy, yes! Sebastian thought as sharp pleasure arrowed through him. She had guessed with the intuition of a born sensualist what they needed. He held her against the wall with the taut weight of his upper body and pinioned her high with the length of his erection.

Held willing captive, she rode the long slow strokes that surged into her, teasing and demanding, begging a response. There in the secret silent darkness she yielded to his rhythm, the rhythm of desire.

When she was sobbing against his shoulder with each rocking thrust of his lower body, he cupped her down low and lifted her an inch higher, heard her gasp of breath and knew he had at last reached the secret center of her, filled her completely with sure steady thrusts that sought something that would last beyond this transient peak of pleasure.

Her hair whispered across his face in chiding reminder that it had been too long since he had last kissed her. Her grasping arms drew pain from his shoulder but it was a distraction almost necessary to keep him from exploding in the pleasure of their union.

He was accustomed to the sensations of pleasure, but his emotions had always remained untapped. But here, with Mignon, he could not separate one from the other. The sensations, hot, delicious, were inextricably bound in more compelling emotions of need and tenderness and— the fear that this bliss, this longing to exist with and in her might quite possibly last forever. But even in the midst of this ferocious dance of desire, he knew, through the fear, it was not going to be enough, this one sweet stabbing of possession.

When their bodies could no longer withstand the exquisite friction, they rode together the silent undulations of pleasure until she broke the quiet with tiny cries of overwhelmed sensation and he gasped in the rough convulsion of ecstasy.

Madeleine heard the woman's laughter as if from the distance of a separate plane of existence. If he had not caught her to him, nestling her face into the opening of his dolman, she might never have realized that someone was passing so closely by. Then the woman spoke.

"Good evening, *mon hussar.*" Madeleine felt a touch on her arm, but the fingers trailed away almost immediately and she knew the touch was meant for Sebastian. "When you have done rendering your service to the *jeune fille,* come to me," the woman whispered in a suggestive tone. "I am thoroughly conversant in all the French vices, monsieur, *soixante-neuf, mais non faire minette?*"

The firm hand at the back of her head was all that kept Madeleine from turning about to answer the woman's presumptions with proprietary anger. After a moment more Sebastian bent toward her, lifted her face from his chest and kissed her very softly. She felt the impression of his mask once against her face and realized that he had redonned his while she had lost hers.

"I cannot believe that woman would behave so—so—" she stuttered when he lifted his head.

"Whorishly is the adverb you search for," Sebastian supplied with a quiet voice. "You have not attended many masquerades, sweeting. I am surprised she did not ask to join us."

"Join us?" Mystification widened Madeleine's eyes. "How could she do that?"

His smile was as jaded as it was tender. "I forget how innocent you are."

"I am not so innocent," she remarked, feeling that this must seem a deficiency to a man of his vast experience.

"No, not so innocent." He stroked the cleft between her breasts with a finger. "And since you were so very glad to see me I shall consider broadening your sensual practices, but only so far. I do not wish you to aspire to the *ménage à trois* or any other act not limited to two."

Faintly embarrassed by his cavalier referral to their torrid lovemaking, she laid a gentle hand on the arm he tucked back in its sling. "How did you hurt yourself?"

He smiled tenderly, the moonlight making blue satin of his lips. "I did not hurt myself. Someone else did it for me. But come, button me up and I will tell you about it on the way to London."

"London?" Madeleine questioned as she reached for his waistband. Instead, she encountered the warm skin and heavy muscle of a bare hip. It occurred to her that the woman who passed must have noticed his overalls were down about his knees. She smiled as she looked up at him in possessive pride. No wonder she had issued the invitation. Sebastian d'Arcy unclothed was a very compelling sight. "Why are you leaving?"

"We are leaving." He bent to place a kiss on her brow. "I've a coach waiting. I came only to fetch you back to London."

A little of Madeleine's joy collapsed as she shimmied his trousers back up over his hips. "I cannot leave just yet."

"Of course you can."

She shook her head "No, you do not understand."

"Perhaps I do," he said a shade more coolly. "When you thought I was a stranger you asked me to take you away. Were you only looking for a dalliance?" She felt his eyes searching her face in the darkness. "You sounded afraid. What were you afraid of?"

She began refastening his buttons. "I cannot explain it all now. But I promise I will."

"Is it De Valmy?" he asked very quietly.

She lifted her head. "You know him?"

"I know of him." Again that note of reservation in his voice. "You are wise to be afraid of him. But not for long."

A steely sound like that of a blade being drawn from its scabbard edged his voice. It drew a sudden chill across her skin. "Why?"

"I should not tell you, sweeting . . ." His hesitation lasted the space of heartbeats. "But you will waste valuable time arguing if I don't. When he returns to London he will be detained by the authorities as a French spy. Then you need not worry about him ever again."

Madeleine's fingers paused on the last button as a shiver raked her spine. "What do you mean?"

"I suspect he will be summarily shot."

"Mon Dieu!"

"Don't waste your pity on him. Think of us. I made a great mistake in letting you go." He pulled her closer. "I want you. Come to London and be mine, Mignon."

Madeleine flinched. He had called her by the wrong name. Suddenly there was layer upon layer of deception between them. "We must talk, there are things I must explain to you, monsieur. Important things."

Sebastian stared down at her in the moonlight. He believed her innocent of plotting to spy for De Valmy. If he was wrong, if innocence could be so skillfully feigned, he did not want to know. "You may explain everything you think you need to on the journey back to London. But go now and change into something warmer, for it may snow again before morning. I will meet you in the foyer in fifteen minutes." He released her and gave her a little push. "Hurry, sweeting!"

She saw the strength in his face and the reckless desire to run away with him decided for her. "I— Oh, yes! I want to go with you. I will think of something."

Madeleine slipped back through the crowded ballroom attempting to avert her eyes from the participants. Even so, it was impossible to miss the orgiastic atmosphere into which the masquerade had degenerated. Couples were scattered in shadowy corners while others dominated the dance floor in unseemly displays. She hurried past them all and out a side door to find the back stairs.

She was relieved to find her bedroom unoccupied, for she did not want to explain to anyone, especially her aunts, where she was going and with whom. She would explain everything to Sebastian on the way to London, about her aunts, about her mother, about De Valmy's part, and perhaps he would be able to help her after all.

So anxious was she to change that she tore a seam at the shoulder as she struggled out of her dress. She paused a moment to gaze at the small tear and then tossed the gown aside. Suddenly she knew she would never want to wear it again because it would always remind her of the folly of this night.

She found a chemise and then laced half-stays over it before pulling a heavier chemise over all. She chose a high-waisted gown of burgundy cashmere and was pulling it over her head when the bedroom door opened and a man's voice said very softly, "Mignon?"

"I am hurrying as fast as I can," she answered in French through the top of the gown.

"I can see that, mademoiselle. But where are you going?"

Madeleine jerked her dress down, her head popping through the opening in alarm. "Monsieur De Valmy."

"A touching scene, effectively played." He came straight across the room. His gaze swept her with insolent mockery. "I had almost begun to believe I was in error about you. Such innocent ways. But I have seen firsthand that you are d'Arcy's whore and that fits very nicely into my plans for you."

"I am leaving tonight." Her defiance sounded deceptively strong to her own ears.

"Yes, by all means, for I need you in d'Arcy's good graces. Move into his home, his bed, anywhere that gives you access to his private papers."

"If you think I can induce him to pay Madame Justine's gambling debts you are mistaken."

"My dear child. That is nothing, a mere inconvenience. I was looking for a hold over you and tonight it's been provided."

"You are not making sense, monsieur."

"Then let me be clear." He caught the loose curl that hung near her left ear and tugged it. "I know you are the marquis's *petite amie.* I know you are Madeleine Foucant. Best of all, you are Ondine Foucant's daughter. Ah, this time you do not jab at me with words. Do you know why this makes me so happy?"

"You will be pleased to tell me."

"Mais oui, I shall. It means, my dear, that better than bedding you I can use you to fuck Monsieur le Marquis of Brecon. Too crude an analogy for your delicate tastes? You surprise me, for you thought nothing of lifting your skirts just now for his pleasure."

Madeleine shuddered. He had seen them, watched them!

"But then, you thought you were alone, did you not? You have my compliments. You are a superb whore. I have great need for one of your talents. Your protector works for the English government. When called upon, he gathers certain intelligence against Napoléon. I suspect he has just returned from France. I need to know what he has learned. And you, dear little daughter of Ondine, are going to get that information for me."

"I refuse."

"Do you? And how do you think your mother will feel when she learns that she must abandon all hope of retrieval from Napoléon's dungeon because her daughter prefers to spread herself under an English marquis?"

"I don't believe you."

"You cannot afford not to. Have you received one message, one word, one sighting of your mother since she left London? I will tell you why not. She is spying for me, for France, for her royal lover whose bastard you are. Oh, yes, I know quite a few things which your ridiculous aunts thought me too stupid to understand. Only the matter of your identity was in doubt until this evening. Your *tante* Justine has two weaknesses. She is very fond of the gaming tables, and equally fond of young men. She warned a young baron away from you this evening with the warning that he must not commit familial incest by bedding both her and her niece in the same weekend."

Madeleine whitened. She did not know whether to believe this profane man, but the method of his knowledge was a moot point. He knew everything.

"If you ever hope to see your mother alive again you will find out what I want to know. Only *I* know where she is and how to bargain for her life. The men who hold her want information. See that you have something for me when I return to London on Tuesday."

"Do not go back to London, monsieur." Her conscience reared up in warning that by speaking she was betraying Sebastian's trust. But, if there was the slightest chance that any of what he said about her mother was true . . . "You will be arrested."

"What did you say?"

Madeleine swallowed traitor's bile. "You swear to me you will save my mother?"

"Don't toy with me, little one. I could tear out your throat here and now."

"Lord d'Arcy told me tonight that you are to be arrested as a spy the moment you return to London."

"Why would he tell you that?"

"Because he was jealous. He thought that I—that we—" She could not finish the thought.

But De Valmy was smiling again. He reached out and patted her chill cheek. "Good girl. I knew you would bring me luck." He stepped closer to her. "Give me a kiss for luck, Madeleine. For if you hope to see your mother again, I will need it."

Sebastian d'Arcy knew impatience was not a virtue but he had often found it useful. After sending a note to his coachman, he had strolled the ballroom and found De Valmy missing. There were any number of places he might be, engaged in any number of acts, but intuition and impatience to be gone with Mignon drove him above stairs. He heard voices and stopped to look in at every room along the second-floor hallway. When he came to the last room the door was ajar and the voices he heard exploded his dream.

"Remember, Madeleine Foucant, your mother's life depends on what you can extract from the marquess. May you find the method as entertaining as you have tonight."

"Where will you go, Monsieur De Valmy?"

"Somewhere safe, thanks to you. I will send for you when I can. Be ready with the information I seek."

Madeleine Foucant. The name was like a bullet passing

through Sebastian's brain, shattering and scattering his thoughts. Not Mignon but Madeleine! The Foucants' little niece! In league with De Valmy. Warning De Valmy! Betrayer! Spy!

Something inside him cracked. Emotions poured forth over the gaping wound of his mind. But it was not the hot murderous rage he expected and had experienced before. This was an ice-cold wrath so frigid it seared closed the torn and bleeding sentiments of betrayal, grief, and ravaged pride.

Madeleine Foucant was a spy.

He had taken her in, taken her to bed, taken her perhaps into his heart. And she had come into his life, into his arms, into his bed and his heart for one purpose: to betray him.

His hand was on his saber, yet his icy seething froze rash action. But to satisfy the blood lust pumping through him he let a scenario play out in his mind. He would slay them both now. He would then explain to Whitehall how he had found them together, overheard their conversation, and taken matters into his own hands. He would be exonerated of the crime of passion. Or, better yet. He was dressed as a French soldier. They were on the Channel coast. He could plant enough clues to make the masqueraders believe that a Frenchman had stolen into their company to commit an act of butchery to terrorize the English with the knowledge of how easy it was to cross the Channel.

Even as he thought it through he knew he would not act. Tempers and emotions were running far too high. No, he would handle this in his own way, in his own time.

He pushed the bedroom door a fraction wider and his heart wrenched in a way that was new. Mignon—no, Madeleine stood in De Valmy's embrace.

"Pardon me," he said clearly in French. "I must be in error."

He saw Madeleine start away from De Valmy but the

Frenchman merely turned with a smile. "No, Monsieur Hussar, you are not. I was just taking leave of the mademoiselle. I leave the field to you, monsieur. *Bonne chance."*

Sebastian stiffened as De Valmy moved toward to door to pass him. It would take so little, only a single thrust from his saber to end this. So little effort. The hand of his sword hilt trembled in bloody anticipation. But the man brushed past him and out into the hall.

He turned his attention on the woman—the spy!—who was pretending to coward before him. A very poor beginning for one of her talents, he thought dispassionately. He needed dispassion or God help them both!

"It is not what you think," Madeleine began, though she found it faintly disturbing to address a man in a mask.

"What do I think, sweeting?" he asked in English.

She hesitated in answering. How much, if anything, had he overheard? How much did she risk telling him? No, she could not say anything until she had time to think about all that De Valmy had just revealed to her. But first, she must mollify Sebastian's very understandable anger. He loved her, and she him. Therefore it did not seem an impossible task.

She took a conciliatory step toward him. "You must think De Valmy is my lover. But I have not taken any lover because . . . I wanted only you." She trembled a little because he was so silent behind that mask and she felt so guilty despite her innocence in the matter.

"De Valmy tried to force himself on me just now because I told him we are going away together. There, does that not satisfy your pride?" she asked sharply when he continued to stare at her in silence.

"You satisfy me. My pride be damned!"

He moved toward her, a stalking movement that made her back up long before he closed the distance between them. "I wanted you from the first day. I still want you."

Despite his admission he sounded more angry than before. "But if you're going to be mine, I won't have you spreading yourself for anyone else. Who is my competition? Beside De Valmy. Who else?" he snarled.

"There has been no one else." Madeleine tried to elude him but he caught her by the wrist and the pressure of his fingers made her whimper.

"No man has smiled at you?" His voice was deceptively calm now, modulated to inspire confidence but she knew him too well to trust it. "No man has touched you like this?" He trailed fingers along her face and then over her mouth. "No man has kissed your lips?"

Sebastian felt her jerk away a second before he would have kissed her, and he knew he had struck a chord of truth. "Who was he? Tell me!"

"Lord Everleigh," she gasped out as he squeezed her arm painfully.

"You lay with Bram?"

With his mask still in place, Madeleine could not tell whether he was more surprised by the man's identity or the idea that she was admitting to having known another man carnally. "He—I kissed him. That's all."

"Why all, *mon coeur?*" How gentle his voice and how cold. "I know my cousin and he isn't the sort of man to leave a lady in—distress."

"I tried to seduce him," she said defiantly, hoping the ring of truth would save her. "But then I changed my mind."

"Why?" The whispered question was as much a threat as an inquiry.

"Because . . . because he was not you."

Sebastian stilled. "That is a very good answer, a clever answer, a courtesan's answer."

"It is the truth." She jerked her arm and was surprised to be released. "Go to the devil, Sebastian d'Arcy!"

"Ah, a hint of the duchess." She heard the smile in his voice. "You remember a little of what I taught you. But then I was not your only teacher. Was I?" He stalked her slowly, herding her toward the bed without her even realizing it. "Tell me what else you've learned. Tell me about Bram and De Valmy. I am truly curious. Call it scientific inquiry, a footnote to my tutelage. Come, don't be shy. This is your chance to confess. You won't get another."

Madeleine kept moving back, one small step at a time. She told herself she had no reason to fear him. She loved him and he wanted her. That was reason enough to throw her arms about him. But she did not dare. She had heard this tone of voice once before, in the music room the day he castigated and humiliated her with his kisses. Her heart beat in sickening thuds. He hadn't even been angry that day. Now he was furious.

She put up a hand in unconscious defense of his advance. "Please listen to me. I have done none of the things you believe. All that I have learned since I left your house is how to be miserable and unhappy without you." A little of her natural spirit returned as he paused a little distance away. "You taught me how to smile at inane conversation, to flirt with self-conceited idiots infatuated with their own consequence. I think the lesson highly overrated. As you directed, I have allowed men to believe that I am a pleasant docile creature of ease. Yet it seems to me that this only encourages men to think of women as foolish creatures incapable of sense and consequence." Her chin lifted. "All in all, I think I should rather be a *chef de cuisine.*"

He paused. "I almost believe you. Except, of course, that I found you in De Valmy's arms. What hold does he have over you?"

"No hold," she lied too quickly and saw an unexpected abyss of more lies open suddenly at her feet. An instant later the bed abutted the back of her knees.

Sebastian reached for her again and this time he was pleased to see her shrink before his touch. "I did not spend valuable time teaching you only to have you waste yourself on offal like De Valmy. You have deplorable taste in your choice of bed partners."

"Does that include you?"

His smile was not pleasant. *"I chose you, ma petite amie.* You have learned a few tricks to please a man. We played our little game tonight and discovered that we still share a certain facility for mutual pleasure."

"I think I have heard this speech before," Madeleine answered in a fury of resentment. "There is no reason for me to deny again that I am De Valmy's mistress, even if I was. You put me out of your life several months ago. Therefore you have no say in what I do."

He tore the mask from his face and his expression made her gasp. "I beg to differ, mademoiselle." He caught the neckline of her unbuttoned gown in his left hand and yanked her close. "You owe everything you have, your home, your safety, even the clothes on your sweet back to me!"

Despite her sudden fear, Madeleine stood up to him as she had always done. "If you want your things back, monsieur, you may certainly have them!"

Her defiance was the final provocation. The notorious d'Arcy violent temper flared beneath the ice of Sebastian's righteousness. His pulse pounded with the demand for vengeance, for punishment of the woman who had so treacherously betrayed him.

"So then," he whispered savagely, "let me have all that I have purchased, my little slut!"

Madeleine could not believe her ears. "What?"

"You heard me." He tossed his mask on the bed and then casually crossed his arms. "You say you will give me back everything I gave you. By all means do so. You came to me with nothing. You shall leave as you came. Undress now!"

"But I—"

He moved swiftly and he had her by the shoulders before Madeleine could elude him. "By God! Do as I say or I won't be responsible!"

She could not believe that he would physically assault her but his expression was so strange, so remote and yet so etched by rage that she no longer trusted her own instincts. If it came to a struggle, she realized with growing horror, it would be one-sided and she would be the loser.

"Release me and I will do as you ask."

He did.

As she pulled the dress from her shoulders, Madeleine closed her eyes and went deep inside herself, willing the moment away.

"Look at me, mademoiselle." His voice was like a slap.

She opened her eyes to find him smiling at her but fury made that smile very unpleasant. "I want to know that you are aware that this time you disrobe only for me, your most generous benefactor."

Madeleine locked eyes with Sebastian but she no longer recognized him. This man, this coldly furious aristocrat, was a stranger. She told herself that the shame and humiliation ripping through her were not hers but belonged to the sordid moment. Even if she had taken another lover, it was her affair. She had a right to love whom she chose, where she chose.

As her gown slipped from her hands she heard the harsh intake of his breath. She could not tell what he thought. She did not dare look at him again. She would shatter.

At last the final garment slipped from her hands onto the floor. Without even a blink, she kicked the clothing toward him, standing erect and naked before him.

The moment of triumph brought Sebastian no satisfaction or joy. Her beauty was like a wound in his heart. Even when bowed to his will, she still possessed a quiet inviolate dignity of spirit. He had not vanquished her for tossing his love away, only shown himself to be the most venial and vindictive of men.

Damn her! Damn his own black soul! Punishing her for not loving him did not ease his soul. Far from it. He had released the beast inside him he had always been afraid was there. His father's legacy. His methods might differ but his capacity for inflicting pain was the same.

Some latent sense of decency within him was appalled by that realization. He reached out with the inexplicable and unconscious desire to comfort the victim of his temper.

Madeleine did not cower or even flinch when his hand touched her bare shoulder. Instead, she looked up at him with a steady gaze of indignation and abhorrence. "Will you now add rape to this delightful scene, monsieur?"

The question snapped the final bonds of his rage. When he backed away from her, it was out of revulsion with himself. For, despite what he had just overheard, despite her betrayal and his thwarted notions of love—despite everything—he still wanted her.

He lifted his eyes to hers. "I apologize for the last moments. I was needlessly harsh."

"Leave me!" Madeleine whispered, wrapping her arms about her nakedness. "Please, go away!"

"You are right." He nodded once as if responding to some internal voice only he could hear. "I am rude and boorish to force myself where I am not wanted."

He turned abruptly and went to the door. When he glanced back he said in a voice curiously devoid of emotion, "I shall remember when next you are in London to send you a token of regard and reward. As I told you once before, it is the way of men to sometimes be cruel. We are quick to anger and just as quick to forget that anger when faced with a beautiful woman."

Madeleine watched in trepidation as he hesitated and then he spoke again. "I find, despite the last minutes, that I am still inclined to make an offer for you. When you have conquered your quite understandable resentment toward me please come to me in London."

Madeleine bit her lip. These were the words she had prayed for yet despaired of hearing for two long miserable months. But now they made a mockery of all she had felt and thought he felt. She longed to hurl a curse at him, to blurt out the real reason she had suffered De Valmy's embrace but De Valmy's final threat stopped her.

If you ever hope to see your mother alive again you will find out what I want to know. Only I know where she is and how to bargain for her life. The men who hold her want information. Move into the marquess's home, his bed, anywhere that gives you access to his private papers.

She had no choice, no choice at all. Still, he had taught her many things, one was that a repentant man was easier to manipulate. Though she might have to come to him later, she must not allow him to walk away this night with her pride as his victory. Oh, but she hated him for the lesson.

She stood trembling with tear-swollen tears that blurred his image. "I warned you once before that I would never again suffer your insult. I never wish to see you again, monsieur."

Still too angry to trust himself to force compliance from her now, Sebastian drew back toward the door. "Mademoiselle may take the rest of the week to think about it. You know my address in London." He clicked his heels smartly like a French officer and bowed. *"Au revoir."*

Madeleine knew she must not stop him but by the time his boot steps faded in the hall she had drawn blood where her nails bit into her palms.

London, December 24, 1803

The streets were covered in a thick blanket of snow at this early morning hour. But inside the d'Arcy townhouse the rooms were warm and well lit. The dining-room table was set with the best china, crystal, and silver for a festive breakfast. The company assembled at this unusually early hour was ready to celebrate with more purpose than usual this Christmas Eve morning.

Sebastian stood alone in the front salon consuming a morning brandy, rare for him, as he waited for the last guest to arrive. He had dressed carefully in a sapphire velvet evening coat with black satin lapels. His waistcoat was white brocade embroidered with gold thread. His white satin breeches, clocked silk hose, and gold-buckled shoes were all new, commissioned expressly for the occasion. The heavy pristine lace peeking beneath his cuffs and cascading down his front was an extravagant expense. Even his sling of black silk had been tailored. In short, he was dressed with a degree of formality rare for a man of his temperament. That was because he was expecting a very important visitor. A very special visitor. A woman. Madeleine Foucant.

He had made his decision days ago, before he sent the invitation to her. He knew exactly what he was doing. He was going to take Madeleine under his protection. He was going to use her to lure De Valmy into a trap of his own making. Then, when he had learned all he could, he was going to get rid of De Valmy without Whitehall's knowledge or consent so that De Valmy would not have a chance to implicate the Foucants as accessories in his spying.

There was a certain gallantry in his thinking. The Foucants had been kind to him when he was young and vulnerable. They had offered him friendship and diversion and acceptance that he had never before known. He was certain that they were incapable of purposeful treason. Their own weaknesses and foolishness must have led them into De Valmy's web of deceit and lies. And so he would save them because they had once saved him.

As for the other, for Madeleine, well, there was no sane

explanation in that. But there was a reason why he would save her, too.

God help him, he had fallen in love at last.

It gave him no joy, no hope for the future, no lightening of spirit or freshening of resolve to amend his life.

It was a match made in hell, but he could not watch as they stretched her pretty neck at the end of a rope outside Newgate Prison. God help him, he could not!

He did not hear the doorbell as it jangled in the butler's hall, but he heard the front door opening and then a light cherished voice. He turned from the mantel, steeled himself, and when the knock sounded on the salon door he said in a voice that managed to sound absolutely normal, "Come."

She wore an enveloping cloak of wine red wool trimmed around the hood and down the front in silver fox. When she spied him across the room, she stopped short so that the cloak swung and shaped in floating grace about her.

"You look well, Mademoiselle Mignon," he greeted, stifling the urge to turn away, to run away. "I trust the Foucant ladies came with you?"

"Oui." She looked cornered as she lifted back her hood to reveal a pale-blue satin bonnet trimmed in cream ribbons and artificial lilacs. But then she straightened and came into the room. "Monsieur Horace says you wished to speak privately with me, my lord?"

"I do." He set his brandy on the mantel and moved toward her. "Allow me to take your cloak. Why did you not give it to Horace?"

Madeleine could not control her start when his hands reached for the frog that held her cloak closed at her throat, but his fingers were nimble, his touch light. "I was not certain I was staying."

"Still angry, are you?" Sebastian whisked the cloak from her shoulders. "I see you wear my mother's butterfly bracelet," he remarked as she lifted a gloved hand to resettle her bonnet. "So much the better. I did tell you it was an engagement gift from my father?"

"I don't remember," Madeleine answered evasively. She had not known how she would feel when she saw him again. It had been ten days since he left Locksley House. He had shaved his mustache and trimmed his chestnut curls, but he still wore a sling. He looked as she first remembered seeing him, flagrantly male, elegantly featured, perfectly composed. But she now knew his other face, the one he kept hidden from the world behind a benign smile of amused tolerance. The truth was there in his blue eyes, their expression as brilliant and cool and distant as an untouchable star. If she were nervous and afraid, then it was because she was still a little angry, or maybe more than angry, *furious*. She could not be certain how he felt even after his invitation and gifts.

She saw his practiced rake's glance move over her, cool and assessing, and she withstood it because she had no choice. "Very nice," he pronounced of her gown of palest blue satin over which a skirt of white sarcenet has been laid.

"I'm glad the marquis approves," she returned smoothly, but he saw the hectic color rise in her cheeks and did not miss the rapid rise and fall of her chest. "Especially since it is you who chose and paid for it."

Sebastian smiled at this small display of spirit. He had, indeed, chosen and paid for it, along with her cloak and her shoes and satin bonnet. "I trust you find your new residence satisfactory?"

Madeleine shrugged. "It serves, my lord."

Once back in London, she and her aunts had moved back into the residence at Queen Anne's Gate. Ever since, she had been trying to work up the courage to come here. But she had heard from De Valmy the night before. A note had come to the house for her, brought by a street urchin. De Valmy was in hiding, but he would get in touch again.

When he did, she was to have for him the information he needed. And so she had come to the marquis's home because she had no other method of attaining what she needed to save her mother.

Sebastian tossed her cloak aside and moved a little away. "Why did you come here this morning?"

Madeleine looked at him and did not mistake his real question. "I have come to say that if you still wish to have me, I should like to be under your protection."

She held her breath as he stared at her. "Nothing else?"

"Oui." She clasped her hands together. "I am not who you think I am."

"You are Madeleine Foucant. Madame Henrice and Madame Justine are your aunts."

"You are well informed," she said slowly, watching for any sign of rage that should warn her to flee.

"Tardily," he remarked absently. "Whose idea was it to beard the reluctant lion in his Kentish den? Henrice's?"

"No, it was mine. My aunts knew nothing of what I had done until ten days ago."

He did not believe her, of course, but on this day, of all days, he did not want to hear her lies. "It doesn't matter."

He moved back to stand before her and took her right hand in both of his. He drew it to his mouth and kissed it with what seemed reverence. "You are here. I am glad." He then leaned so close she could see herself reflected in his azure eyes. "I still want you, Madeleine. I want you very much. Marry me."

"What?" She was too surprised to even blink.

He smiled, a genuine smile of amusement. "Marry me now. Today. I have obtained the special license. The minister waits on the other side of the salon door. Say yes."

Madeleine felt as if the earth had suddenly opened beneath her feet. He caught her as her legs collapsed under her. But the crazy spinning went on and on. She gripped his shoulders as he pulled her weight against him. "Say yes," he murmured against her ear.

Madeleine struggled with her conscience. "I must tell you something first."

"No!" he answered emphatically, and hauled her around to face him. His breath fanned her face. His lips hovered an inch above hers. "Don't spoil things. Just agree to be my bride. No more talk." He kissed her softly. "Say yes."

She simply looked at him, wondering who had ordered this miracle, and this damnation of an answered prayer. "Yes."

He almost believed the emotion shining in her dark eyes. He almost believed the joy swelling in his heart at her response. He almost believed that he looked upon the face of his love and saw that love returned full-fold in the face turned up to his. He almost believed. Almost.

Nineteen

"Good evening, Marchioness."

After nearly a week, Madeleine still jumped when so addressed. It did not help that on this particular occasion she was being so addressed by her own husband. She looked up from the book that had been half holding her attention for the last hour.

Sebastian lounged against the doorjamb of the dressing room that separated his bedroom from hers. He was in his shirtsleeves but he had already donned formal black satin knee breeches, white hose, and black slippers. He looked fit and confident and supremely virile. But the casual pose he struck with arms folded and ankles crossed in a way that drew subtle but unmistakable attention to his groin was an empty tease, and they both knew it.

"Good evening, *mon seigneur.*" She began to rise from the Recamier of cane and brocade where she had been decorously lounging in an attempt not to spoil her evening dress, but he waved her back into it.

"Do not rise on my account, sweeting. 'Tis yet a quarter of an hour before the carriage is due."

He came forward into her room, looking about as he did so. It was a strikingly beautiful room. The walls were newly hung in rose watered silk and decorated with mirrors and paintings. The chairs were upholstered in floral tapestries. Chippendale and Chinese pieces furnished the room and Flemish rugs overlay the floors. A fire blazed in cheerful warmth and the chandelier of French crystal winked merrily in the ceiling. Amidst it all was the huge bed hung with rose silk and cream lace, piled high with bolsters and pillows trimmed with ribbons and lace and pearls and beadwork, ruffles, tucks, and pleats.

Sebastian observed the bed with the critical interest he might have displayed when shown a new balloon design. The principle use of the structure was familiar but the dynamics of this particular specimen was not.

Well he might stare, Madeleine thought resentfully as she followed his eye.

She had expected that first night, after a dizzying day in which she was wed and then introduced to a good portion of the fashionable *haut ton* over a sumptuous wedding breakfast, to meet her new husband in that bed. But he stayed away. The second night she had ventured into his room, resigned to the fact that he wanted some sign of submission from her, only to be told in no uncertain terms that she was not welcome there.

And so she had remained for the last five nights, lying awake and waiting and wondering when and if and in what temper he would come, until she fell into an exhausted, fretful sleep.

It did not help that she started at the announcement of every caller nor that De Valmy had managed to contact her twice since she had become a marchioness. Once, on the street, an urchin had handed her a note. Then this morning, under the subterfuge of a note for her aunts, De Valmy had written that another of his informers had been arrested in France and that if she did not produce useful information by morning at the address listed, he was severing his ties with Ondine once and for all.

She had burned the note, but it had spoiled her day and would quite possibly ruin her life. She tried to tell herself she did not owe Sebastian her loyalty. He did not even treat her as a wife. But could she spy on him and get away with it?

Suddenly their gazes met, each haunted by the memory of their last encounter.

"Why did you marry me?"

She had not meant to ask that question. She saw it took him equally by surprise.

"Why, sweeting, because you are beautiful and young and entertaining."

Madeleine gripped the edges of her book tightly, determined to have the matter out even if it risked his temper. "You could have had all that . . . and more, by taking me as your mistress."

He smiled politely, charmingly. "Agreed. But it would not have gained me your undying loyalty, would it?" He saw the flicker of her lids as an expression of guilt. "And you would not be wrapped in the arms of protection which my name and title provides for you, correct?"

She watched him approach. "Did I need it? What of your theories about the Independent Woman?"

"A pretty fiction." He plucked the book from her hand, turned it over to read the title and smiled. "Like this." He laid the book in her lap, his fingers grazing her upper thigh as he did so. She saw his lids droop at the touch and then he drew away. "Certainly you would be the first to agree with that assessment. In the two and more months you were in London alone, were you able to progress at all toward the lofty goals I set you?"

"You know I did not," she answered. "But that was because I was confused and uncertain of myself. But I was learning, I think."

"Shall I tell you a secret?"

"If it pleases you."

"It does. While my theory held good and true facts, there is nothing any mistress, maid, or slattern wishes for more than to marry a man of title and fortune. And that is why my theory failed. You have won the pot, sweeting! And you did not even toss for it!"

Madeleine bristled. "You are wrong. I did not marry you for your money or your title and you know it."

He surveyed her coolly. "Do I?"

A tiny row formed between her eyes. "I think your theory has great merit, *mon seigneur.* I believe that one day women will be as independent as men. The flaw lay in the method you chose for a woman to achieve this."

Genuinely curious about the workings of her mind, Sebastian seated himself in a side chair a few feet away and asked, "How so?"

"You taught me that independence requires self-achievement. As long as a woman must look to a man for her wealth—whether earned by wedding or bedding—she is dependent upon him. And he, for the protection his name bestows or the coin he has spent, believes he owns her. One day, I believe, women will be allowed to achieve their wealth as many men do, through their own enterprise, industry, and abilities—not their bodies. They will be speculators, adventurers, and merchants. They won't come from the aristocracy, for I have seen your women and they do not aspire to more than what they can wed. But someone with a skill like me, who longed to be a *chef de cuisine,* someday a woman will achieve this. *Oui,* I believe it. When that day comes, men and women will choose to be together simply for the joy they find in one another."

"You may be right," Sebastian murmured, amazed as always by her incisive mind. For the first time it dawned on him that in the arrogant assumption that he knew what was best for this remarkable lady, he might have stolen something very important from her: her dreams.

He glanced around for another topic and then smiled. "My compliments, if I have not already given them, on the new chef you hired. He is a wonder. Are you trading secrets?"

Madeleine colored. *"Oui.* He is most accomplished, but I know some small things he does not."

Sebastian smiled despite himself. He could not imagine another marchioness in all of England admitting that she spent her mornings in the kitchen learning from her chef and giving tips in kind.

His gaze remained speculatively on her as she arched her back to relieve the tension. The thrust of her bosom above the low neck of her evening gown earned his begrudging admiration. "Why did you marry me?"

"Why did you?" she shot back.

"Because I couldn't help myself," he said simply.

For the first time since that night in the Locksley solarium she saw the naked look of longing in his gaze. But she knew by the set of his jaw that he was fighting it. "You don't sound happy. Well, neither am I."

"Isn't that no more or less than what we should expect?" he asked quietly, as if the full extent of their predicament had just dawned on him. "I've yet to hear of a happy marriage."

"I think you must know the wrong people."

"Really? How many blessedly wed couples have you in your acquaintance? Your parents, perchance?"

She flinched. How bitter he sounded. She did not know why she was stirring him up. Maybe just to see if he was as miserable as she. "I think, *mon seigneur,* that they loved better than yours."

"Do you really? And when were they wed?" Her expression pricked his conscience, but he was not prepared to shy away now that she had made them face the moment. "Or perhaps they were happy because they weren't wed. I'm told illicit love is the best. So far, I would have to agree with that, wouldn't you?"

She gazed into her lap. She was going to betray him any day, whenever the opportunity presented itself, for the sake of her mother's life. But, in her heart, she had not chosen against him. "It could have been different between us."

"Why should we want it different?"

She looked up at him across the chasm of hurt and anger. "I could have been a real wife to you."

"You *are* a real wife to me," he returned too lightly for honesty's sake. "And you may as well know that though I'm half French I intend to be an English husband to you. English wives are not permitted lovers. Do I make myself clear?"

"Infinitely," she snapped.

"Then I ask again. Why did you marry me, after you swore at Locksley Hall that you wished never to see me again."

Madeleine closed her eyes. That was the one question she could not answer truthfully. And so she fell back on silence.

He saw her pain, felt his own guilt, and wanted to end it. He had wanted a dozen times a day to beg her pardon for what he had done at Locksley Estate, but his humiliation of her did not seem a crime which could be easily assuaged by guilt or sorrow or contrition. He could scarcely bear to think of what he had done to her.

This time her gaze jerked up to meet his in challenge. He reached into his waistcoat and withdrew a stiletto with a jeweled handle. He leaned forward and offered it to her, handle first. "If you ever have cause, you may use this on me."

Madeleine eyed in horrified fascination the wicked needle blade he held. Then her hand closed firmly over the hilt as she looked up at him. "If you ever hurt me again, I will do you much mischief in return."

As strangely worded as her statement was, he did not doubt the sincerity of it. So then, it was a draw. He would never deliberately hurt her again, but she would never believe that he would not. A pretty marriage.

The sound of carriage wheels was heard below.

Sebastian stood up. "Ah, the moment arrives for our departure for the Holland House Assembly. Since you are ready and I have yet to finish dressing, I must beg a favor of you, Marchioness. I left a pouch in the library in my desk. I will need it tonight. Will you fetch it for me?"

"Certainly." She was glad for any excuse to get away from him.

He took a loop from his waistcoat pocket. She noticed he used his left hand and wondered if his wound still pained him. He never mentioned it, and since he never held her she had little opportunity to know. "You will need the key. The pouch is marked with the emblem of the Horse Guards. It should be impossible to mistake."

For one wild second Madeleine thought: *He knows! he knows!* But, of course, he could not.

She took the key dangling from his fingers, careful to avoid touching him.

"Have I told you how exquisite you look tonight?" His voice held the old husky quality of desire.

Madeleine turned her head away. *"Merci, mon seigneur."*

Sebastian waited until she had disappeared down the main staircase and then slipped back down the servants' stairwell. He shrugged into his evening coat as he went, wincing. His arm was still very tender though he had discarded his sling as bothersome.

He did not deceive himself in what he had planned. He was playing a dangerous game. If he lost he might well hang as a traitor himself. Whitehall might not accept his explanation that he had acted as he did out of duty toward a treasonous wife. He was gambling everything for a fidelity of feeling he had thought he could never experience. He loved a woman who did not and never would believe him capable of the emotion. How droll! How ironic! How just!

Once De Valmy was taken care of, if he and Madeleine

could not settle their differences, he would allow her to return to France and settle a sizable income on her. In a year or two, he would gazette the news that she had died and so they would both be free. By then he hoped with every bone and sinew of his being that—to him—she would be good and truly dead. But he doubted it. He would go to his grave with her name his last thought.

He stood behind a moveable panel in the room next to the library and watched as she searched his desk. He saw her hesitate before opening his pouch. He held his breath as she read through the papers. He saw her shake her head and then push them back into the pouch. What was this? Could he have been wrong about her? Was she troubled by scruples he had discounted as having sway with her? She was French, after all, and their countries were at war.

He had given the matter a great deal of thought as he lay in his empty bed this last week. Perhaps she did not consider what she was doing any worse than what he had done the past two months in France: listening to others' conversations, adding a quiet word here and there to spark an indiscretion, collecting, sorting, shifting information that might be worthwhile for his side. Was she, then, worse than he? Less driven by patriotic zeal? What then the folly but that they, as unacknowledged enemies, had fallen in love? So then it was up to him, the more experienced spy, to outwit and disarm her.

The Foucants had been tight as clams the day after the wedding when he had interrogated them about De Valmy. They would not say why Madeleine had been in his company. Nor would they say where Ondine was, or why. He very much feared they were all in the conspiracy of spying up to their pretty necks. But they had told him how Madeleine cried after he left her at Locksley House, she had admitted nothing but that they'd had a lovers' quarrel and that she feared she had lost him forever.

They were so happy about the wedding, ecstatic. Justine

had wept, crying again and again, *"Merci, le bon Dieu! Merci, le bon Dieu."* Henrice had simply smiled and nodded in satisfaction. Foucants seldom wed.

He had put the fear of the devil in them but warned them not to say a word about their conversation to Madeleine or he would cut off their allowance. But perhaps they had broken that promise. Perhaps she knew he was on to her and that all his careful planning to trap De Valmy was about to come to naught. If the army found the Frenchman first, they might all hang.

He was almost grateful when she suddenly took the papers and stuffed them in her cape. *At last,* his mind cried as his heart pounded with the scent of the chase. At last, the charade was over and the hunt begun.

He hurried from the room to intercept her as she left the library.

He caught her to him and kissed her hard and deep, almost as if he knew it might be for the very last time. He was only faintly disconcerted by the look he saw in her eyes when he lifted his head. He saw sorrow and pain and regret, very deep regret. And he saw passion. *Too late, sweeting! Much too late!*

He swung her around once, then set her on her feet and offered his arm.

Faint with trepidation and guilt over what she was doing, Madeleine stared up into his face as if he were a madman. "What is wrong?" she asked breathlessly.

"Nothing I cannot put right!" He smiled at her, an extravagant luxuriant smile of old. "Come then, sweeting, let us remember our exchange of vows. It's New Year's Eve and we are in love."

The New Year's assembly was a shocking crush. Madeleine and Sebastian sat half an hour in the cold as their carriage waited an interminable time for its turn to drop off guests at the assembly. While he longed to take her in his arms and keep her warm, Sebastian contented himself with watching his wife huddle under the fur blanket he had given her as a wedding present especially for use in the coach. She had questioned his choice of the heavy traveling coach when it was more usual to use the light more decorative barouche in town. He had explained that it was warmer and less exposed to wind, and hoped she would not notice the trunk strapped on the back when they alit.

When at last a footman opened their door and they were admitted past the crowd of gawkers come to view the beautiful dresses of the ladies and to gawk at their favorite nobles and persons of note, Sebastian saw that Madeleine was so anxious she had turned pale as a cream. "Are you ailing, sweeting?"

Madeleine shook her head and searched her mind for a suitable reply. "I do not so much like your friends and they do not like me. I am nobody and they know this. They cannot imagine why you married me."

"Certainly they can, and that is what really disturbs them." He smiled smugly. "I wed where I wished. If you do not come to bed with child within eight months, they will be even more vexed. Now come along, lady wife," he said heartily, rushing her past the press of people and into the brightly lit doorway. "Let's confound them even more."

Once inside, the atmosphere changed so abruptly as to be shocking. There was no space for chairs. The hallway and the main stairway were clogged with visitors. The brilliance of the hundred of tapers winked back at them from the necks and ears and wrists of the ladies. Once inside, the bitter, dry cold was replaced by the damp warmth of the sea of humanity.

The Whig stronghold was imperiously ruled over by Lady Holland, wife of the 3rd Baron Holland. A notorious supporter of Napoléon, the Hollands were considered the most political of hosts. No other salon in England or France could rival Holland House. If there were intrigue afoot this night, Sebastian suspected it would be found within or just without the walls of this most venerable of Jacobean edifices.

After they had been introduced to their hosts, Sebastian turned to Madeleine and said, "I fear I must leave you to make your own way for a few minutes." He patted the pouch she had fetched for him from the library. "If I have not returned in a quarter of an hour, go to the door and ask a footman to signal our coach. I will meet you at home."

"Wait!" Madeleine called in alarm, but Sebastian was drifting away from her through the press of elegantly clad overheated bodies.

Madeleine stood a moment in miserable indecision. She felt abandoned, dismissed, of no further use to him now that he had introduced her as his marchioness. She pulled her cloak a little more tightly about herself. Though she was perspiring from the heat, beneath her gown her body was clammy with anxiety. What was she to do with the papers she had stolen? How long would it take Sebastian to realize that they were missing? Worst of all, how was she going to get them to De Valmy?

"Marchioness?"

Madeleine swung around at the sound of a familiar voice. Making her way toward her was a pretty young woman with hair more golden than sunlight. "Audelia!"

The two young women hugged enthusiastically, drawing the jaded and curious attentions of those about them. The new marchioness knew a *fille de joie!* Several delighted gossips picked up that *on dit* as worth enduring the crush of the assembly.

"What are you doing here?" Madeleine asked when they moved a little apart.

"I came for a glance at Richard." Audelia's pretty face

dimmed. "He is here with his bride, I'm told. Have you seen them?"

"No. I am so sorry," Madeleine added softly. "I have been looking for you. I was told you were—how do the English say?—rusticating in the country."

A bright smile animated Audelia's face. "I was, and found it quite diverting. I've met someone new." Yet her smile did not quite meet her eyes. Her gaze was a little sharper and a little less naive than Madeleine remembered it. "It is more than I expected." She held out her arm to display a new gold bracelet. "But you, the new marchioness of Brecon? I could not believe when I saw it in the gazettes. How did you manage it?"

"I don't know," Madeleine answered truthfully. "I don't know if it will last."

"Of course, it will last." Her throaty chuckle was new, and vaguely disturbing to Madeleine. "Do you think a marquis marries lightly? Besides, it would take an act of Parliament to sunder your marriage. No, you are good and truly wed forever. So tell me, is he as rich as they say? Does he spoil you with jewels and clothing? Do tell me everything about his home."

Annoyed and vaguely upset by Audelia's avaricious interest in her husband's financial holdings, Madeleine interrupted with, "Did you come in your own carriage?"

"Yes, why?"

"May I borrow it?"

Audelia's eye rounded in amusement. "Don't tell me you are off for an assignation? You are but a week wed!"

"No, no, it's only that I feel faint from the crush of people but do not wish to leave the marquis stranded. I will return your carriage as soon as I arrive home."

"Then, of course, take it with my compliments." Audelia caught her by the arm. "Thank you for not snubbing me." Her animated expression softened with genuine emotion. "You are a true friend, not like the others."

What others? Madeleine mused as she settled herself into Audelia's carriage with a shiver from the abrupt return into the chill night. She suspected Audelia had been referring to only one other: Richard Baltry.

Now that the young nobleman was wed, he no longer sought out Audelia. It might be that his bride's family and his own were forcing him to be circumspect until the bride had conceived. Sebastian's lessons had been full of these little niceties of custom among the *ton,* but Madeleine suspected that Richard wanted his freedom. When he again turned for comfort to a *chère amie,* no doubt it would be someone equally young and fresh as Audelia had been when they first met. And so, Audelia had done as she must, found a new protector. And so she would pass from lover to lover until she either found a docile man willing to be a complacent husband or used up her youth and beauty in the attempt.

As often as she differed with her aunt Henrice, she now understood why her aunt deplored the lack of formality among the English which offered no protection of agreed payments and compensation for a mistress's "issue." Yet the English, according to Sebastian, thought the French formality in affairs to be mercantile. *Incroyable!* Audelia's offspring, should she not choose to use the *redingotes d'Angleterre,* would have nothing.

Love, then, counted for nothing if one did not wed. And, according to Sebastian, the *ton* wed only for gain. No wonder they stared at the new marchioness of Brecon with open mouths.

Madeleine gazed sadly out the frosty window. Once away from Holland House the streets were dark and empty, their black silence faintly sinister. Anxious to be done with, Madeleine tapped the front window of the coach for more speed. Once her papers were delivered, she would be done with De Valmy and she could hurry home to her husband.

Her husband. For the very first time, the thought made

her smile. In spite of her reservation over Audelia's choices, something Audelia had said had given her hope.

Sebastian could not divorce her without an act of Parliament. He did not seem the kind of man to make so binding a commitment rashly or lightly. He believed in the rigorous application of the scientific method. There was no gain to be had in marrying her by title, dowry, or even name. Therefore he must have felt he did not require any of those things in a bride. So what, then, he had used as criteria?

She was pragmatic enough not to believe that a shared appetite for sexual matters had snared him. She had read his memoirs. But perhaps she was not entirely wrong about his motives. Even tonight there had been a certain banked lust for her in his gaze. That memory gave her sudden cause to hope.

Perhaps De Valmy would be able to save her mother and perhaps Sebastian would never learn of her betrayals. And perhaps their life together would settle into something like normalcy. And then, just perhaps, she could set about to win her new husband's love and respect.

It was the first glimmer of hope in two weeks and she was young enough and in love enough to build a roaring bonfire of hope from the spark of a possibility.

When the driver climbed down to knock at the address Madeleine had given him, she waited in the carriage. Several minutes passed before the door to the inn opened and a tall, sinister figure wrapped in a black cloak exited and came to the carriage.

Madeleine lifted the latch to allow him to enter. "Monsieur De Valmy," she said without really looking at him, "I have your papers." She thrust them in the dark figure's direction. "Now leave me alone!"

The sounds of other footsteps did not rouse her curiosity until De Valmy suddenly cried out and then disappeared from the open carriage doorway. The next moment hands were reaching into the carriage for her. She screamed once, but the sound was blocked by a leather-gloved hand. She fought and kicked and tried to bite her captor, but he simply tossed her cloak over her head and voluminous fabric hampered her efforts. Then a second man grabbed her legs and she was easily hauled out of the carriage.

He heard a man groan in pain as she butted her head against his chest and then he growled in her ear, "Cease struggling! You won't be harmed!"

With her legs effectively captured at the ankles and thrust under someone's arm and her arms bound to her sides by more heavily muscled arms, she could not prevent being carried away. Strange thoughts floated through her mind as she lay cocooned in her own cloak. She considered what these men might want: ransom, rape and robbery, her jewels surely. Oh, Sebastian would be so angry when he discovered that she had lost his mother's bracelet. Would he be equally sad if she lost her life?

She was lifted up and gently placed on what felt like a leather seat. Another carriage? A moment later her cloak was lifted from her face. She instinctively put up her hands, ready for a struggle. "You!"

Sebastian grinned at her from the open doorway of their own coach. "I'll take that." He snatched from her hand the papers she had been about to give De Valmy and stepped back. A moment later he and his coachman lifted a heavy solid black bulk through the doorway and deposited it at her feet. It was Monsieur De Valmy, trussed and gagged.

Sebastian climbed in and shut the door, seating himself opposite her, with De Valmy between them.

As the coach lurched into action, the interior reflector lamp threw a wild and wicked light upon the sharpened features of the coach's inhabitants. For several long moments each regarded the other in anger and resentment and wary exasperation.

"How did you know?" Madeleine whispered in shame.

"You are not the only one who knows how to listen at keyholes."

Madeleine recoiled, astounded. "How long have you known?"

"You warned him!" Sebastian's voice betrayed deep emotion as he prodded De Valmy with a boot toe. "The night I came to take you away from the Locksleys you told him not to return to London. You let him get away!"

Thoughts shifted quickly through her mind. The sudden anger in Sebastian that night had not been spurred by pride or jealousy, as she had supposed. He was not so angry over the possibility that she had shared her body with De Valmy as with the fact that she had committed treason in warning his country's enemy of a trap. While it should not have made her feel better, because her crime was essentially worse, it did. She lowered her face from his gaze. "I had no choice."

"Did you not?" Sebastian absently rubbed his throbbing shoulder. "Could you not have come to me? Did you think I would betray you?"

"Yes, no—!" Madeleine shrugged. "I thought you would feel duty-bound as an Englishman to turn De Valmy over to the authorities. If that happened, I would never see my mother again."

He stopped rubbing his aching shoulder. "Why don't you explain that statement to me."

She did. As the coach rumbled through the near-empty streets, she told him everything that had occurred since she received the letter from her mother last August. He stopped her to ask a few questions but otherwise listened with an intensity that made her aware of how rare real attention was.

"So then, you see, I thought you must give me, give all of us up," she finished with a gesture of helplessness.

"You don't know me very well if you thought that." He

was silent a long time. "De Valmy is a spy, and a cunning conniving amoral blackmailer. I cannot let him go."

Madeleine gazed down at the man stirring at her feet. She suspected Sebastian had struck him very hard and with a great deal of pleasure. "You are going to turn Monsieur De Valmy over to the authorities." She looked up at her husband. "That will certainly cost my mother her life."

"It might, if that was what I planned to do. You have not asked me what my plans are."

Madeleine's heart beat a little faster. "What *are* your plans?"

He crossed his arms and smiled. "We are going to sea, sweeting, and then to France to fetch your errant mother home, and deliver a dog to his masters."

Madeleine stared at him, feeling the wild surge of hope and love she had been holding at bay. "You would do that for me?"

His tender smile pleated his cheeks and crimped the outer corners of his devastating blue eyes. "Haven't you guessed by now that I would do anything for you?"

It occurred to Madeleine to wonder if any declaration of love had been made in so strange a fashion, over the trussed body of an enemy. She glanced at De Valmy, who was now groaning.

"He knows where my mother is. He said that he is the only one who can help her. That if I didn't do as he asked and spy on you or if anything happened to him, *Maman* would be lost."

"He is remarkably well informed about the actions of Napoléon's spies for a man who professes to work for the royalist cause. How do you suppose he could gain freedom for your mother from his enemies?"

She considered the question. "I don't know."

"I think I do." He bent down and lifted De Valmy from the floor by his bound arms into a sitting position. Furious black eyes accosted him above the gag as Sebastian set the tall, angular man on the seat beside Madeleine.

Smiling, he sat back and laid a booted leg on the seat between De Valmy and Madeleine to keep them from touching. "Now, monsieur, or *citoyen,* or however you style yourself, we are going to have a discussion. You won't need to speak. Just listen and nod. I have possibly saved your life tonight. I say *possibly,* because it remains to be seen if you can be useful to me. So, I give you a choice. You can come to France with us, or you can take your chance with the first English garrison we pass. France?"

The man nodded once, a jerk of angry assent.

Smiling, Sebastian plucked Madeleine from the seat by De Valmy and deposited her beside him in the curve of his left arm but he grimaced as he did so. "Do you have your stiletto, sweeting? Good. You remember how to use it? Then I beg you keep watch a while. I need a few winks."

They reached the English coast just after midnight. It was obvious by then that Sebastian needed more than sleep. In tussling with De Valmy and then with her, he had reinjured his arm. When he tried to help Madeleine from the coach, his hand would not close firmly on hers.

Madeleine made no comment as they boarded the smuggler waiting off-shore for them, but as she listened to the men discussing the proposed plan for reaching France, one thing became increasingly clear.

She had changed into the clothing he had brought for her: heavy woolen breeches and thick wool stockings, a fisherman's sweater, and her red fur-trimmed cape.

"You cannot row ashore," she whispered to Sebastian three hours later as they neared the French coast. "Your shoulder won't withstand the stress."

"I see little choice. The captain won't spare his men to carry us ashore." In the light of the captain's cabin Sebastian's face looked pale and, despite the cold, sweat beaded up on his brow. A fever was coming on.

"Then someone else must do the rowing."

He smiled at her, the first glimmer in weeks of the former amused, worldly man she had first learned to love. "What do you propose we do, my darling wife?"

She smiled smugly. "I'll row. I've done it before."

An hour later, Madeleine clung stubbornly to the oars of a tiny boat as each surge of the tide tried to rip them out of her hands. The ship which had brought them to the France coast had long since been swallowed up by the night. The shelter offered by the secluded cove was the reason the captain had chosen this place as his anchorage.

From the deck of the ship Madeleine had been able to discern the shoreline where the curl of breakers glowed faintly iridescent in the darkness. One hundred and fifty yards from ship to the shore. That's all it was. Even as she was being lowered into the small boat waiting below in the black water, the task set her had seemed one that could be easily accomplished.

Perhaps she should have given heed to the ring of blackened smirking faces that had leered at her just before she was hoisted over the side.

"Mark ye bring yer cargo silently to shore, little one. Else the French will see to it ye'll all drown!"

Those words, whispered by the ship's captain, had been the friendly sound she'd heard as she was cast adrift into the dark night. Now, as she struggled against the current it seemed she had made a pact with the devil himself. Her fingers, cold and aching, had long since cramped as she rowed against the enormous tidal drag. She could no longer tell whether she was gaining toward her goal. Black seawater, all but unseen in the darkness, slapped cold and salty at her face and hands until her whole body was stiff with the chilling damp.

The inlet, carved out of the rocky coast by the action

of the relentless Atlantic Ocean, had severely fluctuating
tides. The captain had warned them that they would have
a very short time between tides during which to negotiate
her way to the beach. She needed to hear the sound of
Sebastian's voice. But she knew that voices carried over
water and that in calling to him where he lay in the bottom
of the boat with the once-more bound and gagged De
Valmy, she might alert the French soldiers who guarded
this shore of their coming.

To bolster her courage she thought of her mother whom
she was trying so desperately to reach.

The image which formed in her mind was one of her
earliest and still happiest memories. She had been six years
old, walking with a beautiful dark-haired lady dressed in
a white muslin gown with wide pink sash and a broad,
sweeping brimmed hat. She had been allowed out of the
nursery for a rare visit to her mother who resided—wonder
of wonders—at Versailles that summer of 1889.

The day was a beautiful blur except for the moments
she had been allowed to row with her mother out onto one
of the placid ornamental lakes. The miniature skiff had
been painted royal French blue and decorated with gold
fleur de lis, the king's emblem. The bolsters on the benches
were gold silk, the blades of the oars painted vermillion.

She summoned from memory the warmth of that summer sun on her shoulders and arms, and the scent of water
lilies lying in dappled light along the rim of the lake. She
called to mind also the well-remembered voice encouraging her from the shore.

"Dip, pull, then lift, *ma belle fille!*"

A tall, handsome man in white cadogan wig and striped
faille coat had smiled and waved and shouted praise to
her, his deep baritone voice the most reassuring sound she
had ever heard. She had never seen the man again, but his
voice was as fresh and unique in her memory as if she
had heard it yesterday.

Was that man her father, she wondered now, the man her mother had risked her life to reach? Why had she not recalled him before!

The sudden shock of a cross-current of choppy water against the boat clicked her teeth painfully together. The men in the bottom of the boat shifted and the boat rocked crazily with the balance of their weight.

With a cry of alarm, she dug in her oars, but the right one caught on something beneath the surface and snapped off, sending a painful shock up her arm. Suddenly the entire boat was lifted and shoved forward as if by Neptune's unseen hand.

Madeleine thought in that scant second of time that she did not want to drown. She had heard it was a terrible death, going down and down and down until the lungs burst from need for air and then the water rushed in through nose and mouth. Involuntarily, she gasped as if the terror had already begun.

Just as abruptly, the boat dropped and she felt the jolt of striking the sandy bottom. Elation burst through her in a prayerful whisper of thanks as she realized they had reached the shallows. The breakers were pushing them in.

Suddenly the black water surrounding her exploded with movement. She heard men's voices, their coarse inflections so pronounced as to make their peasant French seem a foreign tongue, and then the boat was steadied by several pairs of hands.

"Stay to, *mon garçon!*" a voice hissed at her as she tried to climb out.

"Gor! 'Tis a woman!" cried another as Madeleine felt hands slip over her shoulders and then graze her breasts.

"Silence!" came the menacing hiss again. "Bring her with us. There's no time to waste."

Hands reached for her, dragging her from the boat. Someone hoisted her up and she landed across his shoulder. Water splashed her face as he waded toward the beach with an arm cinched across the back of her knees to keep her balanced. They had been told she would be met by the ship's compatriots when she reached the shore. Though it was too dark to see distinctly anything or anyone, she heard the men moving all about her though they did not speak again. Still hoisted over her captor's shoulder, she listened with curious interest to the grunts of the men who dragged her boat to shore. Certainly these were not soldiers or they would have identified themselves as such. But, all at once, Madeleine was no longer certain that the shore was a safer place to be than the empty black expanse of the sea.

Then she heard Sebastian's voice, the murmured replies and quickly stifled chuckles.

As her captor began the steep climb with the others from the beach to the cliffs above, Madeleine hung on with both hands to the thick belt spanning his waist, helpless to free herself. She reminded herself to be grateful for small mercies. At least they were on dry land, on French soil.

They climbed some minutes in darkness, the smugglers' stealth and silence giving their actions a fierce menace. Finally, the ground leveled out as hedges enveloped them on all sides and she knew they had reached the summit.

Madeleine was dumped back onto her feet so quickly the blood left her head in a dizzying rush. Hands caught her familiarly by the arms as the lantern flared about her, pushing the darkness back with yellow light. Finally, she was spun about.

Ten men circled her, their clothes ragged and dirty, their faces bearded and blackened with soot. Their eyes were wild and feral, and the smell of whiskey betrayed their natures, but they did not reach for her.

"*Nom de Dieu!* She's a beauty!" whispered one of them.

Sebastian smiled down at her. "And worth every franc."

"What did you tell them?" Madeleine whispered suspiciously as they moved along the road toward shelter.

"Why, that you are my mistress, of course, a very accomplished, very expensive, very highborn courtesan."

"Men!" she huffed.

He laughed and hugged her with his good arm. "They are in awe of your daring, *mon coeur*. You were magnificent!"

Twenty

During the next two days, Madeleine discovered that Sebastian had a talent for intrigue. As they made their way from the Channel coast to Lille on the Belgium border where he said a faction of rebels with sympathetic ties to the English had gathered, she marveled at his facility with the local vernacular and with his familiarity with the land. Her respect grew for him as she saw that he knew not only the ways of the sons of Normandy but also had the trust of the Gypsies who formed the caravan to which they attached themselves.

Sebastian explained as they went that with the possibility of an imminent invasion, any stranger instantly aroused suspicion. Only the nomadic Gypsies moved freely from town to town without drawing suspicion. In return for guarding De Valmy, Sebastian promised his Gypsy companions several of the gold coins he had sewn into the lining of her cloak before they left England.

So De Valmy sat bound and gagged in one of the caravans during the day and tied to a tree at night.

As for herself, Madeleine had never been happier or more frightened. This journey was not like the one she had made alone in August, wearing the protective garb of a nun. Because her French accent betrayed her as an educated woman, she kept silent as much as possible. She dressed as a Gypsy in peasant blouse, wool vest, man's coat, and heavy woolen skirt with a ruffled red petticoat that showed underneath as she walked. Her head was covered in a scarf with gold coins dangling from it and her feet were encased in boots that had been stuffed in the toes with rags to help her keep them on. She felt conspicuous, a constant magnet for the eye of any man they passed. If not for Sebastian's ever-alert presence, she doubted that she would have survived unmolested.

They walked a good deal of the way, though Sebastian was feverish and sometimes in great pain. He wore his sling unless they were approached by strangers and then he left his right hand rest casually on the butt of the pistol stuck in his waistband, or on the hilt of the sword he wore at his hip. Both weapons were against the law for a Gypsy to carry but no one thought to challenge him. She understood that. For all his pallor and striking blue-eyed beauty, he did not seem in the least soft or vulnerable. He seemed what he was, a man with a purpose.

When they reached Lille, Sebastian waved good-bye to the Gypsies and then put up at a shabby inn called the Grendouille.

She wondered at his choice. It was a low, sinister, dark and dirty place. Mice scurried in the corners and it smelled faintly of the sea, perhaps because it was lit with fish-oil lamps. It professed to be an inn but there were no other lodgers besides the three of them. That night Jacques Girard, the owner of the inn, and Sebastian shared a bottle of red wine and talked well into the night. The next morning the two men left for Paris, leaving Madeleine with De Valmy and Lisette Girard.

For the next two days the inn had no visitors. Madeleine sat in a wooden chair in the common room and watched De Valmy, who was tied in a chair. She also kept a guarded eye on the innkeeper's wife, Lisette.

There was, Madeleine conceded, a compelling kind of attractiveness to De Valmy. Nor was she the only one to recognize it. Lisette, grew hourly more fond of gazing at the tethered Frenchman.

Madeleine did not see De Valmy move or even gaze in the wife's direction during that time. But she had an uneasy feeling when she awakened from a short nap at nightfall of the second day, and found the woman sitting by De Valmy stroking his arm and talking softly.

No, not stroking his arm, pulling at the ropes that tied him. And, more, his gag was missing.

Alarmed, Madeleine scraped back her chair and pulled the stiletto from her waist back. "Back, madame!" She jumped to her feet. "Move away from this man. He is a prisoner."

The woman was quick. She sprang up from De Valmy's side with a jerk of the rope in her hand, but the knot did not give.

Madeleine rushed her, realizing that she could not afford to allow the woman even one more tug. "Move away!" she ordered and held her knife menacingly. She moved forward cautiously as the woman backed from the bar.

She heard De Valmy whisper something quickly under his breath to Lisette and moved to place herself between them.

"Hear me, Lisette. Whatever this man may have told you, whatever he may have promised, it is all lies. He lives by deceit." Madeleine took a calculated gamble in adding, "He will tell a beautiful woman anything."

But it was too late. Whatever De Valmy had promised was enough to make the larger woman stick by her choice. She stared at Madeleine hard and cold and then she reached for a whiskey bottle by the neck and shattered the base against the heavy wooden bar, making a wicked weapon of it.

"*Fille de trottoir!* You wanted him for yourself, Gypsy woman. Now that you have an English noble as a lover, you have betrayed him!"

"You fool!" Madeleine shouted back. "Do you not see that this must be a lie?"

They both turned as they heard the door at the rear of the inn open and saw Jacques Girard enter. He lifted his head, took one look at the scene, and came forward.

Even as Lisette backed against the bar with widened eyes, he knocked the bottle out of his wife's hand and struck her with a fist to the chin, snapping her head back as her knees buckled. He caught her as she fell, murmuring words of regret and cradling her as they both slid to the floor.

The scene so shocked Madeleine that she did not realize someone had come up behind her until Sebastian reached round and plucked the stiletto out of her hand.

As she spun in surprise, he brushed an errant curl from her cheek and said, "Marchioness, allow me to introduce you to Georges Cadoudal. Monsieur, my wife."

Madeleine flamed with embarrassment as she spied the look of surprise on the Chouan leader's face. In her Gypsy garb and tangled dark curls, she knew she must look to the gentleman less like a marchioness and more like a slattern. Despite it, he managed to intone gallantly, "Marchioness, charmed," as he took her hand in salute.

"Monsieur," she replied, blushing deeply as she noticed several other men had entered the room and fanned out behind them, watching her with avid expressions. "I regret the scene you have encountered, but I was most scrupulously attempting to obey my husband's instructions." She glanced at Sebastian for reassurance that he was not angry. He looked haggard, his face unshaved and powdered with travel dust. He had journeyed to Paris and back in a remarkably short time. He must be exhausted, she thought, though his eyes blazed like twin beacons of blue.

Cadoudal looked past her to where De Valmy sat, and his pale eyes narrowed. "Your courage is to be expected, my lady, for I have met your husband several years ago in London. A man of his stripe would only mate with a spirit of his like, would he not?"

Sebastian chuckled at this. "I will leave you two to talk then, monsieur, while I see to our prisoner."

He turned and caught Madeleine's chin in his left hand. He smiled at her, and then, to her great pleasure and embarrassment, gently kissed her before this company of strangers. *"Merci,* Marchioness," he said warmly, "Now do offer Monsieur Cadoudal a chair. He has something very important to tell you."

Still smiling for her husband, she turned to the gentleman and indicated a table at the far end of the room. "Please join me there, monsieur."

Jacques Girard had scooped up his crying wife. "I must see to her," he said to Sebastian and at his nod, the innkeeper carried Lisette from the room.

When they had seated themselves, Monsieur Cadoudal began in a low, steady tone. "I have had the very great pleasure of meeting your mother, Marchioness. A woman of considerable spirit and beauty, like her daughter."

"Where is she? Is she well?"

"Perfectly, I should imagine, Marchioness. When last I heard, she was in Belgium."

"Belgium? But I thought she had gone to Paris to find a—someone."

"Indeed, she has found him. She carried a personal message to the gentleman from me."

Madeleine's heart quickened. "You know this man?"

Cadoudal nodded slowly. "Soon all of France will know him. He is the best hope our nation has to return nobility to the throne. Your mother has joined our cause and is remaining loyally by his side. She has not contacted you because it might compromise our mission. But if you wish, I will see that you are taken to her."

Madeleine did not respond. Her skin was cold and her heart was pounding so hard her hands trembled. The next question she asked would tell her the name of her sire. Suddenly she did not want to know.

She rose quickly from her chair. "Thank you, monsieur, for your encouraging words. I do not know if I can go to Belgium just now."

Cadoudal stood up with her and regarded her through world-weary eyes. "What is about to come will reverse the course of history. We are determined to turn back the clock to the days of the prerevolution. You and your mother will have a place here when that is accomplished. Join us."

Madeleine shook her head, her gaze straying to where Sebastian stood deep in conversation with one of the other men who had accompanied him. "My life is now with my husband, monsieur. Wherever he goes, whatever he does, I want to be with him."

The fervent insurrectionist smiled. "For all we need you, I admire your loyalty and envy your husband, madame. So, for his sake, you must not betray what I have just told you, regardless of what is about to transpire."

He took her hand and kissed it. "Go with God, Madeleine Bourbon," he murmured so low that she was not certain she had heard it. But she did hear the cautionary note in his voice and knew that something was about to occur for which she should be prepared.

Madeleine knew where her mother was, and with whom, and that she was safe. She watched Sebastian as she came back toward the group of men standing about De Valmy. He held the stiletto he had taken from her, held it idly in his right hand, his weak hand. He and the Chouan plotters were speaking conversationally as with a group of friends at White's. But the language was French and the words were sometimes foul ones that she did not understand. But never was Sebastian's tone less than polite.

He glanced back over his shoulder as Madeleine approached. "Ah, dear marchioness, you are better informed, I suppose?"

"*Oui*," she answered cautiously. She looked at De Valmy and saw hatred in his eyes. If not for her, he might have escaped. She looked away as fear brushed against her. "What will you do?"

"Search for your mother. When I have learned where she is." He held her gaze meaningfully for a moment longer, then glanced back at De Valmy. "Perhaps you can help me. There is no record by Parisian authorities of a woman being arrested as a Chouan spy."

"Do you think they wish to spread the rumors of conspiracy?" De Valmy answered.

Madeleine jumped, for it had been so long since she had heard that voice of cultivated contempt she had almost forgotten it. But De Valmy was gazing past Sebastian straight at her. "Ondine Foucant has been interrogated and forgotten."

The chilling words made Madeleine blanch despite what Cadoudal just had told her. Perhaps he was wrong, or misinformed. Interrogations often included torture. Perhaps . . .

She felt Cadoudal touch her almost surreptitiously on the arm. *Remember,* his touch seemed to say, *your husband plays a role.*

Sebastian regarded De Valmy dispassionately. "I have been thinking about what you have told my wife, De Valmy, and there's no logic in it. If Madame Ondine, who agreed to carry a message for your royalist contacts, had been arrested last August, Monsieur Cadoudal tells me his plan would have been abandoned. There would have been no secondary group of conspirators which I personally greeted at Biville on the night of December 10."

"De Valmy knows very well what we have done," Cadoudal said at Sebastian's back. "We paid him well to arrange it."

"Really?" Sebastian saw by the faint contemptuous lift of his brow that De Valmy thought he was among friends. "If my marchioness had been able to steal papers revealing my dealings with the Chouans, your future in Paris would have been made, would it not, son of a jackal!"

De Valmy smiled. "You should know."

Sebastian met his smile. "I know Jules de Polignac . . . The name strikes a bell with you does it?"

De Valmy's smile hardened. "Polignac is known to me."

"His partisan feelings are well known. He is to be part of the third group of Chouans who will shortly arrive on these shores. Ah, you did *not* know that, did you?"

De Valmy's shining black eyes quickened with interest. "Why are you telling me this?"

"Can you not guess?" Sebastian twirled the needle-sharp point of the stiletto before his eyes and saw the realization dawn in the Frenchman's eyes.

"You won't kill me."

"You think not?" Sebastian studied the deadly weapon. "I am not paid to kill England's enemies." His eyes suddenly narrowed. "But I will gladly murder anyone who tries to harm my wife in any manner."

He pointed the stiletto casually at De Valmy's left cheek. "Now I tell you, Ondine Foucant occupies no prison cell in Paris. If that be the case, then my wife has no need of your skills to bargain for her mother's life, does she?"

The Frenchman glanced again from Sebastian to Madeleine, who stood stiff as a pillar in the middle of the room. The insolence in his expression died, but the hauteur did not dissipate. Sebastian had told her De Valmy's history, or at least as much of it as rumor and intelligence could provide. An aristocratic hothead who had sided with the revolutionaries against his own, not out of principle or need, but out of ennui and sheer malicious spite.

"Perhaps I lied," De Valmy said slowly. He shrugged

within his bonds. "Perhaps I know the truth of where she is."

"And perhaps you do not." Sebastian drew the blade lightly down De Valmy's cheek, and a thin bright line of blood sprang up in its path. "Perhaps you lost her once she reached France. Cadoudal says he did not take her to Paris with his conspirators last August. She made her own way once in France. Perhaps you have merely used her silence as a convenient tool of blackmail against the Foucants."

"Perhaps," De Valmy answered with remarkable calm considering that Sebastian had cut his face. "But then why has no one heard from her?"

This time Sebastian shrugged, moving the stiletto from De Valmy's left cheek to his right. "It is a risky business to smuggle a letter out of France. It would be a very expensive mailing. Or, maybe her whereabouts are the secret to her safety. Perhaps she has found the man she sought."

De Valmy's lids flickered as the blade made a slight indentation on his skin. "I know the name of that man."

Sebastian nodded, but the blade did not move. "If not, you will soon think of one. You will do anything to remain alive."

Madeleine held her breath as sweat formed and beaded and ran down her face from temple to jaw, just as it did on De Valmy's.

De Valmy's gaze moved to the Chouan leader. "I have information which would be of use to you, Cadoudal."

"And you have information that could be of use to Napoleonic France, to the insurrectionists on the Rhine, to the Chouans and so forth," Sebastian replied. "No, I don't believe any of us would find your information that compelling."

"Even so, my men will see if we can persuade him to tell us what he knows," said the French rebel leader. "We will soon learn if we have been betrayed."

"He is yours, Monsieur Cadoudal." Sebastian stood up, lifting his blade from De Valmy's face. "Come, Marchioness, this is no place for you."

Madeleine moved toward him, shaking as she watched the blood drip from De Valmy's cheeks onto his black coat. He picked up her cloak from a chair and swung it about her shoulders. "We will continue our own search." His eyes met the Chouan leader's. "Bury him deep when you are done."

"I know who Madeleine Foucant really is!" De Valmy shouted, but two of the Chouan partisans quickly subdued him with blows to the side of his head.

Sebastian glanced back and raised a cautioning hand when the men would had beat him more. "A moment, messieurs."

De Valmy's calculating gaze swung about the room and then came back to Sebastian. "A private moment, my lord. Between gentlemen," he added. "I know something which your wife will personally find very enlightening."

Sebastian hugged Madeleine close with his good arm. "I'm no longer interested, De Valmy. *Au revoir.*"

"Wait!" Madeleine swung out of Sebastian's embrace. "Perhaps if he truly knows something, we should hear it."

Sebastian did not look at her but only at De Valmy. "If you lie to her, you will not induce me to kill you. I will leave that to your friends. But I will make it so that, should you live past this night, you won't ever lust for a woman again. Do you still have something to say?"

De Valmy, clearly shaken, nodded.

Sebastian glanced at Cadoudal. "Will it please you to give us a few minutes alone?"

Cadoudal gazed steadily at De Valmy. "We will wait outside, but we will have our turn."

When the Chouans were gone, Sebastian brought a chair and placed it a little away from De Valmy so that Madeleine could sit.

"What have you to tell us?"

De Valmy smiled. "You do not want my blood on your hands, my lord. I am an agent for Fouché."

Madeleine and Sebastian exchanged startled glances. Everyone who knew anything of political intrigue within France these last ten years knew the name Joseph Fouché. Ex-cleric, ex-Terrorist, ex-minister of general police now out of favor with Napoléon, the tall cadaverous red-haired Fouché was France's spymaster *extraordinaire*. A man of facile wit and surpassing cunning, Fouché was a dreaded presence. He knew everyone's secrets, everyone's weaknesses. Though he no longer held the official position as Napoléon's chief of intelligence, no one crossed him. He lay at the fatal center of a private network of spies and agents more elaborate than any Europe had ever before seen.

"Tell my wife why her mother came to France."

De Valmy's eyes glittered. "To find the comte d'Artois." He turned his black gaze on her. "Your father." He saw Madeleine was not as surprised as he thought she should have been. "Have you heard this before, Marchioness?"

Madeleine shook her head. "No. *Tante* Henrice would only tell me that I was the natural daughter of a very important man, a gentleman of royalty."

"Do you remember your father at all?" Sebastian asked gently.

"Only one vague memory of the gardens at Versailles and a tall, handsome man in wig and silks and laces." She raised her hand in a helpless gesture. "It could have been any courtier."

"I don't think so." *So it is true then,* Sebastian mused in mild surprise. His wife, the would-be Independent Woman and courtesan, was the natural daughter of Charles-Philippe, Comte d'Artois.

"You know what this means, Marchioness?" De Valmy inquired politely. "Your father is the younger brother of

Louis XVI and the comte de Provence, who declared himself Louis XVIII in 1795. Your father is next in line to
the Bourbon throne."

Madeleine gazed warily at De Valmy. It was in his black
eyes, the rage and anger and resentment, that she saw his
belief that the story was true. He had hated his own royal
family enough to abet their assassination. He would use
her situation to his advantage any way he could have. She
shivered and glanced at her husband. "What does this
mean?"

Sebastian smiled at her ruefully. "That the next king of
France, if such a thing ever again comes to pass, sweeting,
might well turn out to be my father-in-law!"

"And for me?"

"It means, my royal wife, that in marrying you I have
risen considerably from my position as a lowly marquess.
I see I shall have to take better care of you after this."

Madeleine stared into his amused gaze. She saw strength
and goodness in him, a man more handsome than the
devil, a man who had almost broken her heart, a man she
had begun to love better than her own life. "See that you
do."

He again turned his attention to De Valmy who watched
them with the intensity of one who knew his life hung in
the balance. "Why do I believe your master Fouché does
not yet know about Madeleine?"

De Valmy smiled. "A man needs security, a bargaining
chip."

"I see." Though De Valmy had confessed to being an
agent of Joseph Fouché, Sebastian suspected that, like
Fouché, De Valmy worked for no side but his own. Yet,
there was something missing, something else that did not
quite make sense. Why would De Valmy have been helping
the Chouan plotters if he worked for Napoléon's master
spy?

It came to Sebastian suddenly that England and France

were not the only sides who stood to lose or gain by the royalist plot against Napoléon. It was well known that Fouché was a very cautious man. He had never been known to instigate a plot, but he also never missed an opportunity to manipulate one once it had been conceived. Fouché was a republican who had been a leader during the revolution. It was common knowledge he did not like Bonaparte's egomaniacal tendencies. There were even rumors that he had been connected to the 1802 plot by General Bernadotte to overthrow Napoléon. The resulting gossip had cost him his powerful position as Bonaparte's minister of police. Perhaps Fouché wanted revenge. If the Chouan plot succeeded, Fouché was rid of Napoléon.

Then again, the ex-minister of intelligence might be looking for a dazzling show of patriotism to win back Napoléon's favor. Could it be that Fouché was using the Chouan plot against Napoléon's life as yet another diabolical strategy to serve his own ends?

Sebastian stared into De Valmy's black eyes. What he read there was a match for his own rapidly calculating thoughts. "If Fouché is aware of Cadoudal's plot yet has not taken action, then it must be because the master spy has not chosen his side."

De Valmy smiled. "You are very perceptive, my lord."

"So, even though the Chouans scheme has been compromised, it might succeed." Sebastian spoke this thought aloud but no other. De Valmy knew he could not afford to tell Cadoudal what he suspected. No matter the odds, the English government would want the insurgents to act. De Valmy knew it, and now so did he.

Sebastian cursed under his breath. Spying was a dirty, ugly game. As an English patriot he must not even warn Cadoudal of Fouché's machinations. Now he understood why De Valmy had told him this. The Frenchman expected him to save his life because if, under torture, De Valmy revealed that he worked for Fouché, the plot would be abandoned.

Sebastian turned to De Valmy with a bright, brittle smile. "You have my felicitations, monsieur."

De Valmy perked up. "Then you see the need to release me?"

"Do not rush me," Sebastian murmured. One other thing was surpassingly clear. Every side in the political struggle would have a use for the natural daughter of the next in line for the French throne. If Madeleine remained in France, Fouché would see to it that she became a pawn for intrigue. No wonder the Foucants had not wanted the name of her sire to be known. He had to get Madeleine back to England at once. To save his country's plot against the life of Napoléon, he had to keep De Valmy from Cadoudal. To do it, he would have to take a calculated risk.

He looked again to Madeleine. "What say you, sweeting? Do I free a spy?"

Madeleine did not really think. "Free him. He will not, I think, come back to England."

After a moment's consideration, Sebastian moved to untie De Valmy's bonds. "Because it is my wife's choice, I give you a sporting chance. That is all. If you show your face in England again, I will help them hang you."

The old guile quickly returned to De Valmy's eyes. "Would the English not find it of interest to learn that you brought me to France and freed me to protect your traitorous French wife?"

Sebastian smiled "They might. But unlike you, I have not relinquished my title. As a lord I am entitled to the full protection of a trial by Parliament. My wife cannot be induced to testify against me. You, however, are a spy and confessed conspirator against the English king. I think I am willing to take my chances among my peers."

"As I've said, you are very clever, my lord," De Valmy answered, but his expression was no longer friendly.

"So I've been told." Sebastian pulled his pistol free and handed it to Madeleine. "Watch the door. I will see that De Valmy—"

De Valmy moved so quickly that Sebastian had no time to react. He drove his fist into Sebastian's wounded shoulder and then lunged for the hilt of Sebastian's sword, dragging the blade free of its scabbard. Sebastian tried to grasp him by the neck, but his right hand had lost its strength and he could not hold the taller man. They wrenched apart.

Madeleine saw lantern light dance wickedly along the yard of steel, saw Sebastian draw the shorter stiletto blade awkwardly with his left hand.

De Valmy smiled. "I think, my lord, that I have need of your wife after all, as hostage now and for ransom later. Unfortunately, I have no use for you."

Madeleine had never before held a gun. She nearly forgot she was armed as De Valmy lunged at Sebastian and he twisted away with movements made clumsy by his pain.

He will never be able to protect himself. The words were a scream in Madeleine's head, and then the scream was in her throat as she lifted her weapon in warning.

A pistol banged, the noise scattering and echoing in the long low-ceilinged room.

De Valmy looked up at her, flat surprise in his face. Blood blossomed on the front of his black coat. The animation left his face as the sword clattered onto the filthy floor. His eyes dimmed as he pitched forward head-first.

Hands gripped her, turned her around. She gazed up into her husband's face. He was looking at her with an expression of pure joy, the same joy that she had seen in his face by moonlight in the Locksley solarium.

"I killed him, she whispered.

"No, Marchioness, that privilege was mine."

They looked round to see Cadoudal standing in the

doorway, his pistol still drawn. He was not smiling. "I begin to believe, Lord d'Arcy, that you were about to betray us."

Sebastian interposed himself between Madeleine and the doorway, which was filling with Chouan rebels. "I had no other desire than to protect my wife. Girard's wife had loosened Valmy's bonds. He caught me off-guard. But, thanks to you, he could not escape."

Cadoudal's brows lowered in thought for several fateful seconds. Then he smiled and tucked his pistol away. "I am satisfied."

"It is better this way," Sebastian said as he and Madeleine drove the innkeeper's donkey cart toward the Channel in the early-morning light. The day was warmer than the last few. The midwinter thaw had momentarily set in. Yet Madeleine snuggled against his left shoulder with both her arms entwined about his. They had spent a near silent but restless night at the inn before leaving at daybreak. The decision had been made. For her sake, they must leave the Continent without ever setting eyes on her mother, whom Cadoudal admitted having seen in Brussels.

"She is happy, *ma fille,*" Cadoudal had said before he left the inn the night before. "Unless you wish to live within the comte d'Artois's small circle of *émigrés,* it would be better if you went home with your English husband, who can protect you."

Madeleine had cried and thought and cried a little more before falling asleep in Sebastian's lap. When he woke her just before dawn, she did not hesitate when he said they must leave France.

"The Chouans could not afford for De Valmy to live after he had been seen to be a liar," Sebastian explained as they rode along. "They would have tortured him to learn what he knew about the plots of others. And, in the end they would have killed him. So then, this was easier."

"You knew he could not get away?"

Sebastian reached up to skim her face with the fingers of his right hand, a little stronger now. "I had planned to kill De Valmy myself."

"Is that what you are for the English government, an assassin?"

Sebastian laughed. "Lord, sweeting, no! I sometimes faint at the sight of blood. But I had to silence De Valmy before Cadoudal could extract certain information from him that would have hindered my government's efforts against Bonaparte. Forgive me, but I cannot tell you what those actions are. Yet, I wanted Cadoudal to think De Valmy's death was an accident." He looked rueful. "I overestimated my strength."

Madeleine studied his face for a long time. "So then, in a way, you were being merciful to De Valmy. He did escape in that he was spared being tortured."

He looked deeply into her eyes. The truth was not quite that noble, but the fact she thought him capable of that kind of gallantry filled him with gratitude. "Thank you for understanding."

Madeleine nodded. "It is better that I did not kill him." She squeezed her eyes shut, remembering the moment when the pistol had fired, how it had jerked in her hand. Her wrist still ached.

"You have made a conquest in Cadoudal. I see that I am going to need to be a very diligent husband."

Madeleine opened her eyes and smiled. "Is that what you want, to be a husband?"

His smile dimmed. "I once thought it was the very last thing I ever wanted. I did not think I could be a husband to any woman."

She saw the look of truth in his eyes but could not quite

believe it. The doubt provoked her to ask, "What are you afraid of?"

As they rode along, Sebastian told her the long and difficult story of his childhood, relived his hatred of his father, the feelings of impotence and rage engendered by the fact that he could not protect his mother. He talked about his fears that he had inherited his father's intemperate character and his tendency to profligacy. Because of that, he feared he would become the kind of man he hated most.

"I have never hated anything or anyone more than myself after that night at Locksley House," he said roughly.

Madeleine nodded and leaned her head against his arm. "You frightened me and you hurt me, but I believe I understand now the real source of your anger. You did not think I loved De Valmy. You thought I had betrayed you, and your country, by warning him of his imminent arrest."

"I thought you must have been in league with De Valmy from the first. I suspected that you had come to Kent under a false pretext to gain entrance to my house and my life. I suddenly doubted what I thought we felt for each other. I suspected it was a sham on your part so that you could spy on me." He saw her eyes widen in amazement. "That does not forgive or excuse what I did."

She nodded. "That is true."

He pulled the donkey to a halt and tied the reins before turning fully to her. His expression was flat, his voice unemotional. "If you decide once we're back on English soil that you want to go to your parents in Brussels, I am prepared to set you free. I will provide all the money and servants you may desire. I will even petition Parliament for a divorce if that is your wish."

Madeleine searched his face for clues, but she could read nothing. It was as though his soul had suddenly disappeared from his eyes. He had once said that he had married her to protect her. De Valmy was dead. She needed no more protection. Only she did, she did! She needed the warm security of his love to hold her life together through the thousand shocks and insults life had to offer. A few magnificent moments were not enough.

A tear slid down her face. "Why should I want a divorce?"

He blinked, a look of surprise the first emotion to return to his face. "You just said you can never forgive or excuse what I did. We have not yet consummated our marriage. You would be free to marry elsewhere."

She suddenly smiled. "Is that the reason why you haven't touched me?"

He looked down at his hands. "It was a consideration." He looked up again, doubt crowding the blue of his eyes. "But also I thought you'd be afraid of me."

Madeleine lifted a hand to his cheek, recently washed but darkened by a week's worth of stubble. "I should not have betrayed you. I should have trusted you more. So then, I do not excuse you, but I do forgive you."

She was astonished to see a single tear bead up under the downward sweep of his red-gold lashes and then slide free, leaving a clear stain of emotion on his gorgeous face. "I love you, Madeleine . . . I just don't know how to protect you."

"You already have," she answered, her own throat swelling with emotion. "You saved me from De Valmy."

A second tear joined the first, laying another track on his cheek. His mouth was tight with pride but no shame for his feelings. "I meant myself." He swallowed. "I won't ever mean to hurt you—"

She put a hand to cover his lips. "Then don't. Don't."

She saw a puzzled look come into his eyes and then the revelation. His eyes crinkled at the corners, and when she lifted her hand away he was smiling. "I do love you."

"I, too. *Je t'aime, mon mari! Je t'aime.*"

"I'm sorry," he whispered as he clasped her close. "I am so very sorry." He whispered it against her hair, against her ear, against her eyelids and her cheeks and then against her mouth.

Madeleine kissed him back with her whole heart, tears mingling on their cheeks.

When, a little later, they could smile and not feel the world shake under the enormity of emotions their gazes contained, Sebastian picked up the reins.

Toward noon he spoke about Meg, his first mistress, how he had lost her to another and why her death reinforced his sense that he was not meant to care deeply for any one woman.

After a lunch of wine and cheese and bread he told her about his years in Paris, how he had met the Foucant sisters and why.

He kissed her with such tenderness that Madeleine did not even mind that what he told her should have scandalized her. She could see in his eyes that it was all a fond but distant memory for him.

Later, he told her about his duels and his need to protect women as he had not been able to protect his mother.

Madeleine took up the conversation from there, telling him why and how she had come to England, her strong reaction when she learned her aunts had arranged a protector for her, how she felt when she first saw him, even why she had chosen to go to him when he did not come back.

When the afternoon turned cloudy, she told him how her mother had always been a beautiful but distant dream, hardly more real than a fairy-tale princess. She would miss her but she could not say it was as great a loss as it might have been—as much as losing him would have been.

During the course of the day, they filled in one another's silence with sympathy, supplied the ends to hanging phrases and unspoken words with the best of intentions, came to understand in a more profound sense the person each now called spouse. Yet, curiously, each avoided the word "love," as if it might be too great a burden for their sensibilities.

Sebastian laughed when he learned she was the nun he had accosted in the alleyway of Queen Anne's Gate. They kissed a little more and clung to each other as their donkey cart rolled slowly toward the Channel coast.

It was late afternoon when they arrived at a prearranged place on the coast.

In a vast open space a strangely familiar shape loomed before the encroaching darkness. A black orb bobbed gently in the sea breeze, tethered by heavy ropes. Slung beneath it was a balloon car of woven wicker.

Madeleine stared at it and then at Sebastian who was grinning like a small boy with his first toy soldier. "Your chariot awaits, Marchioness."

"You cannot mean us to go aloft tonight?" she whispered, as the wicker basket creaked and the ropes groaned, sounding like tree limbs in a stiff breeze.

"Yes. I met a fellow on the road from Paris and he told me about his balloon. He has a license to send her aloft on the coast. I've paid him to allow me to take it to England. Double its worth if it can carry us across." He was moving about as he spoke, lifting things from the back of the cart. He pushed a bundle into her arms. "Get under a wagon blanket and change, I need to talk to our aeronaut. But hurry!"

"Rare warm zephyr from the south, m'sieu," the French balloon pilot greeted Sebastian. "You were in luck earlier. But it is now too late."

But Sebastian had noticed the signs on the ride toward the shore. He had heard the creaks and groans of the balloon long before he saw it on the horizon. He could hear the aeronaut's crew whispering among themselves as they stared at him. He could smell in the breeze the scents of the land at his back. The brainstorm coming on could be the last bit of luck they needed.

He had known that leaving France would not be as easy as arriving. Along this section of French coast closest to England, Bonaparte's troops patrolled with great diligence. They would have to travel for days to the west to find where smugglers operated more freely, but that meant spending valuable time in France. While he trusted Cadoudal, Fouché was bound to hear from some source of Madeleine's existence. When the spymaster did, he would spread an incredibly efficient net in which to snare her. They could not risk being betrayed. It was imperative they leave France today.

Sebastian's scintillating senses surged with the urgency of the moment as his supra-sensitive sight scanned the silk envelope for telltale signs of bulges and seam breaks. "Is she ready?"

"Of course, but soon there will be no light to guide you."

"I don't need light. We need only the wind."

The corpulent little Frenchman rolled his eyes. "You would need the eyes of the owl to see the sea and land at night from a balloon."

Sebastian laughed and slapped him on the back. "Didn't I tell you, my mother was a *chouette.*"

"But the cold, monsieur?"

"You've included the brazier of coals I asked for?"

"Oui, but it is very dangerous. The hydrogen, monsieur, and the wicker."

"We will be careful, believe me. Blanchard crossed the Channel in two hours."

The Frenchman gave a fatalist's shrug and muttered, "Every man goes mad in his own way."

Madeleine came running toward him, her Gypsy clothes traded once more for her fisherman's garb. "I am ready."

Sebastian smiled at her, a wicked happy smile. "I remember the last time we went aloft." He scooped her up into his arms. "Maybe you will want to legitimize our marriage today." He turned serious. "I promise to be gentle."

Madeleine blushed and moved to hide her face against his shoulder. Instead, she nipped his neck in playful anticipation.

He chuckled, lifting her over the side into the balloon car and depositing her on her feet. After climbing in with her, he caught her face in his hands. "The past is done, agreed?"

She nodded. "Agreed."

He leaned out and waved to the balloonist, shouting, "Let go all!"

The groundsmen let go the tether ropes, and the balloon shot toward the gathering dark of the sky. For the first five minutes Madeleine, guided by Sebastian, worked at releasing the multitude of ballast bags of sand while he used the altimeter to check their altitude. Afterward, she settled against the rim of the car to gaze out at the red eye of the setting sun. It seemed a miracle, and impossible that she was flying so high above the world. Only angels and birds and a very few humans had ever seen what she saw. The coast had receded in the gloom of the late afternoon. It trailed away in both directions as a wavy dark line. The Channel was an oily bright shimmer only slightly lighter than the land.

Arms came about her from behind. "Like it?"

"Oh, *oui!*" As she gazed north she saw the dark hump of land that was their goal. "Are we really moving toward England?"

"So far," he answered, his lips nuzzling her ear.

"I am cold," she whispered as she leaned back against him.

He hugged her tighter, one hand rising up to cup a breast while the other went lower and cupped the apex of her thighs. "Come with me. I know a way to warm you."

The direction he had in mind was down, into the woolen blankets spread within the confines of the basket floor.

And so Madeleine did not see any more of the sun that day, nor of the shore of France, nor the approaching horizon of England, nor even of the sky. Her world was encompassed in the width and breadth and depth of her husband's wicked smile.

The next morning a Kentish farmer found his hopsyard miraculously tented in a thousand yards of green-and-gold silk. When he went looking for his benefactor, he found two laughing people in his barn. Of course, he hastily retreated when he saw why they were laughing.

It made a dandy tale, one which made something of a local legend of the naked marquis and marchioness, and a celebrity of the hopsman who sold the silk balloon.

Epilogue

OF BLISSFUL HOURS
AND THE MARRIED MAN

She leaned away to stir the fire, allowing candlelight to play hide-and-seek over the enticing curves and secret folds of her voluptuously naked bottom. The shapeliness of her thighs, the full swelling derrière, the flare of hips below a girlishly narrow waist held me in thrall. I thought of the times when I have entered her in this enticing fashion, the approach from the rear, and came rousingly to life.

She came and leaned over his shoulder "But, Monsieur le Marquis, you are writing about us!"

He smiled. "I know, sweeting. And what's more, I've at last found a publisher."

"But what will the children think?"

He pulled her down beside him and tossed away his quill. "They will think, my dearest darling adorable wife, that we must be the most happily fulfilled couple in England . . ."

He paused for a heated interval during which he began to demonstrate to her just how that delectable condition would be maintained.

After a lengthy discussion of lips and tongues and hands, he smiled lustily at her when she glanced back at him over her naked shoulder. "And," he concluded in full confidence, "they will be right!"

HISTORICAL NOTE

As with any work of fiction, the main characters of *Risqué*—Sebastian d'Arcy, Madeleine Foucant, Henrice Foucant, and Justine Foucant—are my own creations. But the story of the Chouan plot against Napoléon (1803–04) is real.

Georges Cadoudal, the leader of the Chouans, did land with a band of his men in Biville in Normandy on August 21, 1803. Armand de Polignac brought a second group over on December 10, 1803. The third crossing on January 16, 1804, was led by Jules de Polignac and the French *émigrés* generals Pichegru and Lajolais.

Joseph Fouché, the diabolical spymaster, figures largely in this and many other intrigues which swirled about Napoléon during his reign. He kept a private network of agents. Mehee de la Touche who worked in London—like my fictional De Valmy—was one of them. Fact suggests that the Chouan plotters were unwitting puppets of Fouché, who was at that time out of favor with Napoléon. His exposure of the Chouan plot put him back in Napoléon's good graces and he again became minister of police.

But there was one thing Fouché never knew: who was the mysterious prince whose arrival had been promised? Cadoudal never would name him.

There has been much debate about which Bourbon the Chouans had hoped to place on the throne after kidnapping

Napoléon. The possibilities included the duc de Provence (later Louis XVIII), the duc d'Enghien, who was arrested and executed in 1804 though innocent of the plot, and Charles-Philippe, Comte d'Artois. History leans toward the theory that the Chouan plotters delayed action in January in the expectation that the comte d'Artois, living with his wife and mistress in Brussels, would join them in Paris, ready to replace Napoléon. For whatever reason, he did not come.

On January 26, 1803, a Chouan named Querelle, soon to be executed, revealed details of the plot in order to commute his sentence. Pichegru was arrested on February 26, the Polignac brothers on February 27, and Cadoudal on March 29. On June 10, 1804, the court pronounced sentence: nineteen conspirators were condemned to death. Cadoudal died impenitent on June 28. Of the remaining eighteen, Napoléon pardoned twelve, including the Polignacs.

Charles-Philippe, Comte d'Artois, a subtle, patient man, outlived them all to ascend the French throne in 1824 as Charles X.